RELINQUISHING THE AGENT

AGENTS OF ESPIONAGE
BOOK FOUR

LORRI DUDLEY

WILD HEART BOOKS

But he said to me, "My grace is sufficient for you, for my power is made perfect in weakness." Therefore I will boast all the more gladly about my weaknesses, so that Christ's power may rest on me. That is why, for Christ's sake, I delight in weaknesses, in insults, in hardships, in persecutions, in difficulties. For when I am weak, then I am strong.

— 2 CORINTHIANS 12:9-10 (NIV)

CHAPTER 1

n the Lipscomb ballroom, Rebecca Leah Prestcote inched along the full-length damask curtains, hoping to blend in the way the peppered moth camouflaged itself against tree bark.

Servants swept past her, carrying trays of food and drinks. An orchestra played in the balcony as couples danced the square figure of the quadrille.

The room was opulent with gold-leaf coffered ceilings, crystal chandeliers, and large second-story mullioned windows. Beneath the geometric plane of palatial architectural design, the upper echelons of polite society—dripping in expensive fabrics and jewels—danced and mingled.

Rebecca was supposed to appear as if she belonged, but how could she when she felt as out of place as an Australian Cockatoo trying to fit in among the swans gliding in Hyde Park? Her breathing shallowed as if someone drew her corset strings tighter.

She'd never witnessed such splendor in her quiet seaside town of Blakeney. The *le bon ton's* laughter, rich food, and strong drink had fit her papa's lifestyle but remained foreign to her. The study of *Debrett's Peerage* and Thomas Gisborne's conduct book, *An Enquiry into the Duties of the Female Sex*, did little to prepare her for this moment. And to think, this was only a private party. What would she do when she and her cousin attended court and assembly balls?

Rebecca closed her eyes and mapped a mental route to the family's library. If she crossed the dance floor, she could escape into the comfort of a book. Perhaps Lord and Lady Lipscomb's collection contained a volume that would help her research a cure for her sister's condition.

"Corinne, darling. There you are." An elegant young woman with blond curls tucked around a glittering tiara raised a gloved hand. She swept toward Rebecca, leaving the cluster of gathered guests and wafting Rebecca with the rich fragrance of jasmine.

She was being mistaken for Corinne, her cousin? Rebecca pressed back into the curtain's folds. "You've mistaken me—"

"What is this relic you're wearing?" The woman peered at Rebecca over her intricately carved fan. Her expensive floral scent assaulted Rebecca. "Lace? Truly? Are you trying to bring back last Season's fashion?"

"I'm—"

"It's a bold move, but I doubt you could pull it off." She pivoted to observe the crush of guests filling the ballroom and fanned herself. "Mr. Beau Brummel will slice you in two with his sharp tongue. You know how he can be." She passed Rebecca a sideways glance. "I daresay; is that why you're hiding in the corner?"

"Lady Portia." Corinne approached in a sway of lavender silk and taffeta, firing Rebecca a stay-out-of-trouble glare before she offered a gracious smile to her friend.

The lady's brow furrowed as she glanced at Corinne and then peered down at Rebecca. "You're not Lady Prestcote."

Rebecca tilted her chin up. "Actually—"

"I see you've met my cousin." Corinne wedged between Lady Portia and Rebecca, pushing Rebecca deeper into the curtains. "She's Miss Rebecca Prestcote, on my father's side." Corinne leaned close to Portia's ear and whispered, "A poor relation I'm saddled with for the Season."

A look of utter disgust marred Lady Portia's face.

Anywhere else, God. Rebecca pleaded toward the coffered ceiling. *I'll go anywhere.* What was her father thinking? She could never pull off a Season and win the favor of a wealthy gentleman. Father must find another way to save himself from debtor's prison.

Besides, why should she put herself through this torture for a father who was never around—not even when Rebecca's mama had grown deathly ill? He hadn't even been there when she'd passed from this life.

Already the preparations for the upcoming London Season interfered with Rebecca's determination to find a cure for her sister, Madeline. Her mission had become more imperative since Madeline had developed the same symptoms as Mama—shortness of breath, fatigue, and an irregular heartbeat.

If only Rebecca could sneak away to the Lipscomb's library. When she and her cousin first arrived, a footman directed them down the hall past the library's open doors opposite the ballroom entrance. Rebecca's pulse had quickened at the sight of shelves of books. Amid the two-floor rows of tomes, the Lipscombs would certainly own a book on the conditions of the human body.

"I know. She's a complete dowdy." Corinne snorted. "My parents insisted she shadow me before the Season begins."

Rebecca's aunt and uncle had been gracious, allowing her into their home and sponsoring her for the Season alongside their daughter, but did they truly believe she could fit in among the elite? Or were they simply fulfilling a familial obligation to their niece?

Corinne's voice flattened. "To make things even more dreadful, my parents just penned that I'm to attend the Coburn misfit house party in the Cotswolds."

"Oh." Lady Portia drew out the single syllable into three and puckered her lips as if she'd swallowed bitter tea.

"Mama and Lady Coburn became close after summering together in Italy." Corinne sighed as if this were terrible news. "Since then, my parents have regularly attended the Coburn's annual party, but as they're in Prussia meeting the prince, I'm to participate in their stead."

"You must feign an illness." The overly coiffed woman twisted her lips as if in sympathy. "My husband and I attended two years ago. Never again. I still have nightmares of being surrounded by droll Oxford professors who wanted to discuss leeches, diseases, and such."

Oxford professors? Rebecca's ears perked up. Such a party sounded heavenly compared with tonight.

Lady Portia shivered. "I was speaking to one guest who appeared as if she might have been one of us, but then she fell asleep."

Corinne harrumphed.

"Where she stood." Lady Portia gripped Corinne's arm. "Mid-sentence."

"How will I endure?" Corinne expelled an agonized sigh.

"Lady Coburn's annual masquerade party, at least, was enjoyable. Wait..." Lady Portia's gloved hand flew to her bosom. "You'll miss the Carter house party in Surrey. Only those in the highest circles receive an invitation, and of course, I'll make certain you receive one. The Marquis of Wolston will be there. My sister-in-law claims he's already accepted the invite."

Corinne groaned. "I expect Miss Bellecourt will swoop in

and try to snatch him up. It's no secret she's set her cap for the marquis."

"The hussy," Lady Portia hissed. She rose on her toes and eyed the open door to the cardroom. "He's here, you know."

"The marquis? Of course." Corinne's eyes sparkled. "Remember your husband promised to introduce me."

"Indeed." Lady Portia scanned the far section of the room. "I should find Harold and remind him." She swept off on her mission.

Corinne watched her friend stroll away before rounding on Rebecca and leaning in to whisper, "Lady Portia can move ladies to the top or bottom of London's invite list. I know you can't help it, but please act less conspicuous."

"How?" Rebecca gritted her teeth. "I'm so close to the window, I'm practically outside." The late-September air passed through the glass pane, chilling her skin between her gown's capped sleeves and her elbow-length gloves.

"Just don't embarrass me. You look as if you've never stepped foot in a ballroom before."

She hadn't.

Her cousin pulled her away. "I can't believe she mistook you for me." Her eyes narrowed as if homing in on the faults in Rebecca's complexion. "I suppose the Prestcote traits are strong in our family line."

She and her cousin Corinne shared certain features—a heart-shaped face, thick, dark hair a bit on the unmanageable side, wide-set hazel eyes, and apple cheekbones. Rebecca's younger sister, Madeline, resembled their mama with lighter hair and fairer skin.

Corinne shrugged. "Which means you're pretty."

"Thank you." Rebecca perked at the flattering remark, but then frowned. If she resembled her cousin so much that people mistook them, then Corinne had really just complimented herself. Her cousin hadn't always been so mean-spirited—only since Aunt Diana announced that Rebecca would debut along-side Corinne.

Surely, her cousin didn't see Rebecca as competition.

Over Corinne's shoulder, Rebecca spied a man weaving through the crush of taffeta gowns and kerseymere jackets with long strides, staring straight at her. "Lady Prestcote, I believe the next dance is mi—" He reared back as Corinne shifted to face him. "Lady Prestcote?" His gaze bounced between Rebecca and her cousin as if uncertain who was whom.

"Lord Danforth?" When he still seemed confused, Corinne's nostrils flared.

Rebecca had seen that look plenty. Her cousin was about to give Lord Danforth a stern set-down.

Corinne's eyes widened, and her lips parted with a gasp. She turned to Rebecca. "Rebecca, you're a dear. You're going to make my Season."

"What?" Her cousin's moods shifted faster than a weather-vane during a storm. "How?"

"Excuse us for a moment." Corinne held up a gloved finger for Lord Danforth to wait, and when he turned to speak to another guest, Corinne drew Rebecca closer, whispering in her ear. "I'm going to the Carter house party in Surrey, and you're going to the Coburn house party in the Cotswolds in my stead."

"What? No." Rebecca shook her head. "Your parents will be livid if they discover your plan."

"They will not hear of it because you're going to go as me."

"Don't be ridiculous. We'll be found out." Her Season would be over before it began. The upper crust of society despised being made to look foolish. She'd be ruined.

"Think of it." She gripped Rebecca's shoulders. "You'll be surrounded by intellectuals and professors. Even Professor What's-his-name will be there, that one you've gone on and on about."

Rebecca's heart jumped. "Professor Duval?" The man who

lectured on possible cures for the weak heart her mama died from? She could speak to him regarding her research and potential treatment for Madeline. She grasped Corinne's elbows. "You're certain Professor Duval will be there?"

"Of course." Corinne turned so their backs were to Lord Danforth and the rest of the room. "But for this to work, no one else must see us together." She stepped on the lace ruffle of Rebecca's gown and pushed her.

Rebecca stumbled into the curtains.

The sound of ripping fabric was muffled beneath the party's noises.

"Oh, my." Corinne covered her mouth with her gloved fingers in feigned astonishment. "You must be more careful."

Trembling in embarrassment and anger, Rebecca inspected her skirt, lifting the delicate fabric of the gown that had once belonged to her mother. The lace hem sagged on the hardwood floor.

Corinne leaned over and stared at the torn section. "That looks irreparable."

Rebecca and Madeline had spent hours altering the ruffles to fit the more modern trends. All their work, lost in a moment of sabotage. Rebecca stared at the lace, unsure whether to weep or rage at her cousin.

"You must return home at once," Corinne whispered in Rebecca's ear. "Go through the terrace door and follow the stone path to the garden shed. Exit the gate behind it. Take the carriage and have the driver return for me." She shooed her off. "Go on, now."

"I'm not going to let you—" A torn hem provided an opportunity for her to escape the party. She could return to her aunt and uncle's manor and finish the book on heart arrhythmias.

"If you want to meet your precious professor, then you must do things my way." Corinne didn't wait to see if she'd comply. Her cousin smiled at Lord Danforth, who approached once more. She linked her arm through his, and they strolled to the dance floor.

Rebecca picked her way through the crowd and onto the terrace. She had wished to be anywhere else—even prayed for it. Why, then, did she not feel right?

Was leaving a boon—or a problem in the making?

~

*L*ord Daniel Hudson Elmsley, the Marquis of Wolston, held back the thick boxwood hedge branches for a view of his target. His arms ached from the strain.

A chill in the air kept the guests lingering inside. The lack of people wandering the grounds must have kept his targets comfortable enough not to stray far from the terrace, which was fine with Daniel, for the proximity of the house made for his quick getaway if needed. The garden torches flickered in the night breeze and danced shadows across two men's faces.

"Your vote is imperative. The motion must pass, or our medical research will stagnate." Lord Holmes, the chancellor of the Royal College of Surgeons in London, glanced back at the entrance to the garden's alcove.

"For the right price, my opinion and that of other members can be swayed." The parliament member's deep baritone voice sounded familiar, though his identity remained in question as the man refused to step from the shadows.

The chancellor reached into his coat pocket and removed a rolled document. "It's too early for guests to drift far from the food and drink. Even so, we must make this quick."

Wait for it. The bribe was about to be exchanged for the remaining vote needed for parliament to legalize the motion that charity hospital patients, in return for free care, must consent to donate their bodies upon death to the anatomy hospital for dissection. He clenched his jaw at the injustice done to the poor. Many believed dissection could hinder their souls' departure into heaven, yet without charity, they couldn't afford care. The bill would make them choose between living a longer life and the comfort of heaven for eternity.

The marquis was always surprised at the information people divulged when they believed him to be a self-indulgent dandy who enjoyed partaking of spirits overly much. His assignment had called for his collaboration with two other operatives, but Daniel was about to accomplish the mission alone. He could almost hear the accolades of his superior, Lieutenant Scar, for a job well done after months of surveillance. He'd established their motive and was about to witness a money exchange. All he needed was to identify the statesman to take down the bribery scheme.

"A necessary evil." Holmes held the stack of banknotes closer to the torchlight. "But anatomy cannot be learned any other way."

A spider spun a web near Daniel's cheek, growing bolder as Daniel remained still. He blew air out the side of his mouth, and the spider jiggled away.

The politician accepted the notes and counted the sum.

Holmes leaned closer, the harsh torchlight aging the young man and adding dark shadows under his eyes. "No one will be the wiser."

Daniel moved back, careful not to step on the crushed stone path and alert them of his presence. Grabbing his neglected drink, he set his plan into motion, dipping his hand into his untouched spirits and spritzing the potent scent onto his jacket.

This was his chance to expose parliament's corruption and earn his superior's respect. He moved into position. They wouldn't suspect a thing about the harmless marquis, stumbling around drunk as a wheelbarrow, as usual. He'd get a good look at the statesman's face when he bumped into him.

A door opened on the veranda.

The chatter from the guests inside spilled out into the night air, and Lord Holmes glanced at the house. The door closed, diminishing the party's hullabaloo to a dull murmur. Someone was exiting the ball via the far side terrace door.

He glanced over his shoulder to the top of the veranda stairs. A pale blue flash of a woman's skirt dampened Daniel's hope. He stood directly in her path at the bottom of the steps.

Blast.

If he turned, she'd surely recognize him and make a fuss, blowing his opportunity, but if he stayed, it would be obvious he was spying on someone on the other side of the hedge.

The party member stuffed the bills into the inside pocket of his coat.

From the direction of the young lady, the sound of tearing fabric ripped through the quiet of the gardens, followed by a high-pitched, startled shriek.

Daniel released his hold on the boxwood bush and spun. The woman's arms flailed—her hem caught on a trim board on the top step. He raised his arms in time to catch the falling female guest before she tackled him to the ground. Her forehead whacked his cheek as he gripped her in an awkward hug. Her arms wrapped around his neck, and his fingers clasped her back.

Footsteps scuffled behind him, and he caught a flash of a cloak as the conspiring scoundrels darted deeper into the gardens.

The woman in his arms squirmed. Daniel tried to set her down to give chase, but she remained unable to get her feet underneath her.

Confound it.

He tugged, but the hem of her gown refused to give without his ripping the bottom ruffle of her dress completely away.

The sound of footfalls down the crushed stone grew distant. The men were getting away.

He had to let go.

He swung her down and, bending slightly, dropped her the remaining inches onto the grass.

He dashed after his targets.

And cringed at a thud and the woman's startled gasp.

CHAPTER 2

*D*aniel dashed into the garden's shadows. The juniper smell of gin wafted around him as he paused at a dead end—one of many he'd already discovered. He listened. Only the ruckus of the party inside the manor filtered through the thick night air.

He circled back around and caught a hired hack departing with Lord Holmes peeking out the back window.

Thunder and turf.

He kicked a stone into the bushes. Lord Holmes had gotten away, and Daniel never laid eyes on the other conspirator. The statesman could have ridden off with Lord Holmes or could be mingling with the guests, but Daniel wouldn't be able to identify him. How would he report this to Lieutenant Scar? He'd be the laughingstock of the Home Office and surely demoted. After all he'd done to prove himself, losing his target was a significant setback.

Lieutenant Scar had taken a risk on Daniel despite Daniel's grandfather's opposition. The crusty old duke had told the lieutenant that Daniel had been mollycoddled by his mother and had never seen a hard day of work.

The memory of Grandfather's condemnation riled the same tempest as it had twelve years prior, when his disparaging assessment lit a torch within Daniel to prove him wrong.

Once again, you crumpled under pressure. You're weak.

Daniel blamed the woman, but what was he to do? Let her fall?

Guilt caught up with him, and he raced back to where he'd left her.

Rounding the hedge, he skidded to a halt at the vision of the woman he'd dropped in the grass, appearing like Persephone, the Grecian goddess, dragging herself up from the underworld. She lay in a precarious position, her feet tangled in her gown and the hem still caught on the trim board. Several long tresses of dark hair had fallen from her simple coiffure and hung in glorious waves over her back.

Her cream-satin-gloved hand worked to free her feet from their shackles. She murmured under her breath, "...should have hidden in the library."

The library?

Did this socialite enjoy reading, or was she holding a clandestine meeting? His irritation over her interruption switched to curiosity.

"Allow me." Daniel climbed the few steps and unhooked the torn hem from the trim board. He untangled the lacy material from around her slippers. In his pass, his thumb grazed the delicate skin along her ankle. She gasped and jumped, but he continued with his task of freeing her from her bonds. How had she gotten twisted up so...?

She tucked her feet underneath her gown and sat up. Even in the cool darkness of the night, he could feel the heat of her blush. She stared at the ground, seeming unwilling to look him in the eye.

He wound the unraveled hem around his hand and held it out to her.

She glanced up, and their gazes held. "You."

Let it begin.

He knew the following conversation too well. *Yes, I'm the marquis. Did I plan to dance? Actually, I planned to finish the night in the cardroom. Terribly sorry.*

She stiffened, and her brows snapped together. "You dropped me."

He'd been well off his mark.

"My apologies." He aided her to stand.

She had every right to be upset with him. It had been an ungentlemanlike thing to do. How was he to explain such rude behavior?

Frowning, she rubbed her hip while examining her elbow.

He pulled her into the soft light of a garden torch to inspect her injuries. "Are you hurt?"

She snorted. "I've little hope of my pride ever recovering."

In the flickering shadows of the torchlight, he discerned the image of a dark-haired beauty with heavily lashed, wide-set, intelligent eyes. She arched an eyebrow and crossed her arms and gave him an *explain yourself* look.

Unsure how to do so, Daniel stalled by brazenly plucking a leaf from her hair and dusting a few sprigs of grass from her gown. The missing hem offered an ample view of her trim ankles. He forced his gaze back to her face before his thoughts took an unseemly turn.

She leaned in closer.

Was she hoping he'd pull her into his embrace? The temptation was strong, but unwise. He tensed and prepared to move away.

She sniffed. "You're foxed."

By Jove, that's right. He'd quite forgotten he reeked of gin. His supposed drunkenness could play nicely into his hand.

"Indeed," he said a bit too enthusiastically, offering her what he hoped looked like a besotted grin. "I apologize for my muddled mind and ungentlemanlike behavior. I feared casting up my accounts."

She grimaced.

"I didn't." *Don't over-explain.*

"Splendid."

He chuckled at the sarcasm in her voice.

She studied his face in the torchlight, and he waited for her to identify him at any moment with a, *my lord!* Then the fawning over his title would begin, but the dark-haired goddess merely sighed, mumbling, "I'm not cut out for these social soirees." She grunted. "And this is only the start."

"I'd say you're doing quite well."

She snorted. "My hem is in tatters."

"It happens now and again." He shrugged. "A common hazard when dancing."

"I fell down a flight of stairs." Her look of self-deprecation was refreshing and adorable.

"I, too, acted foolishly." He couldn't quell his snort or the urge to make her feel better. "But chin up—you met a marquis."

"I can't be introduced to a marquis." She glanced down at her gown and satin slippers peeking out. "There's no way I can return to the party looking like this."

She must have misunderstood him. Did she truly not know who he was?

Her head tilted, and she blinked, studying him closer. He knew the minute she made the association because her expression fell, lips parting, and he physically felt her gasp as if she'd sucked the air from his lungs.

"*You're* the marquis." Her words held a reverent whisper. She dropped into a curtsy. "Lord Wolston."

How had she not recognized him? A clue regarding his mystery woman—she didn't mingle among the *ton.*

He stepped closer, playing the part of a foxed libertine despite the alarms in his head warning him to keep his distance. He lifted her chin with his knuckle and peered down at her with the same look he used to melt the paramours, wives, and daughters of diplomats. Usually, his aloof finesse flowed with ease, but the disarming innocence in her gaze turned personal. She smelled like the perennial his sister, Alicia, kept in the solarium. What had she called it? "Your scent reminds me of that white-flowering plant with the thick petals."

"A gardenia?" Intelligence flashed in her eyes, and another warning sounded that she'd see right through his personas and uncover his secrets.

"You've heard of them?"

"Interesting fact." A smile tinged her lips, and her eyes sparked. "They're rare and imported from the Pacific regions of Africa and Australia."

He chuckled at another intriguing clue. She either practiced botany or was a devoted plant enthusiast.

The door to the terrace opened. "Wolston?"

Daniel recognized the voice and silhouette of his fellow chap from university, Lord Tremont.

"Where are you? We're moving to the card room for the evening."

Daniel had gone missing for too long. If Tremont caught sight of this beautiful chit with him in her rumpled state, her reputation would be in tatters before the Season started.

So much for maintaining a safe distance. He hugged her to his chest and spun into the shadows, his back shielding her from view.

"Unhand—"

"Shh." Daniel pressed his index finger to her lips. The moonlight illuminated her eyes, expressive pools of shock, confusion, and—a glint of something—curiosity? He leaned a hair's breadth from her ear and whispered, "Someone will discover us."

His damsel stilled, but her curled fingers clung to the lapels of his jacket. Silken tendrils of hair danced in the night breeze, caressing his cheek. The heady smell of gardenias pervaded his nostrils, leaving him dizzy. He allowed his drunken persona to act on its inhibitions, running his finger over her plump lower lip.

By Jove, it was soft.

Her gaze slid to his mouth, and the curious glint returned.

"Wolston? Is that you?" Tremont bellowed.

She glanced toward the house, and the tip of her nose lightly brushed his.

Blast. If Tremont saw them, every gossip monger in all of London would hear of the scandal before morning. He dipped her, and even in the shadows, with only the pale moonlight above, saw her eyes widen.

"Whatever are you doing?" She clung to him.

"Shh!" If he covered her mouth with his hand, he'd drop her a second time.

"Release—"

He pressed his lips to hers and absorbed her startled gasp.

She stilled, and he got the distinct impression this was her first kiss. And that she was analyzing it—perhaps for later comparisons. The curious beauty, delicate and subdued in his arms, stoked a fire to deepen the kiss and make it one she'd never forget.

Justice isn't served by creating another injustice. The niggling voice of his sister invaded his conscience, extinguishing his desire.

Typically, his assignments involved getting foreign ambassadors to divulge confidences. He shouldn't be shocked that kissing a lovely young lady was more enjoyable, but this innocent temptress pressed the limits of his control and better judgment. In his line of work, he'd thought little of finding a wife. Being a spy wasn't conducive to marriage, and he had plenty of time before an heir for the dukedom must be procured.

Suddenly, the notion of entering the institution felt... pertinent.

You cad. You don't even know her name.

A man snorted.

He'd forgotten about Tremont's presence behind him and the threat he posed.

Tremont exhaled and muttered, "Figures."

Daniel peeked out the corner of one eye and saw Tremont leave.

The woman's eyes flew open, and she stiffened as if just noticing their unwanted spectator.

Daniel stroked the back of her head to calm her, reveling in the silken feel of her hair.

The door opened, and orchestra music floated around them.

Her body relaxed, and her eyelids fluttered back closed.

Daniel lingered with a light, shivery kiss, waiting to ensure Tremont wouldn't return.

The door closed, and the music once again muffled.

Daniel lifted his mouth from hers but didn't release her. His chest rose and fell in rhythm with hers, and their breaths mingled. She must believe him the worst libertine ever—and a drunkard, to boot. She had every right to take him to task or haul him to the altar for his indiscretions. He lifted his gaze from her mouth only to find those curiously expressive eyes observing him, and he tumbled into their dark depths.

A distant voice in his brain said, *don't forget your mission,* but his concentration focused on how nicely she fit against him. She was a refreshing change, like autumn's burst of color or the unblemished, fanciful expectation of the first snow.

All the romantic dribble filling his thoughts would please his sisters. He blamed them for reading him so many excerpts from their novels.

Her hand slid up his chest, and his muscles reflexively

tightened. The soft satin of the fingertips of her glove brushed the line of his jaw, and his breath caught at her intimate touch.

"Unhand me!" The heel of her palm rammed his chin, knocking his teeth together and slamming his head back.

Daniel glimpsed the starlit sky and blinked to stop the stars from spinning. He'd sorely misjudged her touch as a caress, considering she'd actually been positioning to pack a good wallop. He released her and grunted.

He deserved her retaliation.

She stepped back, holding up the balled hem like a shield.

"Do that again, and I'll scream."

Quite unexpected.

Usually, ladies fawned over him, or at least his title, but not this dark-haired beauty.

He stepped back into the warm glow spilling from the windows, hooked an arm around the stone pineapple finial on the railing's baluster, and gazed with a heavy-lidded stare at his accuser. "Again, I beg your pardon. Although I saved you from being spotted—and therefore your reputation from being ruined—my methods were, admittedly, unorthodox. But unless I was mistaken, you seemed to enjoy it."

"A Canterbury tale. Every word." She protested rather quickly and looked away, as if to hide her blush. A cloud drifted in front of the moon and further shadowed her face, so he couldn't see if her face heightened in color. She attempted to move around him, but he blocked her path.

"Allow me to escort you to your carriage." He tucked her hand into the crook of his arm. "There are scoundrels out there who'd try to take advantage of a woman alone at night."

"Such as yourself?" She eyed him with a dubious glare and kept a wide space between their bodies as they strolled.

Most ladies of the *ton* would lean or brush against his side.

"Nay, my fair lady. You are safe with me. As it is, my sisters will box my ears after interrogating me tonight. Don't fret. I won't mention your name, for you've yet to offer it."

He paused, waiting for her to supply it. Instead, she peered at him.

"You reek of spirits, but you taste of lemonade." She stepped away, yanking her hand back, and crossed her arms, the lacy ball of trim peeking out from underneath. "Why is that?"

Daniel's breath hitched as warning bells sounded in his mind.

The chit was much too clever.

~

*W*hy was the marquis pretending to be foxed?

Rebecca willed the night air to cool her heated cheeks and studied him.

He stiffened at her comment, and if he hadn't quickly covered his shock, she might have burst out laughing, though the moment didn't call for humor.

Lord Wolston stepped back. A nearby torch shadowed the crease that formed between his straight eyebrows. His masculine features were all planes and angles—a square jaw, pointed chin, and a Roman nose with a slight curve, as if it might have been broken at some point. But a pair of piercing blue eyes rested under thick, fringed lashes the color of sand, and a generous mouth softened his manly aura with a boyish youthfulness.

She needn't focus on his mouth.

He cleared his throat. "I find lemonade helps sober the mind."

Rubbish.

Lord Wolston eyed her, then the house, and twisted to glance toward the garden gate.

She couldn't make heads nor tails of the evening's bizarre chain of events.

He pointed at her mostly detached hem. "Can it be repaired?"

"I hope so." If he was to believe her to be Corinne, she had to make it seem she intended to return to the party. She peered down at the torn fabric so he couldn't see her face as she told a white lie. "My maid is waiting in the carriage to repair it so I can return. She'll be wondering where I am. I should be going." She bobbed a curtsy and strode down the stone path.

"Wait." He gripped her arm.

She'd almost made it to the back gate. "My carriage is right there." She shook off his hold and continued, inclining her chin to the cluster of conveyances and waving as if her make-believe maid waited inside and could see her.

"Very well." He hurried forward, lifted the latch, and swung the gate open.

She nodded her gratitude and started to pass, but he stepped in her way.

She raised her hands to keep from bumping into his chest.

"What is your name?" The intensity of his gaze raised the fine hairs on her arms.

Rebecca, her heart cried, but her mouth said, "Miss Prestcote."

He stepped aside, and she skirted past, counting her steps to slow her stride to the carriages. Was he watching her? *Please go away. Go back inside.* She glanced over her shoulder to see if she was in the clear.

"A pleasure to meet you, Miss Prestcote." He leaned against the gatepost with arms crossed and a smug smile lifting one corner of his mouth.

Could she say the same? Unsure if she should nod or shake her head, she attempted a smile and darted to hide between two carriages. Through a double set of windows, she watched and waited.

After a long moment, he closed the gate and headed back to the house.

She silenced the nagging of her heart. Men were merely a distraction that had cost her dearly and, if she wasn't careful, could do so again.

CHAPTER 3

Thunder and turf. Daniel kicked the fencepost, and pain shot up his leg. What an evening. He'd mishandled his mission and let his target get away. Then he'd taken advantage of Miss Prestcote, a poor, innocent girl entering the social scene.

He hadn't needed to kiss her. Now that the moment was over, he could hardly justify his rationalization that he'd done it to save her reputation. *Truly?*

Ravishing her to keep her from ruin?

He could have told her to run. He could have pulled her deeper into the garden and hidden her.

His big toe smarted, but not as much as his disappointment in himself. The thin sole of his dress shoes didn't offer the same protection as his Hessian boots, and he limped off in pain, retracing his steps to the veranda.

The last thing he wanted was to socialize, but if he didn't make a reappearance at the party, tongues would wag about his disappearance, and he'd hate for Miss Prestcote to be pulled into the gossip despite her torn-hem alibi. He passed the spot where he broke her fall and ascended the steps, remembering her expressive wide-set eyes, those soft lips—*you smell of spirits, but taste of lemonade*—and her keen intelligence.

Mayhap the party wouldn't be a complete bore. If he could get a proper introduction when she returned, he could further his acquaintance with the tempting beauty. He checked on the card game and watched a few rounds, but Tremont and his friends from university shushed him to concentrate on a French emissary who'd placed a high-stakes bet. The dandy was sweating profusely.

Daniel couldn't abide watching a man lose more than he could afford, landing him in dun territory, so he returned to the ballroom and scanned its occupants.

Would Miss Prestcote's maid have had substantial time to mend the torn hem?

Dark hair and a pale-blue gown drew his eye—Miss Prestcote? She must have changed gowns instead. Lord Clifford escorted her off the dance floor to where Lady Portia Heming stood with her husband. *Brilliant.* Lord Heming could formally introduce them.

He sauntered to where they stood near the Italian marble fireplace topped with a large gilded mirror. "Lord Heming, I hope you fared better in the cardroom."

All heads in the group swiveled in Daniel's direction.

Lady Heming fluttered her fan faster and reached over to squeeze Miss Prestcote's arm.

Miss Prestcote's other hand moved to her hair, and she glanced in the mirror as if checking to ensure every strand remained in place. Her lady's maid had re-pinned her hair. His sisters would be impressed by her servant's efficiency. Seemingly satisfied, she issued a daring smile at Daniel.

Funny, her lips had appeared fuller earlier, her nose a little thinner, but it could have been the shadows of the torchlight playing tricks on him.

Lord Heming clapped him on the shoulder. "Not as well as

I'd hoped, or I'd still be in there." He waggled his eyebrows. "At least I'm not the Frenchman." He pivoted to his wife. "Lord Wolston, I believe you've met my wife, Lady Portia Heming."

Lady Heming curtsied low. "My lord."

"Lady Heming." He bowed.

"And this is her dear friend, Lady Corinne Prestcote."

Lady? He thought she'd said Miss, but perhaps he'd misheard. He locked gazes with her and bowed a second time. "A pleasure to meet you, Lady Prestcote."

She fanned her face with her left hand.

If his sisters' notions were correct, positioning her fan in such a fashion meant she desired an acquaintance. *Fascinating.* "Lady Prestcote, would you care to dance?"

"Most definitely." She batted her lashes and met him with a come-hither smile.

Was Lady Prestcote typically this flirtatious? She hadn't been outside. In fact, she'd pushed him away. But then again, he'd surprised her, and she hadn't recognized him. Now, she held up her gloved hand, which he placed it in the crook of his arm before parading her onto the dance floor.

Corinne. The name sounded too cold for the winsome beauty who'd warmed his arms and heart earlier, but it could grow on him.

Lady Prestcote raised her chin and glanced over the other party guests haughtily, as though she used him to get attention and higher standing.

He loathed that exploitation of his title.

Daniel swallowed and pulled her into position for a waltz. Had he been mistaken about Lady Prestcote?

The music began. At least she danced well, and halfway through the piece, he complimented her for being light on her feet.

"My parents only allowed the best instructors." Her hazel eyes met his and held, but his concentration didn't wane, nor did he feel overwhelmed by her nearness as he had earlier. "Lord Brissett from Paris instructed me. Have you heard of him?"

The name sounded familiar. His sisters might have mentioned him, but Daniel shook his head.

"He's well known and in high demand. My parents heard of him during their travels. Currently, they're in Prussia, meeting the prince. Papa is the British ambassador."

Her parents were well traveled. That could explain how she knew where gardenias flourished. So she wasn't the amateur botanist he'd fancied her to be.

He guided her through a turn. "Prussia is beautiful. I've ice-fished there."

She blinked, and her lips parted as if to speak, but she hesitated as if uncertain what to say regarding the topic of ice fishing. "I've heard the Prussian palace is extravagant. My parents say the king throws elaborate parties."

"Prince Wilhelm mentioned they may add a dome to the palace."

Again, his comment met with silence, and his favorable opinion of Lady Prestcote sank faster than a ship with a breach in the hull. He preferred intelligent conversation regarding the sea creatures of the North Sea, the architectural feat of building a dome, or the origins of gardenias over small talk.

Anything over small talk.

She offered him another coy smile. "Mama promised she'd return with an amber necklace for me."

"Collected from the Baltic?"

She blinked at him.

He worked to keep a pleasant expression on his face as his night turned into a complete debacle. She might not be aware that the Baltic Sea was known for its amber stones, but she could at least attempt conversation beyond the banal.

The time had come for him to cut his losses and take leave.

The music ended. He bowed and escorted her back to her friends. He attempted to pass her off to Lord and Lady Heming, but Lady Prestcote clung to his arm.

"I'm afraid I must be leaving." He nodded goodbye to Lord Heming and his wife.

"I have it on the best authority that you'll attend the Carlson house party." Lady Prestcote offered a pretty pout above the handle of her fan.

What did that gesture mean? An image of his sisters giggling on the bed with fans as they practiced what seemed like a secret language flashed through his mind. Handle to the lips meant *kiss me*. His sisters had fallen into a fit of laughter after showing him that signal.

"I'll be there too." She flashed him a coquettish smile, but her shyness was a farce.

Which meant, she'd been pretending outside. Confound it. He was a spy and should have ascertained her fake façade.

"Splendid." He attempted to shake off her grip on his arm with a bow. Unsuccessful, he had no choice but to pinch the fabric of her glove and remove her hand from his arm so he could back away.

He'd hoped this Season would differ from the last. Apparently not.

Lady Heming and Lady Prestcote whispered behind their fans and eyed him as if not recognizing the sardonic tone in his last comment.

Usually, he was an excellent judge of character. He shook his head and grunted. How could he have been so mistaken?

∼

Two days later, Rebecca sat on her cousin's bed in her traveling dress while Corinne pulled out gown after gown from her wardrobe and passed them to a maid to pack.

Corinne peered at Rebecca's feet. "You'll need to wear your own slippers since our feet aren't the same size, but since you're also a tad shorter, a longer hem will hide your worn shoes."

Rebecca refused the impulse to tuck her feet out of view under the bed, staring at her folded hands in her lap.

After the Lipscomb ball, Corinne had arrived home as the sun rose and been all sighs and smiles and raved about how the marquis had singled her out for a dance.

Rebecca hadn't wanted to intrude on her cousin's bliss nor start a competition to win a man's favor. Therefore, she hadn't mentioned her interaction with Lord Wolston—nor their shared kiss. How many times had she relived that moment in her mind, savoring the feelings it stirred but hating herself for it at the same time?

Men were a distraction she couldn't afford, especially a debonair, overconfident marquis, who, if he hadn't been foxed, wouldn't have paid her a second glance.

She'd considered that he'd merely pretended to be intoxicated but ruled it out. If he'd been of sober mind, he certainly wouldn't have paid her any heed, especially looking as she had with her hem dragging and her coiffure coming loose. The tips of her ears burned, remembering how she'd discussed where gardenias originated. If he'd been in a normal state, surely, her bluestocking ways would have appalled him.

Rebecca watched in a daze as luxuriant gowns and undergarments were packed, her own secondhand clothes set aside.

Marriage to a marquis could solve her father's financial issues, but the chances of a marquis choosing her were statistically insignificant enough to be laughable. Rebecca needed to focus on a cure for her sister—without distraction.

"I can't leave without Madeline. What if her condition worsens?"

Corinne shrugged. "Take your sister with you. She can act as your chaperone, and my prior governess, Miss Blakeford, can be your lady's maid." Corinne closed the wardrobe and opened her jewelry box, holding up strands of pearls and simple pendants to accent the gowns.

"But she's a governess. How will you convince her to take the role of lady's maid?" She lowered her voice so Corinne's maid wouldn't hear as she packed. "Wouldn't that be considered beneath her?"

A devious smile spread across Corinne's face as she searched her dresser. "The same way I avoided most of my lessons." She passed several pairs of gloves to the servant. "I know her secret. If she wants a letter of recommendation to continue being a governess, she does whatever I request."

"But that's wrong." A shudder ran through Rebecca.

Corinne's deviousness wasn't evident unless she was crossed. Was the cautious young girl she and Madeline befriended that one summer Corinne visited still in there somewhere?

Corinne shrugged. "You've lived in the country too long." A heaviness weighed her expression as if weary of a long existing burden. "Manipulation is the way of the world, especially in politics. It's not who you know, it's what you know about them."

This charade felt so wrong—the deception, lies, and blackmail. Rebecca couldn't pretend to be Corinne. Why had she agreed to it? Her cousin had a reputation, which would put Rebecca in a quandary. If Corinne expected her to act pretentious and forward, especially with men, her cousin's plan would fail—*terribly*. Rebecca had been an awkward mess in front of the marquis, falling down the stairs, not recognizing him, and punching him in the chin.

Corinne shut the drawer and stilled. "Don't even think of backing out on me." She rounded on Rebecca. "I danced with the marquis, and he expects to continue our acquaintance at the Carlson house party."

Mama would have prayed for God's guidance to know the

right thing to do. Grandmama and Grandpapa would have also, but all their prayers hadn't made a difference in Mama's sickness and death. Since Madeline had become ill, Rebecca refused to stand by and wait to see if God would intervene.

She couldn't lose Madeline. She had to act.

"You said you wanted to meet this professor to cure Madeline," Corinne pressed. "A more perfect scenario isn't likely to come along. You'll even have your sister with you to try treatments." Corinne crossed her arms. "Sometimes you must make concessions. Life rewards action. Being smart doesn't help unless you have the courage to act on what you know."

The maid shut the trunk with a bang.

Corinne pulled Rebecca to a stand. "You must go. Otherwise, you'll always wonder if you could have done more to save your sister."

Rebecca swallowed her misgivings and nodded. Madeline's health must be prioritized over her qualms.

A smile swept over her cousin's face. "Good. Just behave as I said, stick to the plan, and things will go swimmingly."

Rebecca forced a smile.

Swimmingly good, or swimmingly as in trying not to drown?

~

*D*aniel scooted forward on the sofa of the converted townhouse that was now the Home Office and rested his forearms on his thighs as he waited for Lieutenant Scar. Across from him, the lieutenant's clerk worked busily at a small angled desk outside the man's door.

The clerk dipped his quill in the inkwell and furiously scribbled, making the feathered top wiggle. When he finished his paragraph, he held the feather high, presumably re-reading his work.

From Scar's office, his low, rumbling voice rose to a near shout before the door opened and an agent exited. The bloke, with whom Daniel had often sparred in pugilism matches to keep his training fresh, looked drawn and defeated. He didn't make eye contact with Daniel as he passed.

The clerk dropped his pen in the inkwell and peered up at Daniel. "Next."

Daniel slowly rose and, with an ill feeling, glanced one last time at his retreating comrade.

"Don't fret." The clerk peered at Daniel over his spectacles. "Being a husband and parent has mellowed the lieutenant."

Daniel had only met Lieutenant Scar once. Their conversation had been brief, held in a dim tavern, when Daniel had received an overview of his first assignment. Now, as he entered the office, a large sunlit window back-dropped the lieutenant at his desk, turning the man into a mere silhouette.

"Agent Wolston." He gestured for him to sit, and Daniel lowered into the upholstered chair and waited for his eyes to adjust. "Due to an unexpected meeting request from the Prince Regent, I must skip the formalities and get right to business." He signed the bottom of a letter. "Your target got away."

While Lieutenant Scar set the quill aside and removed a folded paper from his desk, Daniel scanned the signed page, deciphering it upside-down. He recognized his name written next to the words *good sense of right and wrong, desires justice above all, and holds potential but lacks the patience and maturity for the assignment.*

His stomach knotted. Not the glowing endorsement he'd hoped for. He exhaled a steady breath. "Yes, sir."

"Why?" Lieutenant Scar shifted the letter aside to allow the ink to dry and leaned back in his chair, lacing his fingers. His hair was longer than most agents, and his collar points pulled high. If rumors could be believed, the man was riddled with battle scars that had earned him his name and reputation within the War Department. The intensity of his gaze alone made Daniel squirm.

"As I was in position to identify the target, a woman exited the building and toppled down the stairs. If I hadn't caught her, she would have landed at my feet, injuring herself and giving away my position. Lord Holmes and his co-conspirator heard the commotion and fled. I gave chase, but they stole away in a hired hack."

"What intel did you obtain on the target?"

Daniel resisted the urge to sink lower in his chair and forced out the disappointing words, "Very little." He recalled the scene from that night. "He was well-dressed, of standard build, and about five foot seven or eight. He stayed in the shadows and said little."

"Your mission was to identify the target. Why didn't you use the assistance the Home Office lined up? We had several agents in the area."

"I believed I could handle it alone. I saw the opportunity and took it."

"You rushed the operation, leaving holes that should have been buttoned up. You're too prideful to seek assistance when you need it."

Heat spread up Daniel's neck.

"More injustices will be done with the target still at large. How many more allegiances will be bought?"

Daniel's jaw tightened.

Lieutenant Scar pulled an envelope off a side table and opened it. "I'm taking you off the case."

"What?" Daniel gripped the armrests.

The lieutenant flashed a warning glare.

"I'll stake out Holmes to see if the Parliament member makes contact." Daniel scooted to the edge of his seat. "I can bring the target in. Don't take me off."

"I have something more pressing."

Daniel nodded, even though inwardly, he sulked. He'd botched his big assignment. Had he lost his chance to prove himself and gain real agency experience? The last thing he wanted was to be used for his social connections to gather information to pass along so another agent could step in and bring down the accomplice or criminal ring.

Would he never see action?

Lieutenant Scar unfolded the letter and scanned it. "I'd have asked Agent Warren to take this one, but he's recently married. Lord Felton's wife just bore their second child."

Those agents received the assignments Daniel could only long for.

Using his palm and the edge of his desk, Lieutenant Scar cleanly ripped off the bottom half of the letter and passed it to Daniel.

He read the handwritten address—twice. "Leafield?" No real spy activity happened in a rural village in the hamlet of Langley. *Hound's teeth.* The lieutenant must have lost faith in Daniel's abilities after one mishap.

"An associate in Edinburgh passed intelligence to the department regarding gravediggers selling bodies for a lofty price to their university. Our associate was informed the bodies had been sourced near Leafield, and I want you to investigate."

"Dead bodies?"

The lieutenant didn't answer, the tiniest quirk to his eyebrow.

Of course, he meant dead bodies. If he'd been referring to alive bodies, he'd call them missing persons. Daniel shook his head. "You're implying I need to intercept a band of resurrection men robbing graves?"

"I implied nothing. That's for you to discover." Lieutenant Scar held the corner of the remainder of the letter and envelope to the candle on his desk, and a flickering yellow flame quickly consumed it. He dropped it into a metal waste bin beside his desk. "Lady Coburn is hosting her annual fortnight-long house party."

Daniel forced his gaze away from the dwindling flame. Capturing a band of sack 'em up men was a higher-level assignment and more action-packed than gathering intelligence. This could be his opportunity, after all.

"I presume you can obtain an invitation?"

One of the many benefits of being a marquis—party invitations were easy to acquire. "Certainly."

"You'll want to stake out the graveyard and follow the robbers back to their source. I need to know who's paying them to exhume the bodies and why."

"I'm to wait at the Coburns until someone dies?"

"Someone already has." Lieutenant Scar bowed his head as if praying for the deceased's family. "A local man, the chandler, who'd fallen down on his luck. He's to be buried in two days' time. Hence, it would be best if you rode to Leafield today."

"Understood."

Lieutenant Scar rose, and Daniel followed his lead.

"God's speed, agent." The lieutenant dipped his head and lowered back into his chair.

Daniel headed for the exit.

"One more thing, Agent Wolston."

Daniel turned in the doorway.

"Lady Coburn's guests tend to be"—he glanced up at the ceiling as if searching for the right words—"interesting, let's just say."

"I'll keep that in mind." Daniel held back his grin until after he passed the clerk's desk on his way out. This was the second chance he'd been hoping for.

He'd attended some strange parties before—costume, themed, stuffy, foreign, and awkward. He doubted Lady Coburn's guests could be more interesting than the opportunity to take down body snatchers.

CHAPTER 4

*R*ebecca stared out the carriage window at Wychwood Forest. The dense woods opened up to the sun setting over rolling hills and a pond, complete with a stone bridge that the carriage rattled over. Large imposing trees lined the road leading to the Gothic manor home. Their leaves hinted at changing into their fall garments, and a few fell, swirling in a gust of wind across their path.

The carriage pulled around the circular drive and parked. Cracked and lichen-covered columns reminded her of images she'd seen in books of the Roman Pantheon. They held up a sizable stone portico. An east and west wing, with two stories of mullioned windows reflecting the red dusk sky, stretched to low Belvedere towers in both directions that crowned each corner.

"Look at this place." Madeline's nose touched the glass as she stared at Griffin Hall. "Our cottage could fit inside a single floor of one of the towers."

Rebecca gazed at the grandeur tucked away in the rural country. No longer would she be Rebecca Prestcote, village bluestocking. Instead, she'd become a social elite and earl's daughter, Corinne Prestcote.

Play the part.

She shook the shoulder of Corinne's middle-aged governess, and poor Miss Blakeford woke with a start. The plain-featured governess had said very little on the eight-hour carriage ride, even though Rebecca and Madeline had tried to include her in conversation. The woman only eyed Rebecca as if leery of what she might do next, or more likely, what Rebecca's cousin might hold against her.

Madeline had commented on a gold bracelet around Miss Blakeford's wrist. *I never take it off*, the governess said, speaking fondly of her niece, who'd given it to her.

"We've arrived." Rebecca smiled at the governess. She could only hope that her soon-to-be lady's maid would eventually warm up to her.

A footman opened the carriage door and helped Rebecca, Madeline, and Miss Blakeford alight. Rebecca held her head high, imitating how Corinne carried herself. She tried not to gape at the imposing entrance as the butler in maroon-and-gold livery swung open the thick oak door for them to enter.

Two red-carpeted sets of stairs mirrored each other on opposite sides of the foyer. Colorful tapestries hung from three second-story balconies, billowing over the marbled white floor. Ghostly busts with unseeing eyes loomed in arched alcoves, and the armor of two knights stood erect in the corners. Crossed swords and the Coburn coats of arms hung on the far wall, contrasting with the muraled dome ceiling painted with blue sky, puffy white clouds, and angels carrying long trumpets.

In such a regal setting, surely, she'd stand out as a fraud.

God help her.

Rebecca looked over her shoulder to gauge Madeline's reaction, but her sister was nowhere to be found. She stepped back and whispered to Miss Blakeford, "Where did my sister go?"

"To the servant's entrance, I presume." Miss Blakeford's expression remained bland.

"What?" Rebecca couldn't keep the panic from her voice. "Why?"

The governess shrugged. "She is determined to act as your lady's maid. She thinks no one would believe someone so young could be your chaperone."

Madeline, her beloved sister...her maid? Rebecca peeked around the butler through the sidelight window of the main entrance door, as if Madeline still stood outside.

"Lady Corinne Prestcote?" A singsong voice called from across the room.

Rebecca swallowed her shock and faced her approaching host.

"Welcome back to Griffin Hall." Lady Coburn entered the foyer, her long satin-gloved fingers extended. She took Rebecca's hands and practically drew them to her chest. "It has been an age." The ostrich feather trimming her white turban waved in greeting above them. Her face held a warm smile, and her eyes appeared sharp but kind. She held Rebecca's arms out. "Last time your mama brought you along, you were in leading strings. Now, you're all grown up." She released Rebecca's hands. "How fare your parents? I miss your mama. Letters do not suffice."

Could she pull off looking and acting like her cousin to people who'd known her? She itched to run and hide in the safety of a book, but she forced a gregarious smile and pretended to be Corinne. "Mama is well and also misses you. She's in Prussia with Papa, who's meeting with the prince. Otherwise, they would never have missed your party."

Lady Coburn clasped her hands under her chin. "I'm so grateful you agreed to join us in their stead."

"Indeed." Rebecca turned and eyed the woman who'd

become her chaperone without Rebecca's consent. "Miss Blakeford has accompanied me as my travel companion."

Lady Coburn gestured to a footman, who'd appeared in the room's periphery. "John can show you to your room and your chaperone to hers. He'll also ensure your trunks are settled. We dine at eight. I do hope you'll join us, but I understand if you'd prefer to take the evening meal in your chamber after the long ride."

"You are too kind." Rebecca dipped a curtsy. "I'm looking forward to freshening up."

"Lady Coburn." A man walked into the foyer carrying a thick opened book. He looked up at the last minute, and Rebecca held in her gasp.

Professor Duval.

She recognized him from the drawings printed on pamphlets advertising his speaking engagements. He was younger than she'd imagined, probably not more than five to seven years her senior. His well-tailored suit fit his lanky physique, which was not uncommon for a man who spent much of his time engaged in academic pursuits. He pushed his spectacles up the bridge of his nose and blinked at Rebecca as if with a donning awareness that Lady Coburn had been speaking to another.

"I'm certain you're weary from your travels. I won't keep you." Lady Coburn kissed the air next to Rebecca's cheeks and waved her off before addressing the professor.

Rebecca hesitated. Professor Duval was the man she'd come here to see. Should she say something? It wasn't proper without an introduction. Perhaps if she hesitated, Lady Coburn would formally acquaint them.

"Right this way, miss." The footmen beckoned her forward, but Rebecca peeked over her shoulder, slowly meandering to the exit.

"Have you seen Professor Matthews?" Professor Duval's

slightly disheveled hair and crooked cravat presented an endearing picture, as though he needed a female's hand to make him presentable. Most likely, his intelligent mind, over-working a problem, couldn't be bothered by trivial matters like appearance.

"I was just speaking with Professor Bell." Lady Coburn tapped a gloved finger to her lips. "I believe Professors Bell and Matthews said they were meeting in the library."

Professor Duval nodded and turned back the way he came.

Rebecca sighed and followed the footman.

"Your bedchamber is on the second floor of the East Tower," the servant said as they climbed the right-side staircase. "Your chaperone will be on the third."

Rebecca followed with steps lightened by hope, Miss Blake-ford behind. She followed the footman down the wainscoted hall past stern portraits of what must have been Lady Coburn's relatives.

What was Madeline thinking, impersonating a lady's maid? The role was beneath a young woman who would one day debut among society...assuming Rebecca could find a cure.

A heavy weight pressed on her shoulders. She had the added pressure to marry well and keep their father from debtor's prison. If, by some miracle, she did find a well-in-laid husband who would overlook being saddled with her papa's debts, perhaps he'd also be willing to pay a renowned physi-cian for Madeline. The thought seemed too farfetched to even hope for. More likely, a future husband would frown upon his wife's bluestocking pursuits of knowledge and command her to desist.

The footman opened the bedchamber door, and Madeline rose from a chair, her head bowed and hands clasped in front, looking the part of a dutiful servant.

Rebecca entered the room in awe, taking in the large four-poster canopied bed with a small tufted settee at the foot. The walls were papered in a cornflower-blue damask print with gold-painted cornices and trim and fabrics picked to match. She shrank into Corinne's impeccably tailored gown, feeling gauche and conspicuously out of place in a room made for a princess.

With a bow, the footman exited the chamber.

"Thank the Lord." Madeline kicked off her slippers and strode to the bed. Flipping back the covers, she crawled underneath and closed her eyes.

Rebecca, who'd been poised to give her sister a good tongue lashing for pretending to be her maid, melted at the sight of her weary frame, looking so small and fragile in the large bed. "Are you feeling unwell?"

A deep sigh passed Madeline's lips. "Just road-weary from being jostled in a carriage for eight hours. Nothing I won't recover from after a good nap." She patted the bed. "You also must be tired. Why don't you rest too?"

Rebecca's nerves were too high-strung, especially after spying Professor Duval. "I think I shall ready for the evening meal and go down early to meet the guests. Or have a servant direct me to the Coburn's library."

She sat on the edge of the bed and grasped Madeline's hand, warming it between her own. "Why did you choose to act as my maid and not my chaperone? I fear you'll be mistreated or overworked. I can't allow it with your condition."

"You know my symptoms lessen after the first frost, and it's chillier in the north, so I should have a reprieve soon." Madeline cracked open her sleepy eyes. "As your lady's maid, I will get to have alone time with you, whereas a chaperone is with you only when you're in the company of others. Besides, we've shared the same bed since Mama pulled me from the crib. I don't think I could stand being isolated in a tiny room in the attic."

Her sister's logic was sound. "Very well, but I'm not sure I like it. You're not a lady's maid, and if I have any say in the matter, you'll never have to be."

Madeline's smile turned into a yawn.

Rebecca tucked the bedcovers snuggly around her sister, whose breathing deepened as she drifted to sleep. "Rest well, my heart."

She moved to her trunk, which must have been brought up earlier, and unpacked, selecting the least wrinkled gown to wear for tonight's meal. She fingered the smooth satin fabric. She owned nice gowns, but nothing as elaborate as the ones Corinne had lent her. Her own dresses had once been her mother's, which Madeline had altered to look more like today's styles. Their family couldn't afford to order the latest fashions from Paris, as Corinne had.

Donning the pale-blue satin, Rebecca bent and contorted to reach all the tiny hooks, understanding better than ever why lady's maids were a necessity when one wore elaborate gowns. Since her mother could never afford more than a maid-of-all-work, she'd been perfectly capable of dressing herself. Now, Rebecca reveled in the material's silky feel, twisting so it swished back and forth around her ankles like the Superb Lyrebird that used its plumage and imitations of other birds' distress calls to secure a mate.

She hadn't finished the book written by Australian ornithologists, chosen from her aunt and uncle's library, but was intrigued by the raw nature of the Australian colonies.

Could Rebecca attract Professor Duval, with her satin plumage and imitation of her cousin, enough for him to divulge his wisdom, or would he see right through her farce?

She tied her hair back in a simple chignon and peered into the cheval looking glass to ensure nothing was missed. The reflection of her cousin peered back at her, and Corinne's shrill voice commanded in her head, *do not ruin this for me.*

She raised her chin. She'd try to keep up appearances for

Corinne, but she wasn't doing this for her. She was here to help Madeline. The Coburn house party presented the perfect opportunity to avoid the distraction of the upcoming Season and its marriage mart and, instead, focus on a solution to heal her sister.

She pulled the covers over Madeline's shoulders, listening to the slight wheeze in her breathing. When her mother passed, the responsibility of Madeline's care had fallen to Rebecca, and she'd promised to be there for her sister as she hadn't been the hour their mama died. All-too-familiar pangs of guilt tightened Rebecca's chest. *Forgive me, Mama. I will put Madeline's health above finding a husband or falling in love.*

Rebecca closed the door softly behind her to not disturb Madeline's sleep. Retracing her steps, she found her way back to the main foyer, where Miss Blakeford stood in the corner awaiting to accompany her. The same footman from earlier showed them to where the meal would be served and then directed them to where guests had already gathered to wait for the dining room doors to open.

Rebecca paused in the hallway outside the salon, the rumble of socializing guests reaching her ears. Was it too late to turn back and sup in her room? She glanced over her shoulder as she walked, determining a means of escape. Her shoulder hit something metal, and a hollow gong sounded.

"My lady." Miss Blakeford kept the knight's suit of armor from rocking. "Are you all right?" She frowned and raised her hand as if to adjust Rebecca's gown but hesitated.

"I'm fine." Rebecca rubbed her shoulder and scanned her puffed sleeve to ensure she hadn't dirtied it.

"It's merely that Lady Corinne is never..." The woman swallowed as if afraid of facing repercussions. Her thumb circled the thin gold bracelet on her wrist. She emitted the last word in barely a whisper. "...disheveled."

Rebecca inspected her blurry reflection in the knight's highly polished shield.

Miss Blakeford was correct, of course. Corinne would never abide an unkempt appearance. A pinned curl had fallen loose and hung down the side of her face. She tucked it behind her ear, pulled down the capped sleeve that had ridden up, and adjusted the crooked tulle tucker she'd added. The low necklines of Corinne's gowns were indecent, and even though she probably never added the bit of lace to hide her cleavage, Rebecca had to, or she'd be pulling up on the front of her bodice all evening. "The long ride has left me out of sorts." She turned to Miss Blakeford. "Better?"

The timid chaperone nodded.

Rebecca raised her chin to mimic how Corinne carried herself and strode into the salon as if she belonged. *Focus on the objective.* Meet the professor and ask him about his latest discoveries regarding the heart.

Professor Duval and his colleagues conversed near an Italian marble fireplace.

Lady Coburn approached. "I'm so pleased you decided to dine with us. Let me introduce you to some of my friends." She cut through the room, guiding Rebecca to the opposite side from where Professor Duval stood.

Corinne had labeled Lady Coburn's guests as misfits, a harsh judgment. *Eclectic* would have been a better word. A nabob dressed in silk Indian garb addressed a man with a wooden leg. A blind man sat at the pianoforte next to a woman in an ill-fitting wig, and a man who must be from the continent of Asia stood off to the side with his hands clasped in front. He bowed to Lady Coburn as they passed.

Against the far wall, Rebecca's host stopped before a fair-haired lady fashionably dressed in a satin cream gown with lace inlay. Her high, rounded cheeks held a pink tinge, and she dipped her angular chin and sipped her drink. An amused smile curved the corners of her lips as she observed the room. The woman appeared to be of a similar age to Rebecca and could easily have run in the same circle as Corinne. Had she reluctantly attended the party, too?

"May I present my dear niece, Mrs. Sarah Evans?" Lady Coburn warmly regarded Mrs. Evans. "Sarah, it's my pleasure to introduce you to Lady Corinne Prestcote, the daughter of Lord and Lady Mercer. Her parents are emissaries and are also away. Perhaps the two of you can find companionship together."

With that announcement, Lady Coburn swept off to greet other guests.

"Please excuse my aunt." Mrs. Evans's cheeks rounded, and her chin sharpened even more with her smile. "She loves a flare of the dramatic."

What could Rebecca say? She didn't know Mrs. Evans nor their host enough to know whether her theatrical tendency was considered a good or bad quality.

"When did you arrive?" Mrs. Evans sipped once more from her glass.

Whew, a question she could answer. "About an hour ago. I fear I haven't made anyone's acquaintance yet."

Mrs. Evans straightened. "I'm honored to be the first. Most of the guests arrived a few days ago, so they're already acquainted." She threaded an arm through Rebecca's and drew her to her side. "Take a turn about the room with me, and I'll introduce you."

Rebecca didn't have time to acquiesce or argue before Mrs. Evans started walking.

"My aunt has gathered a diverse group this year. To our right is Lord Farsley. He caught scarlet fever as a child and lost his sight but has a great ear for music. Lady Farsley is next to him. She is a dear but has a strange habit of plucking out her hair." As if on cue, Lady Farsley touched the corner of her eyebrow and discreetly yanked out a strand. Mrs. Evans introduced Rebecca to Lord and Lady Farsley with bows, curtsies, and warm greetings.

"In the colorful silk robe is Lord McGower. He made a fortune in India as a maharajah."

Rebecca flicked her gaze to Mrs. Evans. "He became a king?"

She shrugged. "Of a small providence but amassed his wealth in trade with China."

"He wears the regional garb. Is he returning to India soon?"

Mrs. Evans chuckled. "He relinquished his holdings, but I'm afraid he finds the Indian attire freeing. The man next to him with the peg leg is Captain Linder. He's shipping off early tomorrow, so you may not have the opportunity to make his acquaintance." She nodded her chin toward the Asian man in the corner. "That's Mr. Kim, a quiet man but another one of Lord McGower's contacts with the silken road." Mrs. Evans turned toward the professor, and Rebecca's heart thumped. "We're about to pass the professors. The one with the spectacles is Professor Duval, who teaches at Oxford. He's with a few of his colleagues, Professor Bell with the beard, and Professor Matthews—he's the one holding the open book and taking notes."

She would be too. "From the look of it, they must be having an interesting conversation. I've heard of Professor Duval. He does speaking events regarding his scientific research. I would love to attend one."

"Truly?"

Rebecca sucked in a breath and pinned her lips tight. She'd already said too much. Corinne would think nothing of a professor.

"I didn't take you for a bluestocking." Mrs. Evans slowed to a stop and leaned against a wingback chair.

Think, Rebecca. Why would Corinne consider attending an

academic lecture? "I-I hear that many of the House of Lords attend. It's practically a covert marriage mart at those things."

Professor Duval must have said something witty because his colleagues laughed.

Mrs. Evans didn't reply.

Did she believe her tiny fib? Rebecca pressed a hand to her stomach.

Mrs. Evans's empty glass lowered, dangling at an angle from her fingers. Her head had tilted back, eyes closed, and lips parted.

Was she asleep? "Mrs. Evans?"

She released a light snore.

Who fell asleep in the middle of a party? In the middle of a conversation? Was she all right? "Mrs. Evans?"

The woman's eyes opened. "That explains your quirk. You're an intellectual. A socialite bluestocking."

Rebecca blinked. Mrs. Evans had resumed the conversation as if she'd never nodded off. Was she the woman who fell asleep while standing up that Lady Portia mentioned at the Lipscomb ball to Corinne?

Her face fell. "I dozed off, didn't I?"

"Um..." Rebecca nodded. "I believe so."

"Don't look so worried." Mrs. Evans shrugged. "It happens all the time. I can't help it or stop it." She sighed, but a slight flush reddened her cheeks. "Now you know my quirk. I doze off at unexpected times."

"You fell asleep while standing." Rebecca couldn't hold back the astonishment in her voice.

"Standing, sitting, talking." She waved her hand dismissively. "The worst time was during a pall mall game. I was leaning on my mallet when I drifted off. Fell flat on my face. Quite embarrassing."

Rebecca tapped her chin. "Do you not sleep well at night?"

"It seems I can't sleep when I want to but expediently nap when I least expect it."

"I wonder if you don't sleep deeply enough. We could set up an experiment where I monitor your nighttime sleeping habits."

"You want to watch me sleep?" Mrs. Evans snorted.

"Goodness." Rebecca grimaced. "When you put it like that, it does sound odd."

"It sounds as though you'll fit in well at my aunt's party." She giggled in a lighthearted, airy manner. "I figure God allows these quirks to keep us humble"—her giggle deepened to a merry laugh—"or to keep us interesting. I do wonder if my dear aunt throws these parties to make me feel more normal."

Mrs. Evans's infectious laugh drew a smile from Rebecca, but it seemed rude to make sport of her affliction. She jumped at the safer line of conversation. "Lady Coburn is a generous hostess."

"Indeed, and I'm touched by the gesture, even if the company is a bit trying at times—not you, of course." She nudged Rebecca. "Every person here has an interesting story, and it's nice to get out and socialize, especially since my husband passed."

"I'm terribly sorry. Was his passing recent?" Mrs. Evans wore a gown of lavender crepe, and Rebecca hadn't noticed the black silk ribbon tied at the waist, signaling she'd entered the period of half mourning.

"It's been over three years, but I still miss him." Her gaze grew distant. "Our marriage was arranged, but we'd known each other since birth and respected one another. He was patient with my sleeping spells and would tease that they gave his ears a break since I tend to babble." She sighed. "He was a good man."

"How long were you married?" Mrs. Evans looked too young to be already widowed.

"Only a few months. He was a captain under the Duke of Wellington and served the Crown well during the Peninsula Wars. We were married after Napoleon's first capture, thinking the war was over, but then Harold was called back when Napoleon escaped Elba. A stray bullet killed him at the Battle of Waterloo. I was told he died honorably, still instructing his men."

"It must have been so hard having been newly married." Rebecca's heart clenched, remembering her sister screaming her name, shouting for her to come quick. The young man who asked Rebecca to meet him had told her to ignore the calls as he slowed the phaeton and leaned in for a kiss. She broke free from his embrace, leaping from the carriage and sprinting home, but she hadn't made it in time, and regret trailed her like a shadow.

"I lost my mother...I mean, my aunt, though she was like a mother to me. I understand how difficult of a time that must have been."

Sympathy showed in Mrs. Evans's gaze. "It's my turn to be sorry."

"Thank you. She had a weak heart, so we knew death was near."

Mrs. Evans glanced toward the professors. "Did you know Professor Duval's research specializes in the heart?"

"Indeed." She nodded. "I hoped to be introduced and speak to him on the topic."

Her blue eyes sparkled. "That can be arranged." She waved over her aunt and whispered in her ear.

Lady Coburn nodded and flashed Rebecca a conspiratorial smile. "Consider it done."

Rebecca's heart leapt. Today could be the day she learned of a cure for her sister.

CHAPTER 5

*R*ebecca twisted the tip of her glove while, across the room, Lady Coburn surveyed each guest as if mentally grouping everyone into pairs for when they dined.

"Etiquette states we must be escorted into the dining room by rank, but since you must be seated next to Professor Duval..." Mrs. Evans watched her aunt speak to the maître d. "No one will think anything of my eccentric aunt switching things up a bit."

"This means a lot to me." Rebecca turned to her new acquaintance. "Thank you, Mrs. Evans."

"Please, call me Sarah." She squeezed Rebecca's arm. "I feel like we're becoming fast friends."

"And you may call me Re—Corinne." She flipped her wrist. "Or just Rin. Some people call me that. You know, as a nickname. I'll answer to whatever." *Stop making a cake of yourself.*

"Rin." Sarah blinked, as if testing out the sound of the nickname. "It's different. I like it."

Across the hall, the dining room doors opened, and the footmen stepped aside.

The guests wandered toward the entrance, where Lady

Coburn paired them, mixing and matching couples. She hooked her niece's and Rebecca's arms and drew them toward Professor Duval, whose back faced them as he spoke to his acquaintances.

Lady Coburn directed Sarah to pair with Professor Matthews, with whom she was already acquainted. Sarah glanced at Professor Duval, deep in conversation with Professor Bell, and leaned over to whisper behind her fan in Rebecca's ear. "He's more handsome up close. Let's hope he's a master in matters of the heart and not merely heart dissection."

Rebecca pressed her knuckles to her lips to quell her nervous laughter, not only for meeting someone she's admired, but even more so at the notion of a romantic interest.

Lady Coburn nudged her closer and cleared her throat to get Professor Duval's attention.

Rebecca sidestepped Sarah for a better view of Lord Duval's profile.

"Morgagni believed he'd discovered the footprints of disease." Professor Duval touched the corner of his spectacles as he spoke. His high widow's peak led to thick, wavy, honey-brown hair. "I, too, have removed fibrous clots from the heart after death—myocardial degeneration."

Myocardial indicated the muscles of the heart lining. Rebecca had read about blockages causing the heart to stop beating in Matthew Baillie's book *Morbid Anatomy of Some of the Most Important Parts of the Human Body* after Madeline had exhibited similar symptoms as their mother.

Lady Coburn cleared her throat once more.

"If the patient has had a myocardial infarction—"

Lady Coburn gripped the professor's upper arm. "Professor Duval, there is someone I'd like for you to meet—Lady Corinne Prestcote."

He blinked at Lady Coburn and glanced back in Professor Bell's direction. He opened his mouth as if to finish what he'd been saying, but Lady Coburn would have none of it. "You may escort Lady Prestcote to the table." She gestured to the dining room before snagging Professor Matthews's arm and guiding him to Sarah.

Professor Duval grunted and removed his spectacles, cleaning the glass with the bottom corner of his waistcoat.

Rebecca worked to summon the courage to speak. The moment she'd longed for left her feeling insignificant and out of place. *Do not make a mull of this.* "It's a pleasure to make your acquaintance." She bobbed a quick curtsy.

He frowned and hooked the ends of his spectacles over his ears.

What would Corinne say? "Lovely weather we're having. Fall is upon us."

"Indeed." His tone was flat, and his gaze fanned over the room as if looking for someone else to engage in conversation.

You're losing him.

She inhaled a steadying breath. *Here goes.* "I've read your work"—she spoke a little too loudly—"and have always wanted to attend one of your lectures."

He issued her a side glance.

She rubbed a fold of her gown between her gloved fingers. *Stop fidgeting.*

The professor held up his elbow for her to take.

Thank heaven.

Was he warming up to her or merely being a dutiful escort? She threaded her hand through his arm, allowing him to lead her into the opulent dining room. Footmen buzzed around the table, filling drinks as guests were seated.

"I'm most curious about the human heart."

"Are you?" Eyeing her, he pulled out her chair and seated her before settling on her left.

Professor Matthews and Sarah sat to her right with the nabob, Lord McGower, across from her. Professor Bell latched onto Lady Coburn and escorted her to the head of the table, bragging about his department's accomplishments.

"Indeed." Rebecca adjusted the placement of her silverware even though it had been set perfectly fine. "I'm fascinated with how the heart pumps blood through our bodies. And that valves open and close, segmenting the blood into different chambers."

He pressed the center of his spectacles with his index finger and studied her as if she were an oddity. "What is your name again?"

"Miss Prestcote. Ah...*Lady* Prestcote."

He snapped his fingers. "The daughter of Lord and Lady Mercer, the Crown's emissaries to Prussia."

"Indeed." He'd heard of her. Well, he'd heard of Corinne, but that was a win.

The footman draped the white linen napkin over her lap and did the same to the professor.

"I would love to hear your thoughts on what causes a weak heart." She met the blue-gray of his astute gaze.

"Are you ill?" His eyes clouded, not sympathetically, but as if leery.

"No, just curious."

"Because I'm not a physician." He exhaled a jaded breath. "Many people seek my opinion for tonics and treatment, but my work is the long-term study of the heart, not quick fixes."

She forced her shoulders to stay erect and not slump in disappointment. He was probably bombarded by people desperate to find a cure for themselves or loved ones, just as she sought for her sister. It must be difficult not to have the answers they sought, and by his reaction, being unable to oblige wore on him. She understood that helpless feeling all too well. "But a better understanding of the heart and its functioning will lead to cures and life-saving surgeries, don't you think? It's why your work is so important."

The furrow between his eyebrows softened, and a slow smile spread across his lips. Professor Duval was handsome in an intellectual sort of way.

"There appear to be several causes of a weak heart—dropsy being one, where fluids build around the vascular organ." He paused as a servant ladled white soup into his bowl.

The creamy aroma of chicken, peppercorn, and bacon rumbled her stomach, but she focused on the professor's answer.

"Come now, Professor." Lord McGower drew his attention. "Such a discussion is not for the weaker sex. Lady Coburn wouldn't have Lady Prestcote swooning into her soup."

"I'm fine. Please contin—"

"Quite right." Professor Bell picked up his spoon and dipped it into the steaming bowl. "Professor Duval, why don't you tell Lord McGower about Oxford's plans to expand our research wing? Perhaps he might want to invest—have the new building named after him." He paused for effect. "McGower Hall."

Sarah caught Rebecca's eye and gave a sympathetic shrug.

Rebecca tried to change the topic back to the heart to no avail. She finally gave up and ate her soup and several more courses without saying a word.

Professor Duval leaned over his plate to say something, and a bit of mashed potatoes stuck to the top button of his jacket.

"Professor—" She touched his sleeve to direct his attention, but he waved her off, thoroughly engaged in the conversation about how much funding the new building would require.

She was forgotten.

Professor Matthews sat forward in his seat, listening to Professor Duval's pitch to Lord McGower.

Rebecca peered at Sarah between Professor Matthews and the seat back. Her eyes were closed, and her head lolled to the side. She'd dozed off again. Should she wake someone having a sleeping episode? Rebecca glanced around to see if anyone knew what to do, but either nobody noticed or nobody thought anything of it.

She could reach behind him and tap Sarah on the shoulder, but would she startle Sarah and draw attention?

She peered at Lady Coburn at the head of the table, but she spoke in low tones to Lord Farsley and appeared unaware.

Maybe a light tap?

Rebecca crept her arm across Professor Matthews's backrest, and with her index finger, tapped Sarah on the shoulder. Sarah's head snapped upright, and she blinked, glancing around the table as if gaining her bearings.

Professor Matthews raised his palms at something that was said and leaned back.

Rebecca yanked her arm away, but her fingers brushed the man's shoulder.

His head swiveled in her direction, and he blinked at her wide eyed. "Lady Prestcote?"

"I beg your pardon, Professor." She folded her hands in her lap, wishing the floor would open so she could disappear.

"It's quite all right, my lady." He sipped his drink, then set it down, a sly smile curving the corners of his lips.

Oh fig. Did he believe she'd been flirting with him?

"So tell me, Lady Prestcote..." He cleared his throat, relaxing. "Are you enjoying your time at Griffin Hall so far?"

"I only arrived this afternoon, but Lady Coburn is a delightful hostess."

He scratched his long sideburn. "Might I be honored to show you the grounds tomorrow with a morning ride?"

How had she drawn the attention of the wrong professor? If only Professor Duval's affections could be as easily gained. She turned to eye the man's back, since he'd shifted to converse with Professor Bell. She would not be so easily disregarded.

"Shall we make it a foursome and include Mrs. Evans and Professor Duval?"

Did Sarah ride? Could she ride with her condition? Perhaps Rebecca shouldn't have involved her new friend—or at least should have asked her first.

"Duval?" At Professor Matthews's bidding, Professor Duval faced him.

I'll be beggared. Rebecca hid her clenched teeth behind a smile. She'd struggled the entire meal to get Professor Duval's attention, yet for Professor Matthews, he was alert.

"I've enlisted you in a morning ride to show the grounds to these delightful ladies." Professor Matthews smiled as if he'd completed a Herculean feat.

Professor Duval nodded, and Rebecca's stomach leapt in victory. His gaze fell to her. "Forgive me for being remiss. You must think me a knave for ignoring your company."

She shrugged. "I admire a man who enjoys his work."

The corners of his mouth twitched with a grin.

Rebecca saw her opening. "I'd love to hear about—"

"An invigorating morning ride might be just the thing to get the heart pumping." Professor Duval peered at Professor Matthews.

Rebecca overlooked his interruption and suppressed a chuckle at his research humor.

"Unfortunately, we shall have to keep it short." Professor Matthews sipped his drink. "We have a meeting in town at noon regarding supplies." He glanced at her, then to Sarah on his other side, and said, "Because I haven't bot-any plants today."

Sarah snorted a laugh but covered it with her napkin.

Professor Matthews grinned at Sarah before setting his glass down and turning to Rebecca. "Botany is my preferred area of study."

"Don't mind his puns." Professor Duval nudged her with his elbow. "He believes he's witty."

Lady Coburn rose. "If the gentleman would like to adjourn for a cheroot or billiards, the ladies shall join me in the rose salon."

Rebecca inwardly growled. She'd finally gotten the professor's attention, just in time for the men and women to separate. *Tomorrow*. She exhaled a breath. Tomorrow, she would take full advantage of the morning ride. There had to be something she hadn't yet tried to help her sister.

Following Lady Coburn's lead, Rebecca and Sarah shuffled into the rose salon, where tea awaited. Rebecca gripped Sarah's arm and pulled her toward two chairs in the room's corner. "I shouldn't have cornered you into a morning ride without asking you first. I'm terribly sorry."

"I should be fine, a bit rusty, maybe, but the challenge should help keep me awake. I'll need to retire early to get as much rest as possible."

"Shall we make our excuses?"

Sarah nodded and drew her aunt's attention before Lady Coburn started pouring tea. "Aunt, I think we shall call it a night. All the excitement has worn me out, and I'd like to be refreshed for tomorrow's festivities."

"I'm afraid the long carriage ride sapped my strength as well," Rebecca said. "Please excuse me and thank you for the scrumptious meal."

"Of course." Lady Coburn smiled. "If you don't recall how to get to your chamber, Sarah can guide you. She's directly a floor below."

Rebecca curtsied to her hostess and stepped into the hallway as Sarah bid her aunt goodnight.

A mirror above a console table reflected Professor Duval and Professor Bell standing next to the servant's exit near the billiards room. Rebecca strained to hear their discussion.

"I should be able to obtain what you need." Professor Bell frowned and jabbed his finger into Professor Duval's chest. "But you must act with more care. It wouldn't hurt to warm up to the other guests, especially those who could financially benefit the university's program."

Professor Duval jerked down on the lapels of his jacket. "I shall do my best." He stomped back into the billiard room.

Professor Bell peeked inside the servant's stairs and then back again at Professor Duval's retreating form. He gestured for someone to follow, but the mirror only reflected the professor as he slipped below stairs.

Odd.

A few seconds later, a footman exited the same way.

"Ready?" Sarah linked her arm with Rebecca's and strolled toward the foyer.

A shuffle of footsteps sounded behind her. Startled, Rebecca spun around to find Miss Blakeford trailing them like a shadow. *Heavens.* She'd forgotten her chaperone's presence. "Mrs. Evans will escort me to my chamber. Go and settle into your room."

"Thank you, miss." The woman curtsied with a guarded look and departed for the servants' stairs.

Rain hammered the paned glass windows, and a flash of lightning illuminated the hallway brighter than the candlelit wall sconces. "I hadn't noticed a storm roll in."

"Indeed. You were a bit distracted." Sarah giggled.

"Was it that obvious?" Rebecca's neck heated. "I've been enamored with Professor Duval's work."

"His work, truly?" Sarah arched a questioning eyebrow.

"I've only just met him." The heat rose into her cheeks and the tips of her ears. "But he is handsome in a different sort of way."

A gust of wind blew from the foyer down the hall, as if

someone opened a door or window, flickering the candles and carrying a chill. Rebecca hugged her midsection.

"Don't worry about his inattention. Professor Duval is like that to everyone unless you're a body he's about to dissect. Then he's riveted."

Rebecca gasped. "You've been to one of his lectures?" As they approached the foyer, a rumbling of male voices ahead bounced off the stone walls. She lowered her voice. "Why didn't you say so?"

"I haven't." Sarah shook her head. "I've only heard."

A footman scurried past at a faster-than-acceptable pace. Rebecca twisted to watch. Was something amiss?

A loud crack of thunder shook the hall, and a second gust of wind blew out the candles. Sarah yelped and hooked Rebecca's arm, yanking her around the corner into the foyer.

Rebecca smacked into a wet wall smelling of male musk, and the room went black.

CHAPTER 6

*D*renched and chilled to the bone, Daniel stood in Lady Coburn's foyer. Longing to crawl into bed with a hot brick to get warm, he handed his wet cloak to the butler.

Thunder cracked, and a woman screamed.

Before Daniel could turn fully, two women rounded the corner, and one ran straight into his wet cloak. She screeched and clawed at the dripping fabric. The material of his hood caught in her coiffure, probably by a hairpin. Blinded, she stumbled back, groping at the fabric.

The butler jumped out of the way of a stray elbow.

The second woman, a young blond who'd accompanied the flailing ghost, gaped at Daniel before glancing at her companion and pressing a hand over her mouth, smothering laughter.

A fine help the lot of them were.

Daniel gripped the distressed woman's shoulders and received a punch in the stomach for his efforts. He grunted.

"Unhand me!"

He yanked the hood off her face and peered into a pair of hazel eyes all too familiar. "Lady Prestcote?"

Her gaze hardened into granite. "You!"

He uttered a half scoff, half laugh. God had a sense of humor. Of course, the same woman who'd thwarted his last assignment would be here, already getting in his way. His jaw tightened as he remembered their previous interaction. Ugh. Soon she'd be using her wiles to gain his attention. His goal was to stop a band of grave robbers. Her goal was to catch a marquis. "Lady Prestcote—"

"Unhand me." A tangle of mahogany tresses fell loose from her coiffure, pins jutting out like tiny spikes.

His rain-drenched cloak left dark water stains on the front of her gown, and a damp lock of hair pasted against her forehead. Her cheeks were flushed from the exertion of wrestling his jacket—or, more likely, based on her heaving chest, flared nostrils, and the sparks spewing in her eyes—from her rising anger. Even mussed and angry, she was temptingly kissable, but she was a bold romp, looking to land a titled husband. That obliterated her desirability in his eyes.

If he hadn't had that last encounter with her at the Lipscomb party and asked a few discreet people about her background and reputation, he would never have learned what a vapid social climber she truly was.

If he'd only met her in the garden, he'd have been delighted to bump into her again, but first impressions were often deceiving. He raised his palms and backed up. "Forgive me, my lady. I believed you in need of assistance, since you appeared to be losing the battle with my cloak."

"What sort of jest is that? Who throws a wet cloak over a passing guest?"

Hers wasn't the response he'd expect from a marriage-hunting socialite.

The butler said, "My apologies—"

Daniel raised his index finger and silenced the man, peering at Lady Prestcote. "You weren't watching where you were going, and you ran headlong into my cloak as I passed it to the butler."

She hesitated, her bottom lip trembling as if seeking a retort, and she didn't let him down. "You could have given a warning."

He spoke to her companion to reiterate the ridiculousness of Lady Prestcote's logic. "Because I can see around corners and should have known you would turn at the exact moment I handed my cloak to the butler."

He nodded at the butler, who bowed and left to dry the damp garment.

Her friend's gaze jumped between Lady Prestcote and himself, and she pinched her lips tight, but her pale eyes danced with laughter. She seemed like a reasonable woman, and pretty, to boot. Asking for an introduction would surely irk Lady Prestcote. "Might you introduce me to your lovely friend?"

The dampness on the lady's gown evaporated into a steam cloud above her head. She hesitated, her rosy lips thinning into a tight line, but propriety dictated the rules. "Indeed." Her chin lifted. "I'm aware of your affliction with meeting pretty women."

The blond woman's pale eyes widened, then crinkled, and laughter snorted out her nose. She covered her mouth with her hand for a second time. At least *she* had a sense of humor.

He flashed his eyebrows at Lady Prestcote. *Touché.*

"Lord Wolston, may I present Miss Sarah Evans?"

Mrs. Evans dipped into a curtsy. "My lord."

"Welcome, Lord Wolston." Lady Coburn rounded the corner with outstretched arms. She scooped up his hands. "I'm terribly sorry you were caught in the rain, but I'm so pleased you've decided to attend our house party. Let's get you warmed by the fire."

Lady Coburn drew up short, spying Lady Prestcote. "My dear, what happened?"

Her hands flew to her dangling coiffure, and she gasped, yanking out a few of the jutting hairpins. "I—"

"Lady Prestcote assaulted my cloak."

"Pardon?" Lady Coburn blinked at him.

Daniel fought to keep a straight face, especially when Mrs. Evans released another snort of laughter.

"I did no such thing." Lady Prestcote's tone was lethal. If her eyes were swords, he'd be gutted and bleeding out.

He clicked his tongue. "The unprovoked attack came out of nowhere."

Lady Coburn gaped at Lady Prestcote.

"Do not fear. No damage was done." He grimaced. "Except for the damage Lady Prestcote inflicted upon herself."

Her eyes blazed.

He shouldn't be having this much fun, but it was all Lady Prestcote's fault. Why did she provoke him so?

Lady Coburn paled. "I apologize, my lord, for any inconvenience. I'm uncertain what came over Lady Prestcote." She glanced her way. "But I can assure you, it won't happen again. Is there something we can do to atone for the mishap?"

"I'm fine. No harm done." He stifled a yawn. If he attempted to gather intelligence on the guests tonight, his mind wouldn't be its sharpest. "My journey was long. I prefer to retire for the evening and"—he peered at Lady Prestcote, hoping she'd receive his peace offering—"have a fresh start in the morning."

"You are too kind, Lord Wolston." Lady Coburn raised a hand to signal a footman.

Mrs. Evans stopped her. "I'd be happy to show Lord Wolston to his chamber and escort Lady Prestcote to her room."

"You are a dear." Lady Coburn cupped Mrs. Evans's cheek before facing Daniel. "Will you require a valet to assist you, Lord Wolston?"

"I prefer to manage on my own." At Lady Coburn's

surprised expression, he added, "Since my last valet left for America, I haven't found anyone fit to replace him. No one can tie a knot like Deters." Nor could another be trusted to keep his espionage work a secret.

"Very well, then." Lady Coburn smiled. "Ring if you need anything. We are grateful for your presence."

A guttural noise sounded on his right. Had Lady Prestcote grunted?

Lady Coburn bid them goodnight and returned to attend to the other guests.

Daniel raised his elbows for each of the ladies to take hold.

Mrs. Evans accepted with an amused grin fixed to her lips.

Lady Prestcote stared at his upturned elbow as if it were the devil's pitchfork. Finally, she accepted his assistance but fumed as they strolled across the foyer's marble floors.

Lightning illuminated the hall, and a gust of wind pounded rain against the roof. The candles on wall sconces flickered and danced as a drafty chill swirled past.

"Wicked storm outside." He nodded to the window, and thunder boomed in response.

"Quite." Mrs. Evans peered around him to check on the stiff and brooding Lady Prestcote.

"I'd initially intended to ride to Chadlington to visit friends, but the sky darkened. Fortunately, I remembered Lady Coburn's hospitality and invitation."

A fierce wind rattled the windows. Mrs. Evans's grip tightened. "I'm glad you could come in out of the storm."

"Only to run into another kind of tempest." He flashed what he hoped was a wry smile and tilted his head in Lady Prestcote's direction.

Lady Prestcote broke her silence. "You are horrid."

"Me?" The right corner of his mouth twitched.

She released his arm and rounded on him.

He drew up short, halting Mrs. Evans.

"I don't know whether you're mad or just maddening." Lady Prestcote jabbed the words at him like his opponent's attack from their fencing spar that morning. "Lady Coburn now thinks I'm the one who's crazed and ill-mannered." She harrumphed. "Assaulted your cloak." Her hands rose, and she smacked them back down on the side folds of her satin gown. "How absurd."

Daniel kept his gaze on the vengeful angel before him, with rosy cheeks and thick waves of dark hair cascading over her shoulders, but leaned closer to Mrs. Evans and said, "Does she speak to all the guests in this manner?"

Mrs. Evans eyed him much as his governess used to do when she wanted him to know *he* was the problem. "She was perfectly calm and polite until your arrival."

"So you're saying I draw out her passionate side?"

"Argh!" Lady Prestcote's hands balled into fists. She spun, hefted her skirts with one hand, offering him a pleasant view of her trim ankles, and trotted up the curved staircase.

He glanced at Mrs. Evans and led her in Lady Prestcote's wake. In the second-floor hall, Lady Prestcote stood a few doors down, trying a knob. It wouldn't budge. She looked to Mrs. Evans, who discreetly pointed to the door on the other side of the hallway. She flounced to the chamber across the way. This knob turned, and she stomped inside, only to pause as if checking herself.

She returned to the doorway. "Good night, Sarah. It was delightful to make your acquaintance, and I look forward to tomorrow." She eyed him with an icy glare that rivaled the driving wind outside. "Lord Wolston."

Before he could bow, she whirled into the room and shut the door.

The smile he'd been holding back erupted in full. He enjoyed this version of Lady Prestcote much better than the one he danced with at the Lipscomb party. Tonight, she reminded him more of the spirited and sharp woman he'd met in the garden and less of the social climber seeking an advantageous match. Perhaps to enjoy this side, he must continue to keep her off-balance. He raised his voice. "Pleasant dreams, Lady Prestcote."

Mrs. Evans eyed him with a bemused smile. "Your room is around the corner."

He followed her about five rooms down from Lady Prestcote, passing a ghoulish portrait of a hollowed-eyed, elderly man in a gilded frame. They stopped, and his focus returned to his mission. He wouldn't allow Lady Prestcote to impede his assignment this time. His priority was catching the body snatchers and getting them to talk so he could unearth and bring down their financial backer.

Mrs. Evans pushed open the door to his chamber and stepped back into the hallway. "I take it you and Lady Prestcote have met prior."

He peeked into the spacious room decorated in rich fabrics of blue and gold hues. "We were introduced briefly at the Lipscomb ball." He turned to face her and leaned his forearm on the door frame. "Thank you for your assistance, Mrs. Evans."

"We are riding tomorrow morning to tour the grounds at ten."

"By 'we,' you mean yourself and Lady Prestcote."

She nodded, studying his reaction.

After witnessing two people verbally spar, wouldn't a good friend try to keep them apart? "Why are you telling me this?"

A sparkle of mischief lit her eyes. "Because it's apparent the two of you hold sentiments toward each other."

"Hardly." He snorted.

"Hmm. Good night, Lord Wolston." She turned and strode toward the stairs.

He leaned into the hallway. "Good night, Mrs. Evans."

She peered over her shoulder, and the bemused smile returned. "See you in the morning."

Unlikely. He grunted and entered his chamber, where his bags awaited unpacking.

The rumors and Lieutenant Scar's declaration were true.

Lady Coburn's guests were *interesting.*

$\sim$

*T*he following morning, Rebecca awoke to her sister opening the drapes. She squinted at the bright light, removed the open medical journal from her chest that she'd fallen asleep reading, and set it on the bedside table. "What time is it?"

"Half-past eight, my lady." Madeline curtsied.

Rebecca struggled to an upright position. "You don't need to act like my maid when it's just us."

"I was merely getting into character." Madeline strode over to a table that held a tray.

Rebecca rubbed her eyes, and they adjusted to the sunlight, bringing her sister's face into better focus. "I thought you slumbered beside me. Did you sleep in my dressing room?"

Madeline shook her head. "But I will if you stay up all night reading medical journals again. The settee in there looks comfortable enough." She carried over a tray with a morning cup of chocolate. "I had to crawl over you to blow out your candle. I tried to put the book away, but you wouldn't relinquish it, even in your sleep."

"I didn't mean to keep you up. You need your rest. Next time, I'll go to the library." Rebecca welcomed the steaming liquid. "You didn't need to bring me a tray."

"What kind of lady's maid would I be then?"

Holding the cup in both her hands, Rebecca inhaled the rich chocolate scent. "How long have you been awake?"

"Long enough to go below stairs and meet some of the staff." Madeline set the tray at the foot of the bed, plucking a second cup of chocolate for herself, and crawled onto the bed beside her sister. "I met a delightful young woman of a similar age. Her name is Lucy Josting. She works for Lady Coburn but attends Mrs. Evans when she visits."

"You make friends so easily."

"Lucy started as a scullery maid and lived with her grandmama, but when funds grew tight, Lady Coburn was kind enough to offer her employment as a maid." She blew steam from her cup and sipped. "Lucy now lives in Griffin Hall. She gave me a quick tour, walked me through the routine, and introduced me to the cook and a couple of footmen. Griffin Hall is enormous. I think our entire home would fit in the front foyer. I now know where to find the laundress, the cups, saucers, the carafe of chocolate, and supplies like writing paper, ink, and spare needles, should you break one while doing needlepoint."

Rebecca frowned. "I hope you didn't overexert yourself."

"I'm fine." Madeline pushed up on the corner of Rebecca's mouth, forcing it into a smile. She giggled and her hand returned to her cup. "Please stop worrying. If I start to wheeze, I'll quit the room pretending my slipper bunched or a hem is torn."

"I'm still uncertain how I feel about you assuming a servant's position." Rebecca could imagine the look of disdain on their father's face. "Papa wouldn't lower himself, not even to save the family from living on the streets."

"Mama would quote from the book of Matthew, 'But he that is greatest among you shall be your servant.'"

Mama's voice rang in Rebecca's memory as she recited the next verse, "'And whosoever shall exalt himself shall be abased; and he that shall humble himself shall be exalted.'" The ache over the loss of her beautiful mother formed a knot in Rebecca's throat. She drank from her cup to swallow the pain that persisted in plaguing her. She couldn't lose Madeline. How would she survive without the people she loved the most in this world?

There must be a cure, and she would find it. There was no other choice.

They sipped their chocolates in silence.

Madeline set her cup aside and rolled off the featherbed mattress. "The true test to see if I can pass as a lady's maid will be taming your thick head of hair."

"I'll be touring the grounds on horseback this morning, so I'll need to don my riding habit." Rebecca downed the last sip, set the cup on the tray, and rose.

Madeline gripped a chair to move it in front of the looking glass.

"Allow me. I don't want you getting winded." Rebecca set the chair before the cheval mirror. "You must take it easy."

Madeline retrieved the borrowed pale-green equestrian gown from the wardrobe and rubbed the soft merino wool before passing it to Rebecca.

Rebecca wiggled out of her night shift and donned the habit, followed by a dark green wool spencer.

"Come sit." Madeline patted the chair cushion and picked up a brush. "Time to test my skills." She set a matching military-style cap with a ruff of fine Mechlin lace on Rebecca's lap to be pinned on top of her coiffure when finished, then twisted Rebecca's hair up into a Grecian style.

"Lucy told me that her grandmama has a similar breathing problem."

"She's found a way to live with it?" Rebecca met her sister's gaze in the mirror. "Is she taking any elixirs or going to Bath for healing dips in the ocean? What is she doing that we haven't tried?"

"Nothing different." Madeline inserted a few pins. "Her

health has declined recently. Lucy is taking it hard, but I'm glad I can be here for her."

Rebecca sat on her hands so she wouldn't shake her fists at God and scream. Wasn't He supposed to be loving? Wasn't He supposed to care?

And how did you show you cared? You were out gallivanting around with a suitor when Mama passed. You should have been there for her and for Madeline.

The familiar guilt twisted her stomach. Mama's death was Rebecca's fault. If only she'd been there to aid Mama in sitting up so the episode might pass. She should have prayed harder, known more, tried more elixirs...

"There." Madeline stepped back and inspected her creation. She held up a hand mirror for Rebecca to view the back of her hair. "How do you like it?"

She'd woven curls and twists into a loose bun at her nape. "It's lovely."

"It's a good thing I've had practice. Woe to the poor maid who first encounters your unruly mane." Madeline flexed her fingers. "You have so much to work with—unlike my fine strands. My hands and arms grow tired."

"You mustn't overexert yourself." She tried to snatch the brush and pins from Madeline's hands, but she twisted, holding them out of Rebecca's reach.

"It's such a splendid color, rich and dark like our cup of chocolate. I've always been a little jealous." She pinned the riding cap on Rebecca's head.

She snorted. "My hair may look nice when fixed, but it's willful and heavy to bear, and the dark color is just another reminder of Papa."

He'd burdened her with keeping him out of debtor's prison and demanded she find a match this Season and marry for money. Her uncle, Corinne's father, refused to bail out his younger brother, stating that it was past time he grew up. At least he offered to aid Rebecca by hosting her Season and helping her land a husband.

Rebecca would have preferred the option of seeking employment. She'd be a good governess. She'd enjoy teaching but despaired of being separated from Madeline. Papa disliked the idea of the duns sending him to prison until she earned enough to pay down his debts. If that happened, Madeline would become a ward of their aunt and uncle, who spent most of their time traveling as ambassadors for the Crown. No one would be there to look out for Madeline's welfare. Certainly, Corinne wouldn't take up the charge.

"He's trying to make amends." Madeline sighed. "Maybe you could show him a little mercy."

"As he showed Mama? I wrote him when she became ill." Rebecca shook her head. "He didn't come. Not even after I begged him. He didn't even come to the funeral."

Madeline set the brush and remaining pins on the dressing room table. "He loved her and couldn't stand to see her ill. It broke his heart."

"It broke our hearts, too, but we were there for..." She swallowed, and her voice turned to a whisper. "*You* were there for her."

Her heart thundered against her rib cage much as it had during her first kiss, when the Benson boy had pressed his lips to hers. Madeline's scream had burst the magical spell like someone had dropped and shattered her favorite snow globe.

"Mama wanted you to live your life, enjoy yourself," Madeline said, as she had so often before.

"I should have been there, and Papa should have too."

"He's been with us since."

"To ease his guilt, or because he needed to hide from creditors?"

A year after Mama passed, Papa walked into the house, his hat in hand, claiming he'd missed his girls. Since then, he'd become an intrusive figure, trying to re-insert himself into their lives.

Madeline had welcomed him, but Rebecca remained suspicious, and for good reason. Several months after he'd settled in, a letter arrived, and he grew panicky. He disappeared, promising not to be gone long, but returned two months later to upend their lives with the news that he'd spent all their funds and needed Rebecca's help to keep the duns at bay.

Madeline added one more pin to Rebecca's coiffure. "A little grace is all I ask."

Rebecca stood and faced her sister. "What do you call trying to save his hide when no one else will? I'd say that's enough grace."

"Indeed." Madeline pressed her lips together, but her lips quirked up at the corners.

"What is so amusing?"

"I've been praying that God would give you more than you could ever imagine." She grinned fully. "And I'm believing He's going to do it."

Rebecca grunted and looked at her watch. She would be late and miss breaking her fast if she didn't hurry. "I must go, but you stay here and rest."

"Yes, my lady." Madeline curtsied.

"You're impossible." Rebecca shook her head and turned, but she eyed her sister as she opened the door. "But I love you."

Madeline blew her a kiss and waved her away.

Downstairs, a footman directed Rebecca to the breakfast room. She entered the buzzing fray as servants filled tea and coffee cups and carried in platters of eggs, blood sausage, and fruits of all sorts. She halted at the sight of Lord Wolston, lounging in his chair on the far side of the long table with the morning sun from the nearby window, highlighting his frame.

His steel-blue gaze slid to hers and stopped her intake of

breath. He issued her the tiniest nod before returning to his conversation with Professor Matthews and Lord McGower.

She scanned the room for Professor Duval, but he had either already broken his fast or hadn't yet arrived. Her chaperone, Miss Blakeford, sat at the opposite end of Lord Wolston nearer the entrance to the kitchens, holding her coffee cup as if it were the only thing sustaining her. Her gaze occasionally strayed to a blond footman stationed in the corner.

The delicious scents drew a growl from Rebecca's stomach, and she moved to the sideboard, filling a plate with fruit, toast, and a bit of egg.

"Good morning, Lady Prestcote." Sarah's voice was cheerful. She heaped a spoonful of eggs onto her plate. "Are you ready for our ride?"

"Quite." Rebecca waited for her to finish gathering her food and suggested they sit toward the middle of the table. She chose a seat far enough away from Lord Wolston not to have to engage with the man but close enough so that, if Professor Duval joined them, she could converse with him.

She sliced a strawberry and noticed that the dark smudges prevalent the night before beneath Sarah's eyes had lessened. "You look well rested. Were you able to sleep through the storm?"

Sarah swallowed a bite of blood sausage and nodded. "For the most part. I should be good for the ride, but just in case, nudge me before I fall off the horse."

Rebecca stopped chewing.

"I'm only funning you." Sarah's eyes crinkled with her grin. "I'll be fine."

Lord Wolston rose from the table and nodded to the gentlemen. He yanked down on the bottom edge of his tailored jacket to straighten it. The frock coat hugged his broad shoulders, and his buckskin breeches outlined his athletic build. Compared to him, the professors looked like gangly twigs.

He strode around the table with a sway of pompous grace and stopped beside her. "Good morning, Lady Prestcote, Mrs. Evans." He tucked his top hat under his arm. "I must see to an errand, but enjoy your ride."

Sarah watched him leave with a disappointed expression.

Did she hold a tinder for the marquis?

Her new friend turned her attention back to her meal.

Professor Bell joined them with Lady Coburn on his arm, taking the spot Rebecca hoped Professor Duval would fill. He spoke of his current position as the Pro-Vice- Chancellor of Research and his nomination to become Oxford's vice-chancellor.

Professor Duval scurried into the breakfast room just before ten and downed a cup of coffee. He seemed eager to be off.

Professor Matthews hovered near Sarah. "Ladies, are you ready for our tour?"

Sarah rose, and they left Lady Coburn and Professor Bell to finish dining.

Rebecca followed them through the marble hallway, past paintings of fox hunting scenes and portraits of Coburn family members from long ago. Sunlight streamed through the open doors of large salons, where pane glass windows cast grid-patterned shadows across the floor.

They walked out the portico exit, filing down the stairs and up the stone path to the stables. The sweet scent of fresh hay hung heavy in the air. Prepared horses stood at attention, and in a short time, they were off, Professor Matthews leading the way and acting as a tour guide with an extra focus on the grounds' agricultural benefits.

Sarah didn't object to him taking the lead, even though she probably knew the area best and only corrected dates and names in a whisper to Rebecca. A blond groom and Rebecca's chaperone rode a fair distance in the rear.

Much of the property was forested, but the manor gardens

spanned an acre. Over a ridge, a natural clearing formed where the Coburn's sheep grazed. They maneuvered through an opening in a rock wall, and the slower pace allowed Rebecca an opportunity to speak to the professor.

"Professor Duval." She sidled up next to him. "When is your next lecture?"

He raised a hand halfway to his spectacles, but the horse shifted, and he gripped the reins as if afraid he'd be thrown. "Next week. I'm speaking on the importance of balancing the body's humors with bloodletting."

"You believe in the effects of bloodletting, then?" A physician had bled her mama, but it had only seemed to make her weaker.

"The buildup of bile poisons the body and can lead to a weakened heart or a disturbed mind. I've seen the wall of a man's heart swell to double its size, killing him. If only he'd come to us sooner, we could have bled him and remedied the issue."

"Have you listened to hearts that have a unique rhythm?" She held her breath. Had he studied patients with similar afflictions as her sister?

"You mean through a stethoscope?" He glanced her way, taking his focus off his horse. "Have you?"

"I purchased one and am familiar with the *lub-dub* sound of a normal heartbeat and the *lub-dub-dub* of an abnormal beat."

"A heart flutter." His steed nipped at her mare, and he yanked the reins to the left, separating the horses. The professor wasn't much of an equestrian.

"Is that what you call it?" She'd read it was called such or a heart murmur. She checked over her shoulder to see how Sarah managed. The dark smudges had returned under her eyes, and she peered at Professor Matthews with a glazed-over smile.

"The medical term is a systolic murmur," Professor Duval said. "It's caused by the heart valves not closing properly."

"Have you ever treated one?"

"Over there is the church and family burial grounds," Professor Matthews said.

She turned again as the man pointed to crooked headstones dotting the hill near the small stone church. "And who have we here?"

A rider emerged to the left of the graveyard and descended the hill in their direction.

Sarah perked up.

Rebecca recognized the silhouette and groaned.

CHAPTER 7

*D*aniel maneuvered his horse down the rocky path.
Mrs. Evans and Lady Prestcote rode alongside
two of the professors. A groom and a woman, who he assumed
must be a chaperone, lagged behind. He'd rushed from the
scarcely attended graveside service of the victim Lieutenant
Scar mentioned to catch Lady Prestcote on her ride. Why he'd
done it, he couldn't say. He waved a greeting and joined them,
turning his horse in a tight and neat circle. He matched his
steed to their pace. "Good morning, ladies and professors.
Lovely day after a stormy night. May I join you?"

Lady Prestcote's lips thinned.

"Of course, please do." Professor Matthews waved him over.

The lanky professor with the spectacles, whom Daniel had
met briefly after breaking his fast, extracted his pocket watch
from inside his jacket and flipped open the cover. "Look at the
time." The man motioned to Professor Matthews. "We're going
to be late if we don't hurry."

"Ah, yes. Our meeting." Professor Matthews nodded. "Perfect timing, Lord Wolston. Would you be kind enough to
continue the tour and escort the ladies?"

"It would be my pleasure." Daniel tamped down the impulse to grin at Lady Prestcote's annoyed expression.

"I'd hoped to show them the old mill dam and the pond." Professor Matthews turned to Lady Prestcote. "I particularly enjoy how the mill harnesses the power of water and converts it into energy, but I believe you'll enjoy the lovely view." The man's Adam's apple bobbed. "Though I admit it doesn't compare to the beauty of such lovely ladies—as pretty as a flower garden." He waggled his eyebrows. "The day is *marigolden* with you around."

Was Professor Matthews smitten with one of them?

Daniel's grip on the reins tightened. Why did that irritate him? He nudged his horse next to Lady Prestcote's mare.

The professors bid the ladies farewell and trotted off toward town.

Mrs. Evans yawned. "I fear all this fresh air has exhausted me. I'm going to return to the main house."

Lady Prestcote steered her horse as if to leave with her, but Mrs. Evans raised her palm.

"You go on ahead without me. The view is beautiful, especially with the fall colors. You won't want to miss it."

"But what if...?" Lady Prestcote stared at Mrs. Evans.

Daniel held back his scoff. Was she worried he might ravish her?

"The groom will ride with me. No need to worry." Mrs. Evans waved her off. "Enjoy the day"—a rueful smile touched the corners of her mouth—"and the company."

Daniel chuckled at the look of betrayal on Lady Prestcote's face as she watched Mrs. Evans ride over the hill to the stables with the blond-haired groom in tow.

Lady Prestcote's chaperone didn't appear pleased to lose her companion and made no effort to increase her pace and join her charge.

Time to form a truce. Daniel positioned his horse to ride

beside Lady Prestcote's. "I'm afraid we've gotten off to a poor start."

Her gaze snapped in his direction. "You mean stealing a kiss at the party, then insulting me in front of our generous hostess? Is that not how you typically make a person's acquaintance?"

He peered at the sky as if thinking it over before matching her sarcastic tone. "I do believe our introduction was unique."

Her lips pursed. "How did I get so fortunate?"

"Right place, right time, I would guess."

The corners of her mouth dipped into a censuring frown.

A bee buzzed near her ear. She startled and leaned away from the insect. In response to its rider's sudden movement, her horse danced nervously.

The bee flew around to her other side, its beating wings dangerously close to the loose tendrils of hair at her nape.

She squealed and leaned away, pulling the reins to the side, turning her horse toward him. Her shoulder bumped his. Her eyes widened with fear as she righted herself, crouching low in the saddle.

His mount grew uneasy, and her horse snorted.

"Hold still and it will leave." He waved to shoo the pesky bug away, but the oblivious bee landed on Lady Prestcote's nose.

She screamed and leaned back. The whites of her horse's eyes showed, and its ears pulled back.

If Daniel didn't do something fast, the horse would bolt, and he had no idea how adept of a horsewoman she was. If the horse reared, she could be thrown.

"Hold still."

The bee floated up to her hairline.

Lady Prestcote cringed.

He snatched the bee with his gloved hand.

She gasped.

The vibrations of the creature's wings tickled his fingers and palm through his thin riding gloves. Pain shot through his hand as the stinger pierced the leather and into the soft part of his palm. He winced and released the bee.

It buzzed away.

"Why did you do that?" Lady Prestcote stared at him, wide-eyed and motionless.

Why had he?

Curiosity swirled in her hazel eyes. They were verdant green with gold flecks and a brown spot between ten and twelve o'clock and reminded him of the meadow they'd passed through, dotted with fallen yellow leaves.

Argh. All the poetry gibberish his sisters had recited to him over the years was affecting his thoughts. Why else would he be comparing her eyes to a meadow? "Sisters." He grunted. "I have sisters, and they, too, are fearful of bees."

"It's not the bee I'm afraid of. It's the sting." She took his hand and opened his palm to inspect it, and for a brief moment, he regretted his gloves.

His horse shifted, and his leg brushed hers. Her gardenia scent drifted past him in waves like the falling leaves. No wonder the bee was enticed.

She released him to remove her glove, revealing graceful and slender fingers, before re-taking his hand. Frowning, she leaned closer to his palm and plucked out the stinger, holding it up for him to see. "You must be protective of your sisters."

"Quite." An understatement if he'd ever heard one. His sisters' protection was why he'd taken up fencing, boxing, shooting, and now, espionage. Never again would he be left weak and defenseless while someone attempted to hurt someone he loved.

"Thank you." Her green-gold eyes swirling with wonder locked on his.

He stilled, spellbound, remembering the feel of her in his

arms, the curiosity in her gaze, and the velvet softness of her lips.

A rosy blush that wasn't merely from the fresh air colored her cheeks.

Was she remembering their kiss too?

She looked away. "For coming to my aid."

"My pleasure." The pain had been worth it to see her awed expression. "Might it suffice to say I've taken the *sting* out of our first encounter?"

A little snort escaped her throat, and her lips curved into a crooked smile. She shook her head at his ridiculous pun as she redonned her glove. Clicking her tongue, she nudged her horse forward. "You sat next to Professor Matthews this morning, didn't you?"

"Indeed." *Egad.* Did he sound like the professor?

His sisters often groaned over his attempts at humor to break the tension—regardless of how creative his word twists. He smiled at her back, pleased to get a reaction. Snapping the reins, he took the lead. "Come on." He glanced over his shoulder at her. "The mill is just up ahead."

Colorful leaves swirled to the ground, and the damp musk of autumn grew pungent. They rounded a bend, and the splashing from the turning watermill wheel sounded before the tree line broke and the mill appeared. The morning sun reflected off the honey-colored stone and illuminated Lady Prestcote's face in a warm glow. Her eyes shone bright as she took in her surroundings.

"This way." He coaxed her around the back side of the mill and over an arched stone bridge. He'd passed this way earlier, surveilling the grounds, and he looked forward to seeing Lady Prestcote's expression at the view. Was that why he'd sought her out? She'd never been far from his thoughts since their first encounter, even after they'd danced and he'd learned she was a vapid socialite.

Whatever she was, the curiosity and perception in her eyes haunted him.

He turned his horse around to face her and reined to a stop. Her gaze homed on the tricky, narrow path. She glanced up at his halt with questioning eyes that widened, and her expression lit like that of a child peering into a confectionary shop window. Her rosy lips parted, and his skin tingled from the rush of air that passed between.

The autumn trees surrounding the pond reflected their colorful mirror images in the still water. The double tower of Griffin Hall on the hill rose tall and proud above the trees.

Her gaze panned the gorgeous view, but all Daniel saw was the dark-haired beauty mounted beside him. His heart slammed against his breastbone.

One of her gloved hands let go of her reins and lowered to her side. The desire to enfold her hand in his and absorb this moment with her physically pained him, making it nearly impossible to abstain. He remained still, noting her every breath, the long sweep of her lashes, and her delicate chin.

Thank you, Lord, for this moment.

Those lashes blinked rapidly, and her graceful chin quivered.

He recognized that look. Had witnessed it on his sisters' faces numerous times. She was about to cry. He patted his pocket to feel for his handkerchief. "Lady Prestcote?"

"My mama would have loved this view." She sniffed, blinking back the tears, but her overly bright eyes sparkled. She hit him with a sad smile that caused him to send up an irrational vow to fix her sorrow and replace her sadness with joy.

"Lady Mercer?" Daniel had never seen Lady Prestcote's parents, the earl and his wife, outside the city, but he'd heard her mother was close friends with Lady Coburn.

"Oh." Lady Prestcote straightened. "Indeed." She nodded

but turned away. "Yes. She...uh...harbors a secret love of nature."

"I didn't know that about the countess." He chuckled. "She and I share that in common."

~

*R*ebecca inwardly groaned at her slip. The stunning view reminded her of the walks in the woods she used to take with her mama back when she was healthy. Mama would stop and soak in the beauty of nature, whether it be a sunset or an unusual leaf.

At that moment, Rebecca could almost feel her mother's hand on her shoulder and the tickle of her breath on her cheek.

She dared to look at her companion.

Lord Wolston eyed her warily, one hand pinching the corner of his handkerchief at the ready. He must think her a veritable ninny for tearing up.

She flashed him a smile to reassure him and combat her unsteady emotions. "If only I were skilled in watercolors, but I doubt any artist could capture this majestic view. It's much too grand to limit to a canvas."

"Quite right." He stared out over the pond, relaxed and in command of the saddle. His horse stood stock still, dutifully awaiting the bidding of its master. The indulgent marquis was accustomed to being in charge, having his way, and accepting the women who flocked to him. The way his shoulders filled out his riding jacket, she could see why they did. She'd had little experience with nobility, but from what she'd seen, the men fell into two categories—stout and rotund or lean and lanky, never having lifted a finger for work. Lord Wolston's athletic build set him apart, as did the ease with which he exuded dignified confidence, signaling he was a leader.

The side of him that protected his sisters and who stopped to admire nature enticed her more than she'd care to admit.

Men are a distraction, Rebecca reminded herself. A marquis would never be interested in the likes of her. Besides, she shouldn't be wasting time out here when she could be in the Coburn library researching a cure for Madeline. "I should be getting back."

His head snapped in her direction, and he frowned. "So soon?"

What excuse could she use?

Miss Blakeford sneezed.

Rebecca had forgotten about her chaperone, who'd trailed them with a dazed look and resigned expression. "Miss Blakeford has been unwell."

Unwell might be a stretch. The woman did appear to be nursing a headache this morning. Well, every morning, evening, and afternoon, to be precise.

"It's kind of you to consider the well-being of your chaperone."

She smiled, but it wobbled.

"We'll head back, then." He inhaled a deep breath. "I could stay outdoors all day. It makes me feel alive." He turned his horse. With a click of his tongue, his mount continued down the path around the pond.

"It's because..." Rebecca pinched her lips tight. The marquis didn't want to hear about her research, nor would Corinne ever discuss science.

"You were saying?" The path widened, and he slowed until her horse came beside his.

Drat. Of course, he'd give her his full attention. She'd been trying to speak to the professor all morning about the human body to no avail, yet Lord Wolston patiently waited to hear her thoughts. She felt the weight of his gaze, and heat rose under the collar of her riding habit. "Because more oxygen is traveling through your blood."

"Oxygen in the blood, you say."

"Hmm." She nodded. "We breathe in the air, and our lungs disseminate the oxygen into tiny blood vessels that circulate via the heart, pumping blood through the body. Oxygen is carried to every cell, energizing them and making you feel alive. At least, according to William Harvey."

"You're well read. I've heard of Harvey's findings, but confess I haven't read them myself yet. What interests you about the health sciences?"

"The heart, mostly."

A lazy grin spread his lips. "Ah, matters of the heart, of which no one is an expert."

"Not the feelings between a man and woman." Heat burned her cheeks, and she lowered her gaze. Once she found a cure for Madeline, she'd research the cause of blushing and determine how to prevent it. "The heart as an organ, how its valves and chambers work, and how it continuously pumps blood through our arteries."

His teasing smile dissipated, replaced with serious interest. "Why specifically the heart? Why not the liver or stomach?"

"My...maid is ill." It pained Rebecca to spout falsehoods. They'd never rolled naturally off her tongue. Her mama could always tell when Rebecca fibbed and punished her for it. "She has a weak heart, as did her mother. My aunt also passed several years back when her heart stopped."

Lord Wolston regarded her with interest as if he could pick out her lies as easily as Mama had. "I'm sorry to hear about your aunt and your maid."

"I want to find a cure to help Madeline."

"Your maid?"

Rebecca swallowed around her tight throat. "Yes."

"A very noble task." He looked surprised and impressed. Or were his brows raised in skepticism?

"One in which I'm single-mindedly determined."

"Why is that?" His tone bordered on incredulity.

The closer she stuck to the truth, the more believable she would sound. "Madeline and I have been together for years and, in a way, grown up together. She's been my encourager, my shoulder to cry on, and my voice of reason. I know it may seem odd, but we've become closer than friends—almost sisters." She glanced at him to see if he believed her small falsehood.

"You are fortunate, then." He nodded. "A friend who is like a sister is a blessing."

They rode in silence the rest of the way around the pond and through a grove of trees, and Rebecca feared she'd lost the marquis's attention due to her bluestocking ways. What was the marquis doing here? Why would he choose Lady Coburn's party over London's elaborate events? Corinne would fly into the boughs when she learned Lord Wolston was in Leafield, and even more so when Lord Wolston wrote her off as dull. Should Rebecca try to redeem herself or, more accurately, Corinne as a socialite?

Lord Wolston peered up the solemn hill dotted with the gray headstones of the Coburn family plots and Leafield's deceased town members. He probably found her just as morbid.

"What brings you to the Cotswolds and Lady Coburn's party? I'd heard you were supposed to attend the Carter's party in Surrey." There. She sounded more like a London socialite—more like Corinne.

He grunted. "Part work and some play. I have holdings north of here that I've been bereft to check upon, and Lady Coburn's invitation arrived at the right time. The storm served as the extra nudge I needed to attend."

The path they followed rounded a bend.

"And you?" He slowed his horse. "I figured you'd be preparing for the Season."

The stables and main house came into view.

A game of shuttlecock seemed in full swing in the yard, Lady Farsley and Lord McGower against Lady Coburn and Professor Bell. A feathered shuttlecock flew over a net that was held in place by two poles.

"I've never seen the added obstacle of a net between the groups of players," said Rebecca, trying to change the subject until she could think how Corinne might respond.

"Lord McGower said it's called Poona and all the rage in British India. Perhaps you'd like a try?" Lord Wolston hit her with a devilish grin that set her heart pumping faster.

She could understand what Corinne saw in the marquis but must focus on her task. "Perhaps once Professor Duval has returned and Mrs. Evans feels rested."

Lady Farsley ran for the birdie, seeming to forget about the net.

Rebecca gasped and cried out, "Lady Farsley, watch out!"

She peered over her shoulder but ran right into it. The net stretched against the poles before ricocheting her into a backward fall, knocking off her wig in the process. She screamed, and Lord McGower rushed over to lend her aid. He scooped up her wig, plopping it back on the woman's head—unfortunately, backward.

"Are you all right?" Rebecca asked, poised to jump off her horse and lend aid if necessary.

Lady Farsley dusted the grass off her day dress. "Only my pride is bruised, but thank you, dear, for your concern."

Lord Wolston settled back into his saddle as if he, too, had been ready to unseat himself and help the poor woman.

Rebecca trailed him into the stable, followed by Miss Blakeford. He dismounted, passing his horse to the blond groom who'd escorted Sarah back to the stables.

"To finish my answer to your earlier question, I'd grown bored of the tiresome London social scene. The Carter party would have been the same." He chuckled. "Lady Coburn's guests are much more interesting." He helped Rebecca dismount, his gaze locking on hers and holding.

He peered at her as he had in the garden at the Lipscomb ball before he'd kissed her, and a spark jumped between them. "I find the company not only delightful, but fascinating."

Remembering her chaperone's presence, even though the woman didn't reprimand her, Rebecca stepped out of his arms. Cool air replaced his hot touch, and she turned before he witnessed the silly and unwanted smile she couldn't contain.

He found her fascinating.

Truly. She must get ahold of herself. A country girl from the seaside town of Blakeney could easily become swayed by a nobleman's charm and charisma, but she knew through her parents how dismissive the elite could be when one fell out of favor.

If she were the daughter of an earl and her sister were hale, then maybe she could dream of what it would be like to be wooed and pursued by the likes of Lord Wolston. But she could boast neither, and she needed to remember that, or her emotional heart would become as broken as her sister's physical one.

CHAPTER 8

*a*t the local tavern, Daniel cupped his hands around his mug of ale, which had grown warm a half hour before. To avoid drawing attention, he pretended to sip the bitter brew. As far as public houses went, Leafield's might be friendlier than those in the stews of London, but it was just as filthy. His boots stuck to the unwashed wooden floors, and the stink of old sour ale assaulted his nostrils. Business appeared slow at the moment, as there were only a few patrons, including one whose head rested on his arms on the table. Daniel might've thought the man dead if not for his steady snore.

The buxom barmaid happily joined him for a drink. She enlightened him about all the town's happenings, with only the occasional interruption to fetch a fellow customer another round. As a spy, being a marquis held both pros and cons. He couldn't go undercover, at least not in England or its territories, for he'd easily be recognized, since his image had been sketched into various political cartoons and gossip columns. Last month, one of the latter depicted him surrounded by eligible young ladies vying for his attention. The following week, an artist drew Daniel hiding in a maid's linen closet as the marriage mart mamas and their daughters hunted him down.

He'd only been caught hiding that one time—and he'd been on assignment—but he let the gossips believe what they wanted.

The greatest perk about being a marquis-spy was the ease with which people freely spoke to him. All he had to do was show interest in them and ask a few leading questions. If they grew tightlipped, he donned a bored expression and glanced around the room as if intending to leave. Panicked and desperate expressions then transformed the guests' or hosts' faces, and the juiciest information and secrets would follow.

People desired to be around him and be seen talking to him —everyone except Lady Prestcote. She'd avoided him the rest of the day after their ride.

Meanwhile, he'd sought the company of other guests. Without raising suspicions, he'd questioned them regarding why they'd decided to attend Lady Coburn's party, hoping to uncover information to aid his investigation.

Lord and Lady Farsley and Mrs. Evans had been coming for years and found Griffin Hall a haven for those who weren't well received among the *ton.*

It was Lord McGower's first year in attendance, but he'd grown discouraged by society's turning up their noses at new money. Daniel had intended to rule him out as a suspect and move on to other guests when the man mentioned he'd lived in Bengal and had seen Tantric Cults, whose members practiced *narabali,* or human sacrifice.

A chill had run down Daniel's spine as Lord McGower spoke of the Indian practice with fascination. Daniel had moved the nabob to the top of his suspect list. Could the man's interest in the Indian ritual have progressed to an unnatural practice of body snatching, for Lord knew what?

The professors—Bell, Matthews, and Duval—were

attending the party because Lady Coburn donated to their research, and Griffin Hall was located close enough to Oxford for their lectures. The fact that the research Professors Bell and Duval were conducting required cadavers moved them onto the suspect list. Once he got the academics speaking on their preferred topics, Daniel had been forgotten, so he'd excused himself and headed into town straight for the nearest pub. He wouldn't need to stake out the gravesite until after dusk.

Barmaids provided the best insight into the local villages, especially any untoward happenings, and this one with reddened cheeks and corkscrew brown curls half hidden under her cap was no exception.

Daniel issued her a grim frown. "I heard about the local chandler, poor chap."

Greta crossed herself. "God rest his soul. Buried him this morn'. No family to speak of, just the vicar and a few of the chandler's best customers, so he was nailed into a pine box." She nodded to the sleeping man at the counter. "He went to the funeral." She clicked her tongue. "A wee bit too early fer the bloke, but if you ask me, he's got his sights set on taking over the chandler shop and was checkin' that no unexpected family members arrived."

They hadn't. Daniel had never witnessed such a lonely funeral, attended only by the vicar, the butcher from the shop next door to the deceased's—still dressed in his apron—and the sleepy bar patron who yawned and checked his pocket watch repeatedly during the quick service.

"The chandler was a quiet fellow, kept to himself and to his bees." She glanced up at the frowning barkeep and rubbed a rag across the tabletop as if to appear busy. "His candles were of good quality, but he never charged enough. Barely kept his coffers full enough to feed himself, which is probably why he never landed a wife."

Where Lady Prestcote had been so reserved, Greta was as open and forthcoming as the loose strings on her corset. Daniel couldn't shake the feeling that Lady Prestcote was hiding something. She'd gone from a reticent damsel to forward socialite and back. One of her personas was an act, but why lie? She'd also avoided his question regarding why she'd attended Lady Coburn's party. What was she concealing?

Lieutenant Scar's voice rang in his head. *If something seems odd, go with your hunch. God may be trying to get your attention— or warn you.*

When he returned, he'd keep a closer eye on Lady Prestcote, but in the meantime, he'd get what info he could on the townsfolk. He gestured to the sleeping patron. "What does he do for work? Why would he want to take over the shop?"

"Mr. Tye?" She stuffed her rag underneath her apron strings. "He's Leafield's ironmonger. Makes snuffs, lanterns, chandeliers, and the like and wants to add the candles to his iron pieces."

"Makes sense that he'd be interested in the business." And he'd have any tools he needed. "I've heard rumors of resurrection men grave robbing down in Langley. You haven't seen any of that nonsense in Leafield, have you?"

"Pshaw." She leaned in closer and lowered her voice. "I heard the going rate fer a male body is eight guineas." She straightened and crossed her arms. "Fer that price, I might sack up the ol' chandler meself."

She wasn't helping him narrow down his suspects. Initially, he'd figured the bodies were being stolen for research since Oxford was so close, but then Lord McGower broadened his mind with the human sacrifice ritual, and now the money factor. He flashed her the smile he used on London socialites. "A messy business, that. I'd hate to see a lovely woman like yourself get her hands dirty."

A twinkle lit her eyes, and her hand moved to his thigh. "I have other means—"

"Greta." The man in the corner held up his mug. "'Nother round."

She glanced at the glowering barkeep and snapped her mouth closed. With pursed lips, she rose and sauntered to the counter. "Keep yer leggings on, Phillip."

The tavern door opened, and a young lad strolled in. His rosy cheeks and stiff-legged walk indicated he'd ridden a long way. "Beg yer pardon." He addressed the barkeep. "I'm lookin' fer Griffin Hall."

"If ye're comin' from London, ya missed yer turn." The barkeep poured a shot of gin into a glass. "What business do ya have at the manor?"

The lad shifted his weight. "I'm to deliver a letter to a Lady Prestcote."

Daniel rose and set a couple of coins on the table for Greta. "I'm going that way. I can deliver it for you." He held out his palm for the missive.

"I dunno." The boy cleared his throat and looked Daniel over from head to toe.

"You look as though you've traveled a long way and could use the rest." Daniel slid a few more coins on the counter. "How about a hot meal for the lad?"

"Gee, guv'nor, thanks." He flipped open his duffle and passed Daniel a red-sealed letter before hopping onto the barstool.

Daniel nodded his thanks to Greta and the barkeep and exited into the fresh air. The sun hung low in the sky. A groom brought him his horse, and he galloped the leaf-lined road back to Griffin Hall.

He passed his horse off to the Coburn groom and sneaked in the side door, then quickly ducked into an alcove as Professor Bell and Professor Duval passed, donning their coats.

Where were those two headed an hour before the evening meal was served?

Daniel surveilled them from the window as they entered the barn, but only Professor Duval rode off toward town. He waited and watched, but Professor Bell didn't return to the house. Where had he disappeared to?

Time was wasting. Daniel climbed the stairs and strode to his chamber, locking the door behind him. Removing the letter from his breast coat pocket, he dropped it on the desk and sat. He stared at the red seal. Should he violate Lady Prestcote's privacy?

He raked a hand through his hair.

Spying was his job, and he couldn't make any more mistakes, or Lieutenant Scar would dismiss him. He couldn't leave anything up to chance.

He turned up the oil lamp and removed the cover, heating the metal of the desk's letter opener. Several minutes passed while it warmed enough, and then he slid the tiny hot knife under the red wax with smooth, even pressure. The seal opened, and he carefully unfolded the letter.

The scripted hand didn't start with a greeting, merely stated four lines.

Do not think of backing out. If you want to see Madeline healed, you must stay and finish your task. Do not tell a soul of our arrangement, or there will be consequences. I will write to you when it's time to return to Buckinghamshire. Until then, only do what I instructed.

The missive was signed with the letter C.

Madeline was Lady Prestcote's ailing maid.

Was Lady Prestcote being blackmailed? Over her maid?

A maid she considered a friend, nearly a sister, but even so...

Either Lady Prestcote was kinder than anyone he'd ever met in polite society, or her maid wasn't whom they led everyone to believe.

Lady Prestcote had made some arrangement and must stay and finish her task—or there'd be consequences.

Could she be involved with the body snatchers? What other crimes could be happening in the tiny village of Leafield? Why else would someone send a cryptic message?

It could be that, with her connections and financial resources, she was acting as the go-between with the resurrection men and the buyers.

Perhaps Daniel should have another chat with Lady Prestcote. Could she lead him to the body snatchers and their employers?

He removed a candle from the writing desk and lit the wick off the oil lamp, replacing the glass cover. Holding the flame under the red wax, he was careful not to catch the paper on fire. Once the hard wax softened, he resealed the letter. No one would be the wiser.

And he had a fresh suspect to watch.

～

*R*ebecca hid in the comfort of the Coburn library, where rows of arched bookshelves stacked with tomes lined the room with a movable track ladder to reach the upper shelves. She pored over a volume on the internal organs to distract her thoughts from her earlier ride with Lord Wolston and the heady sensation of his nearness. Two smaller books on a similar subject were stacked on the corner of the desk. The one she studied now included detailed illustrations of the small intestine, liver, kidneys, and spleen. Bile rose into her throat at the realistic drawings, and she covered her hand over her mouth to keep the tea and scones she'd consumed earlier in their proper place. With her other hand, she dipped her quill and made a side note in her journal regarding one surgeon's speculation that if the kidneys are damaged, the heart, too, becomes at risk.

A man cleared his throat, and she looked up from the small reading nook desk where she'd nestled away to the figure in the doorway.

"Lord Wolston." She dropped her quill into the inkwell, and a splash of ink spotted the corner of her journal.

He seemed calm and collected, but his presence charged the library's dim and dusty air.

"May I?" He gestured to a nearby chair.

She opened her palm toward the seat. "Please."

Ink stained her ungloved hand, and she snatched it back as he dragged the chair over and sat before her. She yanked on her glove and folded her hands under the table.

He settled into the seat, stretching his legs. His Hessian boots brushed her ankles.

She pulled her legs under her chair.

Every inch of him attested to his being an aristocrat, but it didn't make sense why her heart rate would increase in his presence. He may control wealth, lands, and hearts belonging to ladies of the *ton*, but she was smarter than to set her cap on a man like him. If he knew the real her, he'd likely scoff and seek to offer his attentions to another gentlewoman.

His gaze fell to the open book before her and its sketches of internal organs.

She flipped the tome closed lest he be appalled by her gory reading selection or think her a bluestocking. "Was there something you needed?"

One side of his mouth twisted into that smug, lopsided grin. "I confess to being bereft of your company and used the excuse of delivering a letter to seek you out."

Humbug. All of it. He'd already grown bored and sought an

unmarried female to woo as a distraction. Did the young ladies of the *ton* fall for such flummery? He'd need to do better than that to fool her.

With one hand, he flicked open the button of his jacket and lifted the lapel. He reached into the breast pocket with his other hand and removed a letter.

Rebecca stared at the paper with its red seal. It had to be from Corinne, the only person outside Griffin Hall who knew Rebecca's whereabouts. She reached for the missive, but he snatched it back just before her gloved fingers closed on it.

His smile grew, but he offered it to her again.

She tried to seize it from his grasp, but he yanked it away once more.

"What kind of a game is this?"

"I beg your pardon." He chuckled. "It's an old habit from having sisters."

She extended her palm for him to hand it over.

He moved to place it there but stopped. "Wait."

The letter hovered an arm's length from her nose. Could she snatch it from his grip? His reflexes were quick, and she'd only make a fool of herself once more.

"Typically, a token of favor is granted to the messenger for his trouble."

She frowned. "You want me to pay you a coin?"

"Not a coin." His expression sobered, and his eyes flashed. "A kiss."

~

A kiss? Daniel wanted to suck the words back into his mouth. Had he turned into the cad he pretended to be as a spy? God forgive him. He had sisters. If some bloke said what he'd just said to one of them, he'd call the rogue out and demand satisfaction on the dueling field.

Lady Prestcote's eyes widened, and color swept into her cheeks. Her full lips parted in an affronted gasp, and he remembered their soft feel pressed against his. Would a second kiss bring the same electrical jolt that spread to his extremities that their first kiss produced?

What was he thinking?

He was a gentleman, not some blackguard. He swallowed, intending to tell her he jested. But her eyes fluttered closed, and she slowly leaned over the desk with puckered lips.

Whatever he'd been about to say—forgotten. His pulse thudded in his ear, and his gaze fixed on her magnificent mouth.

Thump!

He startled when her blasted books fell at his feet.

The letter ripped from his loose grip.

He chuckled. "Well played, Lady Prestcote."

She folded the letter and stuffed it into the bodice of her gown behind her lace tulle tucker.

"Aren't you going to read it?"

She snorted. "Not in front of you."

Confound it. Daniel clenched his jaw. He'd wanted to observe her expression as she'd read the contents, but instead, he'd been duly chastised for his childish actions. Would she have been angered by the blackmailer's demands or resigned and submissive?

He retrieved the books from the floor and stacked them on the other volume. "Any luck finding a way to help your maid?"

Her deep sigh caused her entire being to rise and fall. "Some information that I must research further. I merely struggle with the concept of the four humors needing to be in alignment."

"Sanguine, choleric, mucus, and phlegm."

"Actually..." She cast a shy glance at the floor before hitting him with her green-gold gaze, "Melancholic and phlegmatic.

Hippocrates listed the four humors as blood, black bile, yellow bile, and phlegm, but Galen associated them with temperaments. Supposedly, if one is out of balance, it will lead to certain conditions until equilibrium is restored. After writing to and receiving responses from those treated by bloodletting, I found no statistical proof it leads to the patient getting better."

"How many patients did you pen?"

"Sixty-eight."

"Truly." His brows shot up. "If blood is only one of the humors, why do the treatments mostly involve bloodletting?"

"Thomas Elyot believed blood has preeminence over the other humors because it's what distributes fluids throughout the body."

"Fascinating. I recall my professors at Cambridge lecturing on such topics, but your explanation is better." He rubbed the scruff on his chin.

A five o'clock shadow.

She gasped. What time was it? She twisted to see the hall clock. Quarter-past six. She jumped to a stand. "It's late. I must ready for the evening meal."

He rose and offered his arm. "May I escort you to your room?"

She stared at his elbow. Could she touch his arm without bursting into flames? If there was any truth to the four humors, then Lord Wolston put her out of balance. Never had a man made her cheeks burn, caused her insides to flip like leaves before a storm, or set her emotions to spin like a compass needle near a magnet.

Lord Wolston cleared his throat once again.

"My apologies." Goodness. She'd frozen, looking at his arm. "I was woolgathering." She curled her fingers around his sleeve, feeling solid muscle straining against the fabric.

"Pray tell, what do you do for sport?" What possessed her to ask such a question? The warmth in her cheeks spread to the tips of her ears.

He cast her a side glance as they exited the library and strolled the red-carpeted hall. An impish smile twitched the corners of his mouth. "I've been known to frequent pugilist clubs and draw a few corks in the ring. I also enjoy fencing and horse racing, although I'm too tall to make much of a go at jockeying."

His pastime pursuits explained his lithe, muscular frame.

"You aren't the typical London socialite," Lord Wolston said in a tone more certain than questioning.

She faltered a step, but he held her steady. Was he catching onto her pretense? "Why do you say that?"

He chuckled. "It's a good thing. When we danced at the Lipscomb party, I got the wrong impression about you. I believed you to be"—the crease between his brows deepened—"shallow." He exhaled with a shrug. "I apologize. You're caring, intelligent, and insightful."

"Um, thank you." Silence fell between them except for the swish of their footfalls on the carpet and the murmurs of other guests in their chambers, most likely dressing for the evening meal. She should say something—explain away her change in demeanor. "I was a little out of sorts at the Lipscomb party." She toyed with the index fingertip of her glove. "I had torn my gown and then happened upon you in the gardens. Plus, there is a certain amount of social pressure when dancing with a marquis."

He stopped at her room. "I'm pleased to get you away from your friends and social influences because I enjoy this version of you." He lifted her hand, his expression serious. "If you need a confidant or assistance, I'm at your service." He placed a kiss on the top of her glove.

She slid her hand from his grasp as soon as it was polite to do so.

"I'm looking forward to continuing our banter at supper." He turned and strode in the direction of his bedchamber, his shoulders swaying with each confident step.

She forced her feet to back into her room. His words rang in her ears...

I'm at your service.

CHAPTER 9

*R*ebecca arrived at dinner early, hoping to speak to Professor Duval, but his presence was missing. She maintained a polite smile despite her disappointment. Guests gathered in the rose salon awaiting the dinner announcement, and a cheery fire in the hearth chased away the evening's chill. She scanned the room, buoyed when she realized that Lord Wolston had also not arrived. The last thing she needed was another scene like the one in the library. The man was an unspeakable cad who should be taken to task.

Standing beside Professor Matthews, Sarah waved Rebecca over. When Rebecca joined their circle to the right of the fireplace, the professor asked, "How was the remainder of the tour of the grounds with Lord Wolston?"

"The millpond was lovely." Rebecca closed her eyes, conjuring the awe and inspiration the beautiful sight had stirred within her. "Especially with the leaves of gold, orange, and yellow."

"Indeed." Professor Matthews cleared his throat. "Griffin Hall's woodlands boast a wide variety of natural British Isle species like the silver birch, which turn yellow, the aspen in a golden hue, and the English oak a yellow-green." His chest puffed as if he was about to announce something momentous. "Two French chemists, Pelletier and Bienamié, recently isolated a chemical they're calling chlorophyll from the Greek words *Cholors*, meaning green, and *phylon*, meaning leaf. They believe the presence of this chemical gives the leaves their green color, and it's the breaking down of this chlorophyll chemical in autumn that causes the leaves to turn various colors."

"How interesting." Rebecca nudged Sarah, whose eyelids had lowered by the end of his monologue.

Sarah straightened and flashed the professor a vibrant smile. "Quite fascinating."

Lord Wolston and Professor Duval strolled into the salon. "I could introduce you to Lord Chelmsford." Though he didn't speak loudly, the marquis's baritone cut through the room's noise. "I guarantee if you have one glass of port with the earl, he'll donate to the cause." Lord Wolston clapped Professor Duval on the shoulder. "It has to be a specific port, so I'll bring the bottle."

Rebecca and Lord Wolston had only a few interactions, but her mind homed in on his deep baritone voice, fluid body movements, and keen blue eyes.

Which locked on her.

She shifted and smiled at Professor Duval next to him.

Lord Wolston urged Professor Duval in her direction. The tailored fabric of Lord Wolston's dark jacket moved like a second skin against his broad shoulders as he strode to their group, a disarming grin on his face.

The professor followed in his wake, his cravat askew.

As they joined their circle, Lady Coburn entered the salon and clapped her gloved hands to draw attention. "The evening meal is served. Please join me in the dining room."

Couples filed to the door, and Rebecca turned toward

Professor Duval, who had ushered her to the dining table the previous day. But he barely spared her a glance.

Lord Wolston raised his elbow. "Shall we?"

Rebecca was supposed to be the daughter of an earl, which, after Lady Coburn, made her the highest-ranking woman in the room. That meant she was expected to walk in on the arm of the marquis. Blast. Why couldn't they mix things up as they had the night before? Why did Lord Wolston have to be there in the first place? Shouldn't he be dancing with her cousin at the Carlson's house party?

Beside her, Professor Duval offered to escort Sarah.

Lord Wolston leaned closer and whispered in Rebecca's ear, his breath tickling the fine hair on her neck. "I promise not to ravish you at the dinner table."

She threaded her arm through his and gave it a tight *behave-yourself* squeeze.

His lips curved in a slow, saucy grin.

Odious man. He seemed bent on distracting her from her goal. She loved her sister too much to divert her purpose. She would uncover a way to heal Madeline's heart if it killed her— or Lord Wolston.

He pulled out her chair and aided her to sit at her place in front of the bone-white china plate and highly polished silverware place setting. One footman draped a napkin over her lap while another filled her water glass.

Lord Wolston sat on her right, Lord McGower on her left. Sarah and Professor Duval sat across the table with Lady Coburn at the head. Lord and Lady Farsley sat at the far end with Mr. Kim and Professors Matthews and Bell.

"A toast to Lady Coburn." Lord Wolston raised his glass, followed by the others. "We appreciate our hostess's generosity and her delightful efforts to bring such an array of fascinating guests together to learn about one another's exploits, giftings, and talents."

"Hear, hear!" echoed Professor Bell and Lord McGower. Other guests nodded their agreement.

Lord Wolston lowered his glass and addressed Lady Coburn. "Tell me about the interesting portraits in the halls. Are they relatives of yours?"

"Quite right." The lady gestured for the footman to ladle the soup into their bowls. "Although"—she fixed a polite smile at Lord Wolston—"I admit, the Coburns have a jaded past as smugglers, and some of the portraits look rather frightening."

Memory of the grimacing, painted faces with hard eyes watching the goings on at Griffin Hall sent an involuntary shiver down Rebecca's spine.

"Smuggling?" Lord Wolston sat back as the footman ladled his soup. "I'm sure there are stories aplenty."

"Indeed. My ancestors used the Evenlode River to smuggle goods during the Continental Wars. The entire hall was built to serve their purposes, with extra rooms to hide their illicit loot. Thank heavens my family found the Lord and changed to landowning and tenancy."

The footman served bone broth soup to Rebecca, and Lord McGower gently elbowed her. "Indian food has a spicy flavor that makes our English cuisine taste bland to me now. Phulkari Pulao is a common dish in India made of four different kinds of rice, often served with a nice curried chicken that I..."

"Professor Duval."

Rebecca's ears perked at Lord Wolston's voice, and her attention drifted while Lord McGower still spoke.

"Tell me about your upcoming lecture." Lord Wolston saluted Professor Duval with his glass before sipping.

Lord McGower tapped a section of bone bobbing in his broth with his spoon, drawing Rebecca's attention back to him. "You don't find any of these in Indian cuisine, just beans, rice..."

She listened to Lord McGower drone on about Indian food throughout the soup course, but her focus returned to the professor as the main course was served. Professor Duval adjusted the corner of his spectacles and raised his chin, blinking as if deciding the level of intelligence the marquis could handle. "My next lecture will be on how the liver produces blood and how the heart transports it through the body."

"Some bloke tried to convince me the heart acted like a water pump." Lord Wolston chuckled as he sliced into the roast. "He wanted to bet on it, but I couldn't be bothered."

"You would have lost." Professor Duval sipped wine, peering at Lord Wolston above the rim.

"You don't say?"

Lord McGower sighed, raising a bite of tenderloin on his fork, staring at it as if it were a dreamy treat. "There are foods that I've missed. You'd never eat this in India." He popped the bite into his mouth. As he chewed, he wore an expression of pure ecstasy.

"There are four chambers to a heart." Professor Duval set his glass down and arranged his beef tenderloin, potato, and asparagus into a makeshift diagram with his fork. "When the right ventricle chamber contracts, blood is pumped to the lungs. It comes in dark red, but at this point, it turns bright red, filling the right atrium and passing through a valve into the left ventricle. When the left ventricle contracts, the blood flows to the rest of the body. It makes a circuit through the body, then returns to the right atrium."

Lord Wolston scratched his temple. "Through a valve, you say?" He raised one eyebrow and flashed a smile at Rebecca. "Is that what causes women's hearts to flutter in the presence of nobility? Is that the cause of their swooning?"

Compared to Professor Duval's keen intelligence, Lord Wolston came across like a greenhorn, half flash and half foolish, yet he'd conversed with her on the four humors in the library. He wasn't a chawbacon. What was he up to?

Professors Bell and Matthews subdued their conversations to listen, but not Lord McGower, who rambled. "Phare is made without meat. Cows are sacred to the…"

Fortunately, he didn't seem to notice she paid him no mind.

"Hardly." Professor Duval scoffed. "Fluttering comes from an imbalance in the blood."

Lord Wolston washed down his bite of beef with wine. "What of the strange heart rhythms heard? You press that device against a person's chest and listen?"

Professor Duval wrinkled his brow. "A stethoscope?"

"Indeed." Lord Wolston snapped his fingers. "Will that tell you if there's a heart problem?"

Rebecca held in her gasp. Lord Wolston was helping her by getting the professor to discuss subjects she was having trouble broaching with him herself. She wanted to glance at Lord Wolston to see by his expression if his direction of the conversation was intentional, but she didn't dare, for fear they might change the topic.

"A stethoscope will alert the listener to any irregularities in the heart's rhythm."

Lord Wolston leaned over his plate. "And what do you prescribe for the patients with irregularities?"

"I'm not a physician." A guarded expression shadowed the professor's features.

"But if you were?"

He shrugged. "It depends on the other symptoms."

"Such as?" Lord Wolston pressed.

Professor Duval picked up his fork and knife and refocused on his meal.

Was he refusing to answer? Rebecca clenched her mouth shut. *Please, God, don't let the conversation stop now.*

Professor Duval slowly chewed a bite of roast, and his Adam's apple bobbed as he swallowed.

"Ankle swelling, heart palpitations, shortness of breath, and tightness in the chest." The words burst through Rebecca's lips.

"I told you." Professor Duval glared at her with the same leeriness he'd shown her the other night. "I'm not some quack selling tonics."

"I'm only curious because my aunt passed away, and what if her death could have been prevented?" She held his cynical stare.

"A family of your means would have access to the best physicians in all of Europe." He scoffed. "I doubt I could provide any names you don't already know."

Rebecca lowered her gaze to her untouched meal and fought back frustrated tears. She picked up her fork and knife and cut into the cold meat.

"When cadavers are dissected, do you find atrophy or discoloration in hearts that indicate a past problem?" Lord Wolston continued as if Professor Duval's set-down never happened. "Are the bodies you receive...? How do I best phrase this?" He rubbed his chin and shrugged. "Fresh? How do you source them?"

His question drew the attention of Lady Coburn and Sarah. Even Lord McGower paused his monologue.

Professor Duval pressed against the chair's backrest as a servant removed his empty plate. He held Lord Wolston's gaze, but he seemed guarded since she'd rattled off symptoms. "Sourcing is a challenge. British law allows only those blokes who've died in prison to be studied for the benefit of science."

Lord Wolston tilted his head. "What does that amount to— one a month? Less?"

"Too few." The professor focused on the chocolate mousse placed before him.

"I daresay." Lady Coburn's lips pursed. "The direction of this conversation isn't meant for a gentlewoman's ears." She changed the topic to tomorrow's activities and the upcoming ball.

Sarah peered at Rebecca across the table and raised her brows with a look that clearly stated, *What was that about?*

Rebecca shrugged. Had Lord Wolston attempted to help her and she'd ruined it? Where was he going with the bit about the cadavers?

One thing was certain. The man beside her made her heart pound and her head ache.

~

*D*aniel set out into the darkness on foot, skating through the shadows toward the graveyard. Professor Duval had avoided him after the men excused themselves to partake of cheroots and an after-dinner brandy on the terrace. Time would tell if the contents of Daniel's glass would kill the potted ivy in the railing flowerboxes where he'd stood, but he needed a clear mind. He'd almost ruined his dandified imbecile façade after Professor Duval—in his smug, uppity way—disrespected Lady Prestcote.

His strides ate up the ground as he recalled the exchange. He'd wanted to give the professor a good set-down, but he needed to gain his trust so he'd be forthcoming with information. He shouldn't have been so direct about the cadavers. Professor Duval appeared to be a prideful but intelligent man, and if Daniel showed his hand, Duval would surely trump him.

The thin sliver of a moon didn't give much light, but yesterday, he'd memorized a clear path to the graveyard and identified a place to lie in wait. He trudged uphill, passing under an oak tree. A lantern illuminated the rounded headstones, but not carried by the men he sought. The night watchman patrolled the grounds.

Daniel treaded carefully so as not to snap any twigs or

crunch on fallen leaves. When the guard turned his back, Daniel sneaked through the gate and settled behind an overgrown holly bush. The prickly leaves scratched his skin and caught the material of his overcoat, but he eased into a crouch several horse lengths from the chandler's freshly dug grave and waited.

To occupy himself, he allowed Lady Prestcote's lovely hazel eyes to float in his memory. He almost laughed out loud, recalling her knocking the books off the table in the library and stealing the letter from his fingers. Men of the Quality underappreciated intelligence in a woman, and many ladies hid their minds to not be deemed a bluestocking, but not Lady Prestcote. She wasn't afraid to speak her piece, and he had come to value her quick intellect.

His sisters had been educated by the best governesses. But when he'd returned from university, Alicia and Eliza had pestered him to teach them all he'd learned so they could converse freely with him on various topics. They were blessed with insatiable minds. Alicia had found a good husband who didn't belittle her intelligence, but would Eliza be as fortunate? Daniel couldn't imagine marrying a simpleton wife. He wouldn't be happy with a lovely bobble to hang on his arm.

Lady Prestcote had intelligence and beauty.

In the graveyard, the shadows shifted, and Daniel's skin tingled.

Two men approached, and the guard swung the gate open. The hinges creaked an eerie sound but not loud enough to draw anyone from the manor or stables. The thinner one pulled an empty cart. The taller of the two dropped what sounded like the clanking of coins into the watchman's open palm, and the guard exited the graveyard, whistling a happy tune. One man started digging, their wooden shovels making quiet work of the unpacked earth. The other set a dark lanthorn on the ground with the quick slide open before picking up his shovel. The lanthorn illuminated their work, but one wrong sound and the quick slide would be flicked shut, shrouding them in darkness and allowing the grave robbers an opportunity to get away.

Lieutenant Scar had instructed him to follow them to their buyer, but Daniel could easily bring in both men, having faced bigger opponents during training. One appeared to be a lad, not yet old enough to marry, though close. The other grave robber was stout, looking to be in his mid-thirties. He could incapacitate the smaller one first, then disarm the larger. As a precaution, he'd tucked bindings into his coat pocket. He could capture the body snatchers himself, interrogate them, explaining that they'd face a lesser sentence if they revealed their buyer, and then hand them over to the local constable while he went after the rest of their ring.

He could almost hear Lieutenant Scar's "well done, Wolston."

The key was in the timing. Technically, a dead body didn't belong to anyone, and stealing one was not considered a criminal act. Unless the dead man's clothes remained on his person, or if the gravediggers pocketed any of the deceased's personal effects, then Daniel could threaten them with jail time.

One of the shovels struck wood, and the larger man grinned. "Almost got 'em."

A few more shovelfuls of dirt flew from the hole, and the taller man dropped a canvas bag and a metal pry bar to open the lid to his accomplice.

The young lad grunted and strained.

"Put yer back in ta it, ya weaklin'," the taller one said.

The canvas bag didn't muffle the crack of the pine lid. The lad tossed the crowbar into the dirt, and the tall accomplice passed a rope to his lackey. The young lad bent down into the grave, the dirt obstructing Daniel's view, but by the shuffling and grunting, he assumed the lad threaded the rope under the corpse's armpits and secured a knot.

The lad hopped out of the hole, passing the chandler's gold pocket watch to his partner and keeping a small gold chain for himself. "A little treasure for you and a prize for me."

Time to apprehend them.

The lad and his accomplice picked up the rope, and the two heaved the dead man from the grave.

While the men were focused on their find, Daniel rose. He sneaked up behind the smaller lad, swiped the discarded crowbar, and slurred his words. "You blokes have some gin to spare?"

The lad jumped and spun, letting go of the rope.

Daniel wacked the side of the lad's knee with the metal bar, and he collapsed, writhing.

The taller one released his hold on the body, and the poor chandler slid back into the grave with a thud.

The accomplice grabbed his shovel and swung it toward Daniel, but he dodged the slow man's swings. The momentum pulled the man's arms to the left, leaving his face unguarded. Daniel punched the man's cheek.

He wobbled on his feet for a stunned moment before falling.

The younger lad scrambled backward, dragging his injured leg.

Daniel tucked the crowbar into his belt and dug into his pockets for the bindings.

The lad's gaze jerked over Daniel's left shoulder.

He spun on instinct.

A wooden shovel missed his head but hit his shoulder, knocking it out of socket. Sharp pain seared through him. *Perdition.* Where did a third perpetrator come from?

The light of the lanthorn snuffed out, leaving Daniel with

only moonlight to locate his attacker. Off balance, he grabbed the crowbar with his good arm.

A tall shadow shifted, and a voice in the background commanded, "Again!"

A fourth?

Daniel attempted to swing before his opponent did. He hit the attacker in the ribs but lacked his usual force.

The mysterious third grave robber didn't go down. He was more agile than the stout man, and the younger one who'd dug the grave now sat staring with a look of horror and holding his wounded leg.

The background voice, the man who'd shouted, "Again," was another person altogether.

Four men against one.

With no choice but to fight, Daniel raised his weapon to strike.

The tall shadow swung the shovel again.

Daniel tried to deflect the hit, but the force was too great. The crowbar ripped from his hands and the blow bludgeoned his head, knocking Daniel to the ground. The blinding pain in his shoulder dulled, and the moonlight dimmed to black.

CHAPTER 10

*E*xcruciating pain dragged Daniel back into consciousness. The smell of dirt oriented him to his position, lying on the ground.

Hands tugged to remove his overcoat, and his shoulder screamed in protest. Muffled voices, as if from underwater, cleared until his mind registered the words. "Don't take him. He's one of the guests—a nine—nobility."

Daniel didn't recognize the raspy voice. He tried to open his eyes but couldn't. Best to let them believe him unconscious and for him to listen. Perhaps they'd reveal their identities and that of their buyer.

"His disappearance will raise alarm. Give me your flask."

The pungent juniper smell of gin filled his nose, and wetness dripped under his collar. The irony of his own trick being used against him wasn't lost on him.

"Dump him at the bottom of the stone steps. Anyone who finds him will think he's deep in his cups and telling a good hum." A shuffling of steps sounded. "You. Set the empty grave back to rights. Make it look like we were never here. The watchman will vouch he'd been in the graveyard all night and not a peep."

A hand wrenched under Daniel's bad shoulder, and the pain sent him back into the darkness.

~

*W*hen Daniel awoke again, he lay at the foot of the stone stairs just outside Griffin Hall. The chirps of frogs and crickets told him his attackers were long gone. His shoulder hurt like the dickens, but this wasn't the first time he'd dislocated it. He slowly rose to a stand, pausing occasionally to allow the dizziness to pass.

How long had he been out?

The moon that had been behind tall trees now hung high in the sky. He guessed it to be well after midnight.

Something dripped into his eye. He blinked and wiped it away with the back of his hand.

Blood.

He felt the tender spot in his hairline where the shovel had hit him, leaving a small gash that may or may not need stitching. It was sticky, which meant he hadn't been out long enough for his cut to scab over. He removed his handkerchief and wiped the blood from his eye and off his forehead.

Holding the cloth to the wound to stop the bleeding, he peered up at Griffin Hall. Even simply breathing caused his shoulder to scream. Who would be up at this hour? Who could he trust not to make a scene? He could wake the help, but he'd prefer to control the flow of gossip instead of unleashing the dam of servant chin-wagging. Most of the windows were dark. One lit window on the second floor drew his attention. He counted over from the right.

The library.

Could his little-miss-bluestocking be reading at this hour? Or was she up awaiting word of a successful body snatching attempt? He found her involvement hard to believe, but the letter he intercepted screamed of blackmail. Mayhap she had no other choice. What lengths would she go to for information to save her maid's life?

He sneaked in through the servant's entrance. The kitchens were quiet, and the fireplace had burned down to orange glowing ash. Gripping his dangling arm to lessen its movement, he crept into the back hall and mounted the stairs to the second floor.

Snoring penetrated the closed doors of a couple of the rooms he passed.

In the library, the glow of the lantern emanated from the same far desk in the far corner where he'd spotted Lady Prestcote earlier, except this time, instead of her nose being in a book, her forehead rested on the pages. She slept with palms splayed on either side of the opened cover, clearly having nodded off while reading. He stopped in front of the desk. If he hadn't been in such pain, he might have found the scene adorable.

"Lady Prestcote."

She didn't stir.

He sidestepped around the desk and leaned closer. The book she'd been reading had a detailed drawing of a human's internal organs. Curious woman. "Lady Prestcote."

"One more chapter," she murmured, "then I'll go to bed."

If she'd been waiting up for the body snatcher, she'd made a mull of it, maybe even more so than he. With a soft chuckle, he said, "Wake up, sleepyhead."

She slowly blinked and lifted her head, her cheeks and lips rosy with sleep and her hair loose and tussled. Her gaze scanned the library until it met his.

Eyes wide, she jerked back with a gasp. The cords in her neck tightened, and she braced as if to scream and wake the whole blasted house.

He covered her mouth with his hand, just in case. "It's me. Daniel. Lord Wolston."

She closed her mouth, peering at him as if he were a ghost haunting Griffin Hall.

"I need your assistance." He gritted his teeth against the pain. "Please."

He felt her body relax. She nodded, and he removed his hand.

"You look wretched."

"You're too kind." He blamed the pain for his sarcasm, noting the typeset print from the book she'd been reading had smudged onto her forehead.

"You're covered in dirt and"—she squinted at his forehead —"is that blood? What happened to you?" Concern wrinkled her brow before she pulled her chin back and waved a hand under her nose. "You smell like you bathed in spirits."

"I was accosted. My shoulder is..." He indicated his limp left arm and clenched his teeth, inhaling through the sharp pain caused by the slight movement. "I need your help maneuvering my shoulder back into its socket."

Her gaze roved over him from head to toe, then she focused on his limp arm. She tapped her index finger to her lips.

"I saw a chapter on how to address a dislocated shoulder." She shuffled the books on the desk, opening one and scanning the table of contents.

"It merely needs a good thrust back into place. If you could—"

She held up a hand to silence him, her finger trailing down the chapter headings. "Bah. Not this one." She pulled the bottom one from the stack and lifted the cover.

"I'm in a good bit of agony. Now's not the time for research."

She ignored him, opening to a page midway through the book.

Daniel's shoulder throbbed with his heartbeat, and his hand on his left side tingled with numbness. Would she help him or not?

She flipped several pages with her index finger.

He scanned the room. A bookshelf corner looked like it might work. Tired of waiting, he strode to the bookshelf.

"What are you doing?"

Oh, *now* he had her attention. He planted his feet and thrust his shoulder into the corner of the bookshelf. Searing pain shot through his body. He dropped to one knee as blackness crept along the edges of his vision.

"Stop." Lady Prestcote hurried over and knelt beside him. "You're going to injure yourself further."

He shook his head to clear the fog and attempted to move his arm. *Blast.* His shoulder remained dislocated.

"I know what to do." She aided him to a stand, careful not to jostle his arm. "You need to lie down on the desk." She moved the books to the chair and placed the one with instructions open on top.

He'd argue with her if the pain wasn't diminishing his ability to think straight. He allowed her to guide him to the desk like a lost child and settle him there. She lifted his legs and swung them so that he had no choice but to lie down, gripping his arm close to his body.

She moved to his side and pried his fingers off his arm, peering over her shoulder at the open book. "This may hurt a little."

A little? Could it hurt more than it already did?

She gripped his wrist and moved his arm into a ninety-degree position from his body while pumping his wrist in small circular motions. It was like a strange handshake.

He sucked air through his teeth, then held his breath.

She raised his wrist above his head, still doing the small handshake-like movements.

And pulled.

His shoulder popped back into place.

Lady Prestcote released a startled yelp as if shocked it had worked.

The intense pain ebbed, and Daniel exhaled.

"Are you all right?" Lady Prestcote's face, lined with worry, hovered above his. Her soft lips were within reach. All he had to do was cup the back of her neck with his good hand and lower her mouth to his. A kiss to celebrate his not being in pain any longer.

"Much better." He reached for her.

But she turned to the open book.

Bloomin' shame, but probably best that he didn't thank her by accosting her again.

"You're supposed to keep it immobile for a few days." She strode to a nearby chair and removed a throw blanket.

He slowly sat up, allowing the counterbalance of his legs swinging off the side to aid him.

She slid the blanket around his elbow, crossing it over his chest.

Her closeness heated his skin like standing near a cheery fire, and her floral scent overrode the harsh smell of spirits. He liked her being by his side and enjoyed her contrast of soft feminine curves and sharp mind. Was this what having a wife would feel like? Stimulating yet comforting? If so, he might need to reconsider his future. As the next in line to the dukedom, he must marry, but he had been in no rush, especially not while he dabbled in espionage.

Her deft fingers tied the sling at his neck, brushing his skin and setting it ablaze.

Squirming to find a more comfortable position, he moved up his marriage timeline.

"You should be more patient." She tightened the knot.

"So I've been told."

"You could have injured yourself further, ramming into bookshelves." She adjusted the sling. "If you lie face down on a table, you can set it yourself."

"Is that so?" To take his mind off the pain, he admired the line of her jaw and the slope of her neck. Such wisdom would help him for next time. A dislocation was bound to happen again in his line of work.

"You'll need to tie a weight to your wrist and let it hang for twenty minutes or more. Gravity will reposition it back into place."

His gaze moved to her rosy lips—so temptingly kissable. He forced himself to look at her eyes, but the silent anticipation that swirled in their green-gold depths, as if she, too, desired to relent to the pull between them, didn't cool his ardor.

She looked away. "You really shouldn't imbibe. It addles the wits and encourages men to fight."

He wanted to set her straight, but he needed to keep his cover. "You're up late reading."

"I found some volumes on various ailments." She gestured to the stack of books.

"I'm going to call you Blue, as in *bluestocking*, from now on."

She raised her chin. "You're not offending me, if that's what you're trying to do."

"Certainly not. It's a term of endearment. I admire a woman with a mind." He leaned toward her and stared at her forehead as if to read her thoughts. "Let me guess what you were studying."

Lady Prestcote shifted back from his closeness, but then held her ground. A delightful flush stained her cheeks.

"You read about an experiment on weak valves and heart flutters." He narrowed his eyes and read the backward print on her forehead. "'We found irregular heartbeats significantly correlate with the flow of blood from one chamber into another. We hypothesized that these valves improperly close, causing the *lub-dub* sound.'"

Her lips parted. She reached for the second book, removing it from the pile on the chair, and thumbed to a page, reading the content.

"Those are the words verbatim." It was her turn to stare at him. "How did you know that?"

He dragged his index finger across her forehead, smudging the ink. "The print transferred to your face."

Her breath hitched.

Oh, she was delightful.

She leaned back and rubbed her forehead with the back of her hand.

"Allow me." He touched the side of her face to draw her closer, his fingertips dipping into the silky strands of hair above her ear. He rubbed the blurred ink above her eyebrow with his thumb. The heat of her embarrassment fairly radiated.

Why did he so enjoy making her uncomfortable?

He licked his thumb and wiped once more, before Blue could protest.

She jerked back. "Wait." She furrowed her brow. "You read that backward."

He shrugged. "It's a nice skill to acquire when you must spy on conspiring sisters who write in journals and pass notes. I can also read upside down."

"You spy on your sisters?" An accusation laced her tone, and she studied him as if connecting a younger Daniel with the current man before her.

"Merely for their protection."

Her expression lightened, signaling she appreciated his answer. "Interesting fact. Did you know that Leonardo da Vinci used to write in secret code so that it had to be deciphered with a mirror?"

"You don't say." He'd studied da Vinci's methods in university, but he enjoyed her enthusiasm for knowledge.

"You might be able to get a job with the War Department or Foreign Office."

"Indeed." Very perceptive and almost on the mark. He must be careful around her. "If my aspirations to be a marquis don't pan out..."

"How silly of me." She hung her head, and he felt like a cad, but it was best for her to believe his working for the War Department a ludicrous idea. "I'm not thinking clearly."

He slid off the desk and shifted to offer her his uninjured arm. "May I see you to your room?"

She glanced at the stack of books.

"They'll still be here in the morning."

Her chin dipped, and a wave of rich mahogany hair fell across one eye. He itched to brush it back, but she beat him to it, tucking the loose tresses behind her ear. She slipped her hand around the crook of his elbow.

The hall clock chimed three in the morning.

He caught her stifling a yawn.

"Tell me about your sisters." She flashed him an askance look.

"Alicia and Eliza are a pair." He slowed his steps, taking his time. Despite his weariness, he enjoyed having her full attention. "Mothering and bossiness come naturally to them both, but it's done out of love."

Light under the crack in the door to Professor Bell's chamber flickered out as they passed. What was the man doing up at this late hour?

Lady Prestcote asked his sisters' ages, and he told her. "Alicia has married—nice chap, but Eliza has her coming out next Season." He shared his nervousness about her upcoming debut. "I don't relish chasing off unwanted beaus."

"Indeed. Men can be a distraction." She stated the phrase as if she'd said it hundreds of times, as if trying to convince herself.

They reached her door, and he stopped, facing her. "Some gentlemen may be a good distraction."

Her gaze cleared as she snapped out of whatever thought plagued her.

He managed to stifle a chuckle at her chagrined expression. He fingered a lock of hair that S-curved over her collarbone. "One in particular may be a much-needed distraction."

She held still, her chest not even rising and falling with breath.

He trailed his finger along her collarbone and felt her shiver before he flicked the loose strand back over her shoulder.

She reached for the door and would have darted inside if he hadn't caught her arm.

"Blue." He whispered his new nickname for her and reveled in how her lips parted. He expected her to demand he not call her that, but she said nothing. He bowed his head. "Thank you for your aid tonight."

"Anytime." She shrugged off his grip and fled behind the safety of her closed door.

"Is that a promise?" He leaned close to the crack. "Because I plan to take you up on that offer."

An audible gasp emitted from the other side.

He strolled down the hall. It had been a terrible night all around. So why was he in such a good mood?

It faded when he reached his chamber.

A dusty footprint marred the carpet just outside his door.

He leaned to examine the track closer.

Definitely male, composed of dirt mixed with something... white.

White dirt?

From the gravesite? Maybe lime residue? What else could it be?

It seemed his suspect had access to the hall and knew the location of Daniel's bedchamber.

CHAPTER 11

*R*ebecca overslept the morning meal, thanks to the strange late-night encounter with Lord Wolston in the library. Had she dreamed the entire episode? She really must stop reading medical journals so close to her bedtime. It was no wonder, with her medical knowledge, that she'd dreamed about falling asleep in the library and aiding a handsome marquis. Her insides fluttered as she recalled the heady sensation of him trailing his fingers along her collarbone and brushing back a lock of her hair.

Foolish greenhorn. Of course, it was a dream.

Madeline ran the brush once more through her hair before setting it aside and gathering the heavy mane.

Rebecca pressed a hand to her stomach to still its nonsense. She must speak the foolishness aloud to drain it of its power. "I had the strangest dream last night that Lord Wolston dislocated his shoulder and I reset it for him."

"Really?" Madeline twisted Rebecca's thick hair into an elaborate coiffure instead of the loose bun she typically wore. Madeline flashed her eyes at Rebecca. "You dreamed about the marquis?"

"I'd been up too late reading medical journals, and he was the most likely one to become injured due to his imbibing." She checked her pin watch for the time. Forty-five minutes past ten.

"Oh?" Madeline handed her a mirror. "How do you know he imbibes? Did he overly toast our hostess during the evening meal to partake more?"

"He toasted once." Rebecca reflected back. "Actually, I don't recall him drinking wine or spirits last evening, but I smelled it on him the night of the Lipscomb party."

His lips tasted of lemonade, but she hadn't told her sister the marquis kissed her that night. She fought down the heat rising in her cheeks. What kind of example would she be setting for her younger sibling?

Out the window, clouds threatened rain, which changed her plans for the day. Professor Duval would most likely skip a morning ride and instead gather with the other professors in the orangery before high noon tea.

Madeline stuffed the last pin to hold Rebecca's hair. She stepped aside, and Rebecca rose. "You look lovely in Corinne's gowns. That shade of green goes well with your coloring. You'll draw many men's attention today."

Rebecca glanced down at the pale sage day dress trimmed with lace. There was only one man whose attention she intended to gain—Professor Duval.

Why, then, did Lord Wolston's teasing smile float through her memory?

"If you see Miss Blakeford," Rebecca said, "let her know I'm awake and will require her services." She had seen little of the governess-turned-chaperone.

"I'll knock on her door before breaking my fast with Lucy and the staff."

"I don't want you over-exerting."

"Truly, I'm enjoying myself." Madeline eyed her with a *stop-*

worrying look. "Lucy and I are becoming fast friends. We talk about boys, getting married, and having children."

Maybe a friend would benefit Madeline. She should be considering her future, not worrying if she'd have one. That was Rebecca's job.

Madeline *would* have a future. She'd see to it.

Professor Duval would help her find a remedy.

"And I'm privy to all the staff gossip."

"Just have a care and don't overdo." Rebecca hugged Madeline and strode from the room, heading to the orangery. Her stomach grumbled, but she must wait and hope finger sandwiches would be served at high tea.

Men's voices drifted down the hall, and she followed them into the warm solarium air scented with green plants and a hit of orange peel. Even on this overcast day, the glass ceiling allowed much natural light into the room, along with a bit of heat. Large pots with orange trees almost as tall as Rebecca created a tropical alcove around a cluster of low-backed chairs.

The men had removed their jackets and draped them over the backs or arms of their seats. Sarah and Lady Coburn sat near Professors Matthews and Bell, and Sarah waved her over to an empty chair between her and Professor Duval.

Rebecca mouthed the words *thank you* to her new friend. Only after she passed between the two professors' line of vision did they clear their throats and rise as belated signs of respect that a lady had entered the room.

"Good day, Lady Coburn, Mrs. Evans, professors." Rebecca fanned out the sides of her day gown and sat next to Sarah.

Sarah smiled her greeting. "We missed you at the morning meal."

"I beg your pardon. I overslept because I stayed up too late reading in the library."

"Oh, I'm looking for a good book." Lady Coburn fanned herself. "What novel were you reading?"

"It was a collection of medical journals on the circulatory system."

Lady Coburn blinked at her. "Your mother has written that you're the furthest thing from a bluestocking." Her lips curved into a matchmaking grin before she turned to the men. "Has one of our knowledgeable professors turned you on to their topics of interest?"

Rebecca glanced at Professor Duval, then bowed her head with a coy smile. Why hadn't she asked Corinne how flirting was done? Was she even going about it properly?

Professor Duval didn't seem to notice. How could she encourage him to speak of his research?

Lady Coburn eyed Professor Duval, who removed his spectacles and cleaned them with his handkerchief. "Although I find this fascinating, we must turn to a lighter discussion than the inner workings of the heart before I grow faint and we put poor Sarah to sleep."

"No need to change the subject." Rebecca blew on the dying ember of conversation, desperate to reignite it. "Professor Duval has a way of making subjects understandable and enthralling."

"That is true." Lady Coburn tipped a graceful nod in his direction.

"It's a challenge to simplify complicated subjects for the fairer sex." Professor Duval hooked one side of his wire-rim spectacles over his ears. "You're the earl's daughter, correct? Lady Prestcote, is it?"

Rebecca nodded as the air deflated from her lungs. He'd escorted her into the dining room, sat next to her, even conversed with her a little. They'd shared a morning ride, and he'd dressed her down not once but twice, reminding her that he wasn't a doctor and couldn't offer cures.

After all that, he didn't even know her name?

Had she truly left so little of an impression on him?

"You ladies feel free to discuss your fanciful topics while

we'll continue our intellectual discussion elsewhere." Professor Bell rose. "Shall we, gentleman?"

No, she couldn't let them exclude her.

Lord Matthews, eyeing Sarah, seemed reluctant to leave. His gaze moved past her. "Lord Wolston, whatever happened to your arm?"

Rebecca shifted in her seat to peer behind Sarah, where Lord Wolston sauntered toward them, his arm bound in a white strip of cloth as a sling.

Merciful heavens. Had her dream been real?

She met the marquis's gaze, and a current flowed between them, causing a repeat of the physical tension she'd felt in her dream—which hadn't been a dream at all. She subdued a shiver.

The events of the night before spun through her mind. She saw pain straining his features, remembered the warmth when she touched his arm, and felt the intensity of his gaze, which turned her insides into a blustery storm of emotions.

Lord Wolston bowed and greeted everyone with a good day. The sleeve of his finely tailored jacket flapped loose by his side, while the knotted sling held his arm close to his body. He placed a hand on the back of Rebecca's chair. "I had an unfortunate run-in with some dastardly fellows last evening on my way back from the tavern. I was a trifle foxed and stumbled upon some resurrection men."

"Resurrection men? In Leafield?" Professor Bell stroked his beard and resumed his seat. "Odd that they'd find business in the country." He grunted a laugh. "Are you certain it wasn't the barmaid's jealous beau?"

Lord Wolston chuckled. "A graveyard isn't the ideal place for a clandestine visit with a lady. Besides, the shovels and wagon were a dead giveaway—pardon my pun."

"So close to Griffin Hall?" Lady Coburn placed a hand over her heart.

Professor Duval resumed his seat, his attention focused on the marquis.

"I fear"—Lord Wolston grunted and patted the back of his head—"in my foxed state, I envisioned myself a pugilist who could fight my way out, but I was no match for the shovel that hit me from behind."

Gasps sounded all around.

"When I came to, my shoulder was dislocated, but fortune smiled upon me, for Lady Prestcote had been reading medical journals in your library and knew exactly what to do to get my shoulder back into place." He bowed to Rebecca. "I owe you a debt of gratitude for your wisdom and quick thinking."

Heat filled her cheeks, and she glanced at Professor Duval, who studied her with interest.

Lord Wolston's gaze burned into the side of her head, so she looked at him and shrugged. "Anyone would have done the same."

"Anyone with fortitude and medical knowledge," Lord Wolston countered. "I was fortunate that you had both."

"Please, regale us with the tale." Professor Matthews dragged another chair into the circle, placing it directly across from Rebecca's seat.

Somehow, it seemed Lord Wolston had stumbled upon grave robbers in this small town. He could weave a fine story, but it was more likely that in his inebriated state, he'd tripped and rolled down a steep hill, knocking himself unconscious. He either dreamed or concocted the encounter. Even so, his delivery captivated the listeners. When he relayed landing a blow and knocking out one of the grave robbers, the men cheered and the women clapped. His tone changed when he spoke of seeing the light in the window and finding a sleeping angel.

She rolled her eyes, and his lips twitched.

"The angel awoke and, employing both wisdom and tenderness, aided me in my time of need."

"You are too kind." Rebecca flashed him a look that hopefully stated, *that will suffice.*

Sarah's gaze slid to Rebecca, one brow raised. Likely, her friend would demand to hear Rebecca's side of the story later.

The warm, orangery air couldn't explain the fiery burn heating Rebecca's face. She prayed no one would ask if they'd been alone or if her blasted chaperone had been present. Reputations had been lost over less.

Cousin Corinne would fly into the boughs if Rebecca ruined her marriage chances. Who was she kidding? Corinne would ring a peel over Rebecca merely for being in the presence of "her marquis." She'd be mortified Rebecca had used her bluestocking ways to set his shoulder. Corinne had refused to come to this party because she wanted to be near the marquis. Rebecca stifled an inappropriate grin. *Oh, the irony.*

"I shall send someone for our family physician right away." Lady Coburn signaled to a passing footman.

"No need." Lord Wolston waved off the servant. "It's feeling much improved. I will forgo shuttlecock for the next few days, but thanks to Lady Prestcote's ministrations, my arm is already healing nicely. If the lady hadn't insisted, I wouldn't bother with the sling, but I've decided it best to follow her excellent medical advice."

"A physician should have been summoned." Professor Duval's fingers lifted from his chin. "If his shoulder wasn't set properly, there could be long-term ill effects."

"It was not the first time I'd dislocated my shoulder." Lord Wolston glared at the professor. "I can assure you that the lady's ministrations were better than my last physician's."

It was kind of Lord Wolston to come to her defense, but what if his words were misconstrued? They'd been alone in the library without a chaperone present. Even though she'd been resetting his shoulder, such physical touch could be considered intimate. A hard knot formed in her throat, and she swallowed around it. She could be deemed a woman of ill repute, her cousin's reputation would suffer, her father would land in debtor's prison, and she would lose her opportunity to wrest a cure for her sister from the knowledgeable professor.

An inner satirical voice mocked her—*nothing to be unsettled about, nothing at all.*

Just the end of her life as she knew it.

"Thank you, my dear." Lady Coburn smiled at her, and by her countenance, her thoughts had not gone where Rebecca's had. "I'm pleased you were there to aid Lord Wolston, so there was no need to rouse the town physician in the middle of the night."

The method she'd used to set his shoulder brought on a debate among the professors and Lord Wolston. As they discussed the pros and cons, Rebecca's presence and that of the other women in the room was forgotten.

Sarah's eyes sparkled as she leaned close to Rebecca, whispering, "I need to hear all the details. Is his shoulder as strong as it looks? What did you talk about? Is he as romantic as he seems? Did he walk you to your room?"

"It wasn't like that." Rebecca fanned her face with her hand. "He was in pain, reeking of spirits, and grumpy."

Perhaps that last had been an exaggeration. He'd started grumpy. And then turned...something else.

The butler cleared his throat and stepped inside the room. "Letters have arrived, my lady."

Lady Coburn raised a gloved hand, and with a gentle sweep, signaled for him to distribute them. He passed one to Lord Wolston, another to Professor Matthews, and several of what looked like invitations and a note to Lady Coburn. He stopped behind where Rebecca and Sarah were seated. "For you, my lady." He held out an envelope.

Sarah accepted it, then passed the letter to Rebecca. "It's addressed to you."

Rebecca took it, surprised to have received a second correspondence. Only Corinne knew her whereabouts. Rebecca recognized the script as her father's, but the letter was addressed to Lady Prestcote.

Why would he pen Corinne a letter? Or had he discovered his daughters' whereabouts in Leafield? Who would have told him?

The other guests held their missives to read later, most likely in the privacy of their chambers, but Rebecca rubbed her thumb along the folded edge and stared at the handwriting as if it could offer some clue of the contents. She shifted forward in her seat, preparing to excuse herself, but Sarah nudged her arm.

"Go ahead and read it."

Rebecca looked toward Professor Duval, but the conversation among the gentlemen had resumed.

Lady Coburn rose and excused herself to see to a matter with the housekeeper.

Rebecca was about to open the letter, but at the sense of being watched, she looked up.

Lord Wolston inclined his chin as if agreeing she should open it.

She swallowed her apprehension and slid a finger under the seal. She removed the folded letter and scanned the contents. Within seconds, her jaw was clenched so tightly that it ached. She slowed down and started again.

Dearest Daughter,

I happened upon your cousin and insisted she confess the details of this plan you concocted.

Rebecca re-read the line, *this plan* you *concocted.* Had her cousin pinned this debacle on her? If Papa had discovered them, then Corinne's plan was already falling apart, and what had she told him? Rebecca continued where she'd left off.

I daresay, I would not have you take such a risk, but since you are already involved, I agree with your cousin that you must see this through, for much is at stake. I understand Lord McGower is to attend. He has come upon a fortune through trade with the East Indies. You should do your best to make a good impression upon him. His new money could be the answer to our troubles.

Our troubles? It took all of Rebecca's will not to wad the letter and throw it into the nearest fireplace. He faced debtors' prison over *his* poor choices, yet she was expected to sacrifice herself on the altar of marriage.

I have an opportunity and have a good feeling about it. If all goes swimmingly, we may put all this behind us. Keep me abreast of any new developments.

Yours truly,

Papa

An opportunity?

Please, don't let it be at the gambling table.

Did he truly think his luck would change? Maybe for a hand or two, but statistics had proved him to be a wretched card player. Her father held few skills for employment, having grown up with everything provided for him, but it was past time he acquired some.

Fed up with him and the dire circumstances in which he'd placed her and Madeline, Rebecca dropped the letter onto the tea stand. How she used to long for a missive to arrive from her father. She'd re-read every one he sent, memorizing the words and the precise curve of his script, wishing to hear of his planned return so they could be a family.

So he could get Mama the treatment she needed.

Rebecca crossed her arms and sat back in her chair. Her gaze passed over Lord Wolston staring at her letter on the table. As if sensing being caught, he quickly refocused on the correspondence in his hands.

Another memory from last night stirred.

Lord Wolston could read upside down.

Sarah's gaze flicked from him to her, a curious smile curving the corners of her lips.

Had he read Papa's letter?

Rebecca snatched it from the table and folded the paper under her arm.

~

last. He'd been caught.

Daniel rebuked himself, regretting his conversation with Lady Prestcote regarding da Vinci, trying to impress her with his reading skills. Not that her letter had been coded, just upside down from his perspective.

It had been penned from Lord Mercer. At least, he presumed such from reading the script addressed to *Dearest Daughter*.

The letter was too vague to link Lady Prestcote to the grave robbers, but the message was chilling—*involved risk* and *much at stake*. What could that reference in the small village of Leafield other than the body-snatching ring he'd been sent to investigate?

Could her cousin be connected to the grave robbers? What sort of plan had Blue concocted?

Confound it. He'd only gotten to the mention of Lord McGower when she'd snatched back the letter. Could he be part of the body snatching ring?

When Daniel's arm healed, he'd convince Lord McGower to spar with him in fencing. He'd heard the man was good with a sword, and maybe one-on-one, Daniel could extract information from the nabob. Lady Prestcote's father, Lord Mercer, seemed interested in the man—or at least his financial status.

He wouldn't marry off his daughter to the nabob, though, would he? Old money rarely mixed with new, and Daniel hadn't heard rumors about the earl being in financial straits. Quite the opposite. The earl was well inlaid. Daniel was even more so, yet she hadn't acted as if she'd set her cap for him. He'd keep a close watch on Lady Prestcote to see if she set her sights on Lord McGower after receiving the letter.

Lady Prestcote stared out the window toward the gardens, looking annoyed.

Was she perturbed at having to redirect her attentions from the professors to the nabob? Despite her inclination toward academic pursuits, Daniel could envision her settling down and setting up a nursery. When she'd tied the sling around his arm, he'd envisioned her making some man very happy. He saw her curled up in a chair, reading a book with one hand, lacing her other fingers with her husband's, her hair rippling in dark waves over the bed pillow. He could picture her kneeling to adjust a tiny cravat on a young child that resembled...*him*.

He swallowed. *You're here to find body snatchers, not a suitable marriage partner.*

Had his overprotective nature produced these feelings? His sisters often stamped their feet and told him to step aside and let them do things for themselves, but he wouldn't allow anyone to hurt Alicia or Eliza.

Not again. *Never* again.

Lady Prestcote stirred that same protectiveness within him. He couldn't abide the idea of her being blackmailed or being somehow involved in a body-snatching ring. He didn't even like the way Professor Duval kept snubbing her. Daniel had been rounding the corner when he'd overheard Duval ask her name, as if he hadn't bothered to remember it. He was dying to give the man a good tongue lashing.

The real challenge was watching Blue admire the professor as if he'd set the stars in the night sky.

Egad. He sounded like a jealous beau. *Keep to the business at hand.*

But the man could be the buyer he'd been sent to identify.

He bristled, remembering a line in her father's letter.

I would not have you take such a risk, but since you are already involved, I agree with your cousin that you must see this through, or much will be at stake...

What could be so grave that the earl would put his daughter's life at risk? And had Lady Prestcote concocted the plan? She certainly possessed the intelligence, but if his discernment was correct, she lacked a devious side. Her expressions gave away her emotions—her vulnerability, her curiosity, her passion.

Could the dark-haired beauty mastermind an evil plan? He remembered her worried frown as she'd flipped the pages to find how best to set his shoulder. He didn't doubt she'd fight for those she cared for, especially considering the great lengths she'd taken to search for a cure for her maid. What noblewoman would stay up to the early-morning hours to help one of her staff?

The kindness Daniel had witnessed in her care for him and her devotion to her maid were enough to draw out his protective side. He'd discover who dared to involve the earl's daughter in a grave-robbing ring. He'd see justice served.

But had he blown his cover—and his only opportunity—by not heeding Lieutenant Scar's orders to follow them to the source?

Daniel had attempted to make it appear as if he'd stumbled

upon the graveyard in an inebriated state, but would his story be believed? He'd failed to apprehend even one gravedigger for questioning. He was right back where he'd begun, only worse, for now there was no fresh grave to watch.

And the thieves would be keeping an eye on him.

Some blackguard had the means to come and go freely from Griffin Hall, and he'd searched Daniel's room the night before. His things had been riffled through. The culprit had attempted to hide the fact that he'd been there, but the clothes in Daniel's drawers had shifted, and the telltale cloth scrap he purposefully folded into the drawer had fallen. Even his bedclothes had no longer held square angles.

The faint footprint he'd seen outside his chamber had come up the back stairs. He'd discovered another on the landing, but no footprints inside his room. The one outside his door had faced outward, a lookout. He'd asked his neighbor, Lord McGower, if he or his Indian valet had seen anyone in the hall the night before, or if they'd heard anyone knocking, but both had denied noticing anything suspicious.

He'd originally intended to keep quiet about the graveyard incident but had to confess to being intoxicated and stumbling into the resurrection men after discovering the ringleader was staying at Griffin Hall. The culprit would be even more suspicious if he'd neglected to mention last evening's events.

The dusty footprints appeared from their size to have been from a male of average height, which didn't fit the description of the lad who probably now walked with a limp or the hulking man who'd hefted the body from the grave. Were the prints left by the one who'd hit him with the shovel, or the one who'd spoken from the shadows?

The boot size was similar to some partial prints near the grave, but the blackguard seemed to have known enough not to step near the fresh dirt.

He eyed the male guests. Could it be one of them?

When Daniel had traced the footprints, he'd caught Professor Matthews sneaking up the servants' stairs with a cup of warm milk. The professor had not yet dressed for bed. This morning, he'd had dirt under his fingernails as he accepted the missive. But, with Matthews's wiry frame, Daniel doubted the man could lift a shovel, much less swing it with any force.

Professor Bell's light had been on when Daniel had walked Lady Prestcote to her chamber, and although the man was short of stature, his feet were large. Face to face, Daniel could easily overpower him, which was all the more reason for the bloke to hit him from behind.

But why would he be involved in grave robbing?

Professor Duval was of average height, and for all of his intellect, he looked lithe, as if he walked or rode horses daily. He already had Lady Prestcote's attention. Could he be the one blackmailing her? Was that why she hung on his every word?

She needed medical advice to aid her maid, but what else might the professor hold over her?

Fresh bodies brought in a pretty penny on the black market as cadavers for anatomists' dissection and study. Was she being blackmailed to fund Professor Duval's purse to pay the resurrection men for bodies like the poor chandler's?

Lady Prestcote sat on the edge of her seat, listening in on the professors' conversation. Her long lashes fanned in a graceful sweep as her gaze bounced from Matthews to Duval. She was riveted.

Mrs. Evans dosed off in her chair, probably bored with the discussion.

Lady Prestcote's stomach growled, and she pressed a hand over it as if to muffle the noise.

He felt famished himself, having missed the morning meal. He guessed Lady Prestcote had done the same. He waved over a passing footman, and lowering his voice, requested scones and finger sandwiches.

"...venesection or bloodletting is still best for pulmonary edema." Professor Duval crossed one knee over the other and laced his fingers in his lap.

Lady Prestcote's lips parted, but only a small squeak emitted before the professor spoke over her.

"Opium from the Orient has a positive effect on reducing fluid in the lungs, but patients can crave the drug and often end up in a stupefied state, leading to opium dens such as Lord McGower described in India."

Professor Matthews shook his head. "They're now popping up in London."

"What of foxglove?" She blurted the words.

Professor Duval snorted derisively. "The scientific name is digitalis. What of it?"

"For arrhythmia."

"That rot is old-woman folklore from Shropshire. Where did you hear of it?"

Daniel gritted his teeth at the professor's arrogance and dismissal of Lady Prestcote as if she were some henwit.

She straightened. "I read Withering's book, *An Account of Foxglove and some of its Medical Uses*." Her voice was strong when she added, "His clinical trials had merit."

"In the wrong dose, digitalis is fatal." Duval adjusted the corner of his spectacles and sighed, as if losing patience with an over-eager child. "Don't play around with things you don't understand."

She notched up her chin. "Then I challenge you to enlighten me."

Good for her. Daniel couldn't hold back his grin.

Her gauntlet thrown, she softened her gaze and changed tactics, affecting a demure pout. "Since you are renowned as the greatest in cardiology and received Lady Coburn's high praise for making tough subject matters understandable, surely you could explain such a complex topic in simple terms."

By Jove, she was brilliant, hitting on the man's ego and inability to turn down a challenge. Perhaps she did have a devious side.

The professor tilted his head. "You said a relative of yours died from a heart condition?"

"Indeed. My ma—aunt." Her eyes widened a small fraction. "She was like a mother to me." Pain tightened the skin around her eyes and darkened their depths. "My maid is exhibiting similar symptoms." Her whispered tone turned pleading. "I want to help her."

"An admirable trait." Professor Duval shifted. "It's unlikely your maid would contract the same disease as your aunt—highly irregular considering their class difference, but what are the indicators?"

"A cough that won't go away. Shortness of breath. Tightness in her chest. Weakness. The symptoms come and go."

"My guess would be angina pectoris, arrhythmia, or a diseased valve. I could have determined for certain if I'd had the chance to dissect your aunt."

Lady Prestcote drew back, wide-eyed, and Mrs. Evans gasped.

Daniel hadn't known she'd awoken.

Professor Matthews patted Mrs. Evans's hand. "He meant for diagnostic purposes, not disrespect."

"The best way to understand is to attend my lecture tomorrow." He flashed Lady Prestcote a smile. "As my guest, you'll have a front row seat."

Professor Bell frowned. "The venue isn't for ladies."

Her face lit with glee, and she outright ignored Bell. "I'd be delighted. Thank you."

Daniel fought the urge to lean between her and Duval, desiring her joyful expression to be directed at him—and *only* him.

"Think nothing of it." Duval brushed her off with a wave of his hand.

How dare he act so indifferent? For being brilliant, the professor was an imbecile.

"Speaking of..." He rose and indicated the other professors do likewise. "I must prepare, and so must my colleagues." He addressed Lady Prestcote. "We can talk more about your maid after my lecture."

"Thank you, sir." Her gaze followed the departing Professor Duval with an expression of longing.

Daniel's good hand curled into a fist.

He would attend that lecture tomorrow, wanted or not.

CHAPTER 12

*R*ebecca had done it. She'd gained Professor Duval's attention and an invitation to his lecture. Think of the intelligent minds who'd be in attendance. She wanted to dance a jig and might have done so if Sarah and Lord Wolston hadn't been staring at her.

A maid entered the solarium carrying a tray. The yeasty-buttery smell of fresh-baked scones filled the air, and her stomach responded with an improper growl. She wrapped her arms around her midsection to silence it.

The maid set the tray on the center table. "These are for you, miss." She eyed Rebecca. "Per his lordship's request." She bobbed a curtsy and left.

Rebecca met Lord Wolston's gaze, and a ripple passed between them—like shimmering sunlight flittering through leaves. Was that something a person could *feel*? Why did this keep happening when he was around? Why couldn't she summon the same reaction around someone closer in status like Professor Duval?

She couldn't hold feelings for the marquis. Corinne would box her ears—or worse, have her head—and a marquis wouldn't look twice at an untitled gentlewoman saddled with her father's debt—one whose only asset was that her blood-lines were modestly respectable.

His Adam's apple bobbed under his cravat. "I missed the morning meal and was hungry. I thought you might be as well."

"I'm famished." The tingle spread down to her toes. "How thoughtful."

He nodded for her to take one.

A considerate gentleman. It hadn't been her first impression of the rogue who'd reeked of spirits and stolen a kiss in the garden. She was seeing a different side of the marquis. She remembered the loving way he'd spoken of his sisters and how he'd saved her from the bee's sting by enduring it himself. Could a man so chivalrous and considerate be a frivolous libertine?

Rebecca plucked a scone off the tray and spread a bit of clotted cream on top. The bite tasted heavenly, melting in her mouth, and she resisted devouring the entire biscuit in one gulp.

He gestured to Sarah, who took one with jam, and then helped himself to a plain scone, eating it as if not for enjoyment but to stave off hunger. He returned for a second and eyed the jam with a frown.

His arm in a sling posed a problem for applying toppings.

Rebecca slathered the scone with jam, and at his indication, added a dollop of clotted cream. She'd often done such for her mama when her condition made her too weak to eat. Drawing the line at feeding him, Rebecca passed the scone to his good hand.

Sarah's gaze volleyed between Rebecca and the marquis over her remaining bite of scone. "You two have become well acquainted."

"I owe a debt of gratitude to Lady Prestcote for her care."

Sincerity sparkled in his expression as one side of his mouth quirked into a teasing grin. "Or should I say, Blue?"

"Blue?" Sarah straightened, her tone begging for an explanation.

"Short for bluestocking. It's my pet name for her, since she's revealed her academic side." He popped the last bite of scone into his mouth, chewed, and swallowed. "When we danced at the Lipscomb party, she had me believing that she was like the other vixens on the marriage mart, willing to exchange their souls for wealth and a title."

"Please, tell us how you really feel." Sarcasm laced Sarah's tone.

"Right, then." He leaned forward, resting the forearm of his good arm on his thigh. "I will." He stared at Rebecca in a way that made her want to squirm like a child about to be disciplined.

"You deserve to be treated with respect." He pointed the index finger of his injured arm at her. "You are beautiful and intelligent, and if Professor Duval doesn't see it, then you shouldn't give him a second of your time." He sat back and said with finality, "You don't need him."

She swallowed an affronted gasp. "He could hold the answer to saving Madeline's life. I would do anything for my... maid."

His eyebrows rose. "Anything?"

"What are you insinuating?" Her voice rose with outrage.

Sarah held completely still, though her gaze bounced between them.

"Merely that you shouldn't put up with his belittling you. The man needs to show more respect for women." A muscle in his jaw twitched. "For you."

"As you displayed in the Lipscomb's garden?"

"I overstepped." He cleared his throat. "I apologize."

Sarah's mouth dropped open.

Rebecca crossed her arms. "You're the last person to be instructing a woman on how to conduct herself."

He blinked and looked away.

A hush fell over the orangery, the only sounds the honking of geese overhead, fleeing south for the winter. Rebecca wanted to fly with them, to be anywhere but here.

He believed her a babe in the woods, cowing to the professor without the self-respect to stand up for herself. His brotherly reprimand proved he didn't see her as a romantic interest at all.

Which...of course, he didn't. Why would she allow herself to think otherwise? For all her intellect, she was a fool.

Sarah stared at her wide-eyed, probably wondering what exactly had happened in the garden and last night in the library after Rebecca tended to his arm. Did her new friend believe her to be a trollop?

The sting of tears only angered Rebecca further.

"You're right," Lord Wolston said.

"What?" Rebecca notched up her chin to clear her gaze from unshed tears and her mind from the confusing swing in the conversation.

"I beg your pardon. I've come across as a cad, and that was not my intention. You deserve better." He exhaled a deep breath. "I hope you can forgive me."

Sarah looked at her with wide eyes, and when Rebecca didn't respond fast enough, she nodded her encouragement.

"Indeed. I mean..." Shock had stolen her ability to think. "Yes, I forgive you. You have conducted yourself as a gentleman since then." Except when he'd tried to ransom her letter for a kiss. She added, "For the most part."

He'd shown redeemable qualities, too, like showing her the grounds, suffering the bee's sting, even considering her hunger. Unlike Professor Duval, Lord Wolston had told her that he thought her not only beautiful, but intelligent. Maybe they had gotten off to a wretched beginning.

"There you are." Lord McGower and Lord and Lady Farsley stepped into the solarium's entrance, carrying rackets. "Would you care for a game of shuttlecock?"

"I must pass." Lord Wolston patted his arm. "I have something I must attend to, but the ladies might join you."

Rebecca jumped at the chance to get away. "I'd love to take part in a game." She turned to Sarah. "How about you?"

Sarah nodded but studied Lord Wolston.

He stood and bid Sarah a good day but stopped beside Rebecca.

She twisted her head to peer up at his square jaw.

"I'd like to start over. Properly introduce myself, the way it should be done by a gentleman." His gaze fixed on her, swallowing her with the intensity in its swirling blue depths. "Meet me in the garden at six before we dine?"

Her heart leapt and clogged her throat, stealing her speech, but she found the ability to nod.

He smiled, and Rebecca lost the ability to breathe.

With a confident gait, he strode away, every inch of him exuding authority and nobility.

Her mouth went dry.

The gardens tonight.

What would Corinne think?

Did Rebecca even care?

Hadn't Lord Wolston's arrival at Griffin Hall already ruined their ploy? Once the Season started, he'd know she'd duped him.

Rebecca swallowed a lump of dread that punched its way into her stomach. She would need to tell the truth and pray he'd be understanding enough not to ruin her debut—even if he had every right to be angry and do so.

At the end of the hallway, he turned with panther-like grace, moving out of sight.

Sarah gripped her hand in a tight squeeze, not hiding her excitement. "I need a moment with Lady Prestcote. We'll meet you at the court in fifteen minutes."

The others left, and Sarah rounded on Rebecca. "Tell me everything."

Rebecca swallowed. She needed her friend's advice, but how could she explain without giving away that she was not who everyone, including Lord Wolston, believed her to be?

~

A game of shuttlecock had turned out to be the perfect diversion for Rebecca from her whirling thoughts. Sarah was a dear, getting her to laugh at their mistakes. Lord McGower and Lady Farsley soundly beat them for several games until Lord Farsley rose from where he sat on the sideline and offered Rebecca and Sarah a lesson. He changed out the birdie for a special one he'd made that whistled through the air and helped Sarah with her timing and Rebecca with her serve.

"Most impressive, Lord Farsley," Rebecca said after he scored a point against Lord McGower.

Lord Farsley's chest rose, and he stood taller. "It's all in the sound, my dear."

Lady Farsley toyed with the hair that comprised her thin eyebrows as she said, "Darling, why don't we show them how it's done?"

Rebecca, Sarah, and Lord McGower stepped aside, and Lord and Lady Farsley awed them with behind-the-back flicks, twirling reversals, and even a between-the-legs return.

Rebecca clapped when Lady Farsley led her husband back to his seat. For a moment, Rebecca had forgotten the man was blind.

"I don't know whether to feel better or worse about my playing." Sarah giggled.

"Worse." Rebecca joined in the merry sound. "I'd say we're a hopeless case."

"I want a rematch." Sarah struggled to hold a straight face as she addressed the others with confidence. "We'll beat you in the next match"—she tipped her head in Rebecca's direction— "after Lady Prestcote spends the day in the library reading up on the rules, tricks, and skills of the game."

A boisterous laugh exploded past Rebecca's lips, and she cupped her hands over her mouth.

Sarah was fast becoming a close friend who knew Rebecca's habits all too well. Rebecca fought to compose herself and caught sight of a rider on the hill.

Lord Wolston sat like a commander of His Majesty's cavalry upon a sleek steed, as if his power and that of the horse had become one. His head turned in her direction.

Though Sarah and the others continued talking as they moved indoors for tea, Rebecca remained frozen. Why did Lord Wolston's demeanor impact her so? Sweeping her into his turbulence, leaving her unable to gain her bearings, unable to breathe.

The curve of a jaunty smile stretched his mouth, and though from this distance she couldn't see the teasing spark in his eyes, she felt it in her chest. Heat swirled in her belly.

Behind her, Sarah called, "Are you coming?"

The spell broken, Lord Wolston nodded and spurred his horse toward the stables.

Rebecca turned and scurried for the manor. She paused on the portico to glance back at the way Lord Wolston had come. Only the woods and graveyard were in that direction.

Where had he been?

~

"*Y*ou're fidgeting."

Rebecca looked at the twisted shawl she'd pulled out to wear later to ward off the chilly garden air.

Sarah took the garment. After shaking out the wrinkles, she draped it over the tufted sofa's scrolled arm where Rebecca sat and then perched on Sarah's bed, leaning against the intricately carved post. "I suppose I could act as your chaperone." She released a dreamy sigh. "I confess to being a romantic, and Miss Blakeford's disregard for her employment could be convenient. If Lord Wolston attempted to kiss you, I could nod off. Mind you, I'd awaken if anything untoward happened."

Madeline, seated near the window in the corner, coughed into her hand. She glanced up, her eyes flashing as if she, too, were rooting for the marquis to steal a kiss.

"How kind. I'd appreciate your presence." *And moral support.* Rebecca stood and paced, but the movement didn't release the tension welling up inside. "We are making much out of nothing. He means to start afresh as friends since we had an inauspicious beginning."

Sarah expelled a romantic sigh as she had when Rebecca told Sarah about how she and marquis first met.

The mantel clock above the fireplace read quarter till five. Rebecca returned to her seat and tucked her hands under her to keep them still. She'd readied too early, and now her thoughts juggled between what Lord Wolston would have in store for their meeting and trying not to listen to Corinne's warning in her head—*do not make a mess of this.*

Where in heaven's name had Miss Blakeford run off to? Sarah's maid, Lucy, who knew the staff and hall better, had been sent to obtain information regarding the derelict Miss Blakeford, who'd once again neglected to report for her chaperone duties. Some chaperone she was turning out to be.

Thankfully, standards at house parties were a trifle more relaxed, but if ever Rebecca needed a duenna, it was now. Lord Wolston's mere presence had a way of putting her at sixes and sevens.

"He wants to meet you in the garden to make up for your first encounter?" Sarah flicked open her bamboo fan and waved it in front of her face. "Your first garden meeting sounded so romantic."

Madeline arched a questioning brow at Rebecca, who shot back an *I'll-explain-later* look.

"Are you certain he said *re-do* and not *reenact*?" Sarah giggled.

"I've accused him of ungentlemanlike conduct." Why had she spouted off so? "He's either looking to redeem himself or will be waiting with pistols to pace off for my attack on his honor."

Sarah snorted. "You've nothing to fear. Gentlemen duel over women, not against them."

The door opened and Lucy filled the entrance. "My lady." She addressed Sarah and curtsied before flashing a quick dimpled smile to Madeline in the corner. "I have an accounting of Miss Blakeford."

Sarah waved her in.

Lucy smoothed her skirts as she entered and closed the door behind her. Rebecca could see why Madeline had befriended the fresh-faced young maid. Her countenance showed they shared an exuberance for life. "Miss Blakeford requested the staff have her afternoon meal and tea brought to her room due to her head ailing her."

"Poor thing." Sarah shook her head. "The change in weather might affect her, as it did my husband. She shouldn't be disturbed. Have her evening meal also brought to her room."

"There is a problem, though." Lucy twisted her apron string around her thumb. "Miss Blakeford isn't in her chamber."

Rebecca frowned. "Where is she?"

"A groom saddled a horse for her an hour ago, and she rode toward town."

Sarah pursed her lips. "If she needed medicine, she should have sent for a maid or a footman."

Lucy lowered her gaze. "A man was seen following her on horseback at the end of the lane." Her cheeks reddened. "Likely, the same chap who visited her room, though no one can say for sure."

A man visited Miss Blakeford's chamber? *This* woman was Corinne's governess? If Miss Blakeford had been expected to instill godly values into her pupil, then it was no wonder Corinne acted so forward with men.

"It's a challenge to find good help these days." Sarah clicked her tongue. When the color in Lucy's face faded, she was quick to add, "Not you, my dear. You're a treasure. Let Lady Prestcote know the moment Miss Blakeford returns. In the meantime, you may go about your duties."

Lucy curtsied and crossed the chamber to straighten Sarah's dressing room.

Madeline rose and excused herself with a curtsy to follow her friend.

Sarah squeezed Rebecca's hand, eyeing the thumb of her glove, which she'd twisted between her fingers.

Rebecca smoothed the fabric, too late.

"You're still nervous, and understandably so." Sarah perched to the edge of the sofa. "Let's do something to take your mind off Lord Wolston and Miss Blakeford. What do you do as a distraction?"

Rebecca couldn't think of a thing.

"For fun? There must be something."

"I read, I guess."

Sarah stood and pulled Rebecca up, hooking her arm. "Then to the library we go."

As they strolled the hall, up the staircase, and toward the library, Sarah said, "My husband used to say, 'Do not fret. Worry won't add another hour to your life, nor a cubit to your height, so why be anxious about such things?'"

"My mama used to quote Jesus as well." A pang of guilt twisted in Rebecca's stomach. Mama would be ashamed that her daughter hadn't been to church in several years, but she could either be sitting in a pew or searching for cures.

"The countess?" Sarah's brows rose. "Lady Mercer quotes Scripture?"

Drat. She must be more careful. She attempted a smile but feared it wobbled from guilt for lying to her friend. "She'll surprise you."

"It goes to show we shouldn't judge. I don't know the earl and countess well, for we don't run in the same circles, but on the occasions we have encountered one another, I found them to be...worldly, I guess."

"They enjoy the life of the Quality."

Her aunt and uncle flittered from party to party and put stock in having the ear of the king. Her father, too, had been struck by the allure of worldly things. When Mama fell ill and could no longer keep up with his lifestyle, he'd grown restless, irritable, and bitter. One autumn day, he simply left. He chose riches and reputation over loyalty to his wife and daughters. He didn't return—not even for Mama's funeral—until Rebecca turned a marriageable age.

Mama had instructed her daughters not to despise their papa. She used to say that God was still working on his heart and that they should pray for him. Rebecca had added him to her prayer list for Mama's sake, but after she passed, Rebecca's prayers dwindled. A year later, Papa arrived on their doorstep a desperate man, shipping her off to her aunt and uncle's care and pleading with her to marry well to save him from the duns and debtor's prison.

If her father knew she had a private meeting with a marquis, he'd be salivating. More likely, he'd be dashing off to ring up a tab or gamble on cards at his favorite club. She never agreed to trick anyone into marriage, only to pretend to be Corinne so she could meet Professor Duval and find a cure for Madeline. Lord Wolston didn't deserve to be lied to or deceived into a marriage where he'd be saddled with an unknown pauper and her papa's debts. All the more reason why Rebecca must dissuade Lord Wolston's intentions or tell him the truth, but how could she do so without him despising her and her cousin? One disparaging remark from Lord Wolston and Corinne's Season would be tainted. She'd recover, but Rebecca's debut would surely be over before it began.

Her heart pricked at the thought of Corinne and Lord Wolston making amends as the Season went on. She could imagine he and her cousin laughing over the good joke she'd played on him. They would make a handsome couple. They were of a similar ranking and lifestyle. Why shouldn't they have a chance at happiness?

She knew why.

Because the more she learned about the marquis, the less she believed the façade he presented and the more she believed his intentions were good. The memory of the way he'd held her in the garden during the Lipscomb party surfaced. He'd stunk of gin, but his breath had smelled sweet, like lemonade. He'd reeked of spirits when she'd set his arm, but he hadn't acted the least bit foxed, nor had she smelled liquor on his breath. And just the night before, she watched him empty his drink into a plant when he believed no one was looking.

Then there was the way he'd spoken of his sisters with such love. He didn't act like a man who'd put frivolous parties and material things over family. Quite the opposite.

But then again, he was a marquis and probably hadn't had to make such tough decisions. Did he not let others see his caring side because of how society clamored to befriend nobility? If so, she should feel honored.

It was time she told him the truth—tonight, in the garden.

"You're awfully pensive." Sarah turned toward the library. "Stop worrying. God has a plan for the two of you." In the doorway, she halted. "Professor Duval."

The man stood next to a bookshelf and peered up from the open volume in his hands. His cravat had been loosened, and his jacket lay on a nearby desk, where books had been stacked atop it. His rolled sleeves revealed his forearms with their smattering of golden hair. He balanced the book with one hand and pushed up on his spectacles.

"Ah, Mrs. Evans. Lady Prestcote." A sheepish expression dipped his chin, and a light chuckle rumbled in his throat. "You've caught me."

"Doing what?" Sarah drew closer to his side, and Rebecca followed, glimpsing the title of the book he read, *An Account of Foxglove and Some of its Medical Uses.*

He sniffed. "I might have been hasty in my dismissal of digitalis as a treatment."

Rebecca perked up, meeting and holding his gaze.

He studied her face as if seeing her for the first time. Heat didn't rush through her midsection, though, nor did she feel swept up in a current as when Lord Wolston looked at her. But a flicker did stir in her chest. Could she hold feelings for Professor Duval, or was that reaction merely intellectual stimulation or the hope of a cure for Madeline?

"I'd heard the rumor of Withering being a lunatic who chased some folk healer for an herbal remedy." He tapped the pages. "But the man documented one hundred and fifty-six cases where he administered digitalis to his patients."

He moved to the desk. "Come and look at this."

Rebecca and Sarah did, waiting while he flipped through several books.

"Ah. Here we go. It says here that with the correct dose, multiple cases have been documented of digitalis"—he glanced at them—"reducing dropsy."

Sarah frowned. "Dropsy?"

"Swelling of the heart." Rebecca leaned over the book he'd referenced, tracing her finger down the words as she skimmed the study.

"Here." He passed her another book. "There's also a bark used in Spain, brought back by missionaries from the southern hemisphere Americas that has shown to steady one's heartbeat."

Sarah yawned.

The professor dragged over a chair for Sarah and offered his to Rebecca.

"Is it possible for me to try these remedies on Madeline?" Rebecca worked to stifle the excitement bubbling within. Could this be what would save her sister? *Lord, please let it be so. Don't take the last of my family from me.*

Her father barely counted, considering he was practically a stranger.

"The dosage must be accurate, lest you poison her."

The thrill of excitement turned cold.

Professor Duval's warm hand covered hers. "But yes. I believe these treatments could help."

Rebecca's breath caught, and she stared at the intensity of his gaze. Had Professor Duval's eyes been that blue all along?

"Look here." He tugged a botany book from the pile and flipped to the section on foxglove. A beautiful hand drawing of the flower adorned the page. "This shows the toxicity levels and doses for a man of average height and weight. We'll need to consider your maid is female and of smaller size and height." He rubbed his chin. "Do you know her measurements?"

"Approximately."

"We'd need exact measurements to calculate correctly."

"I can get them."

She looked to Sarah to convey her excitement, but Sarah's head lolled to the side. She was sound asleep. After Rebecca found a way to save Madeline, she vowed to search for a cure to Sarah's aliment.

Rebecca read about the plant and what dosage could be poisonous. "Do you have a notebook to write this down? I left mine in my chamber."

She checked the time as he shuffled through the pocket of his jacket. Plenty of time remained before her meeting in the garden. She'd glance at her watch again in a few minutes.

Their fingers brushed as he passed her the notebook.

A rush of optimism passed through her. It was the first time the professor treated her as a woman with a mind, acknowledging her intelligence by sharing a discourse of ideas. She reached for the inkwell and feather pen on the desk and wrote the toxicity dosage and men's measurements. "What was the name of that bark they used in Spain?"

"Cinchona bark. It's also used to treat the fevers and chills of the ague. Lord McGower mentioned that our colonists in India mixed the tonic with gin to reduce the bitter taste."

Rebecca couldn't take notes fast enough as Professor Duval paced, reading her various cases. Several had similar symptoms to Madeline and had experienced seemingly miraculous recoveries.

One of these cures could save her sister. *Please, Lord.*

"I don't understand why Withering wasn't taken seriously," she said during a pause in the professor's discourse. "This could be revolutionary for cardiac arrhythmia and the circulatory system."

Professor Duval stopped and peered at her. His hair rumpled where he'd rubbed his head, giving him an adorable, boyish appeal. "This may just work."

Rebecca's hand shook with an excitement she could no

longer contain, and she set down the quill so he wouldn't notice.

"If this succeeds, my lectures will be standing-room only. Oxford will promote me as their chancellor above Bell." Professor Duval placed his hand over hers. "And you could save your maid's life." He didn't smile, but she heard pleasure in his tone. "You could be her heroine."

Rebecca could be there for Madeline, as she hadn't for Mama.

CHAPTER 13

*D*aniel shifted on the cold stone bench in the walled rose garden. The vibrant sunset in hues of pinks and oranges had faded to purples and blues, and a sprinkling of stars emerged, twinkling in their silent laughter as if mocking him for believing an intelligent woman would see through his Casanova façade.

He'd given her every reason to be skeptical of him, and if he'd been advising one of his sisters, he'd have told her to stay far away from the likes of the man he'd represented himself to be.

He'd never considered how lonely he'd become as an agent for the Crown.

He rested his forearms on his thighs, the weight of the day's events leaving him weary. Earlier, he'd retraced his steps at the graveyard and interrogated the sneaky blackguard of a night watchman, who'd refused to reveal who paid him off. Daniel had ridden into town and asked a few store clerks about the men he'd seen, giving their descriptions, but the townsfolk had been tight-lipped. By the time he'd returned to dress and prepare for his meeting with Lady Prestcote, his shoulder ached from the exertion.

Memories of her gentle touch as she'd aided him had spurred him to not be late. He'd had a bounce in his step as he'd enlisted the help of the gardener to pick a small bouquet from the garden, choosing dahlias, aster, and chrysanthemum.

He peered down at the colorful flowers tied with a ribbon in his hands. His sisters would be proud that he'd remembered the plants' names. Alicia and Eliza would adore Lady Prestcote.

A candle still burned in the library window where she'd tended to his shoulder, but it could be any of the guests.

Perhaps she'd gotten caught up in her reading and forgotten the time?

His sisters appreciated a good mind and would enjoy her sense of calm. His mother was a worrier who'd fret over the littlest injury and have the family physician summoned at the first sign of illness. No wonder his grandfather had looked upon him with disgust. Daniel was soft—or at least, he had been. He'd worked hard to toughen up that weak little boy, to become something Grandfather had never thought he could be.

The stars shone brightly against the black sky, and the light from the manor's windows lit the garden path. He suppressed a shudder in the chilly night air and checked his pocket watch. Quarter till seven. Dinner would be served soon.

He checked the time once more to be certain.

Perdition.

She wasn't coming.

I'd like to start over, introduce myself the way a gentleman should. Meet me in the garden at six before we dine. Had he only imagined the spark of hope in her curious, wide-eyed gaze? Usually, he was good at reading people, but not Lady Prestcote. He'd obviously misjudged the pull between them—two misunderstood people who longed for a kindred spirit to care for the side of them they dared not let society see.

Apparently, the pull had been one-sided. He rubbed his chest to ease the ache.

You pompous fool.

Perhaps he deserved to be left in a lurch.

He'd grown presumptuous as a marquis, especially since he'd begun his training. Admittedly, his pretentiousness soared as he'd grown stronger in girth and wiser in the ways of espionage. The women, foreign and domestic, who'd longed to be a marchioness hadn't humbled his ego either.

It seemed Lady Prestcote didn't care a whit about his title, wealth...

He plucked a half-dead rosebud from a nearby bush, not caring about the thorns.

...Or him.

Why did the realization make him want her more?

Clenching his hand, he crumbled the dry rose petals to dust and opened his palm to let the breeze sweep them away. The few that hadn't dried, he dumped onto the seat next to him.

He hadn't felt this vulnerable and helpless since his grandfather had brought him to his fencing club and instructed Daniel to *on guard*. At the age of ten and five, he had picked up the sword and readied his stance, holding his sword extended. His arm had shaken under the mental and physical strain of facing off against his grandfather. He'd used his other hand to steady it.

"That's not how you hold a sword." Grandfather had shaken his head with a disappointed scowl.

"But it's heavy."

"That's because you're weak."

The painful words still rattled in Daniel's mind, and he felt afresh the piercing pain in his heart.

"Since your father's death, your mother has coddled you.

She's raised a fainthearted little mouse. You can't defend your sisters. You can't even defend yourself."

He could still see the muscle flexing in his grandfather's cheek and hear the certainty in his tone as he'd added, "But that changes now."

In the moment, Daniel had thought his grandfather a cruel man—and many times after, when he was hit with a blow to the face, wrestled to the mat, knocked to the ground, or swiped by a saber.

As he grew stronger and earned the man's respect, Daniel was thankful for the firm guidance. It made him tough. Strong. Able to handle anything...

He rose from the bench, leaving the carefully picked flowers behind, and stalked into the house.

...Even rejection.

~

*R*ebecca stopped mid-note-taking and gasped. "What time is it?"

Sarah jarred awake and sat up as Rebecca fumbled to find her watch pin.

Professor Duval removed his pocket watch and flipped open the cover. "Five till seven. Dinner will be served shortly. We should tidy up."

Rebecca stood so fast that the chair toppled behind her. "I lost track of time."

With a furrowed brow communicating he thought she'd taken leave of her senses, Professor Duval bent to right the chair.

"Go!" Sarah shooed her with a wave of her hand. "I will handle things."

Rebecca hitched up her skirts and darted from the room, dashed through the hall, and scurried down the stairs.

Lord, please let him still be there.

She paused until a footman opened the door to the veranda.

Outside, the cold air stole her breath. She pulled her shawl tighter and crossed to the walled rose garden. Shadows altered the colorful plants to black and gray, and the daytime fragrance of cut grass and falling leaves had turned to the musk of chimney fires.

"Lord Wolston?" She called as loudly as she could without drawing attention. No reply came. She pushed onward down the crushed-stone path that jabbed the thin soles of her slippers. The rose brushes clawed at the edges of her shawl.

She'd been engrossed in the thrill of finding a potential treatment for Madeline and her discussion with Professor Duval. He'd spoken to her as he would one of his fellow intellectuals, as if she'd been his equal, and she'd savored the thrill of the moment.

Why hadn't she paid closer attention to the time?

At the far end of the winding path, moonlight spilled onto a lone bench that had something resting on top. She crept to it and picked up a discarded bouquet of flowers tied with a bow.

She pressed a hand to her mouth to cover her shuddered intake of breath.

She'd never forgive herself. How long would this moment echo in her mind? The night she ruined whatever chance she had with Lord Wolston.

How long had he waited?

What must he think of her?

She sank onto the cold, hard seat, her heart answering for her.

The worst.

A future with Lord Wolston might never have been an option, but he'd offered her a chance to start over. He must think she'd thrown the opportunity back in his face. Any hope that she'd be able to tell him the truth and relieve herself of the weight of pretending to be Corinne when around him was over. She'd hoped he might forgive her because her intentions had been good.

But now, he'd believe the worst of her—because she'd earned it.

~

*I*n the rose salon, Daniel leaned his arm on the fireplace mantel and listened to Lord McGower ramble about India's politics. When the man's tone fluctuated, Daniel nodded, making the appearance of listening.

He'd chosen this spot, confident his training from the War Department would allow him to lip read the conversations of the gathered guests for any tidbits that could lead him to the body snatchers. The location also provided a nice vantage to gauge Lady Prestcote's expression when she entered. Would she appear remorseful or smugly satisfied for giving a marquis the cut direct?

Lord and Lady Farsley entertained Lady Coburn near the window overlooking the gardens. Because Lord and Lady Farsley's backs faced Daniel, he could only read Lady Coburn's lips.

"Lord Wolston is here, but..." Lady Coburn's gaze slid past him.

Had they seen him waiting, clutching the pathetic bouquet?

Lady Coburn glanced at the doorway. "Lady Prestcote has yet to arrive."

"I've made a substantial monetary investment in the silk road," Lord McGower said. "Especially now that a treaty has been signed, ending our tiff with Nepal and King Girvan." The dip in his tone signaled a needed response.

"Hmm. Good point." Daniel shifted his focus to the professors in the far corner near the drapes.

Professor Duval rubbed his chin. "The studies point to digitalis as a..."

Mostly likely, he said *potential.* Some words were a challenge to pick up through lip reading, but part of the thrill was filling in the blank information.

"...treatment. Additional studies must be done in a professional setting—"

Duval's hand covered his mouth, scratching his nose, and Daniel couldn't decipher the rest.

He wracked his brain. Digitalis? Wasn't it some flower?

"Someone could die." Professor Matthews's eyes widened. "Foxglove is poisonous."

Ah, quite right. Digitalis is foxglove.

Professor Duval shook his head. "Not in low doses."

"We don't have the funding for another project." Professor Bell held up both palms and shook his head.

At Daniel's side, Lord McGower sighed. "Alas"—his tone turned remorseful—"King Girvan died of smallpox recently."

Daniel glanced at his expression to confirm the man's feelings before replying, "How dreadful."

Movement in the doorway caught his attention.

Lady Prestcote entered the salon with Mrs. Evans. Loose tendrils of hair framed her lovely face. She looked...contrite.

A shawl draped her shoulders, and her cheeks tinged pink as if she'd been outdoors.

Had she finally gone to the rose garden—an hour late—in search of him?

She scanned the room. When their gazes locked, a look of remorse dipped her chin. Good. She deserved to feel dreadful.

Biting her lower lip, she walked toward him, her green-gold eyes glassy with uncertainty. Mrs. Evans veered off toward Professor Matthews.

He wasn't ready yet to speak with her, or to forgive. He

looked to Lord McGower, re-engaging in the conversation about Nepal and some Indian king.

Lady Prestcote hesitated in the center of the room.

He could feel her gaze on the side of his head, and he fought not to give in. His protective nature warred with his ego. Should he hear her reason for being late, or would it be an excuse?

Her shawl slipped off her shoulder, and even in the blur of his periphery, she looked fragile and vulnerable as she adjusted the fabric.

Daniel forced his heart to harden. It was good that he didn't open a well of feelings for her when he was uncertain about her potential involvement with the grave robbers. She'd made her decision not to meet him, and he had an assignment to focus on. He refused to be seen as weak, not in his line of work and not where women were concerned. That was part of why he'd chosen the libertine persona in the first place, which was so contrary to his true character.

Mrs. Evans hooked Lady Prestcote's arm and pulled her aside. "He must be angry." He read her lips, but Lady Prestcote's answer was hidden, her back to him.

She shook her head.

"Whatever were you thinking, snubbing the marquis?" Mrs. Evans pressed her gloved fingertips to her temples. "He may never speak to you again, and I wouldn't blame him. What I wouldn't give for such an opportunity...to be noticed by a pan."

Or rather—*man*.

Other than her falling asleep at inappropriate times, Mrs. Evans would be a splendid match.

Professor Matthews seemed to think so, his expression melting into one of a lovesick calf as she approached. The professor had clearly set his cap for the widow.

Mrs. Evans nodded to Lady Prestcote, appearing to listen.

The lady's shoulders slumped.

"A potential your?" Mrs. Evans's brows rose.

What? Blast. The challenge of reading lips was accuracy.

They both looked toward the professors.

"How wonderful." Mrs. Evans clapped her hands. "It's what you were hoping for."

A potential...what? What had she been hoping for?

Lady Prestcote turned toward Professor Duval, who smiled in her direction, and Daniel knew. The knot in Daniel's chest tightened, and he pounded his fist on the mantel. A potential *match*.

"My sentiments exactly," Lord McGower said. "Confound those uncivilized barbarians."

Daniel blinked at the man. What in heaven's name were they discussing?

The nabob rambled on about the need for the British Raj to take control of his Indian territory.

"Dinner is served." The footmen opened the dining room doors, and guests filed inside. This evening, the seating had been shuffled. Daniel escorted Lady Coburn and sat at the opposite end of the table from Lady Prestcote, which was for the best.

Saffron soup was served, and he inhaled the earthy-sweet aroma, complimenting Lady Coburn on her menus.

He caught Lady Prestcote glancing in his direction on several occasions. He refused to let the remorse in her eyes weaken him. She needed to feel his snub, at least for tonight, but he wouldn't let the sun go down on his anger.

Tomorrow was a new day, and he had a plan for Lady Prestcote.

*R*ebecca's gaze flicked to the marquis for the fifth time in a single minute, hoping to gain his attention so she could apologize, but he either refused to look her way or if he did, he quickly averted his gaze.

How could she have gotten so distracted?

Professor Duval, sitting on her left, finished his last sip of soup. "I've been thinking..." He set down his spoon and adjusted his glasses. "A test and control group are imperative. I shall speak to the townsfolk, or we could set up an experiment here at Griffin Hall to discover the proper quantities of digitalis. You could speak to Lady Coburn about administering it to the staff and monitoring their reactions."

Rebecca stiffened. "But the staff may not have heart ailments, certainly not all of them. We'd be treating something that they don't have."

He snorted as if she'd tried his patience. "Which is why it's a control group."

She understood what a control group was, but it still seemed illogical and possibly dangerous to test a healthy person with something that may have adverse side effects.

A footman removed the professor's empty bowl and set before him and Rebecca each a plate of roasted pheasant and root vegetables.

"Your maid is only one case," he explained. "It's not a big enough sample size."

If the treatment healed Madeline, that was the only sample size Rebecca needed, but the professor was right. The medicine needed to be tested on a larger population of both people experiencing heart problems and control groups before being tried on her sister.

"A test group is necessary to determine the proper dosage." Professor Duval cut his roasted pheasant into bite-sized pieces.

"But what if they're given the wrong amount?" She lowered

her voice to a whisper below the din of the other guests. "Someone could die."

Professor Duval shrugged. "We'll start small and work up until we reach a significant difference. In the worse cases, they'd likely only experience some vomiting."

"But if they become ill, that will keep them from their work, and from their pay. They have families who depend upon them." Lucy's youthful face popped into her mind.

"It's the way science is done. Don't you want to discover a cure for your maid? And think of the good it could do. This treatment could save so many lives. A few cases of nausea are better than people dying." He dipped a bite of pheasant in cream sauce. "If you'd like, we can allow them to decline the experiment, or I can speak to Professor Bell about compensating them, but the university is on a tight budget."

Lord Wolston rose after finishing the main course. He bowed to Lady Coburn, saying something about needing to visit town, and left.

Rebecca's chest felt as hollow as a dried gourd. Could he no longer bear her presence?

She pushed the root vegetables around her plate but couldn't swallow a bite. Her conscience wouldn't settle after the marquis's departure and the professor's suggestion, and neither would her stomach.

But Madeline's life depended on a cure.

Could Rebecca live with herself, knowing she might have found a treatment but didn't have the courage to test it?

Alternatively, she would never forgive herself if she administered the wrong dosage and poisoned her sister.

If she could only be certain that an upset stomach would be the only ill ramifications. What if the treatment was worse than the disease?

"I will begin the experiment immediately." Professor Duval

dipped his head to peer at her above his spectacles. "Would you like to take part, or not?"

Rebecca twisted her napkin in her lap, but Corinne's words popped into her head. *Sometimes you must make concessions because life rewards action. Being smart doesn't help unless you have the courage to act.*

Rebecca inhaled a deep breath. "Count me in."

"Excellent." He dipped his chin, and his lips twitched as if considering rewarding her with a smile.

She would do what she needed to do.

For Madeline's sake.

CHAPTER 14

$\mathcal{T}$he following morning, Rebecca entered the sunlit breakfast room, twisting the tip of her glove after discovering Miss Blakeford was still missing.

A footman scurried past her, wafting the smell of warm chocolate and coffee under her nose before he slid among the tables of guests, refilling their cups.

Lord Wolston lounged in his seat at the table nearest the window, offering Lord McGower his full attention.

Rebecca approached Lady Coburn's chair at the table closest to the entrance as her hostess chatted with Sarah and Lord and Lady Farsley. "I-I beg your pardon, but I have troubling news."

Lady Coburn cut off mid-sentence, pardoned the interruption, and turned to Rebecca, gesturing for her to sit. "Corinne, darling, what is it?"

Rebecca cringed, momentarily forgetting in her worry who she was supposed to be. Lowering into the chair, she swallowed hard and said, "Miss Blakeford has gone missing."

Lady Farsley gasped.

Sarah, already in the know, simply raised a brow.

"Who?" Lady Coburn's gaze skimmed the room, appearing to take a head count of guests to determine the missing person.

As if he could sense her anxiety, Lord Wolston set down his fork and directed his attention her way.

Next to him, Lord McGower continued to talk.

Rebecca lowered her voice, not wanting to cause a scandal. "My chaperone."

It was going to be hard enough to explain to Corinne that her governess had disappeared. But it would be much worse if Corinne heard it through gossip spread all the way to Surrey.

Rebecca tugged again on the tip of her glove, and Corinne's voice popped into her head. *Stop fidgeting. Eligible bachelors of the* ton *aren't looking to marry a nervous Nellie.* Rebecca dropped her hands to her sides.

A search for the Lord and Lady Mercer's missing governess could expose her and Corinne's deception and Polite Society abhorred being duped and made to look silly. Because of her family's connections and title, Corinne could bounce back, while Rebecca's Season would come to a quick halt, along with her papa's plans to avoid debtors' prison. "Miss Blakeford left the grounds yesterday afternoon. She hasn't returned. She didn't leave a note, nor did she inform me or anyone where she was going."

Fig on propriety. Rebecca resumed twisting the glove to calm her nerves.

"How insolent." Lady Coburn pursed her lips. "She must be dismissed at once. A chaperone's priorities are first toward her charge." She squeezed Rebecca's hand and stopped her fidgeting. "Do not fret. She most likely has relatives in the area she went to visit. In your mother's stead, I will give her a good tongue lashing when she returns. In the meantime, Professor Duval mentioned you're to be his guest at the lecture. Perhaps Sarah could accompany you today?"

Sarah wiped her mouth with her napkin. "I would be

delighted, but I cannot promise to remain awake through all the scientific talk."

A footman filled a cup of steaming chocolate and set it before Rebecca.

"I'm fascinated by the topic of discussion, but from my experience attending these events, you won't be the only one dosing off." Rebecca sipped her hot beverage.

Sarah tilted her head. "You've attended other lectures?"

"A couple, usually standing in the balcony where I've had to borrow Mama's opera glasses to see the dissection. I'm excited to be in the front row as Professor Duval's guest."

"Dissection?" Sarah's face scrunched into a look of disgust. "Of humans?"

"Usually, the professors use wooden models carved to resemble the heart that are held up for show. I understand cadavers are difficult to acquire."

Chair legs screeched against the wooden floor, and Lord Wolston rose. He eyed her as he passed, his expression unreadable.

He had every right to be angry with her. She understood the pain of waiting for someone who didn't bother to show. She had worn a hole in the rug next to her cottage window, watching for Papa's return. On the rare occasions he came home, he hadn't stayed more than a couple of days. No matter how she'd pleaded, he wouldn't remain. Important meetings awaited, and political acquaintances were to be had among the *ton*—dukes, earls, prime ministers, and generals. She later discovered, in her father's case, his associations were usually made over a losing hand of cards.

If Lord Wolston knew her identity, he wouldn't stay, either, which was why she should stick to books and aiding Madeline.

Regardless, she must apologize for her tardiness to the garden. A chance hadn't arisen since he'd left during the evening meal for business in town. Rebecca had retired for the night before he returned.

She eyed the doorway. Should she follow him and apologize? Perhaps she'd have a better opportunity later. She sipped her drink, but the warm chocolate didn't ease her guilt, nor the nagging inner voice telling her to do the right thing, even if it might be uncomfortable.

The toe of a boot hit her shin.

Sarah glared at her, nodded at the door, and mouthed the word, *go*.

Her friend was right, of course.

Rebecca excused herself and stood. A strange pressure in her chest rose with her, followed by a quivering of her stomach. On leaden legs, she followed the marquis's steps and caught sight of him as he mounted the stairs.

Her soft-soled slippers made little noise as she padded down the hall and ascended to the second floor, all the while rehearsing what she would say. She'd lain awake for most of the night, working out the best way to apologize. *Lord Wolston, please forgive my tardiness last evening. I was looking forward to our meeting but lost track of time when I discovered a possible treatment for Madeline's heart condition. I never meant...*

Lord Wolston was standing in front of Professor Duval's door. He glanced up and down the hall.

Rebecca shrank back into the stairwell. She heard a latch click and peeked around the wall as he slipped inside the professor's chamber.

Strange.

Professor Duval and his associates had left early this morning for Oxford to prepare for the lecture. Mayhap Professor Duval asked the marquis to check on some experiment in his absence? Could he have brought animal subjects that needed feeding with him to Griffin Hall? Or plants that required daily watering?

If so, a servant would tend to those needs.

A door closed down the hall, and Rebecca spun around.

"Can I get you something, miss?" Lucy stood before Rebecca's chamber with her sweet, childlike smile. She carried bed sheets, likely having been helping Madeline.

"I..." *What do I tell her?* "I came up to retrieve something, but I can't recall what it was."

Lucy nodded. "Happens to me on occasion too. I find it's best to retrace my steps to remember."

"It must not have been that important." Rebecca traipsed down the stairs as quickly as she could without drawing suspicion.

Now she'd have to endure the angst until after the lecture before she could find an opportunity to speak with Lord Wolston.

~

*D*aniel removed his ear from the door, having heard voices.

Had Lady Prestcote followed him? Had she seen him enter Professor Duval's chamber? He would have started his investigation with her room, except he'd heard her maid chatting with another. Glancing toward the ceiling, he thanked God for small blessings.

The professor's room appeared tidy enough, except for a desk stacked with books and loose papers. A musk of book glue and ink hung in the air. He rounded the well-made bed. On the end table, he noted the book's titles, alternating biology and botany volumes. Typically, he didn't hunt a fox in its den. He found it more sporting to blow the horn and give chase. In the frantic haste, his targets tended to make mistakes. However, professors were a different breed. Rarely were they impulsive, preferring tactical planning and strategizing.

The professors had moved up on his lists of suspects. His visit the night before to the tavern and another chat with Greta, the barmaid, proved to be a grand success. Greta had freely gossiped about two fellows, one of them fitting the description of the stout man Daniel had encountered at the graveyard. They'd bragged about making a quick profit off some sly-boots gent, and all they had to do was get their hands dirty. If Daniel could locate the stout man or the lad, he could persuade them to identify their buyer.

Greta had further piqued his interest in mentioning a customer passing through who'd said the townsfolk of Witney ran out a ring of sack 'em up men. His best guess was that academics were growing impatient with the jails not providing enough bodies and had started paying resurrection men a hefty sum for a freshly dug corpse to dissect in the name of science.

Daniel started with the desk and Professor Duval's notes, skimming the pages of his journal. The entries focused on Duval's revelations and questions regarding the heart. A few pages later, he listed sources of donors for funding and next to them, jotted astounding numbers. Science, it seemed, was an expensive profession. Lady Coburn's name and those of her guests were on the list of donors, along with Lord and Lady Mercer, Lady Prestcote's parents.

On another page, the professor had written notes on the benefits of digitalis for dissipating symptoms of arrhythmia. Wasn't that what Lady Prestcote's maid suffered from?

Daniel flipped the page. Lady Prestcote's full name was written across the top and below were two columns, one listing her attributes.

Astute for her gender.
   Can hold a conversation.
   Thirsty for knowledge.
   Attractive.

High social status.

Well-connected.

Childbearing age.

Attractive? Of childbearing age? Daniel's jaw tightened. Did Professor Duval hold a tinder for Lady Prestcote? He moved to the other column listing her negative attributes.

Questions me too often.

Daniel remembered the question she'd posed to him on their first meeting. *If you reek of spirits, why do you taste like lemonade?* Indeed, Lady Prestcote didn't hesitate to pose questions, but Daniel would list that under her attributes.

Titled.

As the daughter of an earl, Lady Prestcote would be expected to marry within her class—an obstacle for the professor, but not for him. An optimistic warmth flooded him.

Too spirited.

Was there such a thing? He could easily remember her eyelashes fluttering closed, allowing him to believe she offered him a kiss. And then the sound of books thumping as she'd snatched the letter from his hands. A light chuckle escaped his lips. Spirited, indeed.

Passionate.

Daniel lurched upright. That word could mean a lot of things. Lady Prestcote was passionate about knowledge and her family. But did the professor see her that way in a physical sense?

Daniel could feel her soft lips melding with his. He could see the alluring way they parted when they'd been in the library together, and again in the hallway after he teased her.

But the image was replaced with one of Professor Duval's arms encircling her.

Daniel's hands curled into fists. The man had a lesson or two to learn about how a woman should be treated, but Lady Prestcote would remain blind to the professor's faults as long as he held the knowledge she desired.

One more reason why Daniel must protect her.

He flipped the page, but the following pages of the notebook were blank. The rest of his search availed little, so he moved on to the other professors' chambers.

Professor Bell's room appeared much like his own. But whereas Daniel's neatness had been honed through his undercover work, he suspected Bell's perfectionism boarded on obsessive. His sparse desktop contained only a candle in its holder. Inside the center drawer, however, he found neatly stacked papers. One pile contained correspondences. Daniel flipped through the letters from students and missives from colleagues, some requesting university funding for their projects. Another pile held a five-page acceptance speech for the vice chancellor position at Oxford College.

Odd. From what Daniel had heard, nominations had yet to be completed for the position.

A third stack held lists—one a page of Lady Coburn's guests, a second noting the household staff by department, including the stable grooms and gardening staff, and a third and fourth list named townsfolk, including the deceased chandler, Greta the barmaid, and a few other locals. Curiously, each name had a number next to it. Some of the numbers had been crossed out and revised.

Daniel could not make heads or tails of what the numbers represented.

He set the room back to rights and proceeded to Professor Matthews's chamber. He opened the door to find a jungle of potted plants growing along the windowsill and covering the desk. A notebook lay open on the corner of the bed. Daniel skimmed pages of itemizations of each plant, the nutrients fed to it, and an assessment of its growth. The man must have brought his experiments with him. Daniel trailed a finger down the list and found that digitalis was there. He located the corresponding plant by its Roman numeral scratched into the pot. An abundance of purple bell-like clusters of flowers bloomed. *Foxglove.* Beautiful yet poisonous. Also, curious because the plant was blooming out of season.

From the window, he heard the rumble of a carriage pulling in front of Griffin Hall's entrance below. He peered down.

Mrs. Evans's blond curls peeked out from underneath a straw bonnet, and Lady Prestcote's shapely figure followed her from the door. Her unassuming gait held a natural gracefulness to it, unlike the practiced sensual walks of the ladies on the marriage mart, hunting for a title. If only a strong wind gust would remove her pale-blue bonnet and allow her thick mass of dark hair to flow over her shoulders and down her back.

He stepped back. *Focus, man. You have a job to do.*

He slipped out of the professor's room and down the hall and tapped on Lady Prestcote's door.

A cough sounded a moment before her lady's maid opened the door.

"I hoped to escort Lady Prestcote to the lecture at Oxford."

Her eyes widened, and she bit back a smile. "I'm afraid she's already left with Mrs. Evans, but perhaps you could catch her?"

Blast. His plan had been to send the maid to see if she could catch her mistress, but he'd forgotten about her illness. He sighed but didn't have to feign his disappointment. Inspiration struck. "You should run to the kitchen and get some tea and honey for that cough."

She opened the door wider to a neatly kept room. The only things out of place were two stacks of books, one on the desk and one on the floor next to the bed. The allure of Lady Prestcote's gardenia scent wafted over him, beckoning him into the bedchamber. The maid pointed to the tea tray at the foot of the bed. "I already have tea, but thank you for your thoughtfulness."

She smiled at him with an odd glint in her eyes, mayhap from her illness.

In the past, he'd easily been able to send maids off on fools' errands or sweet talk them into getting him the information he needed, but he wouldn't do that with Lady Prestcote's maid. The woman pricked his conscience, but why? Was it her illness and the frail look about her? Or was it knowing that Lady Prestcote cared deeply for the poor girl?

He bowed and strode back to his chamber, working on a new plan. Any day now, Lieutenant Scar would check in, needing answers, and Daniel was no closer to knowing if any of the professors were connected to the grave-robbing scheme.

Adding another mystery that confounded him was the question of who dared blackmail Lady Prestcote. Was she involved willingly or unwillingly?

CHAPTER 15

*A*ttendants dimmed the wall sconces. Two strategically placed lanterns drew attention to Professor Duval standing center stage behind a podium alongside a wax statue of a human body, complete with a wax heart and circulatory system.

Rebecca listened with rapt attention from her tight wooden chair on the left side in the front row.

Beside her, Sarah pressed a handkerchief to her mouth every time Professor Duval elaborated on the surgeries he'd overseen. Her gag reflex triggered as he detailed guiding a surgeon through how to do an arterial ligation in cases of profuse bleeding.

Rebecca eyed her friend warily. Thank heaven she'd thought to bring her smelling salts after a man had fainted at the last lecture she'd attended. She leaned close to her friend and whispered, "Do you want to leave?"

Sarah glanced past Rebecca down the row toward Professors Matthews and Bell on the opposite side before shaking her head. "This is important to you. I'll be fine once my morning meal settles."

The next time Rebecca peeked at her friend, her eyes had drifted closed. Whether it was from fainting or from one of her sleeping spells, Rebecca couldn't ascertain, but at least the poor dear was out of her misery.

A door creaked open in the back of the arched-ceiling lyceum, spilling natural light into the dusty and dim lecture hall for a moment. The clapping of booted footfalls indicated that someone made his way up the side aisle to the front of the room.

Who would have the audacity to disrupt a lecture in progress?

Rebecca focused on Professor Duval's explanation of how the heart pumps the blood, circulating it throughout the body. In the wax model, he flicked the right ventricle's valve, explaining that it only flowed one direction.

On her left, the footfalls stopped, but she refused to peer that direction and acknowledge the rude person. Then, he passed in front of her, brushing her skirts in the process, and lowered into the open seat on her right.

Of all the luck. There were plenty of open seats. Why sit next to...?

The smell of sandalwood and leather surrounded her, and she couldn't help but look.

The man glanced at her. Even in the dim light, she recognized his cunning grin. *Lord Wolston.* What in heaven's name was he doing here?

He leaned close to her ear and whispered. "Mind if I join you?"

Did she have a choice?

She nodded but pressed a finger to her lips, focusing her attention on the professor again.

Leaning on his elbow and using his hand to direct his voice to her, he said, "What did I miss?"

She snorted. "Everything."

Grinning, he reclined, his forearm brushing hers as he settled it on the armrest.

She slipped her hands into her lap.

He stretched his legs in front of him, lightly flexing his feet. When he drew them back in, his knee bumped hers.

She pinned hers to the opposite side, curling her feet under her seat.

"Dreadfully sorry." He glanced at her, a wry twinkle in his eyes, before focusing his attention on the stage.

Was he teasing her? Could she hope that he'd found it in his heart to forgive her for her absence in the garden last evening? If only the teaching assistants hovering in the wings would turn up the lamplight so she could read his expression, but instead, she focused on Professor Duval still explaining the basics of the heart.

"There are four chambers,"—he held up four fingers—"just as there are four humors, of which sanguine is the dominant and why we focus on the heart and the blood."

Her mind drifted to Lord Wolston beside her. His broad shoulders filled the entire seat, making Professor Duval appear lanky in comparison. Each time she inhaled, her nose reveled in his enticing musk that wrapped her like a soft, knitted blanket she longed to curl up with.

Professor Duval had smelled of books.

She loved books.

Why did the marquis have to be a marquis? And handsome. She could see why Corinne would set her cap for him. He held an aristocratic air, confident and smooth but with a determined edge, like the heart itself—a smooth muscle yet always alert, always working. He could easily come across as arrogant, like how Professor Duval often put on airs, but Lord Wolston seemed genuinely interested in others, encouraging them to converse. After all, he'd gotten her to speak of Madeline and her heart issues. She thought of him waiting in the garden, flowers in hand.

Her gut twisted. She still hadn't apologized. Perhaps now was the best time, since he couldn't make a scene. She inhaled a steadying breath and leaned in his direction, whispering. "I must apologize for last evening, in the garden."

He turned to look at her, their noses only inches apart.

She swallowed, her gaze dropping to his mouth. She drew back, and he slowly turned to face forward.

As alluring...intimidating...as the man was, she needed to say her piece. "I lost track of time in the library, researching a cure for Madeline. I think I discovered one."

He glanced her way and issued a curt nod, as if to say, *good for you.*

"I ran to the garden as soon as I realized the time and found the lovely bouquet." She placed a gloved hand on his arm to plead for understanding. "I never meant to be rude or hurt you. I'm truly sorry."

He didn't look her way, but his other hand moved to rest over hers.

Had he forgiven her? Could they at least be friends?

Professor Duval paused mid-sentence, his gaze homing on Lord Wolston's hand covering hers.

Rebecca felt like a child caught sneaking a treat from the cookie jar. She tried to pull her hand away, but Lord Wolston's grip tightened. For a moment, she forgot to breathe. Was he asking her to choose? Or informing the professor he had a competitor?

As if either of them wanted her.

But then again, they believed her to be Corinne, wealthy and titled.

Lord Wolston relaxed his fingers, giving her the option to move away.

She slid her hand into her lap.

Lord Wolston would be disappointed when he discovered he'd been flirting with a nobody, linked only to nobility by a father who would strain any suitor's pockets to avoid debtor's prison. It was past time she told him the truth—soon, while her heart could still bear his rejection.

Later. For now, she would focus on the lecture and a cure for Madeline.

The creak of the door in the back of the auditorium opening sounded once more.

Professor Duval removed his spectacles and cleaned them, using his jacket's lapel. He cleared his throat and continued describing how arterial ligations were used to stop the uterine hemorrhaging of a woman after childbirth.

"You're a lying quack!"

The shout was hurled from the back of the room, startling Sarah awake.

Rebecca twisted to see who would make such an accusation.

Professor Duval continued as if nothing had happened. "In an instance of hemorrhaging, it must be determined if the humors of the body are naturally balancing themselves by alleviating the hot blood—"

"Charlatan! Huckster!" The man threw up his fist. "My wife and child were alive until you treated them."

"Mr. Tingley, please." Professor Duval raised his palms. "I'm sorry for your loss, but—"

"She became weaker and weaker after each bloodletting."

"Because of her ailment,"—Professor Duval's voice rose—"not the treatment."

"I told you to leave and not come back,"—he shoved an empty chair in front of him that toppled with a clatter—"but when I wasn't home, you entered my house and proceeded with your quackery."

Lord Wolston glanced at the side door exit and shifted to

the edge of his seat. "On my word, I want you and Mrs. Evans to exit through that door."

Rebecca nodded.

"Bloodletting is a proven treatment." Professor Duval's nostrils flared, and he tugged down on his jacket. "If I hadn't treated her headache, she could have died."

"She did die!" Mr. Tingley screamed.

The professor's lips pinched into a frown. "Not from my treatment. Perhaps God willed it."

Rebecca jolted.

Did the professor believe that? Had God willed her mama's death? Did He want the same for her sister? Was He a good God, as Mama had said, or an angry God, snuffing out lives as He pleased, as the professor insinuated?

Professor Bell stood from his front-row seat on the right side and pointed at Mr. Tingley. "I will not have a plebeian interrupt our university's academic pursuit."

"Better a plebeian than a charlatan!" But the broad-shouldered man rounded forward, putting his face in his hands and melting into tears. "Anna was beautiful. She was life and goodness. She was my everything." His voice cracked. "We were going to have a child."

An ache as deep as the grave wrenched Rebecca's heart. Her mama had been life and goodness—and her and Madeline's everything.

"Escort him from the premises." Professor Bell directed his command to the young teaching assistants, who peered at each other as if to see who'd go first and who'd fetch the constable.

"Let the poor fellow be," someone shouted from the gallery.

A man from the back yelled, "He lost his wife, by Jove. Have some sympathy."

Mr. Tingley's weeping increased.

"Seize him!" Professor Bell bellowed.

Mr. Tingley looked up, the brokenness in his expression

shifting into a look of intense hatred. He leapt over the toppled chair and lunged for the stage, reaching toward Professor Duval. Professor Matthews jumped to defend his associate.

Men scattered, and chairs toppled.

Lord Wolston rose, hauling Rebecca up with him, half carrying, half guiding her and Sarah to the side door. He opened it and pushed them through, then slammed the door closed, leaving them alone.

Sunlight streamed in from an upper window, illuminating a smaller lecture-style classroom. In the room's center, chairs surrounded a rectangular table draped with a sheet. A putrid smell hung in the air, and Rebecca pressed the back of her hand to her nose.

Shouts rang from the hall, followed by the sound of splintering wood.

She and Sarah spun to face the door. "My goodness. Are scientific lectures always so adventurous?"

"Typically, they're uneventful. This is a first in my experience." Sarah's hand held in hers, Rebecca backed down the center aisle, passing several rows of seats.

Another crash sounded, and the door shook.

Rebecca gasped. They continued backing away from the door, just in case somebody were to barrel through.

"I do hope the marquis and the professors are unharmed," Sarah said.

Rebecca remembered the strength in Lord Wolston's arm as she'd guided it into the sling, but Professors Duval, Matthews, and Bell had lanky physiques. Could they defend themselves? She glanced at her friend. "I'm sorry for dragging you into this mess."

"Cease this instant," Professor Bell yelled above the ruckus. "This is a university, not a pugilist club."

Another crash shook the door, followed by a human groan.

With a startled gasp, Sarah jumped back, bumping herself and Rebecca against the cloth-draped table.

Rebecca turned to ensure they hadn't damaged anything.

The long object underneath the sheet shifted.

A hand fell, dangling from an arm, which swung back and forth like a pendulum.

Rebecca's heart leapt into her throat, suffocating the scream that tried to escape. She backed away and stared at the lifeless hand—pale, fragile, and feminine, a thin gold chain flashing from the wrist.

Beside her, Sarah turned.

And screamed. She bolted, pulling Rebecca away in a firm grip.

Rebecca fought to keep upright, though her knees had turned to custard.

Sarah flung open the door to the lecture hall, slamming it against the wall, and dragged Rebecca into the room. A few of the fighting men stilled, straightening as if caught by their wives in their wayward act of fighting. A couple men in the back continued their assaults, but the majority of the attendees had disappeared, probably left to escape the violence.

Apparently, her friend would prefer mayhem and chaos over a dead body.

A couple of the men turned to peer at the two ladies clinging to one another, some frowning at the gentlewomen as if they'd gone mad, barging into a brawl. The fighting diminished as more ears perked up to hear what had frightened the ladies.

Lord Wolston stood between Mr. Tingley and Professor Duval. He stayed Mr. Tingley with a palm against the man's chest, but Professor Duval swiped at the widower, missing by inches. Lord Wolston flinched as pressure rammed his bad shoulder, but as the two men attempted wild swings, his lordship easily thwarted them with his good arm.

Professor Duval's tussled hair stuck out in every direction, his cravat hanging crooked and sprinkled with blood. His bottom lip was split and swollen.

"Gentlemen, calm yourselves." Other than a light mark across Lord Wolston's cheek and his grimace when he shifted his healing shoulder, he appeared unharmed. "This issue will be resolved by the magistrate, not by our fists. Especially not when ladies are present." His gaze met Rebecca's with concern. "Why are you here?"

"There's a body!" Sarah shouted in Rebecca's stead, jabbing her index finger toward the smaller lecture hall.

The men who'd been fighting on behalf of Mr. Tingley shoved away their opponents and turned to Professor Duval, some with murderous looks. His eyes widened, and he shrank away, raising his arms to protect his head as if worried the angry mob would attack again.

"Enough!" Professor Bell climbed onto the stage. "The cadaver was procured legally through the proper channels. By writ of the king, hanged thieves are allowed to be dissected for scientific pursuits that will benefit all of society."

"My brother died after taking a tonic prescribed by Duval," yelled a man with bloodied shirt being restrained by two others. "He wasn't even ill. He took the tonic to keep from getting sick. Then he craved the stuff. Went half crazed when he couldn't get more. Your tonic killed him."

Professor Bell looked down upon the bloodied man. "We don't need to explain our methods to you. You can't comprehend the good we do and the risks we must take to further medicine so that lives may be saved."

"At the cost of lives lost today?" another man yelled. "Or do you only seek to save wealthy and noble lives? People you deem worthy?"

Professor Bell's hands clenched into fists, his face reddening like a fiery log hissing in the fireplace. And about to pop.

"We're people, not experiments," the bloodied man shouted.

Booted footfalls approached.

"Ah, the constable has arrived." Professor Bell pointed at Mr. Tingley. "This man and his band of ruffians attended the lecture with the intent to attack Professor Duval."

The constable sauntered to Lord Wolston and took hold of Mr. Tingley. "It isn't right what happened to your wife, Mr. Tingley. Think of yer children. They need their papa at home, not locked up in a cell."

Lord Wolston slipped out as if to inspect the adjoining lecture room.

Mr. Tingley's shoulders slumped, and his head hung. He wept again as the constable had one of his men escort him out.

Rebecca couldn't tear her gaze from the poor grief-stricken man. What would happen to him? Would the magistrate show pity and leniency? Or would Professor Bell use his position to pressure the magistrate into seeking the full extent of the law?

Lord Wolston closed the door with a soft click, and she felt his reassuring presence over her right shoulder before he spoke. "I'm sorry you ladies had to witness a brawl, but also stumble upon a cadaver." His arm curved around her back, lightly touching her elbow. "Are you both all right?"

Rebecca swayed back into the curve of Lord Wolston's arm, and his protective hold tightened. She told herself she merely needed a moment to relax and let her pounding heart slow, but her muscles longed to turn and feel the fullness of his embrace, and her traitorous pulse continued to race.

Sarah shook her head. "I doubt I shall ever sleep again. As soon as I close my eyes, I'll see that hand swaying." She splayed a palm across her bosom, looking as if she may faint. "And the fighting... When the man leapt over the chair, I thought he might kill Professor Duval. If professor Matthews hadn't jumped between—"

"I believe the lecture has come to an early end," Lord Wolston said. "Let me escort you back to Griffin Hall before someone swoons."

He guided her and Sarah around toppled seats and even some shattered glass as the professors collected broken chairs and righted others.

Professor Matthews glanced their way. The botanist's left eye had swollen shut. It would be black by nightfall. He attempted to flash Sarah a reassuring smile, but grimaced when his cheeks rose.

In front of them, other attendees filed out. Bits of their conversations floated past Rebecca's ears. "Poor bloke. He hasn't been right in the head since his wife died."

"I got a good swing at that one fellow," another man said.

Lord Wolston drew her and Sarah aside and signaled for her coach to be brought around. She admired the way he took command.

A bald man to her right spoke to another man. "This is going to affect Professor Duval's chances of being nominated vice chancellor. Leanings will go toward Bell."

One of the teaching assistants said, "Did you see the marquis take on three men?"

Rebecca's pulse quickened. Thank heaven he'd arrived and sat next to her. His quick thinking had moved her and Sarah out of harm's way. He couldn't have known there was a dead body in the next room. The memory of the swinging hand sent a shudder through her.

A coachman pulled a carriage to a stop, and Lord Wolston opened the door to aid Sarah and herself inside. When they were settled, he climbed in and sat opposite of them, lounging against the tufted cushions as if he witnessed such skirmishes every day. His cravat had loosened, but not a hair lay out of place, nor did his jacket hold a single wrinkle. The sunlight illuminated his square jaw and the red mark he now sported on his cheekbone—the only hint that he'd stood in the thick of a battle. He rapped on the ceiling with his knuckles, and the carriage lurched forward.

The movement caught Rebecca off guard, and she slid off her seat and would have landed on the floor if Lord Wolston hadn't caught her.

"Whoa, there." His stormy gaze held hers.

Her throat went dry.

What was the matter with her? She'd known the conveyance would move when he'd tapped the roof, but she left herself off-kilter by staring at the mark on his cheek. Now that the bruise was within arm's length, she couldn't resist. She gingerly touched the slightly swollen skin.

His eyes widened the tiniest bit.

"Does it hurt?"

~

*B*ack in the lecture hall, Daniel had believed he'd reached the limit of his restraint when he'd been tempted to knock the self-importance out of Professor Duval. He'd itched to plant a facer directly in his nose.

But now, sitting in the carriage wrapped in the Lady Prestcote's gardenia scent as she peered at him with such a tender gaze, every inch of him had to resist yanking this bluestocking into his arms and kissing her breathless.

She touched his cheek. He tensed, fighting his impulse, his reaction far more painful to his bruise than her gentle caress.

"A punch grazed me." He tried to shrug, pretending her tenderness didn't set his body ablaze. "It could have been worse."

"Without your quick thinking,"—Blue's words held an airy quality, her breath caressing his skin—"we would have been in the center of the fight."

"A gentleman sees to the ladies' well-being."

Her chin lifted a fraction of an inch. "I didn't see any other gentleman."

Mrs. Evans cleared her throat. "I think Professor Matthews would have come to our aid if he hadn't intercepted a blow meant for Professor Duval."

Blue's eyes widened as if she'd forgotten her friend's presence, and she sat back in her seat.

Daniel tried to smile at her reaction, to present himself as nonchalant and unaffected, but in truth, he ached at the loss of her nearness.

He shouldn't think of her as *his* Blue, not until he figured out who was blackmailing her and if she'd fallen prey to aiding the body snatchers. Was she being blackmailed to protect herself or her family's reputation? From his research, he knew her uncle was in financial trouble. She seemed to have cared for her aunt dearly. Did she feel pressured to aid him? Or was she in need of funds herself? Had her parents cut her off?

Lord and Lady Mercer must tread a fine line as diplomats. Could they be using their daughter to appease academics who demanded a supply of bodies for science? Was she their liaison? Leafield was a short jaunt to Oxford and a two-day trip to Edinburgh University, both known for their anatomy research. And what of Miss Blakeford's disappearance? Had the chaperone seen something she wasn't supposed to? Had she been sent to the country to be done away with, to disappear—permanently?

He might be jumping to irrational conclusions, but speculating was part of his job. At least Lady Prestcote appeared concerned for her chaperone's well-being.

"It looked as though Professor Matthews took a bad blow. I think he'll be sporting black and blue around his eye for the next week." Concern lined Mrs. Evans's face. It appeared the widow had developed feelings for the professor.

"What happened in there?" Lady Prestcote searched his face for answers. "Why would Mr. Tingley believe Professor Duval killed his wife?"

"Rumors have surfaced that Professor Duval has taken part in unsanctioned experiments...on people."

"Unsanctioned?"

"Mind you, these rumors have yet to be proven." He would dispatch an investigator to the village to verify the accusations he'd heard. If they were to be believed, then Professor Duval had experimented on the poorest of paupers, people with few or no relations. Likely, he'd chosen those subjects to help hide—or bury—the results when his experiments didn't turn out the way he intended. "Further, he was accused of trying to cover up the deaths that resulted from his experiments."

"Surely, they are mistaken." Lady Prestcote shook her head. "Professor Duval is the leading expert in his field."

"Could the deaths have been accidents?" Mrs. Evans frowned.

"Perhaps. An investigation will need to be done."

Mrs. Evans lowered her gaze to her gloved hands resting in her lap.

Lady Prestcote stared out the window, and silence fell except for the clopping of the horses' hooves and the rhythmic sway of the carriage.

He gazed out the window until a light snore reverberated next to Lady Prestcote. Mrs. Evans's chin rested on her chest. The earlier excitement appeared to have taken its toll.

"He said God willed it. That woman's death." But Lady Prestcote's choked whisper ached with personal pain.

Daniel slid to the edge of his seat. "You're thinking about your aunt's death."

She nodded, pinching her lips as if to hold back a sob.

He clasped her hand in his and rested them on his knee.

"God is a loving God. He never wanted His children to suffer or to die."

She peered at him, her hazel eyes glistening with unshed tears.

After his father's death, Daniel had had similar thoughts and questioned his grandfather. He'd been seven years old when his father's ship sank during a storm. Grandfather had sat on Daniel's bed, doing his best to explain life and death to a child.

He recalled the words as if his grandfather whispered them in his ear.

"God gave us free will," Daniel said, "but in the garden, Adam disobeyed, and sin and death came into the world."

"One man's mistake, and we're all to be punished?"

"The world is cursed. We each have a sin nature, but God made a way to redeem us, through Jesus."

"In the end, death wins, though. It takes us all."

Lord, help me be clearer. "Those who believe in Jesus live again. Someday, Jesus will return and there will be a new earth without sin and death."

In her eyes, he saw her processing what he'd said. "Why doesn't Jesus come back now?"

He loved how her curious mind questioned everything. "Because God is patient, not wanting anyone to perish, but for everyone to repent."

"All people? Not just nobility, but servants, paupers, and simple country folk?"

"Of course. Everyone."

"Criminals? Thieves? Murderers?"

Daniel didn't want to admit what he knew to be true. God's mercy went against his sense of justice, not to mention everything he'd learned in his training regarding the king's law. "If they see the error of their ways and seek God's forgiveness, and if they accept Him as Lord, then yes. Even them."

Lady Prestcote's eyes shadowed. "I wasn't there." Her voice was a broken whisper. "When she died."

Daniel's skin tingled. He knew from his experience in intelligence gathering that she was about to reveal pertinent information.

"I was supposed to be caring for her, aiding her to drink, feeding her broth." Her gaze fell to his hand over hers. "A young man from town had invited me for a carriage ride in his new phaeton. I'd held a secret infatuation for him and was delighted he'd picked me over the other girls in town. I'd never felt so happy and full of myself sitting on the high perch of his phaeton. And then Madeline screamed my name. My blood ran cold. Instinctively, I knew. I didn't wait for the carriage to roll to a stop, for him to aid my descent, or to say goodbye. I jumped down and ran. Madeline was standing at the end of the drive, but I didn't stop. I flew inside, but it was too late. She was gone."

Her hand grew cold between his palms, and he rubbed the top to create some warmth. At a time like that, the fact she'd believed she should have stopped and consoled her maid spoke volumes for her character.

"I was supposed to be there. If I had been, then maybe I..." Her words broke off in a choked sob.

...could have saved her? What a herculean task to place on a young woman's shoulders. Was it guilt that now drove her to find a cure for her maid? God, help her forgive herself.

"I vowed I'd never let a boy distract me from my real purpose ever again." She raked her front teeth over her bottom lip. "I wanted to meet you in the garden and planned on it. I dressed and readied in advance, even, but then I went to the library, and Professor Duval spoke of treatments. Unintentionally or not, I let the time slip by, and I... It might have been because...I was scared."

New understanding softened his heart, wiping away the pain of her rejection. "I forgive you."

Tears sprang to her eyes and spilled over, running helplessly down her cheeks until she wiped them away with her fingertips. "You must think me a veritable goose."

"I think you are a tenderhearted woman who has endured a terrible strain after seeing a fight break out at a lecture and then being shoved into a room with a dead body."

Her face blanched.

He wanted to swallow back the words. "I'm a cad. I shouldn't have reminded you of such horrors."

She jerked upright, her wide-eyed expression churning worry in his gut.

He couldn't help but cup her cheeks in his palms. "What is it? What's the matter?"

"Her bracelet." Lady Prestcote's breathing quickened. "I bumped the table, and a hand fell. I just remembered where I've seen that bracelet before."

The frightened look in her eyes was almost his undoing. The urge to protect her sparked like a lit fuse.

"Miss Blakeford."

He frowned. "Your missing chaperone?"

Egad.

CHAPTER 16

*L*ater that afternoon, Rebecca sat at the writing desk, her hand shaking as she penned a letter to Corinne. Madeline paced behind her.

Dearest Cousin,

It is with worry in my heart that I must inform you that Miss Blakeford has gone missing. Lady Coburn notified the local authorities, and search parties have been sent out to look for her, but I fear she may be...

Dead?

Fallen into bad company?

Dissected for the benefit of science as this note was being written?

She turned to her sister. "I can't think of what to say. How can I explain everything that happened when I know so little about what events occurred?"

"Our cousin needs to be made aware, and it needs to come from us, not wagging tongues. Miss Blakeford was Corinne's governess. She might know which family members to contact or have some insight as to why this might have happened." Madeline gripped the bedpost, melting onto the corner of the bed. "I still can't believe Miss Blakeford is dead. Are you sure it was her? You saw the gold bracelet with a silver clasp?"

"I think so." Rebecca set down the ink quill and pressed her palms to her eyes to block out the image of the dangling hand. Sarah had also seen the hand but had been too frightened to recall a bracelet.

Was Rebecca's worry regarding her missing chaperone causing her to envision things? She glanced at the mantel clock —quarter past three.

"Lord Wolston should be returning soon with answers." He'd ridden back to Oxford to get another look at the cadaver to determine if it indeed was Miss Blakeford.

Lady Coburn had asked for an explanation as to why they'd returned so early and then nearly swooned as they recounted the events. She summoned the constable, who arranged several search parties before leaving to locate Lord Wolston to see if the corpse was the missing chaperone.

Lady Coburn instructed Rebecca and Sarah to return to their rooms and rest after their ordeal, but Rebecca couldn't nap. She appeased Madeline with a full recounting. Her sister's usual joyful spirit had fled, and Madeline sat dazed on the bed until she remarked that Corinne must be informed of her governess's possible demise immediately.

How would Corinne react to the news? Would this cause a scandal? If the chaperone had been killed, was her death an accident or something more sinister? How had Miss Blakeford ended up at Oxford?

If she had been murdered, would the killer murder again?

She picked up the quill and finished the letter with Madeline's assistance, leaving many of the questions and details unaddressed until she had better answers.

A branch scraped the glass windowpane.

Rebecca startled at the eerie sound. The wind had increased, swaying the branches of a nearby tree. In the distance, dark gray clouds reflected off the far pond's surface, signaling a brewing storm.

Lord, please let Daniel return soon.

After the trauma at the lecture hall and their intimate conversation on the ride back, she couldn't help but think of him by his given name. She placed her palms where Daniel had cupped her cheeks on the return carriage ride. His hands had felt both gentle and strong. His expression had resonated with concern and assurance that he would protect her.

Why would he pay her any heed after how awfully she'd treated him? She'd outright ignored him while seeking Professor Duval's attention.

She'd seen another side of Daniel the night she'd set his arm and he'd walked her back to her room. His love for his sisters resonated in his words. She could hear in his voice that he would do anything for them, as she would for her sister.

The wind rattled the windowpane. In the foggy distance, a dark figure weaved just beyond the tree line toward the old mill. It was a man, perhaps a party guest or servant, but she couldn't make out who. His gait jerked in stiff strides, lacking Lord Wolston's smooth grace. It couldn't be the professors, who hadn't returned from Oxford yet.

Who would go for a stroll when a storm approached?

She peered back at Madeline. "Who is that walking the grounds? They're going to get caught in the storm."

Madeline moved to the window. "I don't see anyone."

The shape had disappeared.

"Mayhap I'm envisioning things. I can only hope I imagined the bracelet as well, and Miss Blakeford will reappear."

Rebecca could still see that swinging hand in her mind's eye. She pressed the image away as she folded the letter and addressed and sealed the envelope. She stuck the paper in her pocket to give to the butler for mailing. She rose and slid around the desk to stand next to her sister at the window. Leaning against the drapes, she peered down the lane.

Daniel had considered her safety when the fight broke out. He'd taken the bee's sting for her, ensured she ate when she'd missed the morning meal, and shown remorse over kissing her at the Lipscomb party. Though he was a marquis, she'd never seen him talk down to anyone. He spoke to all of Lady Coburn's guests with kindness, as odd as they may be, as if they were equals.

He valued people.

Could she say the same of Professor Duval? Even if he hadn't directly caused Mrs. Tingley's death, he'd disregarded her husband's wishes by continuing the treatments. And then there was the way the professor spoke of his experiments, unconcerned about potential harm to the participants.

A horse and rider appeared on the horizon. The rider was familiar enough that her heart thumped within her.

"The marquis has returned." Madeline stepped away from the window and bent to fluff the wrinkles out of Rebecca's gown.

"You're not my servant," Rebecca said, shooing her sister away. "Leave that for when others are near." She leaned so close to the window that her nose brushed the cold glass, admiring his horsemanship, the fluid way he moved as if one with the horse. As always, he was in command and control.

Her insides did a little twirl.

"Go." Madeline shooed her with a flick of her fingers. "Discover the truth."

Yes. About Miss Blakeford. Despite her body's foolish reactions, this meeting would not be a romantic exchange.

Rebecca exited her room and padded down the stairs.

He'd most likely enter through the doorway off the solarium since it was closest to the stables.

Other than a few servants, the hall was quiet. A sad, melodic tune drifted from the music room, where she guessed Lord and Lady Farley played the pianoforte.

Rebecca passed her letter to the butler, who agreed to see it sent, before she wandered into the orangery. She sat facing the door to await Lord Wolston's arrival.

She must look like a veritable ninny, staring at the door.

Spying a book on the side table, she tried to read, though she couldn't manage interest in the subject of growing fruit trees. Nervous energy tingled her fingers. She leaned the open book against her chest and felt the pulse in her wrist. Was its thundering pace declaring her anxiety over learning if the cadaver was that of Miss Blakeford or excitement for Lord Wolston's return?

Merciful heavens.

She was falling for the marquis.

No, she mustn't.

She had yet to explain that she wasn't Corinne. Surely, when she did, he'd despise her for her deceit.

A footman strode to the solarium door and opened it.

Lord Wolston stomped inside, handing his hat to the servant, and with a yank of his tie, swirled off his cape. No wonder she'd run into a wet wall if that was how he'd removed his cape that first night when he arrived at Griffin Hall.

As if sensing her presence, his gaze locked on her.

Her skin buzzed like bees around a hive.

Did he carry good news or bad?

"Lady Prestcote." He raked a hand through his thick waves of hair, subduing its windblown look.

Her legs rose as if of their own accord, and she set the book aside, never breaking eye contact.

In two long strides, he stood before her. The scent of leather and sandalwood filled her nostrils. His gaze swirled with tenderness, and his brow furrowed with concern. "I'm afraid I have wretched news."

A childish impulse to cover her ears tensed her muscles, but she resisted.

"The cadaver was indeed Miss Blakeford."

Rebecca's breath hitched. She'd seen the bracelet. She should have been prepared for the news, but it still ripped the air from her lungs.

Daniel's strong arm wrapped around her, and he crushed her against his chest.

She hadn't known Miss Blakeford well, and their few interactions hadn't been pleasant, but she was a person—a child of God. A lost soul. Rebecca pressed her face into his solid strength, using him to block out the evil in this world and the outline of Miss Blakeford's lifeless body lying under the sheet.

Rebecca had been the one to pull the coverlet over her mama's still body and close the door so her sister wouldn't see the shell of what their mother had been.

Lord, please don't let me have to do the same to Madeline.

A sob escaped her constricted throat, and Daniel's hand roved up and down her spine. His cheek rested upon the crown of her head, and his breath parted her hair as he shushed her like a father would soothe a child.

She squeezed her eyes tight to fend off the burn of tears and inhaled several sandalwood-filled breaths until the tightness in her throat eased.

Reluctantly, she pulled away.

His embrace loosened, and his hands moved to her shoulders. The warmth in his gaze pushed back the cold numbness encroaching upon her. "I'm sorry," he whispered.

"How did she...?" Rebecca bit her bottom lip. "What happened to her?"

"It's hard to tell." He lowered his gaze and escorted her over to the chairs. He tossed the citrus book on the table and gestured for her to sit. She did, and he swung a chair around and sat facing her, their knees almost touching. "Class commenced while I escorted you and Mrs. Evans back to Griffin Hall. By the time I returned..."

Class commenced. Rebecca's hand flew to her mouth. *My word.* Surely... Surely, Miss Blakeford hadn't been... She whispered the word. "Dissected?"

He nodded before bowing his head as if paying his respects to the dead.

Nausea churned her stomach.

"I questioned Professor Bell on how and where Miss Blakeford's remains had been acquired. He admitted that the professors had pooled their funds to obtain fresh cadavers."

"Miss Blakeford was alive three days ago and seemed hale enough. How could she have died so suddenly? Was she murdered so some cur could fill his pockets, or was there an accident requiring a quick burial? And if so, why weren't we informed?" Her hand slid to her heart. "If no one identified her, would she have had a pauper's funeral—wheeled to a cemetery in a farmer's cart and dumped in an unmarked grave?"

"I've pondered the same questions. Her body didn't appear to have been buried. Not a spot of dirt, which is suspicious. Whether she died from an accident or from a more nefarious means is what I plan to find out. Bell claimed he wasn't responsible for who was hired to...acquire the bodies."

"But someone was."

Daniel nodded but dropped his gaze once more.

"Who?"

He met her eyes, his voice a low whisper. "Professor Duval."

Rebecca's hand slid to her throat. "Oh, my."

"I questioned him. Duval admitted that he'd requested the cadaver but had nothing to do with how and where it was... sourced."

"Sourced?" Her voice squeaked, and she hugged her arms. A human life shouldn't be spoken of as a commodity.

"Forgive my callous tone. Some detachment is necessary to gain information." His mouth tightened. "Timing is of the essence in catching evildoers. I need to search Miss Blakeford's chamber."

Search her chamber? A memory of him entering Professor Duval's quarters this morning flashed in her mind. What was he after? Why would he concern himself with her chaperone's death? Rebecca had hardly known Miss Blakeford, and Daniel had only seen her when their riding party explored the grounds and that morning in the breakfast room. "Shouldn't we wait for the constable? He may want nothing disturbed."

"In my experience, constables tend to not be thorough in their investigations, especially not when commoners are the victims."

"You have experience in situations like this?"

His eyes darkened. A long silence hung between them. What was he reluctant to discuss with her?

But Daniel spoke into the tension. "Years ago, when I was on the cusp of manhood, a madman attempted to kidnap my sister."

"Oh, no." She gripped the armrests, unable to imagine the horror. "How wretched. Was she... Is she all right?"

"Quite, but she and my family were shaken. I'll explain while we search." He stood and held out his hand.

She took it and rose. "I'm not even certain where Miss Blakeford's chamber is located."

He pulled her along in his wake but stepped aside for her to precede him, climbing the main stairs and then again on the servant's stairs to the dormered third floor. He led her down the hallway. The wood beneath her feet squeaked, and the narrow passage offered little to see aside from the broad expanse of

Daniel's back. She heard a door close, then a startled female exclaimed, "My lord."

"Could you point us to Miss Blakeford's room?"

"Fourth door down on the left."

He bowed and continued.

The maid squeezed against the wall as they passed, holding out her skirts as if to curtsy but not having enough room.

Daniel tested the knob and swung open the door, then stepped aside for her to go first.

Rebecca hesitated. Servant gossip would spread if she were found alone in a room with Daniel. She should leave to find Madeline or Sarah, but her curiosity to understand what happened to her chaperone drew her in.

As if sensing her uncertainty, Daniel said, "It should only take a moment. I'll leave the door ajar."

Dim light coming through a small window overlooking the grounds illuminated the whitewashed chamber. An unmade narrow bed rested in the corner, a small wardrobe and writing desk opposite. Clothes were littered across the floor.

"Has someone already searched?" Rebecca frowned at the mess as she entered the chamber. Uncertain what to do or what to look for, she stepped aside for Daniel to pass.

He opened the wardrobe, revealing the traveling dress Miss Blakeford had worn on their ride to Griffin Hall. He sniffed the air. "I don't believe so."

Rebecca also sniffed, recognizing the smell of cinnamon mixed with something else. What was that scent? Saffron?

He reached into the back corner of the wardrobe and held up an empty glass bottle. Lowering it under his nose, he breathed in its scent and studied the container. "Did your chaperone complain of headaches?"

Just the one time that she knew of. "I believe so, yes." How much was a socialite expected to know about her chaperone?

"Miss Blakeford kept to herself but had taken to her chamber with a headache before her disappearance."

He found another empty bottle next to the bed. "I think your chaperone had a taste for laudanum. Probably a secret opium eater." He shook the empty bottle, which had a yellow label. "It appears she'd run out. Perhaps that's why she left the grounds, to find an apothecary to purchase more. I've witnessed stronger men go to great lengths to get more laudanum to stave off illness."

"I had no idea." But Corinne's words echoed in Rebecca's memory. *I know her secret. If she wants a letter of recommendation to continue being a governess, she does whatever I request.*

"Check for letters or correspondences." He gestured to the writing desk before bending to search the pockets of Miss Blakeford's discarded clothes.

Rebecca sat at the desk and assessed the contents, finding a letter of recommendation from the headmistress of her governess school, a Christmas list filled with names and gift ideas, and a letter from her niece wondering when she'd visit.

Miss Blakeford was someone's daughter and someone's beloved aunt. No longer.

Rebecca skimmed for an address she could use to inform the woman's family of her passing, but what would she tell them?

She set the letters down. "What happens after..." *her dissection.* She couldn't say the words. Many saw the practice as a desecration of the human body. "What will happen to Miss Blakeford now?"

"I requested her remains be sent here for a proper burial." He straightened to face her. "I'll speak to Lady Coburn about a small ceremony near the family plot."

"Thank you." His thoughtfulness brought a lump to her throat. She hadn't considered arrangements until now, but he'd seen to everything.

She needed to take her mind off of Miss Blakeford's demise. "You were saying about your sister..."

He bent over the discarded clothes again. "Alicia was six and ten when she had her coming out." He dropped a pelisse onto the bed and picked up a gown, feeling for a pocket. "I was a lad of four and ten."

His pitch raised barely a note, as if the memory pained him, but she caught onto the tension. "You don't have to speak of it." She slid the desk drawer closed. "I shouldn't have brought it up."

"It's fine." He shrugged off her worry, tossing it aside with the gown. "I was a scrawny boy and mollycoddled by my mother, who constantly fretted over her children after my father passed. Alicia was quite lovely—still is—but also young and unworldly. She caught the eye of a middle-aged baron. According to my mother, the baron would never have been in the running for Alicia's hand, and I believe the baron knew that, but Alicia was always kind and didn't know how to turn down a man's attentions. The more polite conversation she held with the baron, the more obsessed he became with her."

Daniel straightened, a shadow passing over his face as he stared past her out the window. "I was home the night the baron's hired man climbed the trellis and sneaked into my sister's room. I woke to a thud against the wall. Sleep clouded my mind when I peeked in her chamber, but I found Alicia gagged with some blackguard binding her hands. I'll never forget the look of terror on her face, and her desperation when she spied me. I yelled, 'Unhand my sister!' I ran at the cad, swinging my fists."

Rebecca could imagine a younger Daniel attempting to fight off a grown man. Affection for him grew within her.

"Back then," he said, "I didn't even know how to make a fist, much less throw a punch. I ended up breaking my thumb. I howled in pain. The man merely snorted. He let go of my sister and clapped a hand over my mouth. He picked me up by my nightshirt and planted a facer, breaking my nose."

Daniel touched his nose, running a finger down the slight curve to the bridge. "Before I blacked out, I saw him toss my sister over his shoulder and climb out the window."

"Oh, Daniel. How terrible." Rebecca rose and reached for him, wanting to comfort him, but he returned to his work as if he hadn't seen—or didn't want her comfort—so she clasped her hands in front of her. She was unable to believe he could have been unaffected. "It was terrible what that man attempted to do, and for a child to witness such a thing."

Remorse etched his features. "I was a disgrace. A weakling, helpless to aid my sister." He closed his eyes. A moment passed before he opened them again. His pained expression had faded.

He stood and continued. "My head throbbed like the dickens when I came to. It hurt to move and to think. Fortunately, our butler heard a thump and saw a shadow out the window. He sent a footman to find a bow street runner or the constable, and grabbing my father's sword from off the wall, he ran outside and halted the abduction. Neighbors heard the racket and helped subdue the hired man. Alicia was returned to us, shaken but unharmed."

"Thank heaven for that."

He raked a hand through his hair. "The baron was apprehended a block away, waiting in a hired hack for his henchman to bring Alicia. Later, the baron's crazy rantings revealed that he intended to whisk her to Greta Green and force her to marry him."

Rebecca murmured her dismay.

"By the time dawn broke, the constable had brushed the situation off as acute infatuation. He was mostly concerned as to why I hadn't done more. It was my grandfather, not the constable, who sought justice and saw to the deportation of the baron and his hired man." A haunted look hollowed Daniel's gaze. "I'll forever live with the regret that I didn't do enough to save Alicia." A muscle in his jaw twitched. "Never again will I be weak. I vowed to never let anyone hurt my family again."

The vehemence of his tone struck Rebecca. His vow was not so different from the one she'd made after her mother's death. She might not protect Madeline with her fists, but she'd do her best to safeguard her by finding a cure.

"I'm sorry." She brushed her fingers along Daniel's palm, longing to clasp his hand and bring it to her lips to show her sympathy. The open door and chance of a passing servant held her back.

He stiffened and pulled away. "I only told you this to lower your expectations. Justice isn't always served. Sometimes we must leave vengeance to the Lord."

"You were a brave boy."

"I wasn't." He shook his head. "I was weak. I couldn't stop him."

"You tried."

"I failed."

"You sounded the alarm."

He stared at her, confusion glazing his eyes as if her perspective contradicted his memory.

Behind him, out the window, the wind blew, bending the trees to its will.

His hand raised, his fingers curved as if to cup her cheek, but at the last moment, his hand curved around the back of her neck. Her mouth tipped up, her breath mingling with his as their gazes remained locked.

He tugged her against his chest, his thumb stroking the delicate skin of her neck and teasing loose tendrils of hair.

She didn't resist leaning into his strength and no longer cared if anyone saw them. The embrace was borne out of a need to be understood and supported. At least that was how she decided to interpret his hold as she relaxed against his warmth and circled her arms around his waist.

He stroked her hair near her low bun.

A pin clattered to the floor.

Her breath stilled as he turned her, his arm gently closing the door. A warning sounded in her mind, but the heady sensation of his fingers slowly withdrawing the remaining pins overruled it. Her hair tumbled over her shoulders. He continued the soothing motion, his hand now closer to her mid-back. His heartbeat thumped against her ear, hers beating in rhythm. She silenced the voices in her mind, screaming that she wasn't Corinne and wasn't worthy of a marquis, too engrossed in savoring the feeling of being held.

The wind blew, rattling the windowpane. She shivered.

He pulled back with a torn expression, as if he, too, mentally battled against what was wise and his heart's longing.

She tensed her muscles to walk away before she forgot who she was and her place, but he stared down at her as if seeing something precious and wonderful.

"Blue..." His voice reverberated in a husky whisper. "I vow to protect you too."

His head lowered, his mouth moving closer.

By Jove. Her head tilted back as if of its own accord, aching for his kiss. He met her lips with a velvet-light touch that sent a rush like a warm breeze over her skin.

"Daniel," she whispered on a sigh.

His arms tightened their embrace, and his lips molded against hers.

A door closed in the hall, and he broke the kiss but smiled against her lips. "I like it when you say my name."

She wanted to reply the same, but she'd lied about her identity. Guilt scratched away at the safe feeling she'd treasured moments ago. She pulled back, and he let her go. "I'm not who you think I am. I'm not like the women of your acquaintance."

"That's what I like about you." He curved his fingers around her ear and along her jaw. "You're my bluestocking."

The lovely sensation knocked all thought from her head. She wavered toward him before remembering he believed her to be Corinne. "No." She jumped back, bumping into the chair and toppling it. "You shouldn't... We shouldn't... It's illogical."

"I know." He steadied her arm, keeping her from falling, then released her and groaned. "I swear I am a gentleman, though I keep presenting myself as if I'm not." He glanced around the room. "This isn't the place or the time. I intend to court you properly but seem to forget myself and my good manners in your presence."

"I..." What had she been about to say? That she forgot herself too? Another reason she should put more distance between them...and tell him the truth.

The thought of it sent her stomach to join the loose pins scattered on the rough floor. She bent, collecting a few, and he handed her the rest as she twisted her hair back into a loose bun.

She would tell him. Just not now, while her lips still tingled from his kiss. She desired to savor this moment for a little while longer. "We should continue our search." She frowned at the desk. "I found nothing to help solve her disappearance."

He pointed to a pile of Miss Blakeford's undergarments. "Would you mind searching those?"

"Certainly." She blushed but picked up a petticoat and searched the pockets. Nothing. She grabbed a corset, hoping to accomplish their task and leave the suddenly warm chamber as quickly as possible. A piece of paper floated to the wooden floorboards.

Rebecca picked it up and unfolded it.

Daniel stopped his search of the clothes and stepped closer, too near for her to keep her focus, and read over her shoulder.

I have what you need. Meet me in the alley behind the tavern at dusk.

Rebecca whirled around to face him.

He eyed her. "Another clue to follow."

CHAPTER 17

*A*lthough reluctant to leave Blue's side, Daniel needed to search for clues before the pending storm washed them away. He made Blue promise that, after she dressed for the evening meal, she'd stay by Mrs. Evans's side until he returned, especially once the professors arrived back at Griffin Hall. He didn't voice the last part, but after finding Miss Blakeford's corpse in Oxford's science wing, the professors—specifically Duval—ranked high on his list of suspects, but he needed proof. Without it, Duval could claim they pooled their funds for the legal procurement of bodies through the penal system.

He reined his horse to a stop near the tavern.

"Eve'n guv'nor." The lad he'd come to know as Sam White tipped his cap and petted the horse's nose.

As he had on his previous visits to the tavern, Daniel tossed the lad a coin to care for his stead before dismounting. He handed Sam the reins. "You didn't happen to see a willowy looking woman come by here a couple nights ago?"

"If you're looking for a woman to warm yer bed, I overheard that Greta is sweet on you."

He ignored the insinuation. "The woman has a narrow face and hollow eyes. She was meeting someone in the alley."

"It's not a rare occurrence to see a doxy or two stumble out the tavern's back door on some bosky's arm." The dirty-faced lad frowned. "Wait. Now you mention it, there was a drab woman who came around—must 'ave been Wednesday eve'n. She wore a gray cloak but kept 'er 'ead down. Not the kind we usually get around 'ere."

"Who did she meet?"

"Bloke stayed in the alley back in the shadows. I never got a good look at 'im." He grinned. "They was gettin' pretty close." He pretended the back of his hand was a woman and imitated their kissing. "I walked away ta give 'em some privacy."

"Did you see them leave or where they went?"

"Naw. I went in the tavern to get me supper. They was gone when I got back."

"I appreciate your help." Daniel flipped him another coin. "If you remember anything else, you let me know. I'm going to look around."

The wind blew, and Sam pulled his threadbare jacket tighter around his neck. "Better 'urry. A storm's brewin'."

Daniel entered the dark alley. The pending storm didn't leave enough light for him to search for clues, so he sneaked in the tavern's back door. Scents of beef stew and body odor greeted him. The cook leaned over a boiling pot and wiped the sweat from his forehead. A few drops fell, a couple into the stew, and one sizzled in the flames below the pot.

"Ah, there's my handsome lovey." Entering from the dining room, Greta set down her tray and placed a hand on her ample hip. "Sneakin' in the back? I hope lookin' for me."

"Greta, you know how I enjoy our talks." He flashed her a wide grin. "I need to borrow a lamp for a bit. I promise to bring it right back."

She offered him a sensual pout. "We can do more than talk, lovey."

"That sea captain of yours will slit my throat. I like to keep my head where it is and not on the wall next to the stuffed deer." He tipped his head toward the taproom, then snatched a lantern off a work table. "I'll take my usual. Also, be a love and find me paper and pen. I'll be back in a wink."

He exited the kitchen and turned up the wick. Holding the lantern high, he paced the length of the alley. A small broken bottle caught his attention, and he crouched down to examine it. He lifted it, careful not to let the bottle's jagged glass cut him. Across the yellow label was written, *Laudanum.*

The contents didn't appear to have left a puddle, though the bottle may have been broken days before, all evidence of its contents long dried. He sniffed the ground but didn't smell hints of laudanum's cinnamon or saffron scents.

In front of the wall, a ragged, broken fingernail lay in the dirt along with a hairpin. The first few rows of the stone wall were scuffed with black. He sniffed and picked up the pungent scent of shoe polish.

Interesting.

There'd been a scuffle here.

The fine hairs on the back of his neck rose. The thought of what might have happened sickened his stomach. He hated to think of what the poor woman had endured.

He rose and held the lamp near the wall. A few long strands of blond hair had caught on the rough stone, the ends dancing with the breeze. If Daniel recalled correctly, Miss Blakeford had been blond. Splatters of a sticky liquid, now dried, had dripped down the wall. He leaned closer, and a whiff of cinnamon caught his nose. Had they poisoned her—forced her to drink the entire bottle at once?

He looked around for more clues, but other than a man's

boot print of average size and what resembled the drag mark of the heel of another boot, he found nothing else of note.

He rubbed his face, and the stubble from a long, weary day —still far from over—scratched his palm. Had the poor, unsuspecting woman come here to meet a secret lover? Did she smile when he held up the bottle of laudanum she craved, only to struggle when he tipped the bottle back and forced the contents down her throat?

How long did it take for drug to have its numbing effect? Did she slip away into nothingness, or did she panic knowing death was near?

He hung his head and silently prayed for the lost soul and her family.

The culprit must be found.

He entered the tavern through the back door and returned the lantern.

The cook turned a spit skewed with a roast, its fat dripping into the fire.

Greta spied him and rushed over, hooking his arm and escorting him to the table she'd reserved with a small slip of paper, inkwell, and quill. While she excused herself to refill a customer's ale, Daniel scratched a quick note to apprise Lieutenant Scar of the new developments. He folded the letter and dripped wax from the table candle to seal it as Greta pulled up a chair next to Daniel's elbow.

He didn't mind Greta's presence. Questions plagued him that needed answers, so he slid them into conversation, and Greta appeared happy to reveal what she knew.

Within minutes, he'd learned of two apothecaries who sold laudanum within a ten-mile radius and one traveling salesman who had already completed his usual spring visit.

Greta had seen a tall man with light hair hovering in the alley a few nights before, but he wasn't a regular, and she hadn't glimpsed him well enough to identify. Tall and light-haired could fit Duval's description. Greta leaned close and said with a waft of gin on her breath, "She's not the only one gone missing."

Daniel's senses leapt to full attention, but he kept his tone light. "You don't say."

Greta nodded. "We had a regular elbow crooker named Pete who stumbled into the tavern half sprung and left top-heavy. The bloke never spoke nothing except, 'give me another blue ruin.' I'd fill his glass, and he'd stare at the back wall all night. No family, no friends—at least, that's what the other patrons say. Almost a month ago, he just stopped comin'. No one's seen him. Couple lads visited his house to pick up some things"—she bumped his shoulder—"if you get my meanin'. They didn't find a body, and the man left everything as if he'd planned to return in an hour. He'd even left candles lit, burned down to nubs. The whole town's lucky his cottage and the surrounding buildings didn't go up in flames."

A burly man at the next table tipped his chin toward Daniel, addressing Greta. "Who's this bloke asking questions?"

"Don't be lookin' to get in a row, Mr. Craig." Greta winked at him. "Finish your ale, and I'll get you another."

"I don't like strangers butting their high-handed noses into our business." He scowled and swigged from his glass, then wiped his mouth with the back of his hand.

Mr. Craig's brogue didn't align with the mysterious voice from the graveyard. The man leaned over the table and glared at Daniel. He knew the type, always trying to pick a fight. His sense of justice balked at having to remain quiet and let the insolent man think he'd intimidated him, but the hour grew late, and Daniel needed to return to Griffin Hall.

Greta held up a finger for Mr. Craig to wait a moment. "Then there was Emma. She was a doxy who used to work the wharf but moved to the country when she took ill. Lively gel when she wasn't havin' one of her spells. She considered the tavern to be her family, since she had none. Then one day, she just disappeared. We thought she'd taken a turn for the worse, but her landlady came here lookin' fer payment. All of her things were still in her room, but she'd vanished."

She rose, and he checked his pocket watch.

"Greta, you're a love." He winked and slid her a good amount of coin for being so forthcoming and for the bowl of stew he'd hardly touched. "I must be going, or I'm going to insult my hostess by my tardiness."

She planted a kiss on his cheek as she tucked the coins away. "Ah, now, luv. If you're looking for anything"—she issued him a sultry bat of her lashes—"you come visit, and I'll give you what you need."

Ignoring that, he tipped a pretend hat to Mr. Craig and thanked the tavern owner, eager to get back to Giffin Hall. He needed to find a way to question the professors regarding the day's events in a way that wouldn't raise their suspicions. Once he did, he'd update Lady Prestcote with his findings.

The memory of her soft lips whispering his name had his heart pounding. The pampered earl's daughter he'd expected turned out to be a delightful surprise whose company he not only enjoyed, but sought. Due to his work and title, he'd spent time in the company of countless women, but Lady Prestcote was the first whose affections he craved. All the more reason to uncover the truth behind the blackmail letter she'd received, because the wall guarding his heart was crumbling.

Outside, he flipped Sam another coin and mounted his horse, spurring him toward the manor home.

This operation had taken a turn. If he captured an underling, perhaps he or she would identify the grave robbers. Then Daniel would be able to prove to Lieutenant Scar that he wasn't a throwaway agent and to his grandfather that he was no longer weak.

It was time to post his letter to update his handler on recent developments. Daniel might not be looking for merely a body snatcher, but a murderer.

~

O vernight, an icy wind had passed through. Rebecca clutched her pelisse tighter around her neck as she and Madeline stood at Miss Blakeford's gravesite. A basic pine box rested next to the freshly dug grave. The local reverend held his hat in place as he marched up the side of the hill to the graveyard. His black cloak billowed in the wind.

"Thank you, Reverend, for performing the service on such short notice." Rebecca bobbed a curtsy, and Madeline followed suit.

He bowed. "If it's only the pair of you, I hope you don't mind if I get right to it. This wind will chill your bones."

A pang of sorrow swept through Rebecca, and tears blurred the leaves raining down from the towering beech trees. Wind howled past the gate and headstones, a fittingly hollow sound. Poor Miss Blakeford. No friends or family stood by her grave, only two people who'd known her a few days.

Rebecca despised death.

She hated that a beautiful life could be swallowed up by the grave. She railed at the sickness that had resulted in herself and Madeline standing before Mama's grave, and she despaired over how she might, too soon, face another marked for her sister.

"Please begin, Reverend." Rebecca pushed the words past the tightness in her throat.

"One moment." The reverend peered over her shoulder.

A gloved hand touched her elbow. "Lady Prestcote." Daniel's firm presence stood beside her.

Why would he come to a funeral for someone he'd hardly known—for someone beneath his station? None of Mama and

Papa's past friends of the Quality had attended Mama's funeral. They'd no longer acknowledged Rebecca and her family since they'd fallen on hard times and out of favor.

Yet here stood the Marquis of Wolston as if his appearance were the most natural thing in the world. He raised his elbow for her, and Rebecca looped her hand through, savoring his strength and warmth.

She peered over to see if Madeline was warm enough, only to find that Sarah and Lady Coburn had joined them, Lucy in tow. The group formed a semi-circle around the gravesite. Sarah flashed Rebecca a sympathetic smile as if to say, *I'm here if you need me.*

Lady Coburn handed Rebecca a delicately embroidered handkerchief in a motherly gesture that brought tears to her eyes. She used the handkerchief to blot them away.

Lucy drew Madeline up against her side, and the two friends huddled together for warmth.

A light banging sounded behind them, and Rebecca looked over her shoulder.

Lord McGower strode to the gravesite in full Indian military guard, a crescent sword bouncing off his hip. Lord and Lady Farsley walked beside him, and Professor Matthews scurried a few steps behind carrying a small bouquet. He placed the flowers on the plain pine box before joining the growing circle.

Tears burned Rebecca's eyes. These people—people she'd known only a week—were here not because of affection for Miss Blakeford but for herself. They'd become true friends.

The reverend started his memorial service by quoting from Ecclesiastes. "'To everything there is a season, and a time to every purpose under heaven. A time to be born a time to die...'"

Weeping, Lady Farsley fingered her wig. Lord Farsley draped his arm over her shoulder.

"'A time to kill, and a time to heal...'"

Sarah's head bobbed, and she jerked back awake.

"'A time to mourn, and a time to laugh...'"

Lord McGower cleared his throat but remained standing at strict attention, his loose garb whipping in the wind.

"'A time to embrace, and a time to refrain from embracing...'"

Sarah's head tipped onto Professor Matthews's shoulder, but he didn't seem to mind.

Rebecca eyed each quirky person in attendance. They didn't have to be here, but they had come.

With the exception of Professor Duval and Professor Bell.

~

*D*aniel placed his hand over Blue's to keep it warm. The reverend kept his message short but respectful. As shovelfuls of earth were dropped onto Miss Blakeford's coffin, Daniel turned Blue back toward Griffin Hall. He felt her shiver and drew her closer to his side.

She peered up at him with a look of awe that made him feel as though he'd charged into battle against all odds and returned victorious.

"Thank you for coming." Her tone held wonder, as if she couldn't believe he'd come.

He tried not to be too insulted. "It was the least I could do."

"But you didn't have to. You'd only seen Miss Blakeford on our tour of the grounds that one time. She was a mere chaperone, and you're a marquis."

"Quite right." He slowed to a stop, needing to convey his own selfish motives lest she think him more than she ought. "I came to show my respect, but I also came for you."

"Oh." Her eyes widened with disbelief.

Blue was nothing like the vapid, pretentious women of the *ton*. She was caring, selfless, and lovely on the inside and out.

To Lord and Lady Mercer's credit, they'd raised a genuine and unassuming daughter.

He must remain on guard, for Blue was the type of woman he'd want to marry and have by his side for the rest of his life. But not yet. First, he must discover her blackmailer and prove himself tough enough to protect her and whatever children the Lord blessed them with. He needed to be quick-witted enough to safeguard his family against all threats. He must succeed with his assignment and show his grandfather, Lieutenant Scar, and his country that he was an asset.

Mostly, he needed to prove it to himself.

They made the rest of their walk in silence. Once inside Griffin Hall, Daniel gestured to the other guests and their host, meandering toward the salon and drawing rooms. "They all came for you."

Her pretty blush reddened her cheeks.

The servants bowed and rushed to take his coat and hat.

"Do you like being a marquis?" She peered at him with renewed interest. He'd never met anyone with such insatiable curiosity.

"I don't believe anyone has ever asked me that question." Chuckling, he aided her out of her pelisse and handed the jacket to the butler. He guided her into the drawing room, where a few other guests had gathered for tea, and led her to a chair near the blazing fire.

Rather than sit, he leaned his arm on the mantel. "My challenge is to one day earn the respect my title holds. I don't believe a title is what makes a person great. The title, Marquis of Wolston, was rewarded to my great-grandfather for his service to the king in battle. He was the one who was great." He shifted to stare into the flames.

"You lead your family, hold political clout as a member of the House of Lords, and influence those who know you." She leaned forward. "Your title gives you an opportunity to make a difference."

Which had been one of his hopes when he'd joined the Home Office. Though perhaps he was helping his country in some way, his persona of a carousing philanderer made it more difficult for him to keep up those appearances as he was expected to do. He'd found a way to serve his king and country, but it bothered him that his guise as a libertine didn't honor his family name. "Me?" Adding a scoff as if it were a ridiculous notion, he said, "Save the world?"

She scooted to the edge of her seat. "But if you could save one person? Would it be worth it?"

"Yes." The single word punctuated the air with more emphasis than he'd intended.

When she smiled, her eyes lit as if they'd reached an understanding. "Then focus on saving one."

Had she, too, endeavored to save the world but instead focused on saving the life of her maid? Her passion to make a difference vibrated from her, crackling the air with potential.

Professor Matthews walked toward them, Mrs. Evans on his arm. She sat next to Blue, and the professor stood on the opposite side of the mantel and made the typical post-funeral conversation—how dreadful a death, but what a lovely service.

He'd questioned Professor Duval late last evening regarding who he'd paid to supply cadavers for his research. The professor claimed he'd had an agreement with Oxford Castle Prison, but they hadn't provided any resources lately. Either he, Professor Bell, or the both of them had to be lying. How else would the dead body of a chaperone who was staying at their same location wind up at the very school in which they were teaching and lecturing?

Greta's mention of others who'd gone missing leaned toward murder, and Professor Bell's wording of fresh cadavers led Daniel further down the path of foul play. Had financial incentives led the resurrection men to commit murder, and the professors neglected to question their undertakings for the promotion of science?

There had to be a way to identify some of the resurrection men and get them to talk. Perhaps if he spoke with the tavern owner about anyone recently paying off their debts.

Daniel nodded, but Blue's words rang in his head. *Focus on saving one.*

If only he knew who the next victim would be.

What did Miss Blakeford, the chandler, and the other missing persons have in common? They were of the working class and tended to be loners—people who wouldn't be missed right away.

Could he narrow the list of potential targets before tragedy struck again?

CHAPTER 18

"$\mathcal{T}$omorrow morning, I'm riding into town to recruit some subjects." Professor Duval, seated on Rebecca's left for the evening meal, adjusted his spectacles.

Rebecca poked at her steaming apple tart with her fork.

Lady Coburn's schedule of events had resumed the day after the funeral. Rebecca still reeled from the tragedy of Miss Blakeford's death and the brawl that broke out at the lecture. Did she dare question the professor regarding Mr. Tingley's accusations that Professor Duval experimented with his wife's health without his permission? Had he unwittingly caused Mrs. Tingley's death? Having read his books and after meeting him in person, it seemed hard to believe he would have done so intentionally. Professor Duval may come across as socially unrefined, but never as evil or having ill intent.

Even though Professor Duval hadn't come to the funeral, his nervous touching of his spectacles signaled his discomfort over her chaperone's death, especially after Miss Blakeford's body was identified as one of his cadavers. "I believe your presence will set the subjects at ease. You may accompany me if you'd like."

Maybe if she accompanied him, she could ensure no one was accidentally harmed. Her time with the professor was drawing short, with less than a week remaining as Lady Coburn's guests. Although she had a hypothesis about how to treat Madeline, nothing had been tested. Rebecca had suggested the use of foxglove as a treatment, but it seemed Professor Duval would proceed with the experiment he'd planned, with or without her. At least he'd foregone his idea of running his trial on the staff.

"You'll not only have an opportunity to make an impact on science"—one side of his mouth lifted in a priggish smile—"but also to obtain direct information that others will have to wait for until my book is released."

She couldn't wait for published results. Standing at another gravesite had only made Rebecca more resolute to find a cure for Madeline, and quickly. Experiments always posed some risks. Wouldn't it be better for her to be there to help mitigate any harm? "I would be honored to join you."

Daniel stepped into the dining room, late for supper, and Lady Coburn had a setting and chair brought for him between herself at the head of the table and Sarah to his right.

He sat diagonally across from Rebecca, who had Lord McGower on her right and the professor on her left. His gaze burned into her forehead as she ate a bite of apples in syrup that was both sweet and sour.

His words regarding Professor Duval rang in her memory. *You deserve to be treated better.*

And then she considered Professor Duval's protestors. *Your science killed him. We're people, not experiments.*

She swallowed and glanced at Daniel.

His lips pursed as if he had something to say but held back. Had he learned more of what had happened to Miss Blakeford? She itched for answers, but when could they find a chance to be alone?

Daniel's meal was delivered, and he relaxed in his seat, shifting his glass in a circle with one hand. When Sarah's head fell, resting on his shoulder, he didn't shrug her off. Instead, he switched to eating with his left hand so as not to jostle her, barely pausing as he spoke to the professors. "In all the commotion, I didn't get a good grasp on who those men were at the lecture yesterday. I'm assuming the knaves hadn't been invited."

"Quite right." Professor Duval sounded weary of having to do another retelling.

To Sarah's right, Professor Bell spoke up. "These groups pop up now and again. They're looking to cause a stir to hurt the university's funding. Science to them is a threat to faith, but King Solomon sought knowledge, and the Book of Proverbs states that knowledge and understanding bring life."

"Wisdom." Daniel sipped from his glass. "Solomon asked for the wisdom of a discerning heart to administer justice, and Proverbs reads, 'My son, let them not depart from thine eyes: keep sound wisdom and discretion. So they shall be life unto thy soul, and grace to thy neck.'" Daniel set his glass on the table, looking as though he'd like to lean forward but not jostling Sarah. "There is a difference between wisdom and knowledge."

Rebecca's heart swelled for the man who offered his shoulder to her friend while proving he valued wisdom over knowledge, handling the learned professors smoothly.

"Ah, we have a theologian in our midst," Professor Bell emitted a derisive snort. "Knowledge leads to wisdom, and to quote Sir Francis Bacon, 'Knowledge itself is power.'"

"So power is the ultimate goal?" Daniel raised his brows, seeming curious, but she caught a glint that turned his blue eyes to steel.

Was he challenging the professor's motives?

Professor Bell's nostrils flared, a muscle in his jaw twitching, but he chuckled. "We only seek to learn to better our society and benefit our king."

"Hear, hear." Daniel saluted with his glass, but his steel-eyes didn't soften the least.

The usually silent Mr. Kim set his cup down, staring at the remaining liquid, and quoted from Confucius, "'Real knowledge is to know the extent of one's ignorance.'"

"Indeed." Daniel saluted Mr. Kim with his glass. "If only we could be so self-aware."

"The men who interrupted the lecture didn't sound as though they were there to hurt Oxford's funding." Rebecca set her fork down. "Mr. Tingley was upset about his wife's passing. I heard no other motive in his accusations."

Daniel flashed her a warning look.

Why? What was he trying to tell her? To watch what she said? Was he afraid she'd reveal their suspicions about Miss Blakeford's death? Or something else? What had he found in the alley?

"I'm certain it was a misunderstanding," she added so Professor Duval wouldn't become defensive and shut her out as he had before. "But why would he believe you had something to do with her death?"

Daniel glared at her. She'd said she'd believed the accusations to be in error. Didn't he want to hear the answers and try to understand Professor Duval's side?

"Of course it was a misunderstanding." Professor Duval pushed his half-eaten tart away.

Professor Matthews nodded, leaning forward to listen from the other end of the table.

"Lady Prestcote was ushered into another room." Professor Bell addressed his colleague as if Rebecca weren't sitting across from him. "A woman wouldn't be privy to the understanding of men."

He spoke as if she were feebleminded, as if a bunch of men coming to blows was too difficult for her to comprehend.

"Indeed. The weaker sex is unable to grasp why men would defend their reputation at all costs. Duels are a prime example." Professor Duval issued her a side glance, as if to gauge her reaction to such an insult. "Yet I can assure you, Lady Prestcote is a uniquely able woman."

Her jaw relaxed at Professor Duval's compliment.

"However..."—Daniel peered at her as if to communicate a message—"she should have the wisdom to use more of her father's diplomacy in her questions."

Rebecca swallowed her shock, stricken by Daniel's rude comment.

Lady Coburn rose, which awakened Sarah. Her cheeks reddened as she looked at Daniel. "Dreadfully sorry."

"Think nothing of it. Happy to be of assistance."

"Ladies, shall we let the men continue their discussions while we adjourn to the salon?" Lady Coburn extended her hand toward the door.

The men rose and pulled back the ladies' chairs.

Rebecca stood, thanking Professor Duval for coming to her defense.

He nodded. "I look forward to our outing tomorrow."

"Indeed." She flashed him a grin and excused herself, eyeing Daniel with a frown as he passed.

She didn't miss when he placed a hand over his heart as if she'd just stabbed him. How could the same man who'd been so caring and kind earlier be censoring and teasing toward her now?

Had this been how Mama felt when Papa had come home? He'd bring her a gift but provoke her, holding it just out of reach. She'd jump and reach on her tiptoes, but Papa would merely hold the gift higher until she gave up. Only then would he hand it to her.

Rebecca couldn't say the same for her heart. Daniel seemed to have snatched it and held it out of her reach.

Confusing, confounded men. She needed to stop letting them distract her from her goal.

~

*A*fter excusing herself to retire for the night, Rebecca climbed the stairs to her chamber, still mulling over the evening meal's conversation. Of all the pigheaded things to say—that she should use more diplomacy. As much as she wanted to know if Lord Wolston had discovered any more information regarding Miss Blakeford's death, she didn't think she could stand being in his presence at the moment.

The arrogance of men. How dare he reprimand her in front of the professors?

She stomped down the dimly lit hall but received no satisfying sound from her soft-soled slippers to cool her ire. Wall sconces she passed barely illuminated the portraits of Lady Coburn's ancestors. Their grim faces suited her mood.

The nerve of Daniel kissing her and then later insulting her diplomacy skills. Just because her father wasn't truly a diplomat didn't mean she lacked the talent.

An arm snaked around her waist, yanking her into an alcove several doors down from her chamber.

She struggled and screamed a muffled wail.

"Blue, it's me." Daniel whispered in her ear.

She stopped trying to scream, but as soon as he released her, she whirled in his arms. "How dare you!"

A sly grin twisted his lips.

The amused expression infuriated her, and she swatted him on the shoulder.

"Ow. Careful." He grimaced. "That could have been my injured shoulder."

"Oh, I know." She lifted her chin. "I was being *diplomatic* to hit the uninjured one."

His chuckle reverberated in her chest. She stepped back to escape his nearness and his enticing sandalwood musk, but he pressed a hand against the wall to block her exit.

"Don't tell me you're still sore over my comment." He touched her chin, his gaze softening.

Eyeing his injured shoulder, she said, "Perhaps I wasn't clear." She raised her hand to swat him again.

He grasped both her wrists. His teasing spark turned deadpan. "I had to deter you from questioning them further."

"Why?"

"We don't know who we're dealing with," he whispered. "The more they think you know, the more you'll become a target."

"A target?" Her words were too loud in the small alcove.

"Shh." He turned his head as if listening and stepped closer, his knee brushing her outer thigh.

She jerked back against the wall.

Heat rolled off him, warming her skin as if she stood too close to a fire. His lips hovered near her ear. She felt his deep inhale, his chest expanding while hers collapsed.

She moved her hands to the lapels of his jacket to keep a buffer between them. Even through the thick fabric, she felt his muscles tense.

He's a distraction. Don't be distracted.

The voices of Lord and Lady Farsley sounded on the stairs.

"We can't talk here," Daniel whispered, his voice so low she could barely make out the words. He pulled her out of the alcove and diagonally across the hall.

She nearly had to run to keep up with his long stride.

He opened a door and swung her inside a dark room.

The scent of sandalwood enveloped her.

Merciful heavens. She was in his bedchamber.

He held the knob to avoid the click of it shutting and stilled to listen.

The voices grew louder. Lord Farsley's shuffle steps stopped outside the door.

Rebecca held her breath.

"What is it, darling?" Lady Farsley asked.

"Nothing, my dear, just the scent of love in the air." Lord Farsley's shuffled steps continued down the hall, and Rebecca breathed once more.

Lady Farsley giggled like a maiden. A moment later, a door opened and closed.

That was close.

Daniel let go of the knob and turned to face her. She skirted around him to exit back into the hall, but he gripped her shoulders.

"I can't be in here." She tried to shake him off. "What if someone discovers us? What if your valet enters?"

"I don't travel with a valet. You're safe with me." He turned on the lamp on the bedside table. "I have information we need to discuss."

"This isn't wise." Rebecca hugged herself and eyed the door, knowing she should leave, but curiosity kept her feet planted.

He turned up the lamp, its light revealing a tidy chamber, nothing out of place except a book that lay open in the center of the four-poster bed. He removed his jacket and tossed it over the corner of the bed, and she gripped her hands at her waist, trying not to be overwhelmed by his masculine form.

Don't be distracted. Her hand squeezed until her fingers numbed.

"I apologize for the impropriety. If there was another place we could talk without servants or guests listening in, I would have chosen it." He moved to the window and drew back the curtain, peeking outside. "Professor Bell's out for his nightly stroll, I see. It seems Professor Matthews has joined him." He gestured to a chair near the second window. "Please have a seat."

She forced a steady pace as she crossed his room, catching his crooked grin as she passed him, but refusing to look him in the eye until she sat. Under the intensity of his stare, she found herself once again wishing she could blend in with the draperies. As frightening as the ball had been, it was nothing compared to this.

He leaned against the bedpost, looking not at all like the weak lad he claimed he used to be. "I visited the alley where the note directed Miss Blakeford to go. There was evidence that she fought against an attacker, scuff marks from a boot, a few strands of blond hair, a broken fingernail, and an empty bottle of laudanum. My theory is that the contents were forced down her throat, resulting in her death."

"Forced? Oh, my." Rebecca should have required the chaperone to attend to her duties and stay by Rebecca's side, but how could she have known what would happen to her? A chill replaced her earlier warmth, and the hairs rose on her arms. "She was murdered?"

"It appears so." He scooped his jacket off the bed and swirled it around her shoulders.

A blast of sandalwood and masculinity overwhelmed her senses as she gripped the fabric to keep it from sliding to the ground. "Thank you."

He returned to leaning against the post. "I've also discovered that Miss Blakeford wasn't the first to disappear."

"There were others?" Rebecca gulped. "Also murdered?"

"Perhaps. Their bodies haven't been located, but their homes looked as if they'd intended to return. I wonder if their bodies, too, might have been sold to the university for science."

"Did you notify the constable?"

"I've sent word to the proper authorities. They're searching the university."

Silence fell over the room. Rebecca stared at the pattern on the rug until it blurred, her thoughts screaming like inmates in a sanitarium. Was Miss Blakeford killed for blood money? Restless uneasiness had her standing. "But why Miss Blakeford?"

He rubbed his chin. "It seems the victims all held little in the way of family, connections, and funds. Almost as if the rogues targeted people whose disappearance wouldn't be noticed."

"But we noticed Miss Blakeford's absence."

"Not right away. We wouldn't have sounded an alarm if you hadn't discovered her remains at the lecture. Most assumed she'd abandoned her duties voluntarily. Remember, Lady Coburn suggested she'd gone to visit family."

"True." Rebecca squeezed her eyes shut. "I should have done more—said something sooner. If I had, then maybe she wouldn't be dead."

"You're not to blame." He stepped closer and touched Rebecca's elbows. "Miss Blakeford sneaked away, informing no one of her plan. You couldn't have known."

Her head tipped back to look at his face, his concerned frown.

"I don't want you spending the day with Professor Duval."

Daniel must've heard her remark as they'd left the dining room that night.

"Why?" She stepped back. "You think he had something to do with the murder? Certainly not."

Professor Duval devoted himself to saving lives, not taking them. She wanted to be involved in the experiment that might discover a cure for Madeline. If Duval was accused of being a part of this...this horrid scheme, it could end their work.

"He wasn't responsible for the bodies brought in for dissection," Rebecca said. "He told you so himself. Doesn't the university provide them?"

"They do through the proper channels, but I believe Miss

Blakeford was murdered and the professors have motive to acquire...fresh bodies for their research. I don't want you with him." Daniel's voice was gruff.

She stiffened at the command. "You have no right—"

"Please, Blue." He softened his tone and rubbed her arms.

His jacket slid to the floor.

He cupped her face. "I want to protect you."

Her stomach climbed up into her ribs. Oh, how she desired Daniel's protection, to be encircled in his arms, and forget who she was—and who she wasn't.

An icy wave washed over her. She couldn't be distracted from her purpose. "To save Madeline, I need to go with Professor Duval."

His lips thinned. "No, you don't."

"He's trying to find a cure. I can't be distracted, or she could die." Proper dosage was crucial, and Professor Duval acted too lackadaisically about it.

"You're acting as though I'm the young swain who took you for a carriage ride the day your aunt passed, not a serious suitor." His hands dropped to his sides.

"Of course, I'm not." Or was she?

Her heart screamed, *tell him the truth*. It was her mother who died, not her aunt. She should have been there. What kind of daughter leaves the woman who raised her in her time of need? But her fears countered, *the truth is too risky*. If he didn't understand her reasoning, Daniel could feel betrayed. If word got out, Professor Duval could feel foolish for being tricked and no longer associate with her. Lady Coburn could ask her and Madeline to leave for lying to her.

"I'm not like that boy. I care about you, and if your desire is to help Madeline, then it's my desire, too, but I need to protect you."

He stared at her as if waiting for her to reconsider and change her answer.

An attachment would only end in heartbreak. Curing Madeline must take top priority. Rebecca couldn't allow her thoughts to be diverted by Daniel's strong chin, slightly crooked nose, or cobalt eyes that fluttered her pulse. It didn't matter that he didn't mind her quirks and admired her intelligence. She couldn't allow herself to be so comfortable in his presence or smile so freely from his teasing.

She was not Corinne.

"I must go." She slid past him and turned for the door.

"Blue." He stepped into her path. "I'm more than a distraction." He gazed at her for a suspended moment, as if seeking her understanding, but her mind refused to consider anything but her sister.

And getting away from this confusing, confounded man.

He released a sigh and shifted her aside, out of line of sight from the doorway. He cracked it open and leaned out into the hallway, looking both ways. "It's clear."

He took her hand and, tucking her arm into the crook of his elbow, moved them both into the hall, making it look as though they were a couple on an evening stroll. He stopped at her door and opened it, bowing as she passed. "Please, consider my request. I meant what I said."

She glanced over her shoulder and caught the consternation in his expression before he closed the door between them.

CHAPTER 19

"*I*t's rather pleasant discussing basic scientific topics with you."

Basic?

Rebecca schooled her facial expression as she bumped alongside Professor Duval in the open, two-seater phaeton on their way into town to visit with potential subjects. He'd offered to drive the open carriage so that a chaperone wouldn't be needed.

"It's rare for a woman to comprehend what the male brain easily grasps." He struggled with the reins, trying to keep the horse from nibbling on the buttercups and grass that grew along the side of the road.

She stilled her tongue, stopping herself from exclaiming that she could not only comprehend, but she could also drive a full team—easily. Unlike him. With her papa having been off gallivanting about, she'd had no choice but to take over his duties, summing ledgers, making small repairs to their cottage, and driving a team of horses to bring their loads of jams, jellies, and picked goods to market to sell.

"You are a unique anomaly." He flashed her a smile. "I hope

I will be allowed the opportunity to...ah..."—he cleared his throat—"study you further."

Study her? Did he mean get to know her better? Was he flirting with her?

Gone was the arrogant professor. He issued her a nervous side glance.

"Are you asking to court me?"

"Um, yes, though the marquis seems taken with you. By no means do I compare to him in title or wealth, but I wanted you to be aware that there are other, more interesting avenues available to you. I would think that someone with a keen mind such as yourself would grow bored without intellectually stimulating conversation."

The arrogant professor had returned. Was he aware of how he'd slighted Daniel?

"You don't need to answer," he said quickly. "We can use our time running the digitalis experiment to test if we are agreeable, and if the results are favorable... Well, I must propagate the Duval family line. I wouldn't want my keen intelligence to die out with me."

Was he funning her?

But when he glanced her way, his expression appeared earnest.

"Thank you, professor." She flashed him a gracious but noncommittal smile. "I shall consider your kind offer."

They bumped along in silence as they drew closer to town, past honey-colored stone buildings and houses that were built close together along the side of the road.

If he could temper his arrogance, could she enjoy a life with the professor? Late-night discussions, sitting in the front row of his lectures, raising a family. Would he allow her to teach their children, or would he ship them off to boarding school? What if she bore him girls? Would he treat them as equals or look down upon his own girls as the weaker sex?

Daniel's face floated in her mind's eye. *I admire a woman with a mind.*

It didn't matter. None of it. Both Professor Duval and Daniel believed her to be Corinne Prestcote, daughter of the Earl of Mercer. When the professor and Daniel discovered that she'd tricked them, their pride would be wounded.

They would both resent her.

"If the digitalis has a positive effect upon the circulatory system, it would afford the university great accolades. I plan to write a book on the findings, so you'll need to take good notes."

She patted her travel writing bag next to her.

"Professor Bell is behind our work, especially since it means additional donors and funding." He chuckled. "It would be amusing if the findings got me nominated for vice-chancellor. Professor Bell and I would be in competition."

Professor Duval turned the horse into the village square where two-story buildings lined the street and storefronts set their wares out for display. He peered at the tavern up ahead and adjusted his spectacles but quickly gripped the reins again with both hands. "What is going on?"

In the square, a large crowd gathered on the green. Mostly men, huddled in a tight circle, cheering and shouting at whatever horseplay was happening in the center.

"The tavern owner promised to write a list of names and addresses of potential subjects we can visit—people with shortness of breath or heart issues." He reined the horse to a stop in front of the tavern, a busy street away from the commotion. "Wait here. I will be but a moment."

A cheer went up from the crowd as Professor Duval climbed down from the borrowed phaeton. He stopped to let a limping young man headed in the direction of the poulterer's shop pass before entering the tavern.

She eyed the tight cluster of people in the square, remembering the brawl from the other day. Perhaps she should go with the professor.

The circle broke as people stepped aside. Between them, a large man fell into the crowd.

She rose, holding onto the phaeton's side, and gripped her skirts with the other to step down.

The spectators caught him and shoved him back into the ring.

The other occupant of the circle moved into her line of sight.

Daniel?

Rebecca's grip tightened on the phaeton's side.

Sure enough, Daniel circled his opponent in the ring. His jacket and cravat were missing, and the sleeves of his billowing white shirt had been rolled midway up his forearms. He raised his hands in fists, holding them to guard his body as he eyed the big, surly man, who charged at him like a bull.

Rebecca gasped and held her breath.

At the last second, Daniel stepped to the side.

The man wasn't agile enough to change direction, his momentum propelling him forward.

Daniel popped the burly man in the stomach, which caused the man to pitch over. He landed sprawled in the dirt.

Some of the crowd cheered while others grumbled.

Daniel's rival pushed up from the ground and launched himself at Daniel, swinging.

Daniel ducked, dodging the swipe, and when his opponent swung again, Daniel blocked the punch and grabbed the man's wrist and pulled. The burly man, again unable to stop his momentum, tumbled into the dirt. He lay still, on his back.

Daniel stood over him, casting a shadow over the man's face.

Rebecca didn't have a clear view but saw the man's legs

retract. She imagined him cringing, preparing for another blow.

Instead, Daniel extended his hand to help his adversary up. The man hesitated but then accepted the aid, and Daniel pulled him upright.

The man remained in a bent position, his chest and stomach rising and falling as he caught his breath.

Daniel clapped him on the shoulder and said something, smiling.

The crowd dispersed.

She felt stunned. She'd known Daniel was strong, having glimpsed it at the brawl the other day. But this had been something else. The man he'd fought must've outweighed him by two stones. Where had Daniel learned to fight?

She'd witnessed a few scuffles in her town growing up, but those men had been ham-fisted compared to the skill and agility Daniel had showed, and his shoulder, though improved, was still injured.

Daniel's voice rose above the din of the street noise as he joined his opponent and walked to a rain barrel near the tavern. The burly man blocked Daniel from her view, but she recognized his voice. "You've got some girth in that arm of yours. One wallop could knock a man senseless."

The man straightened if surprised by the compliment. "I'll be beggared if ye're not as quick as a rabbit."

"Have to be." Daniel turned and scanned the town square. "I like to keep my nose on the front of my face." His gaze landed on her. "Blue? Er...Lady Prestcote."

The burly man followed Daniel's gaze to where she stood in the phaeton. "Perdition. Is she the reason you were asking so many questions?" He whistled. "She's a pretty miss. I can see why you'd go out of yer way to do her bidding."

Chuckling, Daniel strode toward her and extended his

hand. "Please, come down. It's not safe to be standing in a carriage."

He seems taken with you.

Professor Duval's words rang in her ears, and the way Daniel peered up at her with concern in his eyes caused her heart to press so hard against her ribs that she feared it might squeeze through. It didn't help that he exuded sheer masculinity and raw power like the Indian panthers she'd read about.

She wanted to leap into his arms, to ignore the niggling of her conscience that reminded her of her responsibilities and the fact that she'd been lying to him. She wanted to open her heart and experience uninhibited joy.

But she gripped hard to the seat back, afraid to get distracted and fail in her mission. She managed her own joy. If it were up to her, she wouldn't find happiness until her sister was cured.

The horse neighed and backed a step, jostling the phaeton. She wobbled and pitched forward.

Daniel wrapped his arms around her legs, and she grasped his shoulders to keep from falling. The thin material of his cambric shirt did little to hide the muscles that flexed under her touch. His cravat had been removed, exposing his tanned neck and the muscular cords leading down to the hollow between his collarbones. Heat rose into her cheeks, and she dropped her gaze, only for it to slide down his sweat-damp shirt, clinging to his muscular chest and forearms. The heat in her cheeks exploded into a blaze.

His eyes met hers, and she toppled into their rich blue depths. His hands encircled her waist, and he hoisted her out of the phaeton and gently placed her feet on the ground. Even then, she struggled to get her breathing back into a consistent rhythm after feeling the ease with which he lifted her.

The man over Daniel's shoulder chuckled. "Aye. I'd do

whatever the lass asked. Go ahead. Ask yer questions 'bout her chaperone. I won't stand in yer way any longer."

His words snapped Rebecca out of the mysterious spell Daniel had cast upon her. "I don't understand." She broke his gaze and peered at the stranger. "You fought to ask questions?"

"Townsfolk are protective of their own, a trait I admire. They don't take kindly to an outsider snooping around and posing questions to their neighbors and friends, as I was doing." Daniel faced the man he'd fought but kept one arm around Rebecca's waist. "Lady Prestcote, may I introduce you to Mr. Craig?"

Mr. Craig bowed. "Pleasure to meet you, milady. I'm right sorry you had to witness us coming to blows."

She bobbed a small curtsy. "I'm grateful no one was injured."

Mr. Craig grunted. "Only my pride."

"Don't hang your head," Daniel said. "You put up a good fight."

"What of your injured shoulder?" Rebecca frowned at Daniel. "You could have dislocated it again."

"Feels right as rain. Besides, I only swung left-handed."

"You fought injured?" Mr. Craig's eyes widened, and he shook his head. "Don't be letting the townsfolk know that, or I'll never be hearin' the end of it."

"You can count on my discretion," Daniel said.

The door of the tavern opened, and Professor Duval strode out.

Daniel eyed her with a disappointed look.

Spying Daniel and Mr. Craig, the professor faltered a step. "What is going on here?" His expression soured. "By Jove, were you the fellows engaging in pugilist activities?"

Daniel faced the professor. "All in good fun, old chap."

Professor Duval's gaze shifted to frown at Daniel's hand resting on her waist.

Chuckling, Daniel removed it.

"I must be off as well." Mr. Craig bowed to Rebecca. "Pleasure meeting you, milady." He nodded at Daniel and the professor. "Guv'nor." He sauntered into the tavern.

Daniel strode to his horse, tethered near the inn, and retrieved his jacket from his saddlebag. He donned it and his neckcloth, which he tied into a proper knot as he returned to them. "Have you come to town on a shopping excursion?"

Professor Duval's chin pulled back as if affronted. He raised a piece of paper. "We're here to study the effects of digitalis on people known to have shortness of breath or heart palpitations."

"Isn't that plant poisonous?" Daniel peered past the professor, and Rebecca turned to see what had caught his attention.

A young man limped across the street.

"In smaller doses, it has shown promise to be used as a treatment for heart ailments. I intend to conduct a static group comparison to study it."

Daniel's gaze narrowed on the limping lad, and he continued to track the young man as he addressed Professor Duval. "How do you know the dosage? You wouldn't want any accidental deaths."

Her breath hitched. She hadn't shared her fears with Daniel —at least, not yet. Did he hold the same concerns?

Professor Duval's nostrils flared. "What are you insinuating, Lord Wolston?"

"Nothing, of course. Obviously, one can never be too careful. I must beg your forgiveness." He bowed. "There is something pressing I must handle."

He crossed the street, dodging a passing carriage.

What was so important he needed to rush away? Did he know the man with the limp? Rebecca tried to track his movements, but horses and carriages in the square blocked her view.

"I'm an expert!" Professor Duval yelled after him. "All of my experiments are conducted in a professional and safe manner."

She scanned the storefronts along the square, but there was no sign of where Daniel had run off to.

"Shall we?" Professor Duval assisted Rebecca back into the phaeton before climbing beside her and snapping the reins.

She grasped her bonnet in one hand and the side of the carriage with the other as the professor maneuvered a precarious path down the main road, then veered off onto a bumpy lane.

"Beastly primal." He shook his head. "I daresay, it's beneath the marquis to participate in such acts. Lowering himself to fighting. Bah."

The image of Daniel's fluid agility as he'd dodged a blow and used Mr. Craig's momentum against him flashed through her mind. Had he really lowered himself to fighting if he were merely defending himself from attack? Plus, the way he'd aided Mr. Craig up and offered remarks intended to save the man's pride showed he was a gentleman.

If she wasn't mistaken, Daniel and his opponent had parted as friends.

"His daily fencing spars with Lord McGower are fitting for a man of his station." Professor Duval grunted his disapproval. "He should stick to those."

Remembering the marquis's eloquence with his words and the animal magnetism he exuded had heat filling her cheeks again. She shouldn't have enjoyed the possessive way his arm had remained about her waist.

But she had.

CHAPTER 20

*D*aniel followed the lad with the limp from a distance down Leafield's busy main street—until he heard the young man's familiar voice. This was indeed the boy who'd assisted in snatching the chandler's body in the graveyard.

Daniel closed in.

The lad must've heard him coming. He glanced over his shoulder, then looked again. His eyes widened, and he hobbled faster, entering a tobacconist's shop.

Daniel slowed and strolled by the window as if shopping.

The lad limped quickly to the back.

Daniel strolled past another storefront before dipping into an alley and circling to the tobacco shop's rear exit. As he'd expected, the back door flew open, and his target fled out. Turning to tip his felt hat to a worker inside, he bumped into Daniel.

From behind, Daniel grabbed him by the shoulders. "We need to talk."

The lad struggled against Daniel's tight grip. "I got nothin' to talk 'bout. Never seen ya before in me life."

"Don't lie to me." The earthy smell of wet dirt combined

with the stench of unwashed male wafted under Daniel's nose. "What happened to the chandler's body?"

"I-I don't know. I swear on the grave on my pa. I just dug 'im up."

"Who paid you?"

"I-I can't tell. They'd kill me. Honest to God. I'd be a dead man."

"What makes you think I won't kill you?"

The boy twisted his head to peek over his shoulder. "Ain't you nobility? Don't ya 'ave to act noble-like?"

The lad had a point. Daniel chuckled, a deep-throated sound. "Wouldn't that be fortunate for you? If only you were so lucky."

His Adam's apple bobbed with a harsh swallow.

"What's your name, son?"

The filthy urchin pressed his lips tight.

"I can make you talk." Daniel wrenched his arm up until the young man lifted onto his toes and maneuvered him toward the constable's office.

"Wait. It's Giles. Giles Shepherd." A frantic lilt pitched the lad's voice higher. "Where are you taking me?"

"A few nights in jail can loosen those lips."

"Me mum would find out." He wilted, and Daniel fought to hold him upright, but the boy dragged his feet the few steps up the alley. "The whole town would know." His tone changed to a meek whine. "Please, guv'nor."

Daniel spun him around and grabbed his shirtfront. "Tell me who you're working for."

Fear paled Giles's face. "I can't. I'm a bug ta him. The boss would snuff me out and not have another thought about it. He'd make me whole family disappear."

"I won't let that happen." Daniel's grip tightened on Giles's shirt for emphasis. "Nobody's seen us together. No one will know we've talked. Just give me a name, and I'll make sure he's locked up where he can't touch you." Daniel led him up the alley but stopped before they reached the storefront. "Who was it?" He searched Giles's features for answers, but the lad radiated fright.

Daniel was all too familiar with fear, the realization of one's own inability to help. Of crumpling under pressure, clamming up and not being able to speak or even move. He'd worked hard to put those feelings to death. "If you tell me what you know, I'll pretend I never saw you filch from the dead chandler's pockets. Body snatching isn't a punishable crime in England, but stealing is."

"You can't keep me safe." Giles's voice quivered. "Mr. Nash thought his station would protect 'im."

"Who's Nash?"

"The attorney. Disappeared in Langley. He had the ear of the earl and mentioned the people who'd gone missin', suggestin' foul play. Look into what happened to him."

The broken bottle of laudanum and the blood that marred the stone wall flashed through Daniel's mind. Could this boy link Miss Blakeford's death to other murders? "Your employer paid you to kill him?"

Giles's eyes widened. "Don't pin that on me. I won't have nothin' to do with makin' 'em dead, but I dig 'em up."

"Come now, Mr. Shepherd. Give me something to go off of to find this blackguard, otherwise, I'll mention your name in the tavern tonight—talk about how you and I had an informative chat."

Giles studied Daniel's shirtfront before whispering, "The boss always chooses the lowest dregs." He tilted his chin up. "You know, bawdy women, beggars, vagrants, paupers. People who won't be missed. Mr. Nash was the first who had a family and a business. I was right surprised to dig him up till I heard he talked too much. The boss has connections and pockets to let. He'd have me put to bed with a shovel if I even mentioned his name. It don't matter if you're one of the patrician order."

"Who was with you the night you dug up the chandler? Who hit me with the shovel? I need more than what you've given me."

Giles dropped his gaze, flexing his toes and exposing a hole where the sole of the boot had separated. He stayed silent.

"You give me no choice, then." He gripped Giles's forearm.

"Ye're just like the rest of your sort." Giles bucked and thrashed. "Pretending to be noble but not caring about the likes o' me. Ye're askin' me to put me life and me family's lives in danger."

"All I need is one name to go after."

Giles's lips remained tight.

Daniel gritted his teeth. If the lad didn't work with him, then the Home Office wouldn't provide protection. If the so-called boss he spoke of was as bad as he said, he couldn't send the boy home and put the lad's life in danger. He'd been careful for them not to be seen together, but he couldn't guarantee it. There was only one way to keep the boy safe and make it clear Giles hadn't said a word to him.

"You give me no choice." He forced him out of the alley and across the main street toward the sign board hanging over the constable's door. "You're going here for your own safety."

"But guv'nor, please. If me mum hears I'm in the gaol, it'll break her heart."

"I'm certain she'd rather you be in jail than in the grave." He opened the constable's office.

Giles struggled.

"Lord Wolston." The rotund constable rose from his desk and tucked in a loose shirttail. "What an honor to have nobility in our small village. What do we have here?"

Daniel dodged Giles's elbow to his ribs and grabbed his other arm.

"Mr. Shepherd!" the constable bellowed, his face turning red from the effort. "That's enough, or I'll give you a good thrashing." He wobbled toward the cell in the back, keys jingling with each step. "Better yet, I'll fetch your mum and have her bring a switch." He unlocked the barred door and swung it open. "What did the lad do this time?"

Daniel shoved Giles inside the cell. "I witnessed him and another man rob the chandler's grave and pockets. He's confessed to digging up bodies."

"Young Shepherd?" The constable clicked his tongue. "Your pa, God rest his soul, would be sorely disappointed, and your mama's heart just might break all the way through."

Giles sagged against the rear wall and hung his head. "Don't tell Ma. Let her think I'm workin' in Langley. I wouldn't 'ave worked wit' 'em, 'cept we need the money or me siblings would starve."

Daniel's heart ached for the young man and his family, but it didn't change the fact that he needed to keep him safe and get him talking so others could live. He turned to the constable. "Give us a moment."

The man nodded and returned to his desk.

Daniel lowered his voice. "Tell me who else is involved, and I'll consider it." Giles turned and rested his forehead against the cold stone behind him.

There had to be some useful information he could gain from the young man. What of Lady Prestcote? "Does your employer work with a woman, or have you heard of him black-mailing a woman?"

A snort rang inside the dim confines of the cell. "Not bloomin' likely. He don't think highly of the weaker sex. I heard him say that women can't hold a decent thought. They're as reliable as leaves in the wind, goin' every which way."

Daniel exhaled the tension that had gnawed at him since he'd opened the letter addressed to Blue. At least that ruled her out as an accomplice. But someone had been threatening her. Who? Was it somehow related?

Giles sank to his haunches and covered his head as a sob escaped.

Professor Duval's comment from dinner the night before haunted Daniel. *The weaker sex wouldn't be able to grasp the full situation or the circumstances.* Professor Duval had a low opinion of women and their intelligence. Could he be the boss even though Blue was aiding him with his most recent experiments? *Egad.* Blue was alone with a potential murderer.

"I must go." He turned and, on his way out, passed the constable a few coins for his assistance in watching over Giles. "Give it a day or two before contacting his mother. If he talks, send someone for me at Griffin Hall—immediately."

Daniel stepped onto the sidewalk and turned toward the tavern and his horse. A man sat on a bench under the constable's window reading the *Morning Post.* Daniel didn't react when the man set the paper aside and fell into step beside him.

"Lieutenant Scar."

His superior was dressed to blend in with the townsfolk, wearing a well-worn jacket, breeches, and boots. How long had his superior been sitting there?

"I received your message."

"Did I keep you waiting long?"

"Long enough to witness your spar with a local man and hold a verbal battle with the professor."

He'd been watching that long and Daniel had just noticed him on the bench. He inwardly grimaced.

"I was about to get your attention when you darted off after the lad."

Daniel mentally reviewed every interaction he'd had that morning, analyzing his actions from the lieutenant's perspective. Would he be upset that Daniel had engaged in a fight or impressed by his skills and how he'd easily bested his opponent? Did Scar notice Daniel's protectiveness toward Blue? Had he sensed the subtle tension between Daniel and the professor? Scar should at least be pleased with how Daniel had located and jailed one of the body snatchers. Daniel bit back his compulsion to defend his actions. The time for that might come soon enough.

"This way." Lieutenant Scar pointed inside the stationer's shop.

Daniel hesitated, desperate to ensure Blue's safety. But how could he deny his superior?

The lieutenant held the door open. "This won't take long."

Daniel entered the stationery shop, removing his hat but keeping it in hand. The smell of fresh ink and musty books filled the air. Shelves of tomes lined the walls, and milled paper was stacked on tabletops. He nodded to the stationer, who finished slicing a large section of paper with his paperknife and glanced past him to Lieutenant Scar.

"The room you requested is upstairs." The stationer pointed to the staircase. "Let me know if I may be of any service. For a good-paying customer like yourself, I'll be happy to run and get anything you desire."

"You're a gracious host." Scar bowed to the man. "A private room is all we need."

Daniel followed the lieutenant to the stationer's living quarters on the second floor and closed the door.

Lieutenant Scar gestured for Daniel to sit at a rustic kitchen table.

Daniel jerked the wooden chair a bit too hard, scraping the legs against the floorboards. He berated himself for displaying his nerves. The lieutenant would pick up on his every nuance.

"I'd like to question the lad myself." The lieutenant remained standing, a hand on the back of a chair across from Daniel.

His stomach hardened like hot metal thrust into cold water.

Did the lieutenant think Daniel couldn't even handle a young man? He hadn't been given the chance.

"I'd like to try a friendly approach," Scar said. "Invite him to dine at the flat I've temporarily let above the chandler's house. See if a relaxed atmosphere loosens his lips."

Daniel clenched his hands under the table. This was *his* mission. How could he prove himself if the lieutenant interfered?

"The information you sent me changes the assignment." Scar sat across from him, lounging back in the hard chair and lacing his fingers across his middle. "Tell me about Miss Blakeford, her disappearance, and the others."

Daniel explained what he'd ascertained from searching Miss Blakeford's room and the alley, adding the information he'd gathered from Greta at the tavern.

"You'd originally believed Lady Prestcote was involved with the body-snatching ring?"

"I didn't want to rule her out. I'd intercepted a letter demanding Lady Prestcote not tell anyone of some arrangement and to finish her task, threatening consequences. The sender signed merely with the letter *C*."

"Could Lady Prestcote have had a hand in her chaperone's disappearance?"

"Of course not. She's not of that ilk."

"Are you certain your feelings for Lady Prestcote aren't clouding your judgement?"

Daniel forced a deadpan expression. "I admit I'm fond of Lady Prestcote's intelligence, but I'm a professional. I base my opinions on facts and godly intuition."

Scar studied him for a long moment, and Daniel fought not to react to the scrutiny.

"The letter was vague. For all I know, the plan could be to snare a husband, but I presume guilty until proven innocent. A second letter arrived instructing her to 'stick to the plan.' Giles

Shepherd told me that his ringleader holds little regard for females and believes the man wouldn't work with someone of the 'weaker sex.' I admit to chasing a bad lead, but I still wonder if Lady Prestcote is being blackmailed."

Daniel paused to see if his superior had any input or criticism, but the lieutenant said nothing, so he continued. "Professor Duval has moved up on my list of subjects for several reasons. His work requires fresh bodies to be dissected to advance his studies of the heart, and he'd been treating a woman who died. The husband blamed Duval for her death. Also, the professor has verbalized his belief that women are vapid and unreliable."

The lieutenant leaned forward, resting his forearm on the table. "I looked into Miss Blakeford's background. She'd held two positions in her short life, both as a governess. After her first decade serving a small family in Bromley, Miss Blakeford entered the Prestcote's employ when their daughter, Corinne, was three and ten years old. Next month, when Lady Prestcote debuts for the London Season, Miss Blakeford is supposed to resume another governess position in Surrey. Miss Blakeford has never been a chaperone, nor does she have the credentials."

That would explain the woman's poor performance in the role. Had she been blackmailing Blue? No, the letter had been sent from Buckinghamshire. Was Miss Blakeford sent to ensure Blue 'stuck to the plan'? Or had her death been an example of what could happen to Blue if she didn't cooperate with whatever devious plot was being implemented?

Scar leaned back. "However, it isn't uncommon for a governess to fill in if a chaperone has fallen ill and family members can't be present." He tapped his lips with his index finger. "One thing that struck me as odd, though, is that my wife claimed she'd met a Lady Corinne Prestcote in Surrey."

Daniel shrugged. "The Prestcote's summer residence isn't far from Surrey."

"This was three nights ago."

He straightened. "Impossible. Lady Prestcote has been at Griffin Hall for over a week. While I haven't been in her presence the entire time, it would be too great of a distance to travel to and back from Surrey in a day."

"Abby didn't speak directly to Lady Prestcote. Perhaps she was mistaken." Scar's gaze grew distant until he gave his head a shake. "I believe your godly intuition is accurate on Lady Corinne Prestcote's account. Something isn't right. I want you to keep an eye on her, if only because she may stumble upon information due to her interactions with Professor Duval."

"Of course."

The corner of Scar's lips twitched.

Had he agreed too eagerly?

"Professor Duval no longer trusts you."

"What makes you say that?" He'd ingratiated himself well with the professors.

"He sees you as competition for Lady Prestcote's affections. You'll have to use her to get information on his whereabouts and interactions, which means you can't discourage her interactions with Duval."

A jolt ran down Daniel's spine. "That could put her in harm's way."

"The murdered women have all been of the working class, their disappearances hardly noticed. If an earl's daughter went missing, all of England would be up in arms. Her status will protect her."

Daniel wanted to argue, but Lieutenant Scar wasn't finished.

"The Crown wants these disappearances to stop before the king's subjects take note and become fearful, and you need this assignment to be a success after the last debacle."

Daniel fought to subdue his frustration.

"Lady Prestcote's help could save lives. She understands

what the professor is doing and seems to be working alongside him. She's intelligent and capable. She's your best chance, especially since she appears to return your sentiments."

Sentiments? Daniel's breath caught. Why did Scar believe Blue had feelings for Daniel? And how did he know Daniel had feelings for her?

Scar chuckled. "When you've been in love yourself, it's easier to spot in others."

Love? By Jove, what madness was this? Someday, he'd need to settle down and sire an heir, but his career with the Home Office was just developing. He needed to focus on the task at hand. "I don't like sending Lady Prestcote into potential danger. She should at least be informed of the risk, what we're asking her to do, and that the Home Office is watching her back."

Scar shook his head. "You're useless to the Home Office if your cover's blown. Success in this mission will significantly elevate your internal ranking." Scar's eyebrows rose as if to emphasize his point. "Your grandfather would be notified. *By Jove*, he'd be the one pinning the medal on your jacket."

Daniel had vowed to prove to his grandfather that he was no longer weak. Recognition by the Home Office would fulfill his pledge. But what if something happened to Blue? Would it be worth it?

"Be careful not to let Lady Prestcote interfere with the mission."

Daniel's feelings must've been brandished on his face.

Scar added, "She's become your weakness."

Weakness?

Grandfather's voice rang in Daniel's memory. He'd been laid sprawled across the rug after his grandfather's shove. *You're too weak to be my grandson. It's time to toughen you up.* Hearing the word spill from his mentor's mouth sent a flash of heat through Daniel, especially after everything Daniel had done to eradicate all weakness from his body.

"Don't worry, ol' chap." Scar slapped the back of his hand against Daniel's chest. "Not all weakness is bad."

How? Weaknesses left you vulnerable, defenseless. Was the lieutenant saying Daniel being vulnerable to Blue was a good thing?

Lieutenant Scar rose. "Your Lady Prestcote is a clever woman. Trust in her wisdom—and God's."

Standing, Daniel sent up a silent prayer.

Lord, keep her safe and strengthen me with the courage to leave her in Your care.

CHAPTER 21

*P*rofessor Duval drew the phaeton to a stop at a small tenant farm, hopped down, and headed for the door. Halfway there, he seemed to remember that Rebecca was with him. He turned back to aid her descent.

"The tavern owner claims Mrs. Josting has been ill for some time with shortness of breath and heart palpitations." Professor Duval took Rebecca's arm and escorted her up the slate path that had grass and weeds peeking through the cracks. "The family is in desperate need of coin. Mrs. Josting relies solely on her granddaughter for income, which makes Mrs. Josting the perfect candidate."

He rapped the handle of his cane on the front door.

Rebecca hung back, squeezing her gloved fingers tight. She'd ensure no one was mistreated or hurt. *This is for Madeline. For a cure. For science and the benefit of many.*

"Coming." The voice sounded roughened with age.

Rebecca's stomach churned. She glanced back at the phaeton. There was still time to walk away. *But if Professor Duval continues and someone dies...if Madeline's condition worsens and you could have done something...*

Bile rose in Rebecca's throat.

The door opened and a woman with kind, rheumy eyes smiled at them, her wrinkles fanning out like the sun's rays. "Good day."

"Mrs. Josting." Professor Duval introduced himself. "And this is Lady Prestcote. The local tavern owner sent us your way because he's aware of your condition, and I believe we have a treatment that might help."

She tucked a few stray strands of gray hair beneath her frilly white cap. "I didn't expect callers this morning"—she inhaled several ragged breaths—"but please come in, and I'll put on a pot of tea."

Rebecca entered the cottage and stepped aside. Professor Duval followed but selected a high-backed chair near the hearth and seated himself.

Mrs. Josting shuffled into a cozy-looking kitchen with a well-worn wooden table and three wooden chairs. She moved to the stone fireplace and swung a pot over the fire, stopping to catch her breath several times.

"Please, Mrs. Josting." Rebecca fought the urge to assist the woman because she didn't want to offend her. "Don't go out of your way on our behalf. We will only be a moment."

"Heavens, child." She straightened and smiled at Rebecca. "We so infrequently have guests. I delight in entertaining. Please, have a seat. I'll be right in with the tea service."

Rebecca sat on the faded sofa, leaving the other chair near the fire for Mrs. Josting. The simple feminine touches to the warm and welcoming cottage reminded her of her own home. She twisted the tip of her glove.

Professor Duval seemed content to sit and wait. He pulled a packet from his overcoat pocket and set it on his thigh.

"You're planning on beginning the treatment today?" Rebecca whispered.

"Quite right." He patted the packet.

She swallowed hard. "If she agrees, you'll give her only the smallest of dosages."

His lips pursed, but he nodded.

She didn't feel reassured.

She leaned closer and lowered her voice even more. "You must be certain. I will not have any harm come to this dear woman."

"Stop being naive." He exhaled a deep sigh and issued her a patient grin. "Typically, there are side effects to medications. We are monitoring to see if the benefits outweigh the deficits."

"Death is worse than a mere deficit. We're administrating a toxin and must take extra precautions."

"I am a professional." He clipped his words. "This is the way science is conducted. We have a hypothesis, and we test it through experimentation, monitoring the results."

Professor Duval was the expert—renowned throughout the British Isles for his research. Who was she to question his methods? She tucked her hands under her legs to keep from fidgeting. Daniel's warnings not to go with Professor Duval and the encounter with Mr. Tingley had set her on edge.

Mrs. Josting shuffled into the room carrying the tea tray and sat in the open chair, setting the tray on a large footstool. "What brings you out this way?" She steeped the tea. "Are you new residents of Leafield?"

"We're guests of Lady Coburn," said Professor Duval, his tone kind, revealing none of his earlier irritation.

"Ah, staying at Griffin Hall. Lovely manor. My grand-daughter is in Lady Coburn's employ."

Lucy. Rebecca's cheeks, fingers, and toes tingled as the blood left her extremities. *Lucy Josting. Sarah's maid was her granddaughter.*

"Lady Coburn is a generous woman." Mrs. Josting poured tea and apologized for only being able to offer honey and not sugar. She passed them the cups. "Lucy brings home extra food, and she's given a Christmas goose every year."

"I've met Lucy." Rebecca sipped from her cup. "She's a delightful young woman."

A muscle in Professor's Duval's jaw twitched, indicating his dwindling patience.

Mrs. Josting beamed. "I'd do anything for my Lucy. She's a dear, sweet soul." She fingered a locket around her neck.

"Is that a picture of her in the locket?"

"Ach, no." Mrs. Josting patted it. "Lucy's mama, God rest her soul. Lucy's parents were killed in a fire."

"I'm so sorry."

"Bless you, child, but when God calls us home, then it's our time."

Madeline said much the same, accepting the possibility of an early death far too easily for Rebecca's taste.

"I live for Lucy and her younger brother until that time," Mrs. Josting said. "I do believe my grandchildren are why this ol' heart keeps beating."

"Speaking of such..." Professor Duval shifted to the edge of his seat. "We may have a remedy for your heart condition. It has been noted in multiple cases to strengthen the heart's contractions, aiding the blood's circulation."

Mrs. Josting furrowed her brow. "And that will help me?"

"Think of the blood as the oil, keeping the rest of the body working." He adjusted the corner of his spectacles. "Our treatment is in the experimental stage but is quite promising."

Mrs. Josting looked to Rebecca for confirmation. "Indeed. The benefits have been observed and documented. Our plan is to study the proper dosage for the most potential benefit."

Professor Duval held up the packet. "I have a small dosage with me today. You add it to your tea and drink it down."

"You believe it can help an old woman like me?"

"Indeed. It aids breathing and offers more energy to old and young alike."

Mrs. Josting pursed her lips. "I tried an elixir that some traveling physician sold to Lucy. All it did was make me jittery."

"Those quacks selling their untested tonics are problematic to the science of medicine. We're conducting this trial in conjunction with the University of Oxford to monitor the results scientifically."

"I place my trust in the good Lord. He's numbered my days, and I won't leave this earth until it's His will." She glanced at Rebecca, who forced her gaze not to lower. "But I'd like to help you well-intentioned young folk."

Professor Duval's shoulders straightened. "You could be helping thousands of people in the name of science. Think of it. Those who've struggled to get out of bed might be able to chop wood, walk to town, ride a horse, or climb stairs. This treatment could offer people their lives back."

"I could stand to be a little more spirited. Maybe I could get around to some chores so Lucy doesn't have to tend to them all on her days off." She peered at Rebecca. "You know my Lucy. She works so hard, the dear."

Rebecca cleared her throat. "Indeed."

"Very well." Mrs. Josting nodded to Professor Duval. "Let's give it a go. I'm going to ask for one thing in return." She peered at Rebecca. "Promise you'll keep an eye on my Lucy. Put in a good word for her and see that none of the guests takes advantage of her. She's a trusting child."

Professor Duval's head swiveled in Rebecca's direction, impatiently awaiting her response.

"Of course." She'd put in a good word for Lucy, and she could keep an eye on her, especially since Madeline had befriended her, and she aided Sarah. "I'll be happy to."

"Thank you, dearie." Mrs. Josting's smile crinkled the corners of her eyes, and she shifted her attention to Professor

Duval as he opened the packet and sprinkled the green powder into her tea.

She raised her palm to halt him, but he added the entire packet.

Was that a low dosage?

Professor Duval was the expert, but Rebecca gripped the sides of the seat cushion to keep from knocking the teacup from Mrs. Josting's hands as she sipped.

Mrs. Josting grimaced. "A bit of a bitter taste to it."

"Perhaps a half a cup for the first time," Rebecca said.

Professor Duval issued her a sharp look but addressed Mrs. Josting. "A full cup is required for the intended effect." He offered her a sympathetic frown. "The tea does have an unfortunate taste, I'm afraid."

Rebecca raised her brows. "You've tasted it?"

"I've read about the taste."

Mrs. Josting drank the entire tea as the professor waited.

"It might take some time to have an effect," Professor Duval said. "Do you feel any different?"

Mrs. Josting peered at the ceiling as if internally assessing, then looked at the professor. "I can't say I do."

"We started you on a small dose. Note your breathing and if your heart beats slower or faster." The professor rose and returned his half-full teacup to the tray. "We'll begin with a daily dose and gauge the reaction."

"We're leaving?" Rebecca hesitated to stand. "Shouldn't we stay?"

"There's no need." Professor Duval strode to the door. "I'll return tomorrow to check on Mrs. Josting's well-being." He bowed. "It was a pleasure to meet you, Mrs. Josting."

Mrs. Josting struggled to hoist herself from the chair, so Rebecca aided her. "It was delightful to meet you." She squeezed the woman's hand. "I know where Lucy gets her cheerful disposition."

"Thank you, dear."

"Come along, Lady Prestcote." Professor Duval donned his hat and opened the door. "We have more visits to make."

Rebecca ignored him, addressing Mrs. Josting. "Will someone be home with you?"

"My grandson should be back from tending the fields shortly."

"Rest today and note any changes." Rebecca stepped to the door. "If you have any ill-effects, send someone for us immediately."

"Don't fret, my dear. When it's my time, then it's my time to go. It's in God's timing."

Why did Mrs. Josting and Madeline trust in God when life was so fragile?

"Good day to you." She curtsied and exited.

Professor Duval followed her out.

Rebecca glanced over her shoulder. "Do you think it's wise to leave? Shouldn't we wait to see if there are any complications from the medicine?"

"I believed you above a woman's hysterics." He issued her a reprimanding look as he aided her into the phaeton. "Besides" —the professor snorted—"you can't expect for me to wait in that hovel all day."

She swallowed her gasp.

Perhaps Daniel was correct in his assessment of Professor Duval's character.

The professor thought higher of himself than he did of others.

Not only did those others—like Mrs. Josting—deserve better, but so did Rebecca.

CHAPTER 22

*O*nce again, you'll have fallen short, because you're weak.

Daniel gripped the reins tighter, as his horse galloped down the wooded lane.

Lieutenant Scar had assured him Lady Prestcote's title would protect her.

But what if he's wrong? What if I don't get to her in time?

Pushing back the intrusive thoughts, Daniel sent up a prayer. *Lord, protect Blue from ill-intent. Let no weapon forged against her prevail. Help me find her and save her from harm.*

Lieutenant Scar's warning also rang in his head. *Lady Prestcote is your weakness.*

He'd dreamed of being a knight, fighting for king and country and rescuing the damsel in distress. That required not leaving his damsel to battle against a villain all alone. He remembered Alicia's screams as the scoundrel carried her off into the night and how helpless he'd felt, struggling to stay conscious and failing his sister.

He spurred his horse on.

Not this time.

Pinpointing Blue's location took longer than he'd expected,

and the sun grew lower in the sky. The tavern owner had directed him to visit a widow's cottage first, where Professor Duval had shown the most interest in calling. He'd ridden to the location and found an elderly woman standing on a ladder about to climb onto the roof. Blood turning cold, he'd convinced the fragile woman to come down from her precarious perch. She'd exclaimed in a giddy voice that she hadn't had this much energy since she was a young lass. It had taken him precious time to repair the broken shingles, but how could he not? His Cambridge friends would scoff at the manual work, but it was the only way to prevent the woman from reclimbing the ladder.

Thanks to the soft dirt from last evening's rainstorm, he was able to identify and follow the phaeton's tracks. The occupant of the second cottage he tracked them to hadn't been endangering his life with risky home repairs. Mr. Tibbs was painting a landscape, claiming he'd felt a sudden inspiration. When Daniel asked about his recent visitors, the man mentioned that "the pretty little lass seemed a mite troubled."

Daniel begged the man's pardon and left. He needed to get to Blue before something happened to her. Now, his steed careened around a corner, and a break in the trees revealed a quaint house with a rustic porch and smoke puffing out of the stone chimney. The phaeton was parked underneath the shade of a large maple tree. *Thank You, Lord, for directing my path.*

He slowed his mount, and a figure rose next to the maple's trunk.

Blue.

He slouched in his saddle, overcome with relief.

She was a wondrous sight to behold, a mix of contradictions. Alluring beauty with an intelligent mind, a polite and timid mouse with a curiously bold streak.

Bright yellow leaves covered the ground and fluttered down in a steady shower with the breeze, creating a dynamic backdrop for her bewitching outline in a pale-green pelisse, her dark waves of hair twisted into a loose chignon.

He dismounted and moved toward her.

"Daniel?" His worry was mirrored in her widened eyes. A leaf landed in her hair. Without breaking eye contact, she pulled it out and held it between them by the stem. "I mean, my lord."

"Are you all right?" He finally reached her and gripped her shoulders. It took a feat of sheer willpower not to pull her into his embrace.

"Quite," she said in a meek voice.

"Where's Professor Duval?"

"Inside." She glanced toward the house before lowering her gaze. "I couldn't." Her lips trembled.

He removed his cape and twirled it around her shoulders as a means to comfort her and ward off the chill in the air.

She didn't object, merely grasped the edges.

He softened his voice and fixed the collar of his cloak around her, using it as an opportunity to draw closer. "You couldn't what?"

"I want to find a cure." Confusion swirled in her glassy hazel eyes. She cleared her throat, and her voice hardened with determination. "I must find a cure." Then her body sagged. "I just can't..."

He removed a blanket from his saddlebag and arranged it beneath the tree before lowering her to the ground so she could lean against the tree trunk. He tossed his hat aside and settled beside her, ignoring how perfectly she fit there. "No one is more dedicated to finding a cure than you."

"But these experiments... I can't do it. Professor Duval sees the patients as subjects, but I see them as a dear grandmama, a promising artist"—her voice cracked—"and a beloved sister."

The farmhouse was neatly tended, flowerbeds all around. It had a woman's touch.

Did the professor prey upon the weak so he could feel strong? "You believe the experiment could harm them?"

"A low dose shows benefits, but how does he decide the proper amount? It might differ between a man and a woman or vary due to a person's weight or other things. We argued over the proper amount on the carriage ride."

Her eyes clouded, and she appeared so torn—heartbroken. If he wasn't a gentleman, he'd call Duval outside and plant a facer in the man's nose. "Mayhap, God is protecting you."

"But what of the participants? If the foxglove works, it could save lives, but what if he overdoses them?" She gestured toward the house. "How can I live with myself if something happens to one of them?"

"You want to help Madeline."

She nodded and fiddled with a leaf in her lap, twisting the stem around her finger.

"It takes a special person to care for your maid the way you do. Do you remember the question you asked me? 'What if you could save one? Would it be worth it?'"

She flashed him a weak smile. "It would. It would be worth it."

"Then focus on each patient as an individual." He warmed her chilled fingers between his palms. "You have a caring heart. It's commendable that you see people as God's children—His unique creations—each special and loved in their own right. Perhaps God has put you in this position for a reason"—he pushed the words past his lips but vowed to not let her out of his sight until Duval was in custody or proven innocent— "because you see them as people and not as subjects. You have good intuition and wisdom that Professor Know-It-All doesn't. Use it to guard them."

"You're right." She placed her other hand on top of his and sighed a sound of relief.

"Just be on your guard." His grip tightened. "I believe God sent me here to protect you."

"I doubt God would even think of me, as little as I've prayed to Him after..."

"Your aunt passed?"

She nodded.

"He's thinking of you more than you know. My mother always said that God loves us more than a mother loves the babe at her breast, and if my mother's love was any testament, that's a tremendous amount of love."

His words drew a smile from Blue's lips, and his pulse skipped in response. She was constantly in his thoughts. And God loved her more...that was a lot. He squeezed her hand. "We can remedy the lack of prayer."

"Right now?" Her smile fell, and he chuckled.

"Indeed." He bowed his head, clasping her hands between his. "Lord, watch over Blue. Give her Your wisdom to find a cure for Madeline and to aid the people she's spoken to today. Give her a discerning heart regarding the dosage, and if it isn't correct, prompt her to speak—and Professor Duval to listen. Protect the patients from any harm that the overzealous professor may cause. Send your angels to guard them—especially Blue. In Jesus's name, we pray. Amen."

Her long lashes swept up, and a genuine grin curved her rosy lips.

"See, that wasn't so painful."

She chuckled. "It felt nice." Her green-gold eyes glittered, and she blinked away tears, sending a few to drip down her face. "Like coming home to a dear friend."

He wiped the tear tracks away with his thumb. He'd never understand how women could laugh and cry at the same time. Someday, he'd introduce her to his sisters. They'd get along famously.

"I happened upon Mrs. Josting and the artist..." What was his name?

"Mr. Tibbs?" She moved to her knees.

"Indeed. They seemed well."

Her lips parted in a whoosh of breath. "Thank goodness."

"I had to convince Mrs. Josting to stop trying to fix her roof. She said she had the energy of a lass, and Mr. Tibbs appeared hale."

Blue gripped his shoulders. "That's wonderful." She pressed a spontaneous kiss to his cheek and pulled away, a blush heightening her color. Her voice lowered. "I was so worried, but that is lovely news."

Behind him, he heard the front door open, and Professor Duval gave his regards to the person inside. Daniel donned his hat and rose, aiding Blue to stand. He turned to face his prime suspect.

Professor Duval faltered a step, spying him with Blue on his arm.

Daniel tipped his hat.

"Lord Wolston." Professor Duval bowed his head. "I figured you'd be at the tavern by now. What brings you this way?"

"The company, of course." He tilted his head in Blue's direction, ignoring the slight of character the professor had issued. He was playing a part, after all. He'd have to settle for irking the professor with hardy competition for Blue's attention. "I thought I'd join you."

"Unnecessary. Lady Prestcote and I are conducting an experiment. You'd merely be in the way."

"Ah, but if I'm to get in the lady's favor, then I must impress her with my wisdom, and that entails learning everything there is to know about the subject matter—the heart, of course."

A snort of laughter broke through before Blue covered her mouth.

The professor's sour expression indicated he wasn't as impressed.

Daniel aided Blue into the phaeton to sit beside the professor before mounting his horse. "Lead on, good professor. The day grows long, and I have much to learn."

"That's an understatement," Professor Duval muttered, leaning as if for only Blue to hear.

Her gaze darted over her shoulder, giving Daniel a nervous expression.

Why did she appear like a fox trapped between two hunters?

He winked at her.

Her eyes widened at his audacious gesture, and she jerked to face forward.

Surely, this wasn't the first time men had fought over her affections. Her innocent reaction was refreshing. Most socialites would have flirted with him, whether they knew how to go about it properly or not. Even though he'd had limited contact with Blue, they traveled in similar social circles, or at least they would. This Season would be her debut. No doubt she'd be an out-an-outer, greatly sought after.

Lord, thank You for the opportunity to get to know Blue outside the clamor of the Season.

Blue's affection was a competition he intended to win.

CHAPTER 23

"*A* letter arrived for you." Madeline lay under the bedcovers, waving the opened paper as Rebecca entered her chamber. "Guess who it's from."

Rebecca shut the door behind her and locked it before anyone caught Madeline lying abed. "How are you feeling?"

"Much better." Madeline patted the spot next to her.

Rebecca quieted to listen to her sister's breathing, but there was no wheezing sound, and the dark circles under her eyes had dissipated.

"You worry too much." Madeline pushed to a seated position. "I was reading and dozed off a bit, is all." She eyed Rebecca. "You haven't guessed."

"Cousin Corinne." Rebecca sank on top of the coverlet next to her sister. "How did she take the news?"

"You set her bristles with your last letter."

"In the eyes of our cousin, I can do nothing right." Rebecca groaned. "I presume she's upset that I didn't notify her sooner."

Madeline shook her head, but then fought a bout of hacking coughs.

Rebecca waited until the cough subsided. "Did you take the herbal tea I had the staff make for you?"

"Yes." Madeline waved her mothering away. "She's mad that you'd use the excuse of the missing governess to lure her away before the marquis arrived in Surrey. Wait until she finds out the marquis is here."

Rebecca snatched the letter from her sister's hand and scanned the contents.

You are overreacting. I will not allow such dramatics to ruin my Season. The marquis is expected to arrive any day now, and you're making up excuses for me to leave. Miss Blakeford has a fondness for laudanum. She may disappear for a time, but she'll return. Stay put and do not cause a stir.

"Oh, dear." Rebecca dropped the letter into her lap. "She didn't believe the seriousness of my first letter. At the time, we knew something had happened to Miss Blakeford, but I must write Corinne again and inform her that Miss Blakeford was indeed found dead."

"She won't like that letter either." Madeline shook her head. "What do you think she'll be more upset by—her governess's passing or that Lord Wolston is here with us and not with her?"

"We mustn't think such wretched thoughts about our cousin." Rebecca sighed. "She acted gracious toward us until Aunt Diana announced Corinne would be saddled with me during her coming-out. The Season was supposed to be her big moment to attract a husband."

"She feels threatened by you because she must share the spotlight."

"Hardly." Rebecca released an unladylike snort. "She's worried I'm going to embarrass her, and for good reason."

"What tosh." Madeline flipped aside the covers and faced

Rebecca. "You might not have the social experience that Corinne does, but you're a quick learner. After a ball or two, you'll be batting your eyes in the flirtatious manner of our cousin"—she flashed a coy smile over her shoulder in a fair imitation of their cousin Corinne—"or offering a gentleman your own come-hither smile."

"I'm a bluestocking and a farce. When the men of the *ton* discover Papa's debts and that I've no dowry, they will flee."

Madeline's lips pursed into a determined line. "You are loving, wise, and beautiful. There is a man among them who will value those qualities over a dowry."

Rebecca leaned back against the headboard, grabbed a nearby pillow, and covered her face. "What a hobble we're in."

"What?" Madeline yanked the pillow down.

"My finding a suitor keeps me from working to find you a cure, but unless I marry well, Father will be thrown in debtor's prison, and we won't have two pennies to rub together."

"God will make a way."

He didn't for Mama. No matter how hard Rebecca had prayed. Wasn't she better off searching for a cure than leaving it up to the Lord?

"Rebecca." Madeline squeezed her hand. "I know you have reasons to doubt. Even John the Baptist, who announced our savior, doubted. He sent a messenger to ask Jesus if He was the one, or if they should expect someone else."

"And then he was beheaded."

"Indeed, but Jesus told the messenger to report back to John of all the miracles He'd performed. The same ones predicted by the prophet Isaiah. Then Jesus spoke to the people, comparing John the Baptist to Elijah." Madeline reached for her Bible, flipped through the book of Matthew, and pointed to a verse. "'And from the days of John the Baptist until now the kingdom of heaven suffereth violence, and the violent take it by force.'"

"I don't understand. There's violence in heaven?"

The dark circles under Madeline's eyes only enhanced the sparkle of joy in their depths. "John the Baptist expected Jesus to come in a physical way, to take His throne as King to save Israel, but Jesus came and died a violent death to save the world spiritually. The Israelites believed their redemption would come in the natural, but a greater spiritual battle for our souls happened in the heavenly realms. That, at the time, was something the Israelites and John the Baptist couldn't fathom."

"But why did they have to die?" Rebecca blinked away hot tears stinging the back of her eyelids.

"You're asking why Mama had to die." Madeline's eyes shone with tears. "Thanks to Jesus, we don't have to fear death any longer. It's a transition, like a caterpillar turning into a butterfly."

"But we're left to suffer without her."

"We do mourn, but Psalms promises that our weeping endures a night and joy comes in the morning." She smiled through tears. "Think of it. How much closer have we become since Mama's passing?"

"Quite close."

"And Papa has returned to us."

Rebecca couldn't hide her frown.

"Mama's death opened Papa's eyes to how fleeting and precious life can be. He's come to understand the mistakes that he's made and is trying to amend them."

Rebecca lowered her gaze. "He should have been there for Mama. For us too."

"He knows it." Madeline tucked a stray lock of hair behind Rebecca's ear and leaned against the headboard, shoulder to shoulder with Rebecca. "That's why we must try to show him grace."

Rebecca bumped her sister. "How come I'm the one

spending hours studying books, but you're the one who's so wise?"

"It's because all the answers are in here." Madeline patted the Bible in her lap. She peered at Rebecca and her voice turned grave. "I'm not afraid to die."

Although her sister spoke the words softly, they rattled Rebecca like a crack of thunder. She scooted off the bed and covered her ears with her hands, not caring if she looked childish. "I don't want to hear it. I'm going to find a cure. I'm close. I know it. Professor Duval has begun trials."

"Fine." Madeline released a deep sigh. "Then tell me how today went. Is he enamored by your intelligence, or does he feel threatened?"

Rebecca snorted. "You have such romantic imaginations." Her thoughts strayed to the wink Daniel had issued her after declaring he was seeking her affection.

"You're blushing." Madeline scooted closer. "I want to know everything. Start at the beginning."

Rebecca filled her sister in on the day's events, from the professor's confirmation that he'd like to court her to her conversation with Daniel under the maple tree. She left out Lucy's grandmother being one of the test subjects. Madeline had grown fond of the young maid. Would she hold the same concerns that gnawed at Rebecca's conscience?

If Mrs. Tingley's death was an accident, surely, Professor Duval had learned from his tragic error and was more cautious in his proceedings. His reputation was on the line. She'd read over a dozen books on his research. Nothing in those earlier studies had caused her to question his ethics, and the university backed his work.

Madeline fell back into the pillows and fanned her face. "How did you not swoon? Two men in one day declared their intentions to court you." She rose onto her elbows. "They are both handsome but so different. Which one is your heart leaning toward? Professor Duval is intelligent and bookish like you, but Lord Wolston is suave, charming, and he gets you to laugh." She arched an eyebrow at her sister. "You could stand to have more levity in your life. Plus, he's a marquis."

"Exactly." Rebecca shook her head. "Which is why it's impossible. He believes I'm an earl's daughter, but I'm a nobody." She pressed her palms to her eyes. "Even worse, a nobody who has lied to him."

Madeline pulled down Rebecca's hands, a saucy smile twisting her lips. "So your heart is leaning toward the marquis."

"No." Rebecca rose from the bed and paced before the window. "My heart isn't leaning toward either of them."

Liar.

She refused to acknowledge that.

Madeline didn't say a word, but her expression conveyed the same. *Liar.*

"Ugh. How did I end up in this predicament? Papa shouldn't have left us without a pocket to let, and Corinne shouldn't have convinced me to go along with this disastrous charade. But I chose to involve myself in their schemes, so what does that say about me?"

"That you desire to help people."

Rebecca plopped onto the edge of the mattress. "Which is why I should be combing through more medical journals, finding alternative treatments instead of wasting time on things like love, especially a love as far-reaching as Daniel."

"Daniel?" Madeline's eyebrows lifted almost to her hairline. "You're on a first-name basis? You two are progressing better than I'd guessed." She glanced to the ceiling and mouthed a *thank you* to God.

"Don't go getting all fanciful. Professor Duval is a more reasonable choice, but my deception will injure his pride. I can only hope that Lord Wolston will understand our dilemma and hold his tongue once I explain who I am, so that my reputation isn't blackened before the Season even begins." She would summon the courage to explain her reasoning to Daniel tonight. "All the more reason why I shouldn't allow myself to be distracted from my goal."

Rebecca stood and opened the wardrobe. This evening, Lady Coburn would host a ball for her guests and a few select townsfolk. She selected a cream-colored gown with delicate roses and vines embroidered into the bodice and hem. The neckline was too daring for her tastes, and for the first time, she longed for one of her sturdier dresses so she wouldn't feel like an imposter.

She donned the gown, and Madeline aided her with the buttons.

"I must continue my interactions with Professor Duval because of the experiment, but I shall avoid the marquis." Rebecca twisted Corinne's elbow-length gloves in her lap. "It's better that way—for him, for me, and for Corinne. He was supposed to be at the Carter house party dancing with her, not here with me."

Madeline brushed Rebecca's hair. "Who's to say this wasn't how God intended? Indeed, we've been dealt challenges that we wouldn't have chosen, but God uses them. He has a plan for you—for us—in the middle of these storms. We must keep our eyes open for what God is doing."

The gentle, rhythmic pull of the brush settled Rebecca's nerves.

"Love isn't a distraction." Madeline kept brushing until Rebecca's hair crackled with static. "The whole reason you search so relentlessly for a cure is because of your love for me."

"You're my sister. I would do anything for you." She blinked back the sting of tears, overwhelmed by the love for her younger sibling. She remembered their shared history—tea parties, walks in the glen, confidences, and tears.

Madeline gathered Rebecca's hair into a twist. "Then I ask

that for my sake, you won't hold yourself back from love. Live life to the fullest, as Jesus wants you to do. If you hold back from love, you'll miss what Mama and I desire most for you."

"But if I want to save you, then I must focus..."

"Only God saves."

Rebecca's jaw tightened. He hadn't saved Mama.

"We are on this earth to love. Love is the point." Madeline retrieved the hot iron from the hearth and used it to create curls, which she pinned into place. "God says the greatest commandment is to love one another as we love ourselves. It's the reason you agreed to help Papa, why you came here for Corinne, and why you cover for Sarah when she falls asleep."

Madeline finished the task, then set the hot iron back into the fire and threaded a silk ribbon through the curls. "I think you're raising walls around your heart because you feel guilty for not being home when Mama passed. But Mama hated being a burden. She encouraged you to go on that carriage ride with Charles Benson because she wanted you to live your life, to enjoy the opportunities God put before you. I want that for you too. Don't use me as an excuse to hide in a book. Be bold and courageous. Don't be afraid to love."

Her sister issued a challenge that Rebecca longed to accept. But what if she failed? What if she couldn't win Daniel's heart? She'd tried to convince her Papa to stay, clinging to his pantleg and begging him not to go. She'd pleaded with him in letters to come home and received no response. Her father proved how paltry a man's love could be.

Could she put her heart out there again?

Burrowing into books was the safer option.

"All finished." Madeline smiled at Rebecca's reflection in the looking glass. "You look splendid."

Gathered curls crowned her head, and wispy ringlets framed her face. One pronounced curl curved around her neck and nestled like a pendant, pointing toward the bodice of her gown. Perhaps the strange woman who peered back at her from the looking glass could be bold.

Madeline set the mirror aside. "Promise you'll enjoy yourself—for me."

"I don't know if it's wise, but,"—Rebecca rose with a sigh—"for tonight, I shall try."

CHAPTER 24

*R*ebecca descended the stairs with Madeline in tow, acting as chaperone. She stopped in front of a footman and requested the second letter she'd penned to Corinne be posted. This note informed her cousin that her governess was dead, the marquis was at Griffin Hall, and it was he who believed Miss Blakeford murdered. Worrying about Corinne's response would avail nothing and only ruin the night she'd promised to enjoy.

"Lady Prestcote."

Daniel's silky baritone sent ripples of awareness through her. She turned, and he pushed off the wall as if he'd been waiting for her.

He bowed over her hand and, raising it, pressed the lightest velvet kiss to her knuckles. "You look stunning."

Warmth flooded her stomach like the swirl of morning chocolate with the promising scent of a new day.

"May I escort you into the ballroom?" His eyes twinkled, and a leisurely smile quirked one side of his mouth.

She glanced back at Madeline, who shooed her on with the subtle flick of her fingers. Her sister moved to stand with Lucy and the other lady's maids, present to handle torn hems and re-pin coiffures.

He led her down the hall and through the French doors the footmen held open.

As they stepped into the grand ballroom, the master of ceremonies announced their entrance. "Lady Corinne Savannah Prestcote, escorted by Lord Daniel Hudson Elmsley, Marquis of Wolston."

At the announcement of her cousin, Rebecca jolted. She resisted the urge to peek over her shoulder to see if Corinne stood behind her.

Daniel cast her a side glance, but she merely smiled to cover her folly.

Leafield's town officials and well-to-do had joined Lady Coburn's current guests for the evening. The Axminster rugs, tufted sofas, and Queen Anne tables and chairs had all been removed from the ballroom, making the high-ceilinged dance floor appear vast. A five-piece orchestra sat in the far corner and struck the chords of a minuet.

Daniel, being the highest-ranking member, excused himself to open the dance with their hostess. Guests moved to the center of the dance floor, except for Lord and Lady Farsley, who sat near the orchestra to watch or listen, and Mr. Kim, who chose to keep to himself. Sarah and Professor Matthews part-nered, and although Sarah looked weary, her smile brightened at the botanist's attention.

"Lady Prestcote." Professor Duval's assessing gaze roved over the length of her. Two of his gloved fingers tapped his lips while his elbow rested on his other crossed arm. He must have approved, for he dropped his hands. "Your gown suits you."

A compliment. Maybe? Sort of.

"Would you care to dance?" Professor Duval held up his palm.

She placed her hand in his, and they joined in the next set

for a quadrille, following as Lady Coburn called the figures. Professor Duval danced well but did little in the way of conversation. By his bearing, she guessed he was counting the steps.

Lord McGower, wearing a silk Indian-styled jacket that reached past his knees, asked Rebecca to stand with him for the next dance. An array of country dances, jigs, and cotillions followed, with various partners, including Mr. Kim, who turned out to be a graceful and exacting dancer. Rebecca maneuvered through the steps, grateful that Mama had insisted she and Madeline receive private instruction from a professional dance master. She leapt, clapped, and pirouetted with the lively dances, beaming an authentic smile as she swung from Professor Bell's arm past Sarah before hooking arms with Daniel. His grin matched hers.

When the music ended, Daniel approached and asked for the next dance. "You seem to be enjoying yourself."

"Quite." She curtsied. "I promised Madeline I would enjoy a dance for her."

"Your maid?" He took her hand and promenaded her in a slow circle.

"Indeed." She waited until the dance allowed them a moment of conversation. "You probably think it odd for a lady to befriend the staff."

The move called for them to step together. His masculine scent swirled around her as his husky voice vibrated her insides. "It's a testament to your character."

The set ended, but Daniel kept hold of her hand. "Care to take a turn about the room?"

Her heart leapt in a grand jeté, but she merely nodded.

~

*D*aniel promenaded Blue around the perimeter of the room, not missing the occasional glare from Professor Duval. "I fear I've made an enemy of the professor."

Rebecca tilted her head and studied Daniel as if expecting him to elaborate. "Professor Duval?" Her innocent expression questioned him. "Why do you say that?"

"You don't know?" He chuckled.

Her face grew solemn. "Because you question the ethics of his experiments."

Daniel's smile grew, and he shook his head. Blue was an anomaly. She held no pretenses, and a genuine glow radiated from her as if she were happy merely to be in his presence. Not because he was a marquis. Not because he was next in line for a dukedom. Not because he was named the most sought-after catch of the Season. But because she enjoyed his company. "Because you're strolling on my arm and not his."

"Oh." She glanced at Professor Duval, who was dancing with Mrs. Evans.

The professor glanced their way. Daniel dipped his chin in greeting. Did the professor's eyes narrow?

"Daniel."

His chest swelled at her use of his given name.

Her eyes widened. "I mean Lord Wolston."

"Please, call me Daniel. I call you Blue, after all." *Corinne*, in his opinion, was too cold to fit her warmth and natural beauty.

She lowered her gaze, the dark fringe of her eyelashes contrasting against her rosy cheeks. "I'm not who everyone thinks I am."

Neither was he. There was more to a person than what the *ton* saw. She put up a good front, acting the part of a socialite, but intelligence abounded in her bright mind. She cared deeply for people, even her maid. Her heart hadn't yet been hardened by the fickleness of the *ton*. And it wouldn't be if he had any say in the matter.

"I fear I'm a bad person." She blinked as if fighting the sting of tears.

He stopped and turned to face her. "Come now. How can you say such a thing?"

"I wasn't there for Mama when she needed me. I want to be there for Madeline but..." The hollow dip at the base of her slender neck deepened as she swallowed. "I want her to be healed, but I fear I won't find a way in time, and I'm having second thoughts about how the experiment is being conducted. Madeline is my closest friend, and Lucy's grandmama means the world to her."

"Who's Lucy?"

"Sarah's maid. Her grandmama, Mrs. Josting, has a heart condition and is a participant in the trial."

Of course, she'd befriend another maid and the maid's grandmother. He swallowed his grin. "And you're worried the experiment may hurt her."

She nodded.

"Remember what I said?" He continued their stroll.

"Pray and ask God for wisdom, but how can you be so sure He'll provide? I prayed, but God didn't spare Mama's life."

"You mean your aunt?"

"Yes, my aunt." Her lips moved soundlessly as if gathering her thoughts. "We were quite close."

"So you've said." Odd that she kept confusing her mother with her aunt.

She lowered her gaze.

He made a mental note to check his files on her family once more. "I had the same question when my father's ship sank. I didn't like that God's answer to my prayers to bring Papa home safely was no. A boy needs a father. I missed him terribly, and Mama's despair tormented me. But even though I don't understand, Papa's death made my family close in a way nothing else could have. We leaned on God and each other."

He chuckled. "It was my father's death that brought Mama's mollycoddling of me to my grandfather's attention. He decided it was past time I toughened up. I was the man of the house and needed to learn to protect my mother and my sisters. He brought in the best people to teach me how to shoot, fence, and spar."

"And you practice with Lord McGower to keep up your skills." Her face brightened as if putting the pieces together. "Because you rose to your grandfather's challenge, you thoroughly bested Mr. Craig, even though he was much larger."

Daniel basked in her praise. "Although tragic, my father's death changed the trajectory of my life. It set me on a path that I hope would make him proud."

Blue bit her bottom lip as if processing that. "How did your faith become so strong?"

An intuitive question. He should have expected such from this bluestocking. "My mother planted the seed, and my grandfather cultivated it. Mostly though, my faith grew as I've seen God move in my life. The times when I've asked for wisdom, He's provided it. When I needed help with a situation, He provided a solution, in an inexplicable way that can't be explained except for a miracle."

"Miracles?" Her tone held a desperate need for hope.

Lord, give her the understanding to believe. He guided her to circle the room a second time, nodding to Lady Coburn, who kept a mothering eye on them as they passed. "When I was five and ten, my younger sister Eliza fell down an old well when she and I were playing in the woods."

Blue's hand flew to her mouth, her satin glove muffling her gasp.

"I heard her scream and found her. She was stuck a little more than an arm's length down. I dropped to the ground and reached for her, but when she stretched to grab my hand, the ledge she stood on broke loose, and she fell the rest of the way. I heard the splash when she hit the water."

An involuntary shudder spasmed through his shoulders. He'd started his training at that age but had much to learn. "Eliza didn't know how to swim. I screamed her name but only heard splashing and gurgles in response. I was as terrified and helpless as when the baron tried to run off with Alicia."

Blue's fingertips tightened on his forearm.

"I panicked, running into the forest, then back out, looking for…I don't know. A branch or something to help me pull her out. And then a calm, clear thought entered my mind. I knew I needed to go get help. I raced back to the house. Mama was visiting her sister with Alicia, and my grandfather was"—on a mission—"out of the country. The responsibility to save her fell on my shoulders, so I ordered the groundskeepers to grab shovels and a rope and follow me."

Rebecca stared at him with a pale face. "Was she all right?"

He nodded, and Rebecca's body relaxed against his side. She fit so nicely there.

"What happened?" She stepped back to face him, and he felt the loss of her closeness.

"When we returned, I called out and, to my surprise, she answered. I lowered a rope and tried to pull her out, but she couldn't hold on, and the hole was too tight for me to go down. The head gardener thought we could widen the well, but I feared dirt or rocks would rain down on her."

She splayed her hand across her chest. "The debris could have cut off her air supply."

"Quite right. The gardeners and I took turns digging a parallel tunnel and crossed over as soon as water seeped up from the ground. I've never dug so furiously, but breaking through and seeing her was a glorious sight. She leapt toward me into the water. I pulled her and hugged her tight. We were both wet and covered head to toe in mud, but it didn't matter. Eliza was alive."

"Thank heavens."

"Thank God. Getting to her alone was a miracle. I asked how she stayed afloat, and she said she found a rock to stand on. I secured a rope around her and had the gardeners hoist her to the surface. Out of curiosity, and to wash off the mud, I swam to where I found her and searched for the rock."

A shiver ran through him, and the noise of the ballroom faded away. He was back in the cold water of the well, only the sounds of dripping and distant voices of the gardeners reaching him. His body shook with either cold or shock, but he pushed through as his grandfather had taught him. He kicked in deep water but hit nothing solid. "There was no rock."

"What? There had to have been something for her to stand on. A ledge?"

"The walls were smooth. I even dove under and searched. There was nothing. I asked her again later, and she was adamant that there was a rock that she stood upon. She held her palm flat at her waist and said that when she was on the rock the water only came to there." He imitated her gesture with his free hand. "I can't explain it. It was a miracle."

Blue's gaze grew distant as if she was trying to figure a solution to explain away his.

They passed the door to the hallway, and she paused and stiffened.

"What's wrong?" He peeked out to where a footman was speaking to two young maids, dutifully sitting and waiting in the hallway—one of them Madeline.

"Hopefully, nothing," she said. "Just my imagination."

"I have found intuition something to which to pay heed." Where had he seen the footman before? "Wasn't that the footman who was with us when we went riding?"

She nodded. "When Miss Blakeford was with us."

He turned her in a way that enabled him to watch the bloke through the doorway over her shoulder. The distance and the way the footman stood didn't allow Daniel to read his lips.

"I also saw him hovering near her in the breakfast room, and he was the one who returned from the search for Miss Blakeford with nothing to report."

The night he'd been attacked, he'd passed the servant near the stables after he returned from the tavern, but before he headed to stake out the graveyard.

"I have a bad feeling about him," Blue said. "I don't want him speaking with Madeline."

The footman shifted, and Daniel picked up a few words on his lips. *My heart suffers...shared sentiments.* The footman shifted again, leaning his forearm against the wall, saying something that brought smiles to the maids' faces.

"I doubt he'll try anything this evening. The maids know they must stay at the ready in case their mistress needs them." The man was tall enough to fit the muddy footprints left behind at the gravesite. Was he linked to the grave robbers? "Ask your maid what he said to them and tell me tomorrow. In the meantime, I'll keep an eye on him."

The music from the set ended. He dreaded parting from Blue's company, but Professor Duval approached, his mouth pursed as if someone had put too much lemon in his tea. "Lady Prestcote, I believe I'm promised the next dance."

Gasps drifted in the air, and the musicians faltered.

Looking beyond him, Blue's eyes widened. "Sarah!"

Daniel turned to find Mrs. Evans in Professor Matthews's arms, though not in an embrace. It appeared the woman had collapsed.

Blue ran to Mrs. Evans's side, Daniel beside her. He angled them out of the way so Lady Coburn could pass through the gathering crowd.

She knelt beside her niece. "Darling, Sarah."

"She's breathing." Professor Matthews gently laid Mrs. Evans on the floor. "It's merely one of her spells."

"Goodness." Lady Coburn stood and signaled for Lucy.

The dutiful maid rushed over.

"Professor Matthews, please bring my niece into the salon where there is more air."

The seemingly scrawny professor scooped the woman into his arms and did as Lady Coburn directed.

Blue looked at Daniel with wide, frightened eyes.

He glanced toward Madeline, then back at Blue, nodding to say he'd keep an eye on her.

Blue flashed him a grateful smile before following Professor Matthews.

She'd understood his nonverbal communication.

And that pleased him.

CHAPTER 25

*T*en minutes later, Rebecca quietly closed the salon door behind her and stepped into the hallway, only leaving Sarah's side because Lady Coburn insisted. Sarah was napping peacefully on the settee in the rose salon adjacent to the ballroom, attended by her maid and Professor Matthews. Nothing could be done for her friend except to allow her to sleep off the episode.

"Lady Prestcote?" Professor Duval stepped out from under the wall sconce, his face shadowed. Was he still waiting for his dance?

Madeline, seated across from the entrance to the ballroom, coughed into her apron. Thankfully, the swaggering footman no longer loomed over her.

Lady Coburn exited the salon and nodded as she passed before entering the ballroom. The orchestra silenced. "Dinner is being served. Please join me in the dining room."

"Shall I escort you since Lord Wolston escorts our hostess?" Without waiting for an answer, Professor Duval gripped her hand and placed it on his arm.

She glanced back at Madeline, who curtsied and left to eat her meal below stairs with the staff. Would she be safe?

Daniel was exiting the ballroom with Lady Coburn on his arm, but he turned, and his gaze held hers.

He had been watching. She could trust him to protect her sister.

The other guests lined up in pairs as the doors to the dining room opened. She twisted to scan the hallway for the footman, her hand slipping from the professor's arm, but the servant was nowhere to be found. Had Daniel sent him on an errand?

Professor Duval set her hand back where he'd placed it. His exactness was a good reason why she needn't worry about their experiment. Perhaps Daniel was correct in reminding her to be anxious about nothing. She could count on Professor Duval's precise measurements. He led her past Lady Coburn and Daniel, whose warm gaze swept over her.

Heat filled her cheeks. She hoped the professor wouldn't notice as he pulled out her chair. She sat, and a footman draped a napkin over her lap while another filled her glass.

Professor Duval raised his glass and toasted to a successful day. "I sent a footman to inquire how our test subjects have fared."

"Must they be labeled *subjects*?"

"What else would they be called?"

"You could refer to them by name or collectively as patients because you're caring for their well-being."

"It's an experiment." He straightened his silverware with a snort. "Hence, they're test subjects."

"It merely seems impersonal, as if you don't see them as people."

He shrugged. "Of course, that's not the case. In fact, I sent a servant to check on the results, and I'm pleased to note that all test subjects have experienced improvement with only a few side effects."

Her breath caught. "What sort of side effects?"

"Giddiness."

Mild and mundane. Nothing to fret about.

"A slower than normal pulse, purging of the stomach's contents, and in one subject, greenish or yellowish vision."

Her chest constricted. "William Withering had warned in his writings about such occurrences. Perhaps the dosage is too high?"

The footman ladled cream soup into their bowls.

Professor Duval sipped from his spoon and requested salt. He stirred and sipped another taste.

She fought an impulse to demand he respond.

"It's perfect," he finally said.

She gripped the table and frowned at him. "I beg to differ. If patients are having side-effects—"

"My soup." He patted her hand. "It's too early to adjust the experiment. We'll wait a few more days."

She turned to face him and whispered, "But what if one of them becomes seriously ill or"—she forced the word from her suddenly dry mouth—"dies?"

At the sensation of being watched, she glanced down the table to Daniel. His observant gaze locked with hers. Could he read the worry in her expression?

Professor Duval snorted. "There's no need for hysterics."

Hysterics?

He sipped more of his soup, unbothered by her concerns. "Besides, you have forgotten that we are short on time. Lady Coburn is a generous host, but only one week remains before my colleagues and I must return to university."

One week to determine if the treatment could cure Madeline? It wasn't enough time.

Rebecca finished her soup in silence while Professors Duval and Bell discussed which publications to submit the results of the digitalis experiment to and how, if successful, it would give Oxford an edge in the medical sciences over Edinburgh.

She cared nothing about what accreditation and accolades the university would receive. She just wanted her sister to live.

But at what cost?

She would sacrifice her life for Madeline's, but could she sit back while other people gave up theirs for what might or might not become a cure?

Would Madeline allow their sacrifices? Rebecca knew the answer. Madeline was gentle, kind, and not afraid to die, whereas Rebecca couldn't bear the thought of a life without her sister and didn't care whether that was selfish or not.

Maybe it was selfish. But would she really risk the health of innocents to gain her goal?

Daniel had said his father's death brought his family together, and she agreed that Mama's death had made her and Madeline closer and brought their father home—at least for now. But losing Madeline was a hurt she couldn't fathom. What good could God make of that?

The memory of Daniel's story about his own sister thrummed in her mind. Could He do another miracle? *Please, God.*

"I shall require another specimen for a dissection." Professor Duval addressed his remarks toward Professor Bell across the table.

The older man's nostrils flared, and his expression pinched. "The university wants to see results before they raise our budget. You must increase your lectures and publish a book that will entice donors to open their purse strings."

"Another dissection is necessary to document prior heart conditions that lead to death, preferably a specimen that's has sustained damage due to dropsy or heart failure. Digitalis shows promise in preventing swelling around the heart."

She cringed at the casual way Professor Duval spoke of the

dead, as if they weren't real people, someone's son or daughter, father or mother, sister or brother, or spouse. Each was a child of God, yet to him, they were all just *subjects*.

Why hadn't she seen how elitist his thinking was before now? He held little respect for human life. To him, people were expendable, a means to an end. He didn't value people as she did, which was why he had no hesitation in upping the dosages for time's sake. Nor, she now realized, had he held sympathy for the man who'd interrupted his lecture, upset over the loss of his wife.

Daniel's warning rang in her mind. *You deserve someone who will treat you better.*

Did Professor Duval only hold sentiments for her because of the recognition she—or more accurately, Corinne—could bring to his work?

Professor Bell set down his spoon and lowered his voice, leaning across the table toward Duval. "Cadavers are challenging to procure, especially when you require such a specific criterion. Besides, procuring too many when they are in short supply may draw unwanted suspicion. Unless you'd like to waste precious time explaining your deeds before the House of Lords."

"There must be a way. An accurate accounting is crucial, or another scientist could discredit the work." Professor Duval lowered his voice until Rebecca only picked up a few words. "Edinburg University...slums...wouldn't be missed...the essence of time...Leafield...magistrate a favor."

"Indeed." Professor Bell grunted. "It might be considered crime prevention."

"Hmm." Professor Duval nodded and sipped his soup.

Unease prickled her scalp. What were the professors contemplating? She glanced at Daniel, but he was focused on watching Professor Duval. Could he hear what they were saying from the opposite end of the table?

"If the results are what I suspect, then you needn't worry." He spoke loudly enough now for her to hear. "I shall soon receive accolades from the medical and science community. People will flock to my lectures, and the university would then receive recognition and funding."

Professor Bell raised his glass. "A toast to that."

"Hear, hear." Professor Duval raised his glass.

The action drew Lord McGower's attention and he, too, raised his glass. "What are we toasting?"

"Successful experimentation on cadavers," Professor Duval said.

"Gentlemen, please." Lord McGower lowered his glass. "I take issue with this topic, especially so soon after Lady Prestcote has lost her beloved chaperone."

Before either of the professors could defend themselves, the dining room doors opened, and their colleague entered. Professor Matthews supported Sarah on his arm. "We must make our sincerest apologies for being late. Our earlier game of Poona and all the dancing wore Mrs. Evans to a point past exhaustion. She needed a nap." He peered at her with an expression of love that would turn standard trees to weeping. "I couldn't leave my wilted blossom."

Sarah turned her sleepy gaze to his with a smile. "I'm feeling much improved, thanks to Professor Matthews's care and ministrations."

Lady Coburn rose, as did the men. She aided her niece into an empty chair opposite Rebecca. Professor Matthews sat in the empty chair to Rebecca's right.

The main dish of roasted fowl and root vegetables was plated and set before each guest.

Rebecca flashed a sympathetic smile to her friend. "I'm sorry you had such a trying day, but I'm glad you're feeling better and could join us."

A shy grin curved Sarah's mouth. "The day was lovely, not

trying in the least." A blush stained her cheeks. "It's merely that I became overwhelmed with joy when Professor Matthews informed me of his intentions to seek my hand in marriage."

Sarah glanced at the professor, her face showing youthful energy despite the dark circles under her eyes. "My knees gave out, and I collapsed." Her smile widened. "One might say, I lilac'd the ability to contain myself."

"It's as I said." He leaned forward as if desiring to take her into his arms but was blocked by the table. "You and I are *mint* to be."

Rebecca pressed her napkin to her lips to suppress the giggle welling over the blossoming lovebirds. Her gaze met Daniel's.

He looked frustrated, bothered by missing out on the conversations, which only drew more laughter.

She pinched her lips but couldn't hide her smile.

He countered with a matching grin that quickened her pulse.

"Tomorrow, I'd like you to try my herb elixir, which aids in sleep," Professor Matthews said to Sarah.

Professor Bell put his fork down. "A sleeping potion? Are you giving her dwale?"

"Dwale? That's used when a man must be cut open or a bone set, is it not?" Professor Matthews shook his head. "Nothing of the sort." He focused on Sarah. "The housewives' recipe for dwale calls for hemlock and opium. I want Mrs. Evans to sleep, but more so, I want her to wake up."

"What do you plan to use?" Professor Bell asked.

"Valerian, a plant with sedative properties without toxic side effects. I grind its root to make a tea."

"Interesting." Professor Bell rubbed his chin.

Supper and dessert fared better with the presences of Sarah and Professor Matthews, distracting Rebecca from Professor Duval and his quest for recognition. When the meal concluded and the plates were removed, dancing resumed in the ballroom.

Daniel claimed the first dance, and Rebecca relaxed, reassured by his strength and confidence. Unfortunately, the dance didn't allow for conversation. When the set ended, he walked her to Sarah's side, but he seemed reluctant to leave her.

"I fear I won't sleep after my nap," Sarah said, "but after all the excitement today, I should probably try to rest if I want to be in tolerable form tomorrow."

"Thistle be a night I shall always remember." Professor Matthews bowed. "Allow me to escort you to your room."

Sarah and Professor Matthews excused themselves and meandered toward the door, looking more at each other than the direction they headed.

The orchestra struck up another country dance, and Professor Duval strode in Rebecca's direction. Her grip tightened on Daniel's arm. How could she dance with the professor after hearing his callous remarks? She also didn't want to exhaust Madeline, who needed her rest. "I believe I shall also retire."

Daniel's brows rose in question, but he nodded. "Then I insist upon escorting you."

She turned before Duval reached her, hoping he didn't realize she'd seen him coming.

They lagged behind Sarah and the professor, who'd stopped to bid Lady Coburn good night before continuing down the hall.

Madeline rose from her chair, where she'd waited in the hallway, looking a little pale. She trouped down the hall behind them, an appropriate length to allow Rebecca and Daniel a private conversation.

Nevertheless, Rebecca lowered her voice, "Thank you for sending the footman away."

"I sent him to the tavern to retrieve a jacket I left behind."

He grinned. "I can be quite forgetful. Turns out, it's being laundered."

"How terribly absentminded of you." She chuckled.

"You appeared distraught at dinner, and just now seemed eager to avoid Professor Duval. Not that I mind." He flashed her a grin. "Did he say something to upset you?"

They climbed the curved staircase side by side. She tried to find the right words. "I was appalled by the way he discussed finding bodies for dissection as if they hadn't once been someone's son, daughter, father, or mother. He seemed so cold-hearted. Even with the digitalis experiment, he's elevated the task over the people." She shook her head. "I couldn't be around him any longer."

"Was Duval asking Bell for bodies to dissect, or was he telling him that he was going to acquire some?"

"Asking. Why?" She slowed her steps as they approached her bedchamber.

"I'm still trying to figure out the mystery of who was behind the disappearance and murder of your chaperone."

"You think one of them might have had something to do with it?"

"The night I was attacked, the professors were unaccounted for. Lady and Lord Farsley, Lord McGower, and Mr. Kim were playing cards with Lady Coburn. I will speak to the housekeeper and butler to get an accounting of the staff that evening to see where the suspicious footman was that night.

"I'm to spar with Lord McGower after breakfast, but I will find you after that, and we'll talk more." At her door, he bowed over her hand and pressed a kiss to the back of it. "Good night, Lady Prestcote."

She curtsied. "Good night, Lord Wolston."

He turned and nodded to Madeline, who responded with a knowing smile and a curtsy. "My lord."

Her tired appearance vanished, and her smile widened

after he left. Once inside their room, she all but pounced on Rebecca, giddy to hear the details.

After dressing for bed and lying under the covers. Rebecca rolled to face her sister. "What was that blond footman speaking to you about?"

Madeline brushed her off. "Nothing at all. He was merely being flirtatious."

"Something's not right about his lingering around the female servants. Besides, he's below your station."

"Truly?" Madeline snorted and snuggled into the mattress. "Now you sound like Professor Duval."

"That's ridiculous." Rebecca fumed. "I'm merely looking after your well-being."

"I know," Madeline said with a sigh. "You always do."

"What is that supposed to mean?"

"You have a grand opportunity to live your life and not waste it trying to save mine. My life is in God's hands."

"'Waste'?" Saving Madeline was what drove her. "I couldn't live with myself if I didn't try."

Silence fell over the room until Madeline's breathing rose and fell in a steady rhythm.

Rebecca stared at the ceiling, reviewing the day, her sister's words, and the determined look in Daniel's eyes. He'd confided in her, yet she hadn't been truthful with him. The longer she waited, the harder it would be to tell him who she really was.

Her heart craved to be treated like someone he could love just a little longer.

CHAPTER 26

The following morning, Rebecca broke her fast with Sarah. The other guests were scarce, probably still asleep after the late night.

"Pardon my simple gown." Sarah flicked the front tie on her day dress. "Lucy must have overslept. I dressed myself this morning because I didn't want to tell on the poor dear."

The blond footman had been hovering over Lucy and Madeline last night. "Are you positive she overslept? Perhaps we should check after what happened to Miss Blakeford."

Sarah blanched, quickly waving over a maid and instructing her to wake Lucy and report back. The maid hurried to oblige.

"I do hope she's all right." Sarah stared out the window at the sun peeking through the drab gray sky. "I will not let worry ruin my good mood." She conveyed how wonderful Professor Matthews had been to her over the past week.

"I believed after my husband passed that I would never find someone who could love me despite my episodes, but I have." Sarah's face glowed. "He doesn't see me as odd but as a woman who occasionally suffers from a sleep disorder. He wants to understand what leads to my 'expedient naps' to see if there might be a way to control or regulate their timing. He believes I may not sleep in a deep enough state."

"Interesting." Rebecca had wondered the same.

"He's going to have me try some herbs to help me relax into a deep sleep." She sighed. "Isn't that lovely?"

"Charming, indeed." Rebecca smiled at her friend. "I think the two of you will make a splendid pair."

Sarah leaned over her plate of eggs and sliced ham. "And what about you and the marquis?"

Rebecca's fork stilled halfway to her mouth. The glob of egg that quivered on the end of the prongs felt much like her stomach at the mere mention of Daniel's title. "We danced, but that is all."

"I told you everything." Sarah pouted. "Yet you hold back on me. The two of you kept gazing at one another across the table and across the room. Then you walked the perimeter of the room together three times around." She arched an eyebrow. "I don't see him singling out attention from any of the other women at the party."

"You're the only other unmarried woman in attendance, and now you're taken. Lord Wolston was just being polite." But it was more than that, and Rebecca knew it. He'd confided in her about his past and his faith. The ballroom and music might as well have drifted away because Daniel had made her feel like she was the only woman in the room —the only woman in all of England. The only woman for him.

That would change when he discovered she was a fraud.

She wanted to cover her face with her hands and sob. Only one week remained of the house party, and then the official London Season would begin. She and Corinne would make their debut, and Daniel would learn she'd duped him.

And then he'd never speak to her again.

"It's more than that." Sarah set her fork down. "Why do you suddenly look as though you swallowed a sea of sorrows?"

Rebecca wanted to explain, but Sarah's expression shifted to one of pure glee. Her hand lifted, and her fingers wriggled in a wave.

"Good morning, Lady Prestcote." Professor Matthews's tenor voice deepened into a husky roll. "Mrs. Evans. Are you ready to try my sleep elixir tonight?"

"Indeed." She patted the chair next to her, and the professor sat, his full attention on his bride-to-be. "I have confidence your theory shall work," she said. "You have such knowledge of plants. I couldn't be in better hands."

He beamed and eyed Rebecca. "Her flattery is a bit mulch. Don't be-leaf it."

He and Sarah giggled over his pun, and Rebecca couldn't help but smile at the jovial lovebirds.

Sarah sighed at the professor, and her expression sobered. "I wanted to ask you about a conversation I overheard this morning. I'd dozed off in the drawing room in a wingback chair. Professors Duval and Bell woke me arguing. I don't believe they knew I was in the room, for my chair faced the hearth, and they stood behind me. Their subject matter gave me pause."

Professor Matthews placed a reassuring hand over hers, encouraging her with his expression to go on.

"Professor Duval said something about the workhouses in North Leigh and the ones on Corn Street in Witney. They're in poor condition, and people must be dying there daily. He encouraged Professor Bell to have his drudge ask around to learn if a person who died had trouble breathing or fainted often."

Rebecca gasped. Were the professors looking for an experimental group for testing, or were they speaking of body snatching?

"Professor Bell said he may have a local option." Sarah shook her head and gazed at Professor Matthews. "They spoke in such a business-like manner, as if they were purchasing a horse to drive a cart or plow a field."

"I wouldn't concern yourself." Professor Matthews flashed a reassuring grin. "It sounds as though Professor Duval has asked for Professor Bell's help in sourcing test subjects for a double-blind experiment."

"Ah, I see. Then I worried over nothing."

The two shifted their conversation, seemingly forgetting Rebecca was there at all.

She saw her queue to leave. "I shall afford you two the luxury of some privacy." She rose and pulled her shawl back up around her shoulders. A footman removed her plate as she bid her friends good day.

She wanted to believe Professor Duval's professionalism wouldn't allow him to stoop to procuring bodies by illegal means, but he held an inflated view of himself and treated servants and commoners as beneath him, not as God's children.

The maid Sarah had sent to wake Lucy descended the servant's stairs, and Rebecca stopped her in the hall. "Did you locate her?"

"My lady." She bobbed a curtsy. "She's not in her room, and no one has seen her." The maid twisted her apron. "She wouldn't go home without tellin' Mrs. Johnston, the house-keeper, and it's not like Lucy to miss the mornin' meal."

Rebecca's stomach tightened. She'd promised Lucy's grand-mother to watch over her. *Lord, please not Lucy.* "Go, right away and tell Mrs. Evans and Lady Coburn. Let any one of us know if you see her."

The maid scurried into the breakfast room, and the butler stopped Rebecca in the foyer to hand her a letter. She took it, recognizing her father's handwriting, and stuffed it in her pocket before wandering up to her chamber to check on Madeline.

Her sister was sleeping. Instead of waking her, Rebecca left to go to the library but stopped outside the door upon hearing Professor Duval and Professor Bell talking inside.

"It's a controlled experiment," said Professor Duval, "single-blind."

"What of the extraneous variables?" asked Professor Bell.

Thank heaven. It seemed the professors were conducting an experiment and not murdering paupers to dissect their bodies.

Turning so as not to interrupt them, she scurried back down the steps and kept going until she reached the main floor. A footman opened the patio door, and she exited, breathing in the fresh air.

Daniel had said he'd come looking for her after sparring with Lord McGower, but would he think to find her walking the grounds? She could sit in the orangery, but others would soon gather there, and she wasn't in the mood to talk about the weather, fashions, or the latest hearsay written in the gossip columns. Turning back to the footman, she said, "If Lord Wolston comes looking for me, tell him I'm out taking a stroll."

A team of gardeners raked leaves blowing in from the surrounding Wynchwood Forest. The rhythmic scraping along the ground didn't ease her nerves, but she knew a place that just might do the trick. She trekked up the hill and scurried past the local parish's graveyard to sit in view of the millpond.

The sight once again left her in awe. A fiery landscape of yellow leaves with bits of orange and brown contrasted with the blue sky and reflected in the shimmering pond. The mill stood like a stone marker to remind visitors that, despite the heavenly scene, they remained in the earthly realm.

A rock jutted out of the ground nearby, and Rebecca used her shawl to dust off a spot to sit. She summoned the courage to open the letter.

Dearest daughters,

The most amazing, wondrous occurrence has happened. When I was down on my luck and sleeping in the gutter, a good citizen woke me up and brought me into his home. He cleaned me up and gave me his clothes and spoke of the same man your mama always tried to tell me about, but I'd refused to listen.

I've accepted Jesus into my heart. I've changed my ways and must beg your forgiveness for all the trouble I've caused you. Someday, I hope you'll find it in your heart to forgive me.

The man helped me find employment on a ship that sails to Antarctica. The sum I will make for the deployment will pay all my debts, so my dearest Rebecca, you no longer need to hold the burden. I regret that I haven't been there for you, and my only sorrow is that this voyage will keep me away for a year or two. Upon my return, I pray we can have a fresh start.

May the Lord keep you safe and watch over you in my absence.

Yours truly,

Papa

Rebecca reread the letter, soaking in the words. All those prayers Mama asked her to pray had finally been answered. Her papa had given his life to Jesus. Rebecca was the only one who remained hard-hearted. Had she hidden her heart from God because of her mother's death? Or had she feared that if God saw her failures, He'd reject her—as her earthly father had?

But had He?

Rebecca lost account of the passing hour as she watched the reflection of the clouds across the water. One floated past, and the sun's rays spilled down on her shoulders as if her mother was above, calling her *my darling sunshine.* She could picture her sweet mama's smile and feel the warmth of her hand upon her cheek as she cupped her face and told her she was a special little girl, a gift from God.

Tears sprang to Rebecca's eyes.

But I failed you, Mama. I left you for selfish reasons. I wanted to meet with that boy. To be kissed by him. It's my fault that I never got to say goodbye and tell you one last time how much I love you.

Would she fail Madeline too? If she didn't go along with Professor Duval's experiments, would he tell her the results, or would he make her wait for his book as he'd commented earlier?

Another cloud blocked the sun, and a chill ran along her skin.

"I'm sorry, Mama." Her words were broken with a choked sob.

Across the water, the leaves shimmered in the light breeze, making them appear to be on fire. It reminded her of the Bible story her mama read to her as a child of the burning bush, where God spoke to Moses.

The memory of Mama's voice filled her head. *Moses had been afraid to act. He was frightened to go back to Egypt because he'd murdered an Egyptian, but God had already forgiven him. God gave him the wisdom to know what to do and when to do it, and He provided Aaron, Moses's brother, to walk alongside him.*

Mama had set the Bible aside and added, *Knowledge is learned, but wisdom is granted by God and must be lived.*

Rebecca missed her mother so much, it was an ache in her chest. Mama had trusted God. Madeline did, too, and now Papa had put his faith in Him.

Even Daniel spoke of God's miracles. What had she missed that others saw?

Faith is the substance of things hoped for, the evidence of things not seen.

Ah, more of her mother's words. No, God's words from the book of Hebrews, recited from Mama's lips.

Rebecca tipped her head up and let the sunlight fall upon her face. "All right, God," she whispered. "I submit. I can't do this alone. I need Your divine wisdom, Your divine intervention. Madeline is ill, and I haven't been able to find a cure.

"Lucy is missing, and I don't know where to look. The harder I try to save people, the more I fail. My attempts become null hypotheses. I'm blocked at every turn, but You made a way for Moses. Your ways are higher than mine. Mama, Madeline, Daniel, and now Papa even trusts in You." She laced her fingers and pressed her hands to her chin. "I'm choosing to trust You with my heart too."

She exhaled a deep breath, gazing at those fiery-colored trees. If only she could hear God's voice telling her what to do. Which way to go.

A dark shadow stepped out of the fire.

Rebecca blinked to clear her vision.

Walking out of the forest, a man carried a large sack over his shoulder and strode alongside the pond. Whatever was in the bag was too lumpy to be flour. He paused to wipe his brow before disappearing inside the stone mill.

Rebecca stiffened. She couldn't be sure, but the man had resembled the blond footmen. What was he doing going into an old, inoperable mill? And whatever was he carrying?

Her blood chilled despite the warmth of the sun.

Could Lucy be in the sack?

CHAPTER 27

*D*aniel returned from his meeting with the constable and Giles Shepherd, which took longer than he'd anticipated. The boy still refused to talk and burst into tears when they threatened a hearing to be held in a fortnight. The young man's sobs still echoed in Daniel's conscience, but he must see justice served for those families who wondered if their loved ones found peace after death.

He entered Griffin Hall and made inquiries about Lady Prestcote's whereabouts. He asked her maid, Mrs. Evans, and even Professor Duval in the library, but no one had seen her after the morning meal.

Daniel fought to quell the panic rising in his chest. Was Blue in trouble? Had her blackmailers contacted her again? Or worse, had the same culprits who'd abducted and poisoned Miss Blakeford attacked his Blue?

His knees nearly gave way at the thought, and he gripped the rail lest he tumble down the stairs.

He found Lady Coburn in the orangery and asked if she'd seen Lady Prestcote. Blue hadn't joined the guests for the high noon tea, nor had she seen her, so he inquired about the suspicious blond-haired footman who'd been among the staff last night.

Lady Coburn frowned. "I don't employ a blond footman."

"But he was in the foyer last evening." Lord McGower strode into the orangery and sat across from Lady Coburn. "I saw him speaking to some of the lady's maids. I thought you might frown upon such fraternizing, but I didn't want to spoil your evening by mentioning it."

Lady Coburn smiled. "You are too kind."

The memory of Alicia being stolen out the window flashed through Daniel's mind. "Have you seen Lady Prestcote?"

"Indeed," Lord McGower said. "Walking up the hill toward the cemetery."

Daniel's heart leapt into his throat. "When?"

Lord McGower scrunched his lips and glanced at the ceiling. "About an hour ago, I believe."

"Thank you." Daniel bowed, trying to appear calm. "I must beg my leave." He did his best to keep his steps controlled and not dash for the nearest exit.

Lord McGower's hearty laugh followed him. "I hope she gives you a good tongue lashing, after the thrashing you gave me in our sparring match."

He forced a laugh and stepped outside.

Once he reached the grounds, he bounded up the hill in a full sprint. Past the graveyard and around the stone path to the mill and pond. He spied the loveliest sight he'd ever seen. *Blue.*

Her rich mahogany hair glistened in the sun, highlighted with shades of auburn. She wore it up in a simple bun that looked like a sophisticated coiffure on her. One escaped tress curved around her elegant neck. The light breeze molded the cambric material of her day dress to her feminine curves and floated past her other side in rippling waves.

His heart pounded in his chest, but his joy in locating Blue differed from the elation he'd felt pulling his sister from the well.

He was falling in love with the beautiful bluestocking.

The revelation struck him like a blow to the cheek, knocking his senses sideways.

All he could see were those inquisitive hazel eyes peering up at him after their kiss, after she set his arm, and each time they'd connected on the ballroom floor. He loved their flecks of green and gold—like fallen yellow leaves on a lawn. He loved her quirks, such as befriending her maid. He loved how she lit up when she learned something new, often using the words *actually* or *interesting fact* before blurting out something she'd learned.

But as he drew closer, something seemed off. He'd assumed she'd bent to pick something up, but she didn't straighten. No, she was crouching behind a rock and peeking over the top as if trying to stay hidden. His muscles tensed and ears perked up, listening for extraneous sounds, but only caught the snipping of the gardener's hedge clippers in the distance. He scanned the surroundings, but nothing appeared out of place.

"Blue?"

She twisted to face him, her palms against the rock. She seemed to relax at the sight of him, then frantically waved him over and turned back to the pond.

He bent and, continuing to scan for enemies, darted to crouch beside her. "What are you looking at?"

She nodded at the stone mill. "I saw the blond man enter the mill carrying something about thirty minutes ago. He hasn't left."

"You don't say..." He studied the two-story mill for movement, but even the wooden wheel was stationary. The pond hid one side of the lower cellar floor unless the wooden dam was lowered, allowing water to flow into the creek that snaked into the forest. The mill offered a spacious hideout. "I inquired about the servant speaking to your lady's maid and discovered Lady Coburn hasn't employed either a blond footman or a blond groomsman."

Blue gasped. "Then what was he doing inside Griffin Hall? And why would he be going into the mill?"

He glanced at the honey-colored stone structure, searching the windows for signs of movement. "You say he was carrying something?"

"A large sack with something heavy inside." Blue peeked over the rock. "You don't think he could have been carrying a body?" She pressed a hand over her mouth and murmured something he couldn't make out.

He pulled her hand away, and fear trembled in her fingers.

"Sarah's lady's maid, Lucy, is missing. Sarah assumed she'd overslept, but she wasn't in her room, and none of the servants had seen her. You don't think Lucy..." Her eyes conveyed her horror. "The footman was talking to her last night. What if he hurt her?"

If only he could assure Blue that the maid was safe, open his arms and offer her the solace her innocent hazel eyes begged for. But he couldn't, not when there were body snatchers and murderers nearby. "Pray she is safe."

Blue squeezed her eyes shut and whispered a quick prayer.

He studied the mill. Only one exit. The windows were too small or too high to escape. Apprehending the murderer would please Lieutenant Scar and gain Daniel his desired status within the department. But as he considered the horror of what Miss Blakeford had suffered—and now perhaps the Coburn's lady's maid—a righteous anger welled up. He must stop this dastardly villain before someone else was killed. Whether it helped him gain status at the Home Office or not was irrelevant.

There was no movement. Had the footman sneaked out without Blue's notice? What if there was a hidden exit? He felt his side, confirming his pistol was in place. He didn't want to make any hasty mistakes as he had at the Lipscomb party, letting the men get away. What if the man had carried a person in that sack? What if there was still a chance to save the victim?

In his periphery, one of the mill windows darkened.

Daniel squinted to discern if something or someone was in there—a person or some animal taking up residence—but it was gone as fast as it came.

A bird squawked overhead and flew across the pond, landing on a tree branch on the other side. He glanced back at the window but only saw the tree line's bright reflection. The shadow must have been from the bird.

"I'm going to investigate. You stay here."

"I'm coming with you," she said. "I promised Lucy's grandmother I would watch over her."

Could he keep her safe? He could defend himself, but if there were assailants inside, would he be able to defend her? "I don't know what we're going to find."

"I'll linger back a bit." She gripped his sleeve. "I can run for help if need be. I just need to know if Lucy is..."

Alive.

"You're to stay behind me. You understand?" He waited for her nod. "I will not let anything happen to you. If I tell you to run, you do so immediately. Sprint to the house and don't look back."

The chords in her neck tightened as she swallowed, but she nodded once more.

Keeping to the forest that ringed the pond, they edged toward the mill. As they neared it, he extended his arm to ensure she stayed behind him. He crept quietly over the crushed stone walkway and onto a wooden porch, which creaked.

He put a finger to his lips and pointed at the board. Blue stepped around it. He had her stand out of sight from the door and windows, her back pressed against the exterior wall, as he cracked open the door. "Stay here," he whispered.

Sunlight spilled in from the high window, twinkling the dust particles floating in the air. A heavy grinding stone stood still and silent. Footprints littered the dusty floor. Boot markings, large enough that they belonged to a man, were scattered, not in any particular direction.

He slipped into the damp, grainy-smelling room and listened for any noise. The room's only contents were a cane chair, a large stone grinding wheel, and a narrow wooden staircase leading above and below. Daniel silently skirted the perimeter to the far window and peeked out.

The sun had lowered to the tops of the trees and cast a shadow over the west side of the pond. The honking of geese rang like warnings and coiled tight every nerve in his body. He climbed a ladder to the hopper floor and peeked onto a catwalk but saw nobody. The only life inside was a sleeping bat in the eave's peak next to the thick beam and pulley system used to lift the sacks of flour.

He descended the first few stairs of the spiral wooden staircase to the machinery floor on the left of the grinding stone. Crouching, he peeked into the dimly lit room below. The heavy scent of milled grain rose from the abandoned shop. Interlocked gears stood dormant. No sign of the footman.

He signaled for Blue to enter but to leave the door open.

She gripped the doorframe, her gaze darting about the room.

"The place is clear. I'm going down to inspect further." Each wooden stair groaned under his weight, but nothing stirred in the shadows. The tiny north side window cast the room's only light, but enough to get a good look around. More scattered boot prints overlapped. There were animal footprints, as well, most likely rats. He swiped the thick coating of dust and examined it. The white flour residue was left from when the mill had been operable.

Daniel gritted his teeth in frustration. He wanted answers to the disappearances of these women. He wanted the body snatchers caught and locked up in Newgate Prison. But at the same time, he felt relieved there wasn't a present threat or a dead body.

The top stair creaked, and Daniel spun only to glimpse Blue's slippered feet and trim ankles as she descended. She crouched and peered at him.

"He must have left." There were no other entrances or exits. Only a worn millstone leaning against the wall.

Blue continued down. "What of the large sack?"

"No sign of it."

"It couldn't just disappear." When she reached the floor, she spun in a circle, inspecting the room with a furrowed brow.

He tapped the walls, but the thick stone revealed little. Leaning over, he scrutinized the footsteps, but the only pattern he could make of them was a circle around the perimeter and back up the spiral stairs. He re-inspected the stone floor of the hopper and the catwalk to no avail.

"I don't understand." Blue glanced around the space. "I didn't imagine the man entering the building."

"I believe you. The footprints prove someone has been here and often, by the number." He paced back and forth in front of the millstone. "We must have missed something."

"We searched every room." The setting sunlight now hindered their search. "As much as I want to keep searching"— she rubbed her temples—"tongues will wag if I don't return soon."

Blue was right, but he hated to give up. The murderer needed to be stopped. Why weren't the clues coming together? Two servants had gone missing, both female. One appeared to have been murdered and sold for dissection. Lucy's status was unknown. According to Greta, other townsfolk had gone missing, also of the working class, and tended to be loners or not have family.

Fresh bodies sold at a high price and provided motive for murder, and cadavers were needed at the university. Four men had been present when he was attacked at the graveyard. He'd gotten a good look at two, but the other two remained unidentified. Could the two unknown be Professor Duval and Professor Bell, or one of them and the blond footman?

He held the door open for Blue and offered his elbow, and they strode back toward Griffin Hall. Daniel paused and peered back over his shoulder one last time at the abandoned mill. The setting sun shone off the top two windows, but all was still.

"Unless he somehow slipped into the water and swam across the pond without coming up for breath, I don't see how he got away." Blue sighed a defeated breath. "I pray we'll discover Lucy has returned when we get back to the hall."

"I hope so too." He patted her hand. "If she's still missing, then it's suspicious that this so-called footman, who wasn't hired by Lady Coburn, spoke with her last night, and a blond-haired groom was the last person seen with Miss Blakeford before her death. Who else have you seen the footman or groom speaking with?"

"Professor Bell signaled for a footman to follow him before he ducked into the servants' hall. I can't recall the color of the footman's hair, though." Blue paled and her voice lowered to a whisper. "Sarah overheard Professor Duval arguing with Professor Bell. Professor Duval is determined to prove the effects of digitalis, but first, he must document how dropsy is caused by a swelling of fluids around the heart. You don't think he could murder people in his desire to document prior heart conditions so he could prove digitalis prevents them?"

"Since hearing Mr. Tingley blame Duval for his wife's death, I've been suspicious of the professor. He has motive because he'd benefit from bodies being available, but would he risk hanging for murder in the name of progressing science?"

Blue furrowed her brow. "You've been considering this for some time?"

Blast. He forgot how perceptive she was. "A friend of mine who works with the Home Office heard about Lady Coburn's guest list and asked me to keep my ears open and keep them abreast of any suspicious behaviors or actions."

She blinked as if processing this new information.

He continued, "My friend is investigating how Miss Blakeford's body wound up at Oxford."

Her slight nod indicated she'd accepted his explanation.

"Duval also would gain financially and his reputation would soar if he linked digitalis to a reduction in dropsy, but his need for specific bodies belonging to people with heart ailments makes his task more difficult. How many deceased criminals with weak hearts are available?"

"Not many, and the timing could take years, but if someone were to hasten their deaths..." Blue paled. "He also thinks little of people who are of a lower class or lesser status than himself."

He guessed she was thinking about her maid. Would she be next to disappear? He'd overheard Professor Duval proclaim he needed a cadaver of a person with a diseased heart to dissect. They were bold enough to kill Blue's chaperone. A lady's maid with the weak heart they require would be tempting. Would they still come for her, knowing how hard Blue had worked to find a cure to help her servant-friend?

"Indeed, but he's not the one obtaining the bodies. It's Professor Bell's job to source and fund the cadavers. He's under a lot of pressure to appease his colleagues to win their nomination for chancellor. He'd also gain prestige for himself and funding for the university if his colleagues publish and receive accolades from the lecture circuit."

"Is that why he hangs on Lady Coburn's arm, hoping to woo a rich widow's endowment?"

"Interesting question." He hadn't considered that angle. "I've also spotted him and Duval leaving the hall at night out the servant's entrance."

"In the direction of the mill?"

"It was too dark to tell where he went after entering the barn. Only Professor Duval rode off." Daniel considered the professor's whereabouts over the past several weeks. "I've also spotted him and Professor Matthews leaving."

"You don't believe Professor Matthews could be involved? He's so dear to Sarah."

"Better to know if he has had any involvement before banns are posted."

"Quite right, but I do hope he's not. For Sarah's sake."

"Agreed. However, I know he grows poisonous plants and has brought some of them, including digitalis, with him to Griffin Hall."

"Professor Duval probably obtains the leaves from him."

He issued her a stern nod. "I passed Professor Matthews on the stairs the night I was accosted in the graveyard, and he had dirt under his fingernails the following morning."

"But he's a botanist. He probably has dirt under his nails often."

"I've checked when his gloves have been off at meals and they've been clean, but most gents would wash up before eating." Horses neighed in the stables as they passed, nearing the west wing entrance. "According to my friend, he'd also visited the chandler the day he died."

"To purchase candles?"

"Indeed, quite suspicious." His eyebrows lifted. "Why would Professor Matthews need candles when he could just ask Lady Coburn for some?"

"Maybe he purchased something else. Perhaps we should check the chandler's ledgers."

He paused at the edge of the patio made private by a large boxwood hedge. "My friend within the Home Office did but was focused more on the names than on what they purchased." He wasn't ready to part company just yet. "I'll have him check again."

The setting sun cast a yellow glow across her features, heightening the color of her eyes, which shone a spring green, like the rolling hills of the English countryside. Except for the golden fleck from ten to twelve in her right eye. Like her eyes, Blue was unique.

"Your eyes are an amazing color."

The pink in her cheeks deepened into a blush.

"*Blue* may be a misnomer. I could call you *green*."

She snorted. "As in green with envy or as in ill and about to cast up one's accounts?"

His laugh sprang from deep in his chest. "How about verdant?"

She shrugged a dainty shoulder. "Better."

"My verdant Blue." His arm curved around her, drawing her close. She fit perfectly against him.

Desire darkened Blue's eyes.

His gaze lowered to her mouth.

"Daniel, we mustn't." Her words were a breathy whisper.

It took all Daniel's willpower to pull away. Did she not realize yet that he was a possessive and protective man? Did she not understand they were meant for each other? *God, thank You for putting Blue in my life.* He couldn't resist cupping her cheek. "You're like a ray of sunshine, chasing away the gloom. I'm so grateful for you."

He searched her eyes and saw them soften—with hope or perhaps love? Or was he reading too much into her reaction? "You are someone I can trust as my sounding board for all my suspicions, a woman with keen insights and an intelligent mind."

His fingers dipped into the silken threads of hair at her nape, and he glided his thumb along the warm satin softness of her cheek.

He shouldn't kiss her, but the urge nearly crumbled him to his knees. "Blue, when I picture my future, I see you."

She inhaled a ragged breath, but then drew back. "Daniel, there's something I need to confess, and I fear I have let you down. Betray—"

"Have mercy, milord." A woman's voice pleaded behind him.

He turned, pushing Blue to shield her with his body.

A ragged woman with a toddler on her hip waddled down the steps of the servants' entrance and strode toward them. From under her cap, her blond hair jutted out in all directions. The toddler rested his head on her shoulder, sucking his thumb. Dirt smudged their foreheads, and their clothes were threadbare.

She knelt on the ground before Daniel. "Please, milord. Have mercy on me boy. Tell me where they've taken him. He's only a lad, a little misguided because his pa liked the blue ruin, but me son's got a big heart, and he's only tryin' to put food in his siblings' bellies."

Daniel had never seen this woman before. But he thought of Giles Shepherd, the boy he'd had arrested. "Are you Mrs. Shepherd?" He cupped her elbow and aided her to rise with the child.

"Your humble servant, milord." Tears welled in her eyes. The toddler on her hip peered at his mum. His face scrunched and lower lip protruded as if he, too, were about to wail. "Please don't let me son rot in Newgate. Have mercy."

"Mrs. Shepherd, he's not in Newgate."

"Give him another chance to stay on the straight and

narrow." She gripped his sleeve. "I can't bear to think of him locked up with vermin and criminals. Tell me where they took him."

He clenched his jaw not to look back and see Blue's expression. Did she think him a monster? "Mrs. Shepherd." He tried to guide her away from Griffin Hall. "It's best if we speak—"

"Gillie acts all tough, but truly, he's a peaceable lad." To Daniel's horror, she lowered to her knees again, begging him. "His little siblings adore him. They've been beside themselves without their eldest brother." Tears streamed down her cheeks. "Please, milord, they miss him so."

"Please, Mrs. Shepherd." Daniel helped her back to her feet. "I hold no ill will against your son."

She burst into tears. "I just want to know where you took me boy. The constable said you took him."

Took him?

Daniel dared to look back at Blue, who stared wide-eyed at Mrs. Shepherd and warily at him. *Blast.* Lieutenant Scar must be questioning Giles. Of all the bad timing.

Professor Matthews and Mrs. Evans rounded the hedge and halted at the sight of the bedraggled woman.

"Pardon," said Professor Matthews. He tugged Mrs. Evans closer to his side and up the few patio stairs, veering toward the French doors. "Terribly sorry to interrupt."

"Wait." Blue brushed Daniel's arm as she sidestepped around him. "Any word on Lucy?"

Mrs. Evans shook her head. "I had another maid assist me in donning a walking gown. If there was a family emergency, Lucy should have informed me."

"Could she have mistaken today for her day off?" Blue voiced the question he'd been about to ask.

"I hope so, because then she'll be back to help me ready for the evening meal." Mrs. Evans's sigh held a wishful tone.

Blue peered at him with a worried expression.

"You don't think something happened to her?" Mrs. Evans eyed them both, and her face blanched. "Lucy's disappearance isn't like what happened to Miss Blakeford, is it?"

Professor Matthews patted her hand. "Let's not jump to conclusions, my dear."

The toddler squirmed in Mrs. Shepherd's arms, trying to get down.

One thing at a time. "Mrs. Evans, would you be so kind as to escort Lady Prestcote inside?"

"Of course." Mrs. Evans hooked Blue's arm. "We'll check together on Lucy's return."

He held Blue's gaze and tipped his head the slightest bit in Mrs. Shepherd's direction. "I will explain when I return."

Blue nodded, but a thousand questions clouded her gaze before she walked away. He watched them leave before turning back to Mrs. Shepherd.

Moments before, he'd resisted pulling Blue into his arms for another kiss like the one they'd shared at the Lipscomb party. Now he'd be hard-pressed to explain his actions. Would she think him a complete cad for desiring justice over mercy? Or would she understand there were other lives he must protect?

CHAPTER 28

$\mathcal{R}$ebecca followed Sarah and Professor Matthews into Griffin Hall through the patio doors.

"My lady." Madeline's voice rang from the servant's hall.

Rebecca turned at the sound of her sister's voice.

Madeline stepped out of the dim corridor into the light of the parlor. Dark smudges haunted her eyes.

"Excuse me one minute." Rebecca held her impulse to run to her sister's side and see what the matter was. Instead, she curtsied to Sarah and the professor and strode to her sister.

"What is it? Are you unwell?" What if she was having a spell? She never should have left Madeline's side.

"Lucy is missing." Madeline took Rebecca's hand between her clammy palms. "She's been gone all day, and it's not her day off. I'm worried for her."

"Sarah and I were about to check on her. I'm hoping she went to call on her grandmother."

But if Lucy had done that and not returned, then her grandmother must be terribly ill. Could her sickness be due to Professor Duval's administration of digitalis?

Rebecca pushed off the prickly mantle of fear. "Go back to

our chamber and stay there. Do not speak to anyone until I find out if Lucy is all right and her disappearance isn't associated with Miss Blakeford's. I will be right there to let you know what I learn."

Madeline hurried back down the servant's hall.

Rebecca's mind whirled as she followed Professor Matthews and Sarah toward the east tower and Sarah's chamber to see if Lucy had returned. While they chatted about wedding plans, Rebecca mulled over questions demanding attention. What if Lucy was still missing? Should a servant be sent to check on Mrs. Josting? Who was Mrs. Shepherd, and where was her son? Was this one more person to be added to the list of those who'd mysteriously disappeared? Why did Mrs. Shepherd keep asking where Daniel had taken her son? He couldn't have been involved in the boy going missing, yet he hadn't denied it.

She and Daniel had just listed the reasons why each professor was suspect. She'd never considered if Daniel had a motive. There were a lot of unanswered questions regarding the marquis. Why had he chosen to attend Lady Coburn's party when he'd planned to be elsewhere? Why did he pretend to dip deep in his cups when she'd never seen him even sip spirits, and why did he chase after some young fellow in town? Why did he personally do the sleuthing instead of involving the constable or a detective?

Professor Matthews leaned closer and whispered in Sarah's ear. A blush heightened the color in her cheeks, and she smiled. "Such flattery, professor."

Watching the romantic couple warmed Rebecca's cheek where Daniel had cupped it, and his words rang in her mind. *When I picture my future, I see you.*

She had lost her heart to a marquis. Had she not sought answers to Daniel's odd habits because she hadn't wanted to pop her dream bubble?

As they neared Sarah's chamber, Sarah waved over the

housekeeper instructing a maid. The housekeeper's keys jangled as she approached. "Has Lucy turned up yet?"

"No, my lady. I don't know where that girl is off to. It's not like her to run off without telling me where she's going. I will deal sternly with the lass the moment she sets foot in Griffin Hall."

"Send someone to her grandmother's house to check on her and her grandmother's wellbeing," Rebecca said.

"And notify me the minute Lucy returns." Sarah dismissed the housekeeper. "That will be all."

"Yes, my lady." The housekeeper spread her apron and curtsied before heading toward the kitchens.

Sarah turned to her fiancé. "You're worried too."

Rebecca followed Sarah's gaze to Professor Matthews, who was rubbing his lower jaw with a frown.

"Something has been troubling me, especially now that there's been another disappearance."

Sarah notched her chin. "What is it?"

His Adam's apple bobbed. "I fear someone has been tampering with my plants. Specifically, my foxglove. I approached Professor Duval, thinking he'd used some for his experiment, but he claimed not to know anything about it."

"When did that happen?" Rebecca asked.

"A few days after our arrival was the first time."

Rebecca stepped closer. "It's happened more than once?"

"Twice, but I've yet to check on my plants today."

Sarah gestured to the staircase. "Then I suggest we do so."

Professor Matthews gestured for the ladies to go ahead of him and spoke as he climbed the stairs. "I received word from a colleague that the examination of Miss Blakeford revealed signs of poisoning." He took Sarah's arm as they strode down the hall. "Not merely a laudanum overdose."

He stopped in front of his chamber and swung the door open to a small forest of plants. His room appeared more like a terrarium than a bedchamber. He moved to the plant labeled *foxglove.* "It has been tampered with."

"How can you tell?" Sarah touched a leaf.

"Look here. Another limb clipped as happened two days ago." He pointed to stubs where the leaves had been removed. "And here." He moved his finger to where a root looked dug out. "They've been careful not to make their scavenging noticeable."

"If your plant was tampered with shortly before Miss Blakeford disappeared and she was found to have been poisoned, and you said it was tampered with again a couple of days ago right before Lucy went missing..." Rebecca swallowed. "You don't think..."

"Oh, dear." Sarah clasped a hand over her mouth. "Poor Lucy."

"Do not fear." Professor Matthews moved to another plant and fingered its leaves with a smile. "If someone tried to poison Lucy, they'll be shocked when she awakes feeling refreshed from a grand slumber."

Sarah looked to Rebecca and back to her intended. "I don't understand."

Rebecca stepped closer, understanding dawning. "This isn't digitalis." She eyed the other plants and spied the foxglove in the far corner in a pot labeled *valerian.* "You switched the labels."

"Bright young lady." The professor nodded as if she were a student who'd given the correct answer in one of his classes.

"So there's hope for Lucy?" Sarah's hand covered her heart.

"One can never know what men with evil intent will do." He pursed his lips and grunted. "But it helps her chances."

Thank You, Lord.

Another plant caught Rebecca's eye, and she leaned in to examine it. "Is this soapwort?"

"Indeed, it is."

"Did you buy it from the local chandler?"

"I did upon my arrival. I like to make my own soap. Do you also?"

"I was merely wondering." Rebecca smiled.

Professor Matthews had purchased soapwort, which was often used in candle making. His answer and actions were enough proof for her to exonerate him from any wrongdoing. His visit to the chandler's shop on the day the man died was coincidental.

Now she could focus on how to help Lucy. Had she woken up alone and scared somewhere in a sack? Could it have been her in the bag the footman carried? They'd searched the mill and found nothing. Had he seen Daniel and her approaching and relocated? Where else could he have taken Lucy?

She should return to the mill for a second look, but doing so could be dangerous.

Perhaps she should wait for Daniel.

~

*D*aniel calmed Mrs. Shepherd as he walked her back to the rooms she let above the apothecary's shop. "You have my word that he is unharmed and shall be returned as soon as everyone's safety is ensured." He bowed, excusing himself. "It shouldn't be long now—not more than a week."

Because time was running out for the remainder of Lady Coburn's party. He needed to work fast. After leaving Mrs. Shepherd at her door, he jogged to the main street.

At least he'd narrowed the mastermind down to one of the professors. But which one, or were they all complicit?

The ledgers.

He snapped his fingers and strode several blocks to the chandler's shop.

A *closed* sign hung on the door, and he skirted around to the back entrance not to draw curious eyes. Giles's hackneyed accent rang from upstairs. Before Daniel made his presence known, he moved to the chandler's desk and flipped open the ledger to the last page.

Soapwort plant – Professor Richard Matthews. Soapwort was useful in making candles but also in making soap and cleaning clothes. So Professor Matthews had made a purchase from the chandler.

He climbed the stairs, entered the chandler's quarters, and halted.

"Lieutenant?"

Lieutenant Scar sat playing a hand of cards with Giles in the front drawing room. He tossed a card into the pile before acknowledging Daniel.

Giles eyed Daniel warily before frowning at the discard.

"I heard Mr. Shepherd's voice." Daniel tugged down his jacket to tidy his appearance. "I expected to see the constable."

"The constable had some work to tend to, and I was called into the area on assignment." He fingered another card as Giles drew.

A different assignment or to take over his?

"I figured you'd eventually return to the chandler's apartment. I relieved the constable and recruited Mr. Shepherd. It didn't suit to have him locked up when he could be collecting intelligence in the field." He winked at the lad. "I've kept him under close surveillance. We may have an agent in training."

Was this the new tactic the lieutenant had mentioned?

Daniel didn't need Giles's help or Scar's. He could apprehend the villains on his own. He swallowed. How many women would disappear before he'd get over his pride? "What did Mr. Shepherd find out?"

"The lieutenant had me meet with me employer to see if he had another job." Giles's face brightened, and he sat up straighter. "He said, he ain't got no work—"

"Hasn't any work," Lieutenant Spark's corrected.

"He hasn't any work for a grunt like me." Giles enunciated the words. "But when I pressed him, he said that something is goin' down tonight, but it don't involve digging up no bodies."

"*Doesn't* involve digging up *any* bodies." Lieutenant Scar raised a single eyebrow. "If you want to go undercover, you're going to have to learn to speak properly when needed."

"I shall, milord." Giles's proper accent needed work. "I promise."

Lieutenant Scar shifted in his chair to face Daniel. "Mr. Shepherd led me to one of their henchmen."

"You followed me?" Giles stared at the lieutenant.

"Of course." Lieutenant Scar folded his hands and set them on the table. "You've refused to divulge any names."

Giles huffed, crossing his arms and pouting.

Lieutenant Scar looked to Daniel. "The one I saw has access to Griffin Hall."

"Let me guess. He's tall with blond hair."

"Indeed."

"He pretends to be a groom or a footman and was last seen with Miss Blakeford." Daniel gave himself a mental shake and focused on Lieutenant Scar. "Another woman has gone missing."

"Indeed. It's the reason I was summoned. Lady Coburn contacted the constable threatening to bend the ear of the king. The constable informed her that we already have our man on it, but he sent for me, anyway." Lieutenant Scar's gaze held a wistful look. "I'd hoped to be heading home to my wife."

Giles scooted forward in his seat. "Who was the victim?"

"A lady's maid. A nice young woman named Lucy Josting."

"Lucy!" Giles jumped up and grasped his head. He started to pace. "No, not Lucy."

Daniel glanced at Lieutenant Scar for an explanation.

"Giles is sweet on a girl named Lucy."

"Help us, then." Daniel banged his fist on the door frame. "Give us the intelligence we need to save her."

My power is made perfect in weakness.

Weak? He couldn't afford to be weak this time. Another woman has disappeared. Power lay in strength, and he had to be strong if he didn't want the blood of other victims on his conscience.

This was Daniel's opportunity. He gripped the lad's elbows, lifting him from his seat, and forced him to look him in the eye. "Enough, Giles. Innocent people are being murdered. You'll be an accomplice if you don't tell us who's behind this."

The young man's face took on a greenish hue as though he might retch. Tears welled in his eyes. "I can't." His voice cracked. "I don't care if ya lock me up or if they kill me, but I've gotta protect me mum and family."

"We can protect them." He glanced at Lieutenant Scar, who nodded his affirmation. "We'll move them to another town, give them new names and opportunities to work for nobility."

Giles groaned and shook his head. "Leafield is our 'ome. It's our family and all we've ever known. I can't uproot 'em. We ain't got nowhere else. Our blood and sweat is in Leafield's dirt. My ancestors 'elped build Griffin 'all and laid the foundation fer the chapel under Sir 'enry Unton of Bruern. My pa worked as a potter turnin' Leafield clay into jars. These are our people. We're born on Leafield dirt, and to Leafield dirt we return."

Daniel let the young man go and paced, his fingers curling into fists. There had to be a way to force Giles to talk. He could feel Lieutenant Scar's gaze on him, and Grandfather's voice echoed in his memory. *The boy's soft. He's weak.*

He couldn't handle this. He was being bested by a lad. More people would die because of him.

"Blast it all." He gripped Giles's shirt front. "People are going to die."

The kid's fearful gaze met his. "And their blood's more precious than my family's?"

"What about Lucy? What about her blood? We can prevent her death if you'd just cooperate."

Giles pressed his lips together, his gaze hardening with a deadened, glazed-over look. No information would be forthcoming tonight.

Daniel dug his hands into his hair. There had to be a way to make Giles talk. *Lord, give me wisdom.*

Blessed are the meek, for they shall inherit the earth.

What did that mean? How did that apply to getting names out of Giles? He must be hearing God wrong. But what should he do instead?

CHAPTER 29

*R*ebecca entered her chamber, her head spinning from the tampering of the digitalis plant.

"How dare you!" Corinne shrieked.

A pit opened in Rebecca's stomach, and she drew up short at the sound of her cousin's voice. She'd known a day of reckoning would come. She should have told Daniel the truth earlier. Corinne's arrival meant her chances of telling him herself had lessened. Swallowing past the tightness in her throat, she forced a steady tone. "Corinne."

Her cousin glared, her hard eyes filled with accusations. "Did you think you could ensnare Lord Wolston out from under my nose?"

Rebecca glanced at Madeline, but her sister stood wide-eyed and stiff in the corner. Rebecca met her cousin's accusing scowl. "I had no idea he was going to be Lady Coburn's guest, and neither did you."

"You should have written me the moment he arrived, but you didn't." She stepped around the bed and past her trunks, consuming the space between them until Rebecca's back flattened against the closed door. "He sees right through you to the dowdy bluestocking pauper your papa handed over, begging for us to help you find a merited match."

Had she spoken with Daniel? A defensive muscle twitched in Rebecca's jaw, but Corinne's words held more than a hint of truth. It had always been inevitable that their trickery would be revealed. She had no right to wish for more time, but she did. She needed one more moment with Daniel, one last chance to explain.

Corinne pointed a sharp finger at Rebecca's chin. Her cousin's dangling earbobs appeared to tremble with malice. "You've overstepped. The marquis is *mine*, and I will ruin you if you've hindered my chances."

"So you've seen him?"

"Looking like this?" Corinne peered in the looking glass. "I daresay not. I shall change and freshen up first. I must look my best to redeem his opinion of me."

Rebecca relaxed against the door for a moment. She still had a chance—however slim. "I'd had little interaction with him until Miss Blakeford...until her...until she was found." Other than their kiss in the Lipscomb's garden, their tour of the grounds, and when she reset his dislocated shoulder. "I'm terribly sorry about your governess." Rebecca's heart softened. Had grief exacerbated her cousin's anger? "We had a small burial ceremony, and many of the staff and guests attended to honor her." The guests had come out of care for Rebecca, having never met Miss Blakeford. "And also, you." Since technically, the guests thought she was Corinne.

A shadow crossed over Corinne's features, sucking the gusto out of her wrath, but a moment later, it was gone. "She was bound to wind up dead with her cravings for laudanum."

"Why didn't you warn us of her inclination toward the medicine?" Rebecca pressed forward, and it was Corinne's turn to back step.

Corinne's nostrils flared. "I didn't see how it mattered."

"Didn't matter? Do you think it matters now? Because she's dead."

"Why did Lord Wolston pay you attention after her death?" Corinne notched her chin. "You acted the part of a distraught noblewoman to draw sympathy. Is that it?"

How wretched was Corinne's thinking. As if she would use poor Miss Blakeford's death for personal gain. "Of course not."

Corinne snorted. "Such a pathetic attempt probably went unnoticed. You have no clue how to draw a man's attention."

Egad. Would her cousin have used such a ploy?

"Our cousin is probably famished from the long ride." Madeline edged around the trunks and squeezed around Rebecca, making her escape. "I'm going to bring up a tray from the kitchens."

"I'll be partaking with the guests. I inquired about Lord Wolston's whereabouts, and he's ridden into town. The poor marquis has to find his entertainment elsewhere. At least he's still expected for the evening meal." Corinne strode to the wardrobe, threw open the doors, and examined its contents. "Tonight's the masquerade, correct?"

"Indeed, but—"

"You'll help me dress until Madeline returns with the tray. Meanwhile, you can bring me up to date. It's time I rectify the mess you've created."

"*I* created? This was your idea."

"And it was terribly executed. You were supposed to pretend to be me, but you probably acted bookish and bored him with your bluestocking ways, droning on about diseases and heart conditions." Corinne sighed as if daunted by the heavy task created for her. "The marquis must believe me a terrible bore."

Blue. The tenderly whispered nickname echoed in her memory. *I consider it a term of endearment. I admire a woman with a mind.*

Could he find it in his heart to forgive her?

"We can't be seen together." Corinne selected a taffeta gown with a sheer overlay and tiny lavender embroidered roses. "As it was, I had to use a side entrance to avoid being spotted. You and Madeline will have to rise before the guests awaken. My lady's maid and driver are lodging at the tavern in the center of town. My driver will return you to Buckinghamshire."

"I can't leave. We're..." Running an experiment. No. She could no longer take part in an experiment that could hurt the patients. She would find a less risky method to help Madeline.

"You're what?" Corinne crossed her arms.

"We must say goodbye to our friends."

"Are you mad?" Corinne clapped a hand to her forehead. "We'd be wreathed in scandal. I will use my charms to turn this around tonight. I'll win the favor of the marquis, and then I will tell him why you pretended to be me."

"You can't blame this on me. The falsehood was your idea."

"The desire to help your sister is the best excuse we have. Otherwise, your Season will be ruined before it begins. You'll be a social pariah." Corinne turned and pointed to her back.

Rebecca began unfastening the hooks and buttons, but her mind whirled. How could her cousin do this to her? Was it Corinne's plan all along for her to take the fall? Her aunt and uncle would surely find out and be furious. No. Corinne must be improvising. She'd never anticipated Daniel coming to the Coburn party.

Daniel.

How could she leave without explaining her side to Daniel or to Sarah? They'd both come to mean so much to her. And then there was Lady Coburn, who'd been a lovely hostess, Lord and Lady Farsley, who'd shown her how to play shuttlecock, Lord McGower teaching her all about India, and the professors...

In a short time, they'd become like family.

Rebecca's heart clenched. She'd miss them terribly.

"It's ludicrous to think the guests will believe you're me." Rebecca couldn't shake the hollow feeling. "They'll know right away. We look similar, but there are differences." She hugged her midsection. "I've come to know and respect Lady Coburn and the rest of those in attendance. They are intelligent and kind people."

"Hopefully, kind enough to show some forgiveness." Corinne shrugged. "My only concern is the marquis. Lady Coburn's guests don't run in my social circles. They can say what they want, but anything negative they report will be discredited because my friends saw me at the Carter's party." Corinne stepped out of her day gown. "I need you to review everything that's happened since you first arrived."

Rebecca guided the lavender taffeta dress over her cousin's head. As she buttoned the long line of tiny fabric-covered buttons, she told Corinne of her interactions with Lord Wolston, Lady Coburn, Sarah Evans, and Professor Duval. Her cousin stopped her periodically to repeat any informal forms of address, such as her calling Mrs. Evans *Sarah*. Corinne's lips thinned into a straight line when she learned Rebecca was on a first-name basis with the marquis.

Madeline returned with the tray and set it aside to aid Rebecca with Corinne's coiffure.

When they finished, Corinne studied herself in the mirror. "I must look my best for the marquis. If I'm appealing enough tonight, he'll forget all the boring dribble he's had to endure and be grateful for my company. I presume he's investigating my governess's death to strum up excitement, so he doesn't perish of boredom. I knew I'd need to invent some mystery to keep my mind occupied if the marquis wasn't in attendance."

Daniel hadn't seemed bored, but then again, what did Rebecca know about how the *ton* amused themselves. She'd attended two parties thus far, not a large enough sample to draw any significant conclusions. The longer she listened to

Corinne, the more she doubted she'd made any impression on Daniel or the guests. Maybe they'd only acted kindly to her because they thought she was the earl's daughter.

"Fix this curl." Corinne pointed to her hair. "It looks out of place."

Madeline removed the pin and replaced it in the exact same spot, eyeing Rebecca with a vexed look.

"You can pack while I'm dining. It shouldn't take you long. That way, you can leave at first light."

"What?" Madeline peered at Rebecca and shook her head. "I'm not leaving until Lucy is found."

Corinne's gaze rolled skyward. "Who's Lucy?"

"She's Sarah's lady's maid," Rebecca said.

Madeline was right. They couldn't depart without knowing they'd done everything they could to locate Lucy. Rebecca also couldn't leave until she'd spoken with each of the participants in Professor Duval's experiments and explained the potentially dangerous side effects caused by higher dosages of digitals that William Withering listed in his findings. They could then make informed decisions on whether to continue the medication.

"You're going to risk our family's reputation on a missing maid?" Corinne rose and shook any wrinkles from her gown. "She probably took another job or went on holiday and didn't have the decency to inform her current employer."

"She didn't." Madeline frowned. "You don't know Lucy."

"This discussion is going to make me late for the evening meal." She slipped on a demi-mask adorned to resemble a butterfly which covered all but her eyes, lips, and chin. "We can't afford to be seen together. If you want to check into the inn at the tavern and stay there until Lucy turns up, that's fine." Corinne wagged her index finger at Rebecca. "But you must stay out of sight. Madeline may come and go from the inn on a limited basis."

Madeline eyed Rebecca.

Rebecca, usually given to weighing and measuring her options and seeking creative solutions, could only conjure the image of Daniel's smile.

Lord, forgive my deception. Let the consequences of my actions fall upon my shoulders and not those who've shown me kindness. Please soften Daniel's heart to show undeserved mercy for my folly, and also soften Lady Coburn's heart and those of her guests. I never meant to hurt them or make them believe I played them as fools.

"Wish me luck." Corinne swept from the room with a smile.

As the door closed behind her, Madeline snorted. "Am I imagining it, or did she become tyrannical in our absence?"

Rebecca chuckled a hollow laugh. She remembered visiting Corinne when they were young, witnessing how her parents flittered about, barely acknowledging their daughter. On one occasion, Corinne's parents had sent her to visit Rebecca's family's humble cottage. How withdrawn her cousin had seemed at the beginning. But by the end of her visit, she smiled, laughed, and ran around outside with enthusiasm. She'd cried when the coach with the Mercer crest arrived to take her home.

A stern elderly nanny had stood by the open conveyance door. Rebecca's home wasn't elegant and grand like her cousin's, but she'd never doubted the love of her mother and her sister. She'd felt overwhelmed with gratitude for her humble family as Corinne hugged them all with a tight squeeze before being led away.

"I think she's merely lonely."

Madeline sighed. "I suspect you are correct, but that makes her no less horrid to be around." She brought the tray to the bed. "I have wonderful news despite the dark cloud our cousin's arrival has cast. I spoke to a servant who said he knows where Lucy is."

"Thank heaven." Rebecca glanced at the ceiling with sincerity and offered a silent prayer of gratitude. "I was so worried she'd wound up like Miss Blakeford. All I kept thinking was how I was going to give the news of her disappearance to her grandmama. Where has she been?"

"He said it was a secret and that he'd show me later."

A secret. Lady Coburn had over thirty footmen on staff, and she didn't want to frighten her sister, but Rebecca wasn't going to take the chance that Madeline spoke to the suspicious blond footman. "No." She wagged her finger at Madeline. "I don't want you speaking to anyone, especially footmen. I shouldn't even have allowed you to fetch our meal. You're to stay by my side from now on. Understood?"

Madeline chuckled. "There you go again, being overprotective. Don't worry. I promise to be careful." She inhaled the scent of beef stew. "I'm famished. Packing can wait until our stomachs are filled." She bowed her head. "Lord, bless this food in which we are about to partake. Amen."

"Amen." Rebecca echoed her, but instead of sitting and eating, she tidied up the ribbons and used hair pins, trying to conjure a creative way to explain and apologize to Daniel without Corinne quashing her attempt.

Madeline yawned. "The tea tastes different. I wonder what leaves they used."

Rebecca picked her teacup off the tray and sipped. "Mine tastes like it always does." She set the cup down and scooped up the traveling dress Corinne had discarded on the floor. She hung it on a hook to be cleaned and pressed when her cousin's actual lady's maid arrived.

Her sister expelled another loud yawn. "He said he added some extra sugar into mine because he knew I'd like it."

Rebecca's head snapped in Madeline's direction.

"Isn't that nice?" Madeline raised her arms in a stretch, arching her back.

"What man?" Rebecca moved to her sister's side. "Who is he?"

Madeline peered back at her with a heavy-lidded expression. "The footman who carried the tray—the one who knows where Lucy is."

"The blond footman?" A cold sweat broke over Rebecca's skin.

"He said I'm sweet and deserve some extra sugar." She smiled a lopsided grin and flopped back onto the pillows with another sleepy yawn. "I know it's all flummery. I warned Lucy to pay him no heed."

Rebecca jumped on the bed, straddling Madeline with her arms. "The blond footman?"

Madeline closed her eyes. "I think he's Nordic."

"Dear Lord, help us. You've been poisoned."

"Don't be silly." Madeline curled onto her side and tucked her hands under her head. "I'm just tired"—her voice weakened—"is all."

"Madeline." Rebecca tapped her cheek. "Don't go to sleep." She sprang from the bed and dashed to the water pitcher. She brought the entire carafe over and, gripping her sister's bodice, yanked her into a seated position.

"Rebecca!" Madeline's eyelids popped open.

"Drink this to dilute the poison."

"Poison?"

She squeezed Madeline's mouth open and poured in the water. Her sister drank some but most of it leaked out with a cough and sputter.

"You're going to drown me." Madeline confiscated the pitcher and set it aside. Her eyes appeared glazed, and she acted slightly intoxicated. "No one wants to poison me, silly. Come lie down and tell me a story like we used to do."

Rebecca paced. What had been put in the tea? Laudanum? Digitalis?

Picking up Madeline's empty teacup, Rebecca sniffed the inside, but the odor didn't smell like cinnamon or saffron. She frowned. The musk smelled like sweet oak—with a hint of dirty socks.

She shook Madeline, who opened her eyes. "Does your vision seem yellowed, or does the room have a green cast?"

Madeline shook her head.

"Does your head ache, or are you having any cold sweats?" Rebecca examined her sister's fingernails and lips for a bluish tint, but they looked pink and healthy.

"No."

"Do you feel you might cast up your accounts? Or is your heart pounding in your chest?"

"No and no." Madeline's eyelids fluttered closed, and her words slurred. "I feel very relaxed, like it would be lovely to close my eyes and sleep."

Sleep. Professor Matthews had switched the labels on his digitalis and valerian plants. He'd said the valerian would make a person sleepy, but that he didn't have enough for it to be toxic. Unless the culprits brought their own digitalis—and the way they'd raided the professor's stock, that seemed unlikely— perhaps Madeline would be all right.

Rebecca found a botany book from the stack she'd borrowed from the library and flipped to the page on valerian. She scanned the effects of consuming the root—sleepiness, vivid dreams, dizziness.

God, please let her tea have been only steeped with valerian.

She shook Madeline awake.

"I'm getting up, Mama. I'll be right over to help."

"It's me. Rebecca."

Madeline blinked, but her gaze remained heavy-lidded. "I was having the most wonderful dream. We were back at the cottage and Mama was there." A crooked smile grew on her lips. "It was so real. I could see Mama's face and smell her scent."

"Are you feeling dizzy?"

She frowned. "A little."

Thank heaven. Her symptoms lined up with the effects of valerian more so than laudanum or digitalis.

Now what? Would the footman come by soon to collect his victim?

She couldn't allow him to find Madeline.

Was this how Lucy disappeared?

Think, Rebecca, think.

She and Madeline should hide, but where?

Trust in the Lord with all your heart.

Madeline is my heart. I would do anything for her. Please, Lord. Help us.

Where would no one think to look? Where would they be safe and protected?

Daniel.

She remembered how Daniel spoke of his sisters, his concern and care for them, how he vowed to protect them. And her.

Daniel could be trusted. She knew it in her heart, but Corinne said he'd ridden into town.

Time was of the essence.

His room was down the hall. She needed to get Madeline out of here before the footman returned for her.

She pulled on Madeline's arm and hooked it around her own neck while sliding her other hand around her sister's waist. "We need to go for a little walk, and I need you to help me."

Madeline's eyes flicked open, and she groaned. "I just want to sleep."

"And you can. Just not here." She hefted Madeline to her feet and half carried, half walked her to the door. Cracking it open, Rebecca peeked out to ensure the hall was empty before stumbling under Madeline's limp weight down the corridor and around the bend to Daniel's door. She didn't dare knock lest she draw the villain's attention. Instead, she hugged Madeline to her side and leaned to support her weight while she lifted the latch and entered his room.

The scent of sandalwood hung in the air. His space was neat and tidy, just as it had been the last time she was here. They could hide here and be safe.

Madeline spied the bed and crawled on top.

If you could save one, would you?

Her own words haunted her. Could she pose as Madeline to save Lucy? Should she go back to her room?

The idea was mad. The footman could show up at any moment.

But what if Lucy could be saved?

She didn't know if Lucy was even still alive.

Lean not on your own understanding.

Mama and Madeline said this verse often, but what was God trying to tell her? *God, what would you have me do?*

She could try to get information out of the footman when he came for Madeline, but that would be neither safe nor logical.

His ways are higher than our ways.

Rebecca covered her face with her hands. *Being smart doesn't help unless you have the courage to act.*

Truly? Corinne's words?

Then again, God could use anyone. Was He trying to tell her to go after His lost lamb? Perhaps if she had time to prepare, figure out a backup plan, hide a weapon, and station watchmen, this might be a good idea.

Lord, I'm scared.

Be strong and courageous. The Lord your God is with you wherever you go.

What if a servant entered Daniel's chamber in the meantime? Would they carry Madeline back to her room?

She studied Daniel's room. The large four-poster bed sat

high off the ground. Rebecca could hide her sister underneath and then go for help.

Wisdom is granted by God and should be lived, Mama had said.

"God, I'm trusting You." She pulled Madeline off the bed and grabbed a pillow. "I'm sorry, Madeline, but you're going to have to sleep under the bed. I need for you to stay hidden."

Madeline didn't put up much resistance. She allowed herself to be moved to the floor, snuggled against the pillow Rebecca handed to her, and proceeded to sleep on the floor next to the bed.

Rebecca lifted the bed skirt and shimmied her sister beneath, letting the covering fall back into place. No one would know she slept under the bed unless they peeked under the dust ruffle. Should she leave a note just in case? She strode to his writing desk, dipped a feather in the inkwell, and scribbled on a sheet of paper.

Daniel,

Madeline was poisoned by the blond footman, but Professor Matthews switched the plant labels, so I believe she was only given a sleeping elixir. The footman claims to know where Lucy is. I'm going to try to save her. Please look after Madeline. She's not my maid. She's my sister. I hope someday you can forgive me for pretending to be Corinne. I'm truly sorry for the deceit and any harm it may have caused.

Sincerely,

Rebecca Prestcote

Where could she hide the note where Daniel would find it? She glanced around the room. A Bible lay on his nightstand, a ribbon marking his place. She turned it toward her, flipped the cover open, and slid the note inside. She placed it on the bed, hoping he'd notice that he hadn't left it there and look inside. She paused as she strode to the door.

Lord, watch over Madeline. I entrust her into Your capable hands.

She opened the door and once again peeked into the hall. Nothing stirred, so she slipped out of Daniel's room and headed for the stairs, praying Daniel was back from town. If he wasn't, then she'd approach Professor Matthews and Sarah for their aid.

Rounding the bend at a brisk pace, she scurried down the hall. Her chamber lay on the right. Had she left it open a crack when she carried Madeline?

The door flung wide, and the blond footman exited with a fierce expression.

She drew up short and gasped.

His head snapped in her direction.

Rebecca froze.

His eyes narrowed.

Run!

Snatching her skirts to one side, Rebecca attempted to turn and run. She made it three steps before he slammed her against the wall. Her muffled scream was cut off by his hand covering her mouth.

"I saw you enter the drawin' room seconds ago." His hot breath hissed against her ear. "Some game you're up to. No one knows you're here, do they?"

His words sent a chill through her bloodstream.

"No one ta sound an alarm if you go missin'."

Kicking and bucking, she bumped the wall, knocking the portraits of past Coburns crooked. The painted smugglers were the only witnesses as the man dragged her into her chamber and shut the door.

They wouldn't say a word.

CHAPTER 30

*D*aniel hurried through Griffin Hall's main entrance doors, nodding to the butler. He checked his pocket watch, passing the main stairs toward the dining room. They'd be announcing the evening meal at any moment, and he'd wanted to talk to Blue beforehand, since they'd so often been seated at opposite ends of the table. He turned into the foyer and caught sight of Blue's graceful form ahead, her dark hair up in an elaborate coiffure of silken curls. He lengthened his stride to catch up to her but barely reached her side as they neared the entrance to the drawing room where everyone gathered.

"Blue."

She didn't turn.

He touched her elbow. "Blue."

"My lord." She spun and hit him with a brilliant smile under a butterfly mask before falling into a deep curtsy. "My gown is a shade of lavender."

Blast, he'd forgotten tonight was the masquerade dinner. He'd have to send a footman to retrieve a mask for him.

"Do you like it?" She posed with a hand on her waist, offering him a pretty pout.

"The gown? Uh...yes. Of course." She seemed off. Was this behavior because she'd witnessed Mrs. Shepherd's display?

"You're not wearing a mask." She pressed a graceful hand to the side of hers.

He didn't have time for small talk. The doors would open to the dining room any moment. He searched for some place private to tell her about Professor Matthews's purchase logged in the chandler's ledgers. "We have much to discuss."

She curved a possessive hand around his arm. "I would be delighted." She glanced into the drawing room and then down the hall. "Shall we find a quieter spot"—she flashed a seductive smile—"to talk?"

He pulled her aside next to a suit of armor in the hall within sight of the drawing room but where they wouldn't be heard over the hum of the gathering guests. Not only did she look a little different, but her countenance was off. Was it the elaborate gown and hairstyle replacing her usual simple elegance?

"Professor Matthews purchased soapwort from the chandler. It was the last entry in his ledgers." Did her face seem fuller, or was it merely that unusual smile, which seemed so wide it bordered on unnatural?

"How fascinating." She looked away toward a few guests meandering toward the dining room.

That wasn't the response he'd expected. "I can explain about the episode outside."

"Please do."

So she was angry.

The Coburn butler cleared his throat, and the footman opened the doors to the dining room. Lady Coburn, dressed in a peacock mask with blue and green feathers fanning from the back, announced the evening meal and instructed them to make their way inside. She approached Daniel with Lady and Lord Farsley, who were dressed as Napoleon and Josephine.

Lady Coburn glanced at Blue's hand on Daniel's arm and addressed her. "You're paired with Lord McGower tonight, my dear."

Blue issued a grunt of disapproval and murmured something under her breath.

"I'll find you after to talk." He removed her hand but gave it an affectionate squeeze.

Blue hit him with another of those strange, wide smiles and curtsied. "Of course."

Lady Coburn frowned as Blue strode to the fireplace, where Professors Bell and Matthews appeared in a deep discussion. Both wore their usual garb with mere demi-masks.

Odd. Lord McGower and Professor Duval stood in the opposite corner. Neither wore a costume that would render them unrecognizable. Lord McGower had chosen to dress as a Hindu solider, and Professor Duval wore his spectacles over his demi-mask. Lord McGower crossed the room and bowed to Blue as her escort.

"She doesn't seem herself tonight." Lady Coburn's peacock feathers quivered when she handed him the same demi-mask that the professors wore. It seemed he wasn't the only one who'd forgotten.

"Agreed." Daniel thanked her and tied the mask around the back of his head. He offered her his arm, led her across the hall to the dining room, and stopped at the head of the table, followed by Lord McGower and Blue, who progressed to the far end.

Lord Farsley piped up beside Daniel. "Where is Lady Prestcote tonight?"

"What do you mean, darling?" Lady Farsley rubbed her husband's arm. "We were with her moments ago."

Daniel faced Lord Farsley.

"That wasn't Lady Prestcote." His unseeing eyes stared straight ahead. "I was going to ask to be introduced to the new visitor."

The other guests filed in and stood, waiting for their hostess to be seated first, except for Professors Bell and Duval, who remained in the hallway.

Lady Prestcote issued Daniel a sultry glance down the length of the table.

The back of Daniel's neck tingled.

He faced Lord Farsley, his voice low. "What makes you say that?"

"For one, they don't smell the same. Lady Prestcote smells fresh, like a bouquet of gardenias, while the new guest reeks of expensive French toilet water."

"Couldn't she have worn a different perfume tonight?" Lady Coburn glanced in Lady Prestcote's direction but averted her gaze when the imposter turned her way.

Daniel stepped closer, hoping Lord Farsley would pick up on the need for a more private discussion. He lowered his voice. "The newcomer resembles Lady Prestcote, but I, too, notice some slight differences." Since Lord Farsley couldn't see the woman, he wasn't fooled. "What else is different?"

"Lady Prestcote has a slight country accent," he whispered, "while our visitor's dialect is closer to the city—most likely, Buckinghamshire."

Daniel stiffened. If that woman wasn't Blue, then where was she?

"Oh, my." Lady Coburn eyed Daniel as he aided her to sit and the other guests took their cue to also be seated. "I barely spoke to her, but she did seem...well, different. Surely, there must be some sort of explanation. They look similar enough to be sisters. What should we do?"

"Let me handle this." Daniel bowed to Lady Coburn and

strode toward the imposter. Lord McGower nodded as he approached, and he bowed to the man and the supposed Lady Prestcote. "I beg your pardon. There is an urgent matter that needs attention. Lady Prestcote, would you come with me, please?"

Uncertainty flashed in her eyes, but she nodded. "Of course, my Lord. I do hope there's not a problem."

She was most definitely an imposter. There were no gold flecks in her green eyes that sparkled with curious interest, and her face lacked Blue's delicate chin. A rounder chin graced the fraud's face, giving it a fuller look.

"That is to be determined." He pulled out her chair and offered his hand to aid her to rise.

She stood and, once again, leaned a little too close to the length of him.

Daniel ushered the stranger into the hall.

Professors Duval and Bell, still outside the dining room, silenced their conversation and nodded a greeting, watching them pass.

Daniel pulled her into the now-empty drawing room, and against propriety, closed the door before facing her.

After a glance at the closed door, she hit him with another seductive look. Her gloved hand ran down the lapel of his jacket. "What is all this about?"

He narrowed his eyes. "Who are you?"

"Whatever do you mean?" She emitted a hollow laugh. "I'm Lady Corinne Prestcote."

"No, you're not." He roughly brushed her hand aside.

"I am Corinne Prestcote, daughter of Lord and Lady Mercer." She raised her chin and crossed her arms, giving her bosom an extra lift.

Daniel focused on her green eyes. "There is no brown spot in your eye. If you're truly Corinne, then who has been posing as you these past few weeks?"

"I... It's merely..." He could see her mind working out the best angle for another mistruth. Her lips thinned and she muttered, "It's her reputation more at stake than mine." She shrugged one shoulder. "That's my cousin, Rebecca Prestcote. She was being a love by filling in for me here so I could attend the Carter party." She stepped closer. "Neither of us wanted to miss out. We figured no harm could be done."

He remembered the letter addressed to Lady Prestcote that he'd opened and the scripted letter C of the signature. This romp of a woman was the blackmailer, but for a different cover-up. At least he knew for sure that Blue...Rebecca Prestcote hadn't been involved in a body snatching ring. Though he itched to step away from this woman, doing so might show weakness and only encourage her.

Her chin tipped up, and her lashes batted. "You and she must have gotten close if you noticed that dreadful brown spot in her eye."

Dreadful?

He tried to wipe the image of Blue's face away, but a cheap replica stared up at him. While he'd given her his heart, she'd been lying to him. A pang in his chest stole his breath.

Blue hasn't been forthright, but neither have you.

He'd been as honest as a spy could be, though. He had a plausible excuse. What was hers?

His teeth set on edge. "Your cousin agreed to this pretension?"

"Happily."

"Why? How did she benefit from the ruse?"

Corinne Prestcote fingered the lapel of his jacket before meeting his gaze. "Her father has practically gambled himself into debtors' prison. She was eager to come, desperate to make a match that will pay down his debts."

The woman's words didn't ring true, not based on what he'd come to know about Blue. She didn't have it in her character to maintain a ruse once a man inquired about her hand in marriage. No, there had to be a different reason she would agree to this.

Pieces from the night at the Lipscomb party started to fall into place. It was Blue whose gown had ripped, whom he'd caught falling down the stairs, and whom he'd kissed that evening. She must have left the party. Later, he'd been introduced to Corinne Prestcote and mistaken the aggressive, manipulative, and title-hunting cousin for Blue.

Blue cared more about looking for a cure for her ill maid than about landing a husband.

Except, if her family was poor, then could she afford a lady's maid?

"Who is Madeline?"

The real Lady Prestcote sighed as if growing weary. "Madeline is my other cousin."

Her sister.

Another Miss Prestcote. He would have to mentally refer to them by their given names to keep them all straight. Now he understood Blue's emotional attachment to her maid, who wasn't her maid at all but her sister. Thus, her determination to find a cure made sense.

He summoned past conversations with her. She'd accidentally referred to her beloved aunt who'd passed as her mother. Why had he dismissed the seriousness of her slip earlier?

Because he'd been too concerned trying to protect a woman he believed was being blackmailed.

"They couldn't afford a lady's maid, so her sister filled the position for propriety's sake. I offered my governess to act as her chaperone, and now I'm devastated by her death." As if to prove her point, she swiped a gloved finger beneath her dry eyes.

Devastated, indeed.

Could Lady Corinne have been behind Miss Blakeford's

disappearance? His gaze narrowed. Or Lucy's? "Where are your cousins now?"

"Upstairs in my chamber, packing to leave."

"Leave?"

"I'm here now." She stepped closer, and her rich perfume assaulted his nostrils. Her leg brushed against his before she straightened the knot in his cravat. "There's no reason for them to stay."

Blue wouldn't leave without saying goodbye. Or would she leave thinking she was doing the right thing? He remembered the remorse in her eyes when she'd said, *I fear I have let you down.*

He must find her, shake some sense into her, and get her to understand that all he asked of her was her love. She didn't need to pretend to be someone else or try to impress him.

Come to think of it, she'd done nothing of the sort. She'd been herself, nothing but herself, the entire time he'd known her. Kind, generous, loving, and intellectual, his bluestocking. His Blue.

She'd shown him her silly faults, such as her tendency to fall into the strangest predicaments with torn hems and wet cloaks, how she twisted the tip of her glove when nervous, and the lovely blush that colored her cheeks when his affections embarrassed her, but he loved those most of all.

He stepped around Corinne and headed for the door that led to the foyer.

"Wait!" She scurried to catch up with him. "Where are you going?"

He pivoted and placed a hand on the knob. "To find her."

"My cousin?" She pressed a hand to the door and hit him with another seductive smile. "Why, when you have the better version?"

"Because I love her." He brushed Corinne's hand away and opened the door.

"What?" Her mouth gaped open. "That's ridiculous."

Daniel stepped into the hall and nearly collided with Professor Bell, still speaking with Professor Duval.

Corinne followed. "I don't know why you're going to such lengths for a penniless pauper." She grabbed his arm. "My cousin is a nobody. Hardly anyone even knows she exists."

The professors glanced at Corinne before eyeing each other.

Fury filled Daniel's chest and must've bled into his glare because she yanked her arm back as if bitten by a spider.

He begged the professors' pardon and sidestepped around them, breaking for the stairs.

"Wait." Corinne scurried to catch up. "She's only using you."

He didn't dignify her comment with a response as he mounted the stairs.

"All she cares about is books." Corinne, huffing and panting, followed him to the second floor.

At least that skimmed the truth, the only words from Corinne's mouth that did. Blue did care about books, but she also cared deeply about her sister, a missing maid named Lucy, Lucy's grandmother, the subjects Duval may have poisoned, Lady Coburn, and her quirky guests.

And him.

Blue had showed her love in how she cared for his shoulder, valued his opinions, sought his help, and leaned on his strength.

Lady Corinne dogged his steps. "She'll turn you into an oddball recluse like the other guests here."

"Splendid." His long strides ate up the hall runner. "Then I'll be in excellent company."

He reached Blue's door and knocked.

"You *like* these people?" Corinne's incredulous pitch screeched in his ear.

"Quite." He knocked again. "Blue, open up."

"Allow me." Corinne squeezed past him and opened the door. "Rebecca, it's past time you told the marquis about your papa and his desperate condit..." She strode to the foot of the bed and glanced around. "Madeline?" She crossed to the door to the dressing room and opened it.

In the doorway, Daniel's gaze fell upon the wrinkled bedcovering half pulled onto the floor as if someone had yanked on it. The tray on top perched precariously on the edge. It held two plates, the food mostly untouched, and two teacups, one empty and the other with tea sloshed into the saucer. The end table next to a reading chair had been kicked over, and books lay toppled on the floor, one with its cover open.

Fresh scratches in the bedpost, light wood against the dark stain, caught his eye. The way they were spaced apart told him...

Were those from fingernails?

A cold jolt ran through his veins, seizing his breath.

Blue had been taken by force.

He'd vowed to protect her... and failed, just as he'd failed to protect his sister.

Please Lord, not Blue. Images of Miss Blakeford's cold, dissected body lying on the lecture hall table popped into his mind, changing to Blue's dark hair, fuller lips, and smoother skin.

His chest tightened as if a vice squeezed all the air from his lungs. He wouldn't imagine Blue lying there. *Lord, help me find her.*

The Lord is her protector.

"They must have left already." Corinne turned with a snort and flung open the wardrobe. "She couldn't even bother to bid anyone farewell." She paused and stared at the shoe hooks. "How odd. She didn't pack her slippers or half boots."

What if he was too late to save Blue? Daniel fell to his knees.

God's power is made perfect in weakness.

Corinne gasped.

For when you are weak, then you are strong.

He closed his eyes. *Lord, I'm a weak vessel. I need Your help. Guide me to locate Blue, her sister, and Lucy before it's too late. Be my eyes and ears. Protect them. Be their front and rear guard. Don't let any weapon forged against them prevail. I thank You for Your goodness and mercy. Amen.*

He forced air into his lungs, and with a new sense of purpose, he pushed his fears aside, allowing his mind to take over.

He needed to think straight. He needed to behave as if this were any other case.

"What's wrong?" Corinne was frozen, staring with horror as he knelt on the floor.

"I believe they were taken."

Her gaze strayed to the overturned table and then to the bed. She paled and drew her elbows in tight, as if someone might jump from the shadows and snatch her.

Lord, what now? He wanted to alert the staff and search the house, but he couldn't panic. Mistakes would be made. No clues could be missed.

He studied the room. There was a light-colored spot on the rug. He leaned to inspect it, seeing the faint shape of a heel. A fine coat of white powder created the outline.

What was it?

He ran a finger through the white powder and brought it to his nose. It held no scent. Could it be flour? Did the kidnapper work in the kitchens?

"Miss Blakeford had an affinity for laudanum." Corinne's voice was a faint whisper. "Her death wasn't by her doing?"

He stood and examined the tea tray, lifting the emptied cup

to his nose. It smelled of sugar and green tea leaves, but had something else been added? Could Blue and her sister have been drugged like Miss Blakeford? Arsenic was an odorless white powder. Were they poisoned? He set the teacup back on the tray. "There was evidence of a struggle in Miss Blakeford's case too."

"Oh, my." Corinne's hand moved to her throat. "How could this be? I never thought... imagined..." She slumped against the wall. Her gaze turned distant, her expression vulnerable. Gone was the self-absorbed socialite.

"Rebecca and I argued." Remorse laced Corinne's tone, but finding Blue took precedence over recounting her regrets.

He scanned the room for any other clues.

There were two women missing. Were there two abductors? If so, wouldn't there have been more signs of struggle? If one had been held at gunpoint, then the other might have gone willingly.

"I can't let that be their last memory of me." Corinne pushed off the wall. "Let me aid you." Her tone turned pleaded. "Please, how can I help?"

She'd only slow him down and get in his way.

For when you are weak, I am strong.

Tears slid down her cheeks. She crossed the room and took his hand. "They're my cousins. Please let me help."

Perhaps he could find a purpose for her. When he nodded, her frame sagged with relief.

"I'm still working out a plan. Please, find the maid who cleans the room. Ask if she saw anything out of the ordinary and tell her to stand guard at the door. I don't want anyone entering or exiting who could tamper with or destroy evidence, including you."

She nodded and rang the bell pull.

"I'll be right back." He needed to retrieve his weapon. All his senses warned that he—and now Blue's cousin—raced toward danger. He needed to be ready. He jogged down the hall to his bedchamber and opened the door.

Strange. His Bible rested on the bed.

A corner of a piece of paper peeked out between the thin pages. He removed it and skimmed the contents.

The footman knows where Lucy is. I'm going to try to save her.

Why would Blue foolishly put herself in harm's way, and where was Madeline?

Look after Madeline. She's my sister.

Look after her? He didn't even know where she was, but the note indicated she wasn't with Blue.

He strode to the bed, lifted the top mattress, and removed the gun hidden underneath.

The sound of fabric sliding against fabric startled him, and he jerked back, losing his balance and landing on his backside.

A soft snore sounded, and peeking out from under the dust ruffle was a feminine pinky finger.

Blue!

He yanked up the dust ruffle.

A young woman lay under the bed, sound asleep, but it wasn't Blue.

He shifted so more light could spill into the dark hiding spot. He knew that face… Madeline, Blue's maid—er, sister.

He reached under and shook Madeline's shoulder. "Miss Prestcote."

Her eyes fluttered open, and she stared at him with a curious expression that reminded him of Blue. How had he never noticed the resemblance before?

"What are you doing under there? Where's your sister?"

"Rebecca said you'd find me." Her voice was thick with sleep. "Said you'd keep me safe."

Safe. That confirmed that they were in danger. He gripped her upper arms and gently pulled her out, careful not to bump her head. "Where is your sister?"

He lifted her and then guided her to sit on the bed facing him.

"I don't know." Her eyelids hung heavy, as if reopening her eyes after blinking was a struggle. "She said there was something in my tea. It made me sleepy."

"You were drugged? By whom?"

"A footman." Her eyes closed and didn't reopen.

He gave her a shake.

Her eyelids opened, and she widened her eyes as if she was working hard to stay awake. "He said he made my tea with three sugars just the way I like it."

The teacup had smelled of sugar. Was it to cover any strange taste or odor?

"Was your sister also drugged?"

She shook her head. "I made the second cup, and she barely sipped her tea."

"Did you call for me?" Corinne approached the door.

She must have heard him call for the Miss Prestcote who'd been under the bed.

When she saw her cousin, she rushed to her take her in her arms. "Madeline! You're alive." She pressed her cheek into Madeline's shoulder. "Forgive me for how I acted. I was so worried about you." She glanced around. "Where's Rebecca?"

"I don't know." Madeline's voice cracked, gaze locking on Daniel. "If she's not with you, then"—her lower lip quivered—"then *he* might have her."

Corinne pulled back. "'He'?"

"The footman." Madeline tried to rise.

Daniel stilled her with a hand. "First, we must get some fluids in you to flush out whatever laced your tea."

Corinne rose and moved to ring the bell pull, but Daniel stopped her. "It can't come from the kitchen without oversight, or she could be poisoned again."

"Rebecca told me it was valery...valerian...something that

puts you to sleep." Madeline rubbed her temples and squeezed her eyes shut, as if trying to force her memories to surface above the fog of grogginess. "That's why I'm sleepy and not dead. I think she said Professor Matthews switched labels or something."

Whatever that was about, it was Daniel's turn to slump with relief. Professor Matthews's quick thinking meant there was hope that Blue had not been poisoned.

"How about I go oversee a pot of coffee?" Corinne offered her cousin a weak smile.

"Meet us in the salon across from the dining room." She left, and he turned to Madeline. "I don't want you out of my sight, but I need to inform Lady Coburn what's happening and confirm with Professor Matthews regarding what was laced in your tea. Do you have the energy to walk downstairs? I can assist you."

With Daniel's help, Madeline pushed to her feet. Together, they made it down the stairs and to the salon. Daniel signaled to a servant and asked him to interrupt Lady Coburn. Moments later, she rushed into the room.

"My lord?" The peacock feathers of her mask swayed back and forth. She pulled the mask off, setting it aside. Worry lined her forehead. "I beg your pardon for all the mischievousness." She flicked a curious glance at Madeline, then returned her focus to Daniel. "Did you find the real Lady Prestcote and send the imposter on her way?"

"Please, have a seat." When she did, he relayed the events of the evening.

Lady Coburn seemed at first outraged and then frightened on Blue's behalf.

Corinne joined them, followed by a maid who handed Madeline a cup of coffee with cream. Daniel stopped the maid before she departed and questioned her about the blond footman.

The young servant tucked the empty tray under her arm and curtsied. "I know who you mean, but I never heard his name, nor did I ever see him do any work. Nothin' but talk from the likes of him. Mr. Severin saw him—"

"Who's Mr. Severin?" Daniel asked.

"Pardon, my lord. He's the butler."

"Please continue."

She bobbed another curtsy. "Mr. Severin saw the footman actin' sweet on Lucy. He grabbed him by the collar and tossed him out on his ear. I saw the bloke several days later in the house talkin' to another maid and thought Mr. Severin must have hired him back, but I kept a wide berth from the trouble-maker after that. There's no fraternizin' among the staff, and I like my employment."

"I appreciate your honesty." Daniel nodded.

The maid looked to her employer, and Lady Coburn said, "That is all. You are dismissed."

When she was gone, he turned to Lady Coburn. "I must interrogate the guests and staff one by one to see if anyone else saw anything suspicious, and I must do so now."

"Indeed." Lady Coburn frowned. "Professors Bell and Duval were called away because someone had fallen ill."

"Did they say who?"

Lady Coburn's gaze drifted to the ceiling. "I don't recall the name, but it was a man. An artist, perhaps? He was part of the experiment."

Daniel recalled the pair of professors whispering in the hallway. Was it due to the man becoming ill, or were they planning a hasty getaway?

He'd chase them down if need be and demand they lead him to Blue. His hands gripped the armrests to rise.

My power is made stronger in weakness.

Why was that verse continually popping into his head?

Mrs. Evans peeked around the door and focused on Lady Coburn. "There you are. I wondered if something was amiss."

Lady Coburn waved her in, and Professor Matthews followed, along with Lord McGower and Lord and Lady Farsley.

The professor nodded to Daniel. "May I help?"

You're too prideful to seek assistance when you need it. Lieutenant Scar's voice rang in his mind.

Lord, forgive my pride.

"Indeed." Daniel stood. "I need everyone's assistance to find Miss Rebecca Prestcote. She's been kidnapped."

Lady Farsley gasped, and Lord McGower's jaw dropped.

Mrs. Evans looked puzzled. "Rebecca Prestcote?"

"She and her cousin switched places so that Rebecca could find a cure for her sister Madeline's ailment." He gestured to Madeline. "Rebecca, the one who tended to my shoulder, the woman we've all come to know, has been kidnapped, and I need to know if anyone has seen a blond footman who was pretending to be part of the staff and, if so, your last recollection of him." He looked to Lady Coburn. "Would you interview the servants regarding the whereabouts and actions of our mysterious blond footman?"

"Of course." Lady Coburn rose and rang the bell pull for the butler.

"I want a search party to scour every crevice of Griffin Hall, its grounds, and the surrounding woods. Even the land and homes of neighbors."

Lord McGower straightened. "I'll see to it."

Daniel was going to have a look around in the mill one more time. "Lord Farsley?"

The blind man tipped his chin up.

"Have Miss Madeline show you to the chamber where Miss Prestcote was taken. There is a fine white dust on the floor. See if your heightened sense of smell can identify it."

"Right away, my lord. Lead on, Miss Madeline." Lord Farsley held up his arm for Madeline to lean on, and Corinne aided her from the other side.

Daniel strode to the door.

Corinne called after him. "Where are you going?"

"To get more help." He nodded his thanks to the quirky group he now called friends.

It was time to hunt down a pair of missing professors.

CHAPTER 31

*T*rapped in a storage room of the kitchen's root cellar, Rebecca stood, breathing hard and leaning against the stone wall, after her captor pushed her away with a shove. She fought the sleepy effects of the valerian tea her captor had forced her to drink while he stood near the door, the only exit to the small, dank room. He leaned on an old barrel, waiting with bag in hand for her to succumb to what he believed was poison. The front of her gown was drenched with the overflow of what had been poured into her mouth, and what she coughed out after he'd released her nose, allowing her to pull in glorious air. She thanked God that Professor Matthews had switched the plants, and she was smelling the strong odor of valerian root and not the spring-green scent of digitalis.

She didn't dare scream again. When she had tried before, she'd received a blow to the head strong enough that she'd lost consciousness, though she didn't think she'd been out for long. The side of her face still throbbed. She needed all her wits to fight the sleepiness from the valerian plant. It was imperative that she remained conscious, and that her captor believe the opposite.

"I know all of Griffin Hall's hiding spots." The blond footman crossed his arms, and a sack protruded from underneath. "Me mum used to work here. Gave birth to me in this very room, set me in a basket, and finished her work." A twisted smile marred his youthful face. "The lords and ladies don't take kindly to servants fraternizing. Ol' Mr. Severin would 'ave let me mum go if he found out she had a child. We'd have been beggin' in the streets." He snorted and draped the bag over his shoulder. "Mum said I should be grateful." He lifted the lid of a barrel, removed an apple, and took a bite.

The heavy-leaden feeling of Rebecca's limbs increased until her legs could no longer hold her weight and she slid to the floor.

Her captor chuckled. "The only thing I'm grateful for is learning all of Griffin Hall's secret passageways. Since I met the professor, the knowledge has paid handsomely. He only wants the ones who won't be missed." He raised his apple in a kind of salute. "I guess we have that in common. Except, I won't be missed after I take the money and purchase a ticket across the Atlantic. You won't be missed after they remove all your organs and gizzards." He took another bite and spoke with his mouth open. "Mum always said it was what's on the inside that counted."

He laughed at his own joke, letting spittle and little pieces of apple fly.

She listed the side effects of digitalis to keep her mind awake. Perhaps she should pretend to be having symptoms. She stared at a spot above his head to make her vision appear glazed over. Stifling a yawn, she exhaled as if short of breath and gripped her chest.

"It won't be long now." A wicked grin spread over his face. He picked up another apple and threw it at her.

The fruit hit her collar bone, spun somewhere up near her forehead, then dropped back down into her lap. She cautiously curved one finger to hold it in place and slid it into a fold of her skirt, for there was no telling when or if she'd get another meal.

He studied her non-reaction to the thrown object and rubbed his palms greedily.

Lord, give me Your wisdom to help save Lucy and myself.

She allowed her eyelids to flutter closed and her head to slump against her chest.

Lord, guide Daniel. Make his path straight to me.

"All right. Time's a-wasting, and I want me money."

A bag was tossed over her head, and she gripped the apple as he jostled her into the sack. When he threw her over his shoulder, she stifled a grunt and bit her lip to hold in the pain in her midsection as he bounced her with a shrug to adjust her weight.

"Time to meet the professor."

For once, Rebecca understood how her sister had felt when she'd said that if it was her time, then it was her time. She would happily meet her Maker, if that was God's will. Her only regrets would be in not saving those she loved and not telling Daniel the truth about her identity. And her feelings for him.

Lord, if this is my time, then I will come home to You with open arms, but don't let my death be in vain. Help me save others from a similar fate.

∼

*D*aniel's search of the mill once again led to nothing. It was more of a challenge to see in the dark, but nothing had changed since their last visit. He wracked his brain for where else they could be hiding Rebecca as he knocked on the wooden door of the Shepherds' home. The patter of running feet was followed by whispers and giggles.

"Back in bed with ya." Mrs. Shepherd's voice penetrated the

door. "Clara, go tuck them back in while I see who's at the door."

A curtain shifted.

"Who is it?" she asked in a stern tone.

"Lord Wolston." He stepped back into the moonlight so she could see his face through the window. "Mrs. Shepherd, I can take you to see your son."

The door flung wide. "Giles?" Mrs. Shepherd held a lantern up at him. "You mean it?"

"You have my word."

"Will you let him go?"

"He is free, but I'd like to discuss a problem I need help with first. I'm desperate to stop the murder of a young woman."

Her eyes widened. She turned and hollered, "Angela, watch the little 'uns." She grabbed a shawl from off a hook and swung it over her shoulder with one hand, careful not to hit the lantern. "Take me to my son."

Daniel aided Mrs. Shepherd onto his steed and guided his horse to the chandler's store as he informed the woman of current happenings. He'd hoped seeing his mother could guilt Giles into helping him identify the culprit and lead him to where Blue might be kept. The woman who'd dared to confront him outside Griffin Hall remained quiet as if waiting to see if he'd hold up to his word. He tied his mount to the hitching post and aided her down.

He knocked on the chandler's door, peering up at the second-floor window.

Mrs. Shepherd shifted and drew her shawl tighter around her shoulders.

Daniel pounded on the door a second time and stepped back, clasping his hands in front of him. A curtain above shifted.

"You do know that the chandler passed several weeks ago?"

Without turning, he could feel Mrs. Shepherd eyeing him as if he'd lost his senses.

He knocked again.

"Enough of the racket," Lieutenant Scar yelled. "I'm coming and this better be urgent." The door opened a crack and then fully once the lieutenant identified him. "I'll have you know, I'd just fallen asleep."

"Lieutenant, I'd like you to meet—"

"Ma!" Giles trooped down the stairs to stand beside Lieutenant Scar.

"Gillie." Tears glistened in her eyes, and she pushed past Daniel to cup her son's cheek, then wrapped him in a fierce hug.

"I'm sorry, Mama." Giles choked back a sob.

Lieutenant Scar backed into the store and motioned Daniel inside. "I'll put on some tea, and you can tell me what you've learned." He climbed the stairs and Daniel followed.

Giles and his mama ascended behind him, his mother giving the young man an earful for all the worry he'd caused her.

In the chandler's rooms, Daniel relayed what he knew of Blue's kidnapping and how Professor Matthews switched the plant labels, offering hope that Lucy and Blue could still be alive somewhere. He turned to Giles. "I know I'm asking you to risk your life and the lives of your family, but I'm begging for your help. I know Miss Prestcote has risked her life to save her sister. Now she's trying to save Lucy."

"A woman of standing risking her life for a maid? Not even her own?" Incredulity hung in Giles's voice.

"Her heart is bigger than her stature, but she's trusting that I'll help her. I can't do that without you."

When I am weak, then I am strong.

Daniel clasped his hands and begged. "I will give you anything within my power. Anything. Please."

In the background, the tea kettle whistled.

Giles hung his head. "I..."

His mother whacked him on the shoulder.

"Ow."

"You're gonna help him, and you're gonna do it for Lucy."

"But Mama, you don't know what my employer's capable— ow!" He rubbed the shoulder she'd smacked a second time.

"So you'd leave Miss Lucy and Miss Prestcote in the clutches of this monster?" Mrs. Shepherd nodded to Daniel. "Townsfolk look after their own, and Lucy's one of us."

Lieutenant Scar brought over the kettle and cups. "Mrs. Shepherd, my wife usually steeps and pours the tea. Would you do us the honor?"

While she was occupied doing that, Giles scooted out of her reach.

Lieutenant Scar pulled over a wooden chair and sat. "Helping out Lord Wolston would go far with my contacts at the Home Office."

"It would?" Giles's eyebrows rose.

"Quite."

Giles glanced from his mama to Lieutenant Scar and then to Daniel.

Daniel held his gaze and prayed.

"I want my family protected," Giles pleaded.

Protecting his family meant everything to Daniel too. He'd fought and sacrificed to ensure no one would ever hurt those he loved. Blue had become one of them, and he'd vowed to protect her.

"Done." Lieutenant Scar accepted the teacup passed to him. "A forgotten uncle will purchase the house next door tomorrow and move in. One shout, and he'll be on your doorstep."

Giles's jaw fell slack. "You can do that?"

"You have my word." Scar sat back and sipped from his cup. "You'll also be reporting to him for training."

A wry smile turned up the corner of Mrs. Shepherd's mouth.

"I'll be beggared." Giles blinked with a dazed look.

"But first, we rescue Miss Prestcote and the maid in time." Scar glanced at Daniel. "There'll be a reward for their safe return."

Daniel nodded. He'd pay anything to get his Blue back.

"Provided by the Crown, of course," Lieutenant Scar added with a smug smile.

"All right." Giles exhaled an unsteady breath. "I'll tell you who's in charge."

A lump formed in Daniel's throat at the goodness of God, who worked through Daniel's superior and a young lad to answer his prayers.

Lieutenant Scar leaned in. "Who are we up against?"

Giles scooted to the edge of his seat and lowered his voice. "Name's Bell. He hasn't ever said so, but I heard someone else call him a professor."

Daniel snapped his eyebrows together. "Not Duval?"

The lad shook his head. "No. Never heard of that bloke. Just Bell."

When Lieutenant Scar met Daniel's gaze, he guessed his superior had also suspected Duval.

"The man's slick as a greased pig and as wicked as one of Satan's demons. He uses the other professor as a scapegoat if things don't go as planned."

"Did Bell plant rumors that Duval killed Tingley's wife?" Daniel asked.

"Poor Miz Tingley overheard a conversation she shouldn't have, and Bell had his henchmen add some arsenic to her medication even though she was a four."

"A four?" Lieutenant Scar's brow furrowed.

Giles stared at his laced fingers. "I didn't know what I was getting meself into, but that's how he works. He lures you in with what ya think will solve all yer problems, but then he's got you by the throat. He gives everyone a value and calls us poor folk as ones or twos."

The book in Professor Bell's chamber flashed in Daniel's memory. It had listed names with numbers next to them.

"The lower the number, the more dispensable they are. Loners without friends or family he calls ones because ain't no one gonna notice them gone."

Daniel cleared his cinching throat. "Like the chandler and Miss Blakeford."

"How did you obtain this information?" Lieutenant Scar leaned his elbow on the armrest and crossed one leg over the other.

"It takes a while to dig up a body." Giles rubbed the back of his neck as if remembering the ache. "I worked with a bloke only a few years older than meself. Name's Hugh, the professor's right-hand man. I got him talkin' to pass the time. He had a nice face, and the professor used him to lure in women, promising 'em marriage." Giles shivered. "He's evil as sin. Gets his jollies out of the fear in their eyes and watchin' 'em fight for their last breath."

Nausea rolled in Daniel's stomach. "Does he have blond hair?"

"That's right." Giles nodded.

"Do you know where they take the"—Daniel inhaled a steadying breath to finish—"bodies?"

Giles shook his head and stared at his hands.

Daniel dug his fingers into the underside of his chair as he thought of Blue in that wretch's grasp. Helplessness rooted him to his chair, and he felt as though he peered through the eyes of his four-and ten-year-old self. He needed to act. He had to find Blue, but he didn't know where to search. He hadn't felt this helpless when he'd learned about the death of his father, nor when some lovesick chap had tried to steal his sister and marry her. He hadn't even felt this helpless when Eliza had fallen down the well.

Lord, protect Blue—protect Rebecca.

"How long have you worked together?" Daniel asked Giles.

"Winter was rough on my family, with me Pa gone, leavin' Mama with little mouths to feed." Giles's eyes shadowed. "I started grave robbin' with 'em as soon as the ground thawed for the extra money."

"So you've done several jobs with him."

"Three in all, including the one where you nearly broke me leg."

"Did Hugh speak of traveling far, or did he disappear for several days?"

Giles shook his head.

"What about his clothes?" Daniel rubbed his chin. There had to be something about the man that would give away where he was hiding out. "Did he reek of anything, or did he have to dress differently? In warmer clothes, or cooler, in uniform, formal or professional?"

"Wait." Giles straightened. "I do know where he was afore was cool and damp. When night come, Hugh complained 'bout havin' to shake off the chill, and one time I bumped into him, and his clothes were damp."

Outside in the woods? Daniel wracked his brain for other damp areas. "A root cellar or basement?" He'd have to ask Lady Coburn.

"So now we know our target, but where do we find him? What is our plan?" Lieutenant Scar shifted to face Daniel.

Our plan? Daniel had messed up his last mission. Why was the lieutenant looking at him as if he could figure out how to rescue them? Lieutenant Scar had more experience. Shouldn't he come up with a plan?

Giles and Mrs. Shepherd seemed to wait for him to respond.

My grace is sufficient.

The Apostle Paul's words rang in his head. *I will boast of my weakness, so that Christ's power may rest on me.*

"I don't have one—not a complete one, anyway," Daniel said. "I'm open to suggestions." He scanned the people in the room. "Here's what I know. Professor Bell has been playing God. He believes he's smarter than anyone else, including his colleagues. He has a book listed with the names of all the staff and guests at Griffin Hall, each with a numeric value next to them—how he ranks them." He nodded to Giles, who'd given him that information. "From what Blue's sister relayed—"

"Sister?" Lieutenant Scar straightened.

"No one, not even I, was aware that Rebecca Prestcote was pretending to be her cousin, Lady Corinne Prestcote."

"Why?" Scar wore a baffled expression. "What was her motive?"

If the situation weren't so dire, Daniel would have chuckled to see the fearsome Lieutenant Scar appear puzzled. "Rebecca" —her real name sounded strange on Daniel lips, but it suited her more than her cousin's name— "hoped to obtain first-hand knowledge from the professors about a cure for her sister, Madeline, who acted as her lady's maid. The abductor looked to kidnap the maid for dissection due to her unique heart condition, but Rebecca hid Madeline, and she was kidnapped instead.

"I don't know if Bell will have had the courage to kill the daughter of an earl with a nine next to her name. However, Corinne yelled in the hall that Rebecca was a nobody who wouldn't be missed, and it's possible the abductor heard that." He rubbed his temples. "While I was discovering that Miss Madeline had been drugged and that Miss Rebecca Prestcote had gone missing, Bell and Professor Duval left—supposedly to handle someone from Duval's experiment who'd become ill, but they could be making a getaway."

"If you give me directions to the house"—Lieutenant Scar buttoned his jacket as if prepared to leave immediately—"I can track them."

"Naw." Giles snorted. "The professor likes to watch the dig, or body exchange—probably the killin', even." He glanced at his mother. "But I don't have nothin' to do with those. The professor wanted to ensure things went smooth-like, sometimes watching from the crowd or hiding in the shadows. He's the one who hit you from behind with the shovel. His pride won't let him leave. He'll return to Griffin Hall."

"Then let's use his pride as his weakness." Daniel leaned in. "Here's what I propose..."

~

*R*ebecca counted the footman's steps and did her best to listen to the sounds over the man's panted breath and the crunching of leaves to determine her whereabouts. His shoulder pounded into her midsection, and her head spun from the sleeping potion. But she must remain vigilant if she wanted to survive. From inside the sack, she had no way of leaving behind clues for anyone to discover which way the footman carried her.

He tromped uphill.

It had to be the hill to the graveyard.

Oh Lord, please don't let him bury me alive.

Help Daniel find me in time.

Would he be furious when he saw Corinne and she told him about their pretense? Or would he be happy that Corinne, with her culture and highborn status, had resumed her rightful place? Would he even notice her disappearance?

His handsome face floated through the darkness, clouding her mind. Instead of the bag that smelled of male stench and flour, she imagined Daniel's arms holding her again. She couldn't have mistaken the love in his eyes before his mouth descended upon hers for a heart-rending kiss. She hadn't gone out of her way to impress him—quite the opposite. She'd tried hard to be herself. She certainly hadn't attempted to make him fall in love with her since Corinne had set her cap for him. Yet he'd made Rebecca feel safe, loved, and protected.

If she were killed, would he protect what she loved? Would he take care of Madeline?

Yes. She knew it in her heart he would, which was why she'd left Madeline in his chamber. He'd care for her sister as he cared for his own.

But would he dedicate himself and his resources to finding a cure?

Trust in the Lord with all your heart and lean not on your own understanding.

Lord, my life is in Your hands. I should have given my heart to You sooner, as Madeline did. She has always trusted You. Forgive me for my stubbornness. I'm trying to trust You in everything. Help me have faith.

The raspy barking of foxes sounded in the distance. She must be near the forest. She listened intently and picked up the faint croaks and peeps of frogs, which grew louder by the second, which meant they were approaching the pond. Was he taking her to the old mill that she and Daniel had searched?

The peeping grew louder, and her captor stopped. He breathed heavily, jostling her against his shoulder. Hinges squeaked, and his boots clapped on wooden floorboards. He closed the door, diminishing the sounds of the frogs.

Boards creaked. He dropped Rebecca to the ground— thankfully, feet first—but her elbow hit hard. She wanted to rub the ache away, but she didn't dare move.

"Well done. Let me have a look at her."

Professor Bell? Rebecca forced her body to remain limp and lifeless as the footman jerked and tugged on the sack, yanking it off. A cold draft up the back of her meant her gown had lifted, exposing her legs inappropriately, but she didn't dare adjust her skirts. A final heave lifted her upper body as the bag tore away. Her hair fell in her eyes, her ribbon having fallen out a while back. She remained slack, tilting and falling to the ground. Her shoulder and head hit the wood floor and bounced. Pain wracked her skull, but she was still alive—at least for the moment.

"Perdition!" Professor Bell shouted, but then his voice lowered. "You good-for-nothing. You've fouled it up again. This isn't the one with the heart condition. You were supposed to take the maid."

"You didn't mention nothin' about any heart condition. She was the only one in the chamber, and I figured one woman was as good as another."

"You're not getting full pay for this. I needed a diseased heart for Duval to dissect. This will delay his research. Timing is crucial. I need him to finish his experiments before he's arrested for the death of his subjects so that I can take the credit for his research and become chancellor."

One of the men paced—probably the professor—his footfalls vibrating against her cheek pressed to the cold floor.

"I had no choice. The chit recognized me and was going to scream." The footman's voice pitched to a whine. "I did what you said. I gave the maid the tea and went to the chamber and nabbed a woman after the earl's daughter left."

"She's the earl's niece," Professor Bell said. "I overheard the earl's daughter speaking to Wolston. I can't sell this corpse to the university. Duval will recognize her. You're going to have to sell her body to the university in Edinburgh."

"But it won't be fresh after two days of travel. It'll start to smell. I won't get a proper price for it."

Professor Bell's voice turned sinister. "Then next time, bring me the right one." Footsteps shuffled. "If that maid has gone and told her mistress and the staff's looking for a kidnapper that fits your description, then you're useless here. I'll have to send you north. Your pay will suffer because the bodies you'll procure won't be as fresh when they arrive."

Air fluttered her loose hair about her face as the footman scooped something off the ground. He gripped the back of Rebecca's gown, yanking her upright, and slid the bag over her head. He pinned her upper body against the stone wall as he worked the rough burlap over her midsection and legs. This time, she slumped lower to the ground, protecting her head from hitting the floor.

"At least you weren't foolish enough to nab the earl's daughter." Professor Bell snorted. "Lord and Lady Mercer have the ear of the king. We would have had to destroy the evidence then, and neither of us would have been paid."

The footman grumbled something unintelligible.

"Put her with the other, then return to the main house, but stay hidden and await my instructions. I will see if obtaining the maid is still a possibility."

Not Madeline! Rebecca held in her scream.

The footman grabbed the top of the bag and heaved with a grunt. Her neck bent at an odd angle, and her knees crumpled, almost hitting her chin. He grunted some more, and chain links ran over metal. The pulley system that used to haul grain? The bag was hoisted upward. By the warm air, she must have been moved into the upper room. The crane stopped, and the bag swung back and forth. The soothing motion, along with the sleep potion she'd drunk, could have lulled her to sleep—if not for the fear that this might be one of her last moments on earth. Such a thought was enough to keep her awake.

Footfalls mounted a set of creaking stairs. "Here we go, beauty."

He lifted the bag, must've unhooked it, and shuffle-stepped across the room. He dropped the bag, and Rebecca landed on her hip with a thud. Thank heaven she landed on wooden boards and not a stone floor. The wall her feet leaned against shifted back, followed by the sound of wood scraping against wood. What was happening? The wall was moving? She remembered what she'd seen of this mill before and could picture nothing that slid in such a manner.

A secret door. It must be. No wonder she and Daniel hadn't been able to determine how the footman had disappeared.

The bag was hooked onto another chain. The vile footman lowered her down. But then she bumped into something. Due to her odd position within the sack, she was too large to fit through whatever opening this was.

The cad's curses echoed in the empty room, and the floorboards bounced as he jumped, the sound of his landing only inches away.

"You got to"—he picked up the bag and dropped it—"get in the hole." Her hip smarted where it scraped against the side of the hole in the floorboards. She tried to curl into a tighter ball to fit better.

"I said, get in the hole." His booted foot connected with her back and head. Pain radiated around her skull and down her spine. And then she was dropping, falling through the air from darkness into deeper darkness.

I failed to save Lucy and even Madeline. I'm sorry, Lord.

CHAPTER 32

$\mathcal{D}$aniel stationed Giles, Mrs. Shepherd, and Lieutenant Scar near the Griffin Hall exits. Lieutenant Scar had to monitor both the French patio doors and the side door, but he could handle it. Daniel described both the footman and Professor Bell to Mrs. Shepherd and taught her the signal—the sound of a nightingale's cry—in case she spotted anyone arriving that fit the footman's or Bell's description. Then Daniel entered Griffin Hall through the servant's door to sneak up and find Lady Corinne and Miss Madeline. A footman carrying a stack of dirty dishes to the kitchens indicated the guests were close to finishing their meal and would soon be adjourning to the salon for the ladies and the billiard room for the men.

Before he reached the servants' stairs, the signal reached his ears. Not one signal, but two. One came from the main entrance where Giles was stationed. The other called from behind him at the servants' entrance from Mrs. Shepherd.

It seemed the footman and Professor Bell had arrived at the same time.

Daniel made haste, mounting the stairs. He prayed for

God's protection and wisdom, and for their plan to work. Upstairs was quiet, so he slipped down the hall and entered Blue's chamber to find Lord Farsley, Madeline, and Corinne awaiting him there.

The moment the door clicked shut behind him, Lord Farsley stood. "Flour." His unseeing eyes peered through Daniel's chest. "The substance on the floor was flour."

Madeline appeared more lucid than before as she stood. "I sent the housekeeper to search the kitchens. She's trustworthy and has been very worried about Lucy. She found this." Madeline held out a pale-green hair ribbon. "It's the hair tie Rebecca was wearing." Her voice wobbled, but she was a strong girl. "The housekeeper found it in a rarely used back storage room, along with a freshly eaten apple core."

"Did she search all the storage rooms?" Hope sparked in Daniel's chest. "Especially the ones where they keep the flour?"

Madeline nodded. "She only found the hair ribbon."

"This is all my fault." Corinne covered her face with her hands, and Madeline consoled her, even though it was her sister who'd gone missing.

"God is in control." Madeline placed a hand on her cousin's back. "His truth will be her shield and buckler. No evil will befall her because He's sent His angels to guard her. God will deliver her."

"Amen." Daniel soaked in her phrasing of Psalm ninety-one, trusting God that it wasn't too late. "Miss Prestcote."

Both Corinne and Madeline peered at him.

"Pardon. Lady Prestcote." For efficiency's sake, he was going to call them by their proper names. "Corinne. I need you to pretend to be Rebecca."

"How will that help?"

"We're going to convince Professor Bell that he's kidnapped the wrong Prestcote, the earl's daughter. When he panics, he'll lead us straight to her."

"Professor Bell, you say?" Lord Farsley gripped the bedpost. "I never liked the smell of that man, dank and musty like death."

"You believe Professor Bell kidnapped my sister?"

"I know he did." Daniel held Madeline's gaze. "But he wasn't without assistance. We're going to find your sister and Lucy and attempt to bring down the whole criminal ring."

Madeline clasped her hands as if ready to pray. "You think he'll fall for it?"

"Of course." Corinne straightened. "If I go missing, then a scandal will break. All of England's attention would turn to Leafield, their focus on my disappearance. Investigators would link my vanishing with Miss Blakeford's death and her body turning up at the university."

Daniel agreed, even if her words proved she thought highly of herself. "Madeline, your help will be needed to pull this off. Can you coach Corinne on your sister's mannerisms and how to act like Blue...er, Rebecca?"

Madeline issued him a weak smile. "I like your nickname. It's fitting." She gripped her cousin's hand. "Let's get started."

"Indeed." Corinne scooted to the edge of the bed. "We'll do whatever it takes."

"Good." Daniel moved closer, kneeling on one knee to whisper the rest of the plan in case the blond footman lingered within earshot. "For this to work, we have to each play our part." He peered into each of their faces and squeezed Lord Farsley's hand. "Together we function as a family, as one body."

"As long as I'm not the eyes," Lord Farsley teased.

"My friend...." Daniel stood. "You're our nose, and I'm thanking God for what that nose has done for us already."

A smile twitched at the corners of the man's lips, and a blush crept up his neck. "Then let's go find our girl."

This was what he'd gotten wrong with his assignment at the Lipscomb party. He'd believed he had to prove himself by going it alone. Maybe both God and Lieutenant Scar had been trying to convey to him that he would have had a greater impact with a team—and with God's help.

~

*R*ebecca awoke to someone shaking her, which caused her head to pound. She pressed her palms to her temples and groaned.

"You took a bad fall." The weak voice was familiar.

Lucy?

Rebecca opened her eyes. A dark shadow hoovered next to her. Moonlight from a high, narrow window cast a blue tint to what looked like a dusting of white snow inside a stone room. "Lucy, is that you?"

"Indeed, miss." Her voice sounded listless, so unlike her bubbly self.

"Oh, thank God!" She pushed upright off a sack of flour, stepped out of the bag still around her ankles, and hugged the maid. "We've been so worried. I promised your grandmama that I'd look out for you, and then you disappeared, and I didn't know how to tell her the news."

"I'm alive." She barely returned Rebecca's embrace.

Rebecca pulled away. "I'm so relieved I found you."

Lucy's face was pale, her lips dry and cracked.

"Are you all right?" If the footman believed Lucy dead, then she'd probably had nothing to eat or drink in at least a day and a half.

Lucy shrugged. "Thirsty, but I don't mean to complain."

"When was the last time you ate or drank?" Rebecca dug into the sack.

"Yesterday was terribly busy with the ball. I forgot to eat. Hugh was kind and brought me a cup of tea." She frowned. "I fell asleep and woke up here. I don't rightly know what happened."

"You're dehydrated." Rebecca pulled the apple out of the sack. She'd read a person could only survive three days without water, and Lucy had gone almost two. *Thank you, Lord, for quick action. If I'd waited longer...* Rebecca swallowed around the knot forming in her throat, handing Lucy the apple. "Here, eat this." It wasn't as good as a cup of water, but the moisture in it would suffice for now.

Lucy cupped the fruit as if it were manna from heaven and took a bite.

Rebecca scooted to lean against what she assumed was several sacks of flour while Lucy devoured the fruit.

The young maid's shoulders straightened a bit after each bite.

"Thank heaven those flour sacks broke your fall," Lucy said, nibbling on what was left of the core.

"My head throbs where I was kicked through the hole in the ceiling." Rebecca flexed her toes and circled her shoulders. "But nothing appears to be broken. How long was I out?"

"Ten minutes, maybe twenty." Lucy started to get up, but Rebecca stilled her with a hand. It was best to conserve their strength if they were going to survive. "Someone kicked you?"

"The blond footman—the one, I assume, gave you the tea—and Professor Bell are behind our kidnappings." Rebecca peered into the darkness, trying to make out anything that could be useful for escape or to draw attention.

"Hugh?" Lucy's deep exhale bounced off the stone walls, mixing with the distant trickle of water. "I thought he was sweet on me."

"He attempted to sweet talk Madeline also." They would need a water source until someone came for them. She listened to trace the sound. *Please God, let Daniel find us before Professor Bell returns.* She felt around on the ground for anything that could be used as a weapon, but all she found was a small rock. "Hugh gave Madeline a cup of tea too. Laced with poison." She explained how Professor Matthews had switched the labels on the plants. "Otherwise, we'd be dead."

"The rogue." Lucy spit the words like a curse. "Why?"

"To sell your body to be dissected for science."

"But how did you end up here?"

She gave the maid the short version of events.

Lucy scooted to her knees. "But people know you were taken. They may not search for a maid, but they'll search for you."

"There are people looking for you—Mrs. Evans, Lady Coburn, Professor Matthews, Lord Wolston, to name a few. But I'm not as important as you think." Rebecca explained their farce and that Madeline was actually her sister.

"Lord Wolston will search for you. I saw how he looks at you."

Did he love her? Her heart told her yes, but her head listed her faults, the biggest being that she'd deceived him. Next in line, the fact that she wasn't of his station and thus wasn't a suitable bride.

Why hadn't she told him the truth earlier? Would he forgive her?

Even if he didn't, he would come for her.

Earlier, she'd been so sure he'd protect Madeline and come to her rescue, but fears crept in like mice along the room's perimeter. Hope seemed foolish in this dark, forgotten space, like an ember from a fire landing on stone, its spark quickly dying.

Would Daniel come for her? Papa had never come for Mama, not until it was too late.

CHAPTER 33

$\mathcal{D}$aniel found Lady Coburn and her guests in the solarium, their masks removed. Lady Coburn gripped the back of a chair as her butler and housekeeper appeared to be reporting in regarding their search of the hall. Lord McGower entered through the patio entrance and announced that a search of the grounds and surrounding areas had commenced.

Professor Bell lounged in a tufted chair, one leg crossed over the other and fingers laced across his stomach as if nothing were amiss. As if he committed kidnapping—or murder—every day. He sat closest to the hearth, its fire twisting and dancing over his shoulder.

Mrs. Evans was the first to spot Daniel and shifted in her chair to face him.

Professor Matthews followed her lead.

Lady Coburn peeked over her shoulder and waved him in. "Lord Wolston, I'm glad you could join us"—she leaned to see past him—"and Lady Prestcote?"

He stepped aside and allowed both Corinne and Madeline to step into the room.

Corinne kept her chin a little lower than she normally would, her hands clasped in front of her instead of floating like ribbons in the breeze as she moved.

Daniel cleared his throat. "May I have everyone's attention to clear up a benign trick that has been played upon us?"

Madeline inched closer to Corinne. Whether to provide a united front or to offer her reassurance, Daniel couldn't tell. He gestured to them. "May I introduce to you Miss Rebecca Prestcote and her younger sister, Miss Madeline?"

Corinne somehow managed to blush as if embarrassed. Perhaps she was smarter than he'd first believed—or at least more cunning.

The guests' expressions were a mixture of surprise and confusion, but Professor Bell jerked upright in his chair.

"The woman who was with us earlier tonight in the drawing room was their cousin, Lady Corinne Prestcote. She is the daughter of Lord and Lady Mercer and is currently in need of rest after her long journey from London."

Professor Bell's grip tightened on his chair's armrests, his gaze bouncing between the ladies and the exit.

Mrs. Evans harrumphed, eyeing Lady Corinne through a narrowed gaze. "I thought you acted different than the pampered socialite I read about in the gossip columns."

Daniel glanced at Lady Corinne, whose smile tightened at the corners. Perhaps he should have let Mrs. Evans in on their subterfuge. She'd come to know Rebecca quite well in the last couple of weeks. She might not be fooled, but would she give them away?

"I know what you all must be thinking." Daniel raised his palms. "I, too, found their audacious tomfoolery distasteful, but it's all due to a misunderstanding. Lady Corinne erred in accepting two invitations, not realizing the dates overlapped. She sent a missive to explain that her cousins would attend temporarily in her stead until she could join us here at a later date, followed shortly after by her parents."

Professor Bell turned deathly pale, his Adam's apple bobbing. He scooted to the edge of his seat as if ready to excuse himself and head for the door.

"The missive was detained and returned due to a mishap, but Miss Rebecca and Madeline Prestcote were unaware and uncertain how to proceed when Lady Coburn assumed they were Lady Corinne Prestcote and her maid."

"Oh, my." Lady Coburn placed a hand over her heart. "I hadn't seen Lady Mercer's daughter in an age. I had no idea."

Corinne, pretending to be Rebecca, curtsied. "It's our fault for the confusion, and I beg you to forgive us."

"Certainly, my dear. I'm merely glad it was cleared up before Lord and Lady Mercer arrived."

"I admit..." Lady Corinne sighed. "I did enjoy being my cousin for a spell."

Madeline nudged her with her elbow, as if to let her know she was acting out of character.

Lady Coburn tilted her head, taking on a mothering expression. "When shall we be expecting your aunt and uncle?"

Madeline bobbed a curtsy. "Corinne said they should arrive any moment now."

A loud yawn erupted from Professor Bell. "I beg your pardon." He rubbed his eyes and stood. "It seems the day's excitement has taken a toll on me. I think I shall retire for the evening. Lady Coburn, thank you again for your hospitality." He bowed to Daniel, Madeline, and Corinne. "I'm pleased you've righted your wrong. I may still need reminders of who is who tomorrow. Good night." He slid past them and exited.

When his footsteps had faded, Daniel whispered to Madeline and Corinne, "Explain to them the truth." He left to follow the professor, keeping his steps light as he crossed the hardwood floors in the foyer toward the back of the hall.

Professor Bell exited onto the patio.

Lieutenant Scar's nightingale's song with a few extra notes signaled for Giles to follow.

Daniel strode down the hall but used the servants' exit so Professor Bell wouldn't spot him, keeping an eye out for Bell's henchman. Where might that dastardly footman be?

Daniel waved Mrs. Shepherd inside, where she'd be safe, and crept into the night to chase after the professor.

Professor Bell half walked, half ran through the gardens. Where was he headed? The stables were to the right. Did he plan to skirt the perimeter of the property? Did he suspect Daniel was following him and wanted to throw him off the trail? Or was Bell going somewhere else? To the graveyard?

Lord, please don't let Blue be buried in a pine box.

A shadow emerged on his right from behind the hedge. Lieutenant Scar.

Another shadow sneaked along the low brick wall on the opposite side. Giles. The lad moved quickly, and his inexperience showed as he tailed the subject too closely. Daniel tried to signal him to hang back.

Giles stepped on a twig that snapped with a loud crack.

Professor Bell turned at the edge of the garden and held his oil lamp high.

Giles, Daniel, and Lieutenant Scar froze.

"I know you're there. Show yourself." He swung the lantern in Giles's direction.

Daniel lowered to a crouch in the shadow of a bush and lost sight of Scar, who must have hidden as well.

"I see you, Shepherd," Bell said. "I can smell your plebeian squalor stench." He lunged forward, grabbing Giles by the shirtfront. "Why are you here? Why are you following me?"

Giles' eyes widened. "I-I was supposed to help Hugh."

Footsteps approached.

"He lies." The blond footman strode past Daniel to Giles.

Daniel readied himself to pounce if Giles needed him.

Hugh reached toward his belt, where the blade of a knife glinted in the moonlight.

Daniel pulled out his blunderbuss and pointed it at the footman. "Stop right there."

Professor Bell jerked the lantern in Daniel's direction and swore.

The footman paused as if he would comply, but then lunged for Giles, wrapping the arm holding the knife around the lad's upper body. He spun to face Daniel, giving him a clear view of the blade tip pointed at Giles's throat.

Lieutenant Scar stepped out from the shadows. He must have stayed low behind the hedge and crept around to flank the professor's left side and put him in his sights. He pointed his gun at Hugh and, with a slight chin raise, indicated that Daniel should move his aim to Professor Bell.

Professor Bell stepped behind Hugh and Giles, using them as a shield.

"Release the lad," Daniel said. "Tell us where you're keeping the women, and we'll go easy on you." He spoke with authority, forcing his voice to remain even.

Professor Bell chuckled. "I was merely out for my nightly stroll."

"The Prince Regent will not look kindly on someone harming a daughter of the peerage." Daniel kept his gaze on the knife poised so closely to the boy's throat.

"I haven't the foggiest idea what you're talking about." Professor Bell leaned around the footman. "Help!" He yelled toward the house. "I'm being attacked. Help!"

Daniel glanced at Lieutenant Scar, who kept his weapon leveled on Hugh.

The patio door opened, and Lord McGower ran out, his curved Indian sword raised.

Professor Matthews followed. Behind him strode Madeline,

Corinne, Lady Coburn, and Mrs. Evans, walking close together and approaching with leery steps.

Lord McGower stopped when he spied Professor Bell and then looked to Daniel for guidance.

Professor Bell stepped around the footman. "Lady Coburn, thank heaven. I was just out for my nightly stroll when these men accosted me. Lord Wolston..." He peered over his shoulder and nodded at the footman.

Hugh's eyebrows lifted.

"...pointed his gun at me." Bell cautiously moved toward the house, Lady Coburn, and her guests.

The footman shifted his hold on the knife, and his arm tensed.

He was going to slit Giles's throat.

Bell continued. "And these other fellows—"

"No!" Daniel feared he was too late to keep Hugh from killing Giles.

A gun exploded.

Hugh jerked and the knife flew into the grass.

The ladies screamed.

Hugh shoved Giles in Lieutenant Scar's direction, blocking another shot. Gripping his wounded shoulder, Hugh used a low stone bench to leap over the hedge and dart toward the graveyard.

"Watch Bell," Lieutenant Scar shouted before giving chase, scaling the hedge in the same manner as Hugh.

Professor Bell froze halfway to Lady Coburn.

Giles stumbled, feeling his throat and sagging with relief on one knee when he found his neck still intact. He crawled away from the professor.

Bell clasped a hand over his mouth and acted astonished, but Daniel had glimpsed the man's wicked grin before he covered it. "Bloodthirsty animals."

Daniel sidestepped to Giles. "Are you all right, son?"

"You both said you'd protect me." His voice shook as he rose. "You promised." He crossed his arms as if to keep them from shaking, but his entire body trembled. "Y-you kept your promise. Thank you."

Out of the corner of his eye, Daniel saw Bell inch toward Lady Coburn.

Daniel stepped into his path. "Stop where you are, Bell."

Lord McGower raised his sword, blocking the professor's way.

"What is this?" Bell feigned innocence. "You should be apprehending them. They just shot at a man."

Daniel holstered his weapon. He needed tempers to calm and Professor Bell alive to tell them where he was holding Blue.

"Where are you keeping my sister and Lucy?" Madeline stepped toward the professor.

"Your sister?" The professor gave Madeline a scathing glare as if she were beneath even acknowledging. His smug expression was made even uglier in the lantern light. "I believe the only person who might have known that is on the run."

No. Daniel lunged at the professor, grabbing his shirtfront. His other hand formed a fist, ready to pummel the answer out of the rogue.

The arrogant professor smirked.

Daniel lifted him onto his toes and glared at his arrogant face. "Take me to her!"

"Hit me, and I'll drag you before the House of Lords," Bell said with a sneer. "I've done nothing wrong."

I will boast about my weakness.

He had to find Blue. He wanted her in his life. He wanted her to meet his mother, his sisters, and his grandfather. They would adore her.

He wanted to wake up to her smile every morning and have discussions about grand ideas as they broke their fast.

Professor Bell leaned left to plead with the guests. "You see?

He's out of control, about to strike an innocent man. You are all witnesses."

The gazes of the group burned into Daniel's back.

I will boast about my weakness, so that Christ's power may rest on me.

He released Bell, who brushed wrinkles from his jacket and shirtfront.

Lord, give me Your wisdom. Don't let Blue's blood be on my hands.

"Professor Matthews." Daniel waved him closer and noticed a crowd had started to gather in the gardens, not merely the guests but the servants and some of the curious townsfolk from the search party. "Could you please tell Professor Bell what you did with the plants?"

Matthews stepped forward. "Someone had been tampering with my digitalis plant, so I swapped the signage with the valerian plant, which causes drowsiness but not death."

Bell's eyes widened the tiniest bit, but he recovered from his shock quickly. "What are you saying? That you think it's linked to the missing women? Do you believe they were drugged?" He feigned a stunned expression. "Then every effort must be made to locate the women." He locked gazes with Daniel like a mutinous pirate. "Time is of the essence. Think of all the ills that could befall them. They could starve to death while we search, get sold into slavery, be raped or beaten."

The image of Blue suffering and calling his name—it was too much to bear.

Professor Matthews stepped to his side, as if to embolden him.

Professor Bell chuckled. "It seems you must have had feelings for the earl's daughter, or are they for the little nobody who pretended to be somebody?"

The all-too-familiar feeling of helplessness and of being weak tried to overwhelm Daniel once more. He couldn't find

Rebecca or protect those he loved on his own. He couldn't thwart Professor Bell or bring down a murdering ring of criminals by himself. He wasn't strong enough to fix this situation, but God was. *Lord, please help me.*

As if the Lord Himself responded, Madeline raised her voice. "The Lord stands in defense of Rebecca. You may see her as weak, but she's wise and she'll survive. You'll see."

Daniel stared at Blue's sister, supposedly suffering from heart illness, who seemed stronger than himself. She dared to confront the arrogant professor, mocking his certainty that he held the upper hand.

Coming from the direction of the stables, Professor Duval's head of unruly hair could be seen above the gathered crowd. "Whatever is going on?" He pushed past the groomsmen and staff. "Why is everyone outdoors?" He halted, spying Lord McGower holding Professor Bell at sword point. "What is this?"

"Perhaps you should be questioning Duval," Bell said. "Ask him where he's hiding the women." He pointed at his colleague. "Duval's the one who requires cadavers for dissection."

"Me?" Duval jolted. "What women? Whatever are you talking about?" His chin drew back and his brow furrowed. "Professor?"

"He's the one whose clients kept ending up dead." Bell hurled his venomous accusations. "Ask him about his current test subjects."

Duval's shock seemed genuine.

Daniel had suspected the professor, but no longer. He allowed Duval a moment to clear his name before his friends and colleagues.

"I've just returned from checking on Mrs. Josting and Mr. Tibbs." Duval adjusted his spectacles. "It seems someone approached them and told them I'd sent an additional dose to be administered. Mr. Tibbs took it and had an adverse reaction, but fortunately, he has stabilized and is resting. Mrs. Josting didn't trust the look of the imposter and didn't take it." Duval reached into his pocket and pulled out a small paper bag, which he sniffed. "I brought it back for Professor Matthews to confirm. Oddly enough, it seems someone tried to give them a dose of valerian."

Matthews strode to Duval and took the packet, which he sniffed before peering inside. "Valerian, and Professor Duval wasn't present when I informed everyone that I switched the plants."

"You did what?" Duval sounded mortified. "Someone could've gotten hurt."

"Did Mrs. Josting give a description of the man?" Daniel asked.

"Indeed." Duval cleared his throat. "She said he was a tall, blond-haired fellow."

The gathered guests murmured. Lord Farsley spoke up. "He must be Bell's henchman."

"Why would you sabotage my work?" Professor Duval's tone rang with disbelief, but his expression held a look of betrayal. "You need me. My efforts raise funds for the university."

"It didn't make sense to me at the time," Lord Farsley said, "but I overheard Professor Bell tell that servant 'if things get out of hand, make things sticky for Duval.' I think he was using the professor as a last resort scapegoat." Lord Farsley snorted. "Or scapegallows."

"Confess, Bell, and tell us where you're hiding Miss Prestcote." Daniel stepped toward him. "Pinning your crimes on Duval isn't going to work, and your false accusations are falling apart."

"I've done nothing wrong." His smug, twisted smile returned. "Unless you can produce an eyewitness—which, of course, you can't, because I haven't been involved in any crime —I will be taking my leave."

"Not so fast." Giles held a palm up to stop the professor. "I was there when you paid your men for the bodies you had us dig up."

Lord McGower pointed his sword at Professor Bell. "I'll keep this bloke under watch."

McGower was an excellent swordsman and could be trusted.

"I have some questions for the professor." Daniel nodded to McGower. "Bring him into the solarium. Lieutenant Scar will want to talk to him when he returns. I have a feeling the choice between the gallows or Newgate Prison might persuade him to offer more information."

"In the meantime," Lady Coburn said to the staff who'd gathered, "I want the search party to regroup. Every inch of the grounds and hall should be searched."

Giles nodded. "Ma can wake the town and get everyone searching. They all know Lucy's family, and townsfolk have each other's backs."

Mr. Kim, the quiet Asian man who kept to himself to the point that Daniel frequently forget he was a guest, spoke up. "I will help with the search." He pressed his palms together and bowed.

Mrs. Evans stepped forward, hooking Professor Matthews's arm. "We'll put on some strong tea and coffee for those searching, and we can take a later shift when others grow tired. I tend to sleep more during the day than at night, anyway."

Corinne moved to stand next to Madeline. "I'll help find my cousin."

Lady Farsley twisted the hair of her wig and reassured Daniel. "We'll find her." She looked to Giles. "We'll find them both."

"Miss Prestcote smells like gardenias," Lord Farsley said. "If you smell flowers this time of year, then you're getting close."

He looked to Daniel. "I won't be good in the searching, but remember, I'm the nose."

Daniel's throat grew tight at the quirky crowd, people society often mocked or overlooked. They might not be the most desirable guests, but he'd choose them over the fanciest fobs in London. These people were a force. And they'd become like family.

Lord, You're right. I will boast in my weakness, because when I am weak, You are strong.

And then, something Lord Farsley had said triggered a memory. "Farsley, you said Professor Bell smelled like something. What was it?"

"Dank and musty, most of the time."

Daniel whipped around to face Giles. "What was it you told me about Hugh?"

Giles scratched his chin. "He complained about the chill, and that one time, his clothes were damp."

Blue would be found near water.

An image of the white footprint flashed in Daniel's mind's eye.

Lord Farsley had said it was flour.

Blue had thought she'd seen someone go in the old flour mill carrying a bag, but he'd checked the mill earlier and found nothing. He remembered Lady Coburn's brigand ancestors. Could there be a hidden room?

"The old mill." Daniel raked a shaky hand over his head. *Thank you, God!* "He's hiding them there."

McGower gripped the back of Bell's collar and gave him a shake. "Thought the cold would keep the bodies fresher for dissection, did you?"

Professor Bell smirked.

Daniel had been inside the mill twice, though—after Lucy was taken. If she'd been there, wouldn't she have called out to them?

But by Bell's reaction, he was keeping them there. Daniel was sure of it.

There must be an explanation.

He turned to Lady Coburn. "You said the Coburn family made their fortune in smuggling? Any chance the mill was used as a hideout, or a place to stash their treasures?"

She closed her eyes. "Yes, I believe...there were rumors." When she opened her eyes, there was a spark in them. "And there's a window on the outside that no one can see from the inside. It must be a secret room."

Daniel looked to McGower.

"Go. Bring back our friends." McGower nodded. "I will keep an eye on Professor Bell until you return to have your talk."

Daniel inhaled a deep breath and nodded to Giles. "Let's go find them."

"I'm coming too." Madeline straightened her back, lifting her chin as if daring him to argue.

Corinne hooked one arm with Blue's sister, and Mrs. Evans attached herself to the other.

Daniel didn't have time to argue with them. "Just hang back and be quiet."

He led the troops around the garden and past the graveyard. True to their word, the ladies and other guests remained silent and kept a distance of several carriage lengths behind him and Giles.

The chirping of frogs in the pond intensified as they approached the old mill, silhouetted by the moon reflecting off the water.

A shadow shifted near the entrance, and Daniel paused. Giles stopped beside him and held a hand back, signaling the others to stop.

A nightingale's cry silenced the chirping.

"It's the lieutenant," Giles whispered and then echoed the bird's call.

Daniel twisted and raised both palms to tell the others not to follow. He touched Giles's shoulder, and crouching low in the shadows, ran to the lieutenant.

The lieutenant had his gun raised and pointed at the door.

Daniel unholstered his and held it at the ready. He and Giles came alongside the lieutenant and pressed their backs to the cold stone of the mill's exterior wall.

"I tracked him here." He nodded to the bloodied handprint on the wooden door. "He's wounded in the shoulder and losing some blood, but I must have only nicked him. He entered a few seconds ago."

"Then we don't have much time." Giles bounded for the door, but Lieutenant Scar stopped him with a hand.

Daniel understood Giles's urgency, but he'd barreled into situations before, and they hadn't ended well. They needed to handle this properly, or someone could get killed.

"Does he have a weapon?" Daniel asked.

Scar shrugged. "His knife flew into the grass earlier, but anything could be hidden inside."

Daniel swallowed a new sense of panic.

Hang in there, Blue. We're coming.

CHAPTER 34

*T*he damp night air grew chilly, and Rebecca and Lucy huddled together beneath the discarded flour sacks. Their attempt to lock in body heat seemed futile against the cold, damp stone sucking the warmth right out of them.

Though Lucy shivered, her skin was hot to the touch. Rebecca hugged her closer.

Lucy sneezed. "I fear I've come down with a bit of a chill." She sneezed again.

"They're going to come for us, and then we'll get you a nice warm cup of tea and some biscuits with clotted cream and then tuck you in bed and let you sleep for a week."

Lucy laughed a weak giggle. "That sounds lovely. I can almost smell the biscuits baking in the oven."

Rebecca tucked Lucy's head into the crook of her neck and rested her cheek against the crown of Lucy's head. When her friend dozed, Rebecca allowed herself to do the same.

Pounding jarred her awake. She sat up straight.

Lucy groaned and stirred.

Wood slid against wood.

She'd said it, over and over—that someone would come for them. She'd thought about who that would be.

Daniel, of course.

She'd even prayed.

But deep down, she'd doubted.

Now, she was afraid to breathe, afraid the noise would float away on the mist or be drowned in the water she couldn't see, its dripping, torture to her parched throat.

Footsteps sounded above.

Rebecca crouched on her haunches. *Daniel?*

Should she shout out to be found or stay quiet so they could remain alive?

Lucy gripped her arm. "It's him," she whispered. "Hugh's back with another body. He's the only one who knows about this place. We must be quiet." Her rapid breaths revealed her panic. "Hide under the sacks and pretend to be dead."

"Quiet until we know for sure," Rebecca whispered, wrapping a protective arm around Lucy. She picked up the palm-sized rock to defend them and draped the canvas bag over her body but peeked from underneath.

Wood scraped across wood as the false wall in the hopper floor slid open.

The chain rattled along the pulley.

There was a thud as someone jumped to the floor above them, followed by a groan. Was the sound that of a man in pain, or had it been the floorboards?

The trap door lifted.

Rebecca raised the stone. *God protect us.*

Lucy sneezed.

A man jumped down. Not Daniel. Hugh, his expression one of an enraged monster. He yanked the sack off Lucy. "You're supposed to be dead."

Lucy screamed.

He grabbed her throat. "This time, I'll make certain."

Rebecca swung the rock with all her might, hitting him.

He gripped his head and staggered against the stone wall. A slew of words Rebecca had never heard spoken spewed from his lips as he gave his head a shake.

She raised her arm to hit him again, but he grabbed her wrist and twisted until the rock dropped from her fingers.

He pounced on her, knocking her to the ground. His hands found her throat and squeezed, choking her.

Rebecca clawed at his tight hold and thrashed, trying to roll side to side, but his weight overpowered her. *Lord, help me.* She couldn't get free. Flashes of her mother's smile, Madeline's laughter, and Daniel's loving gaze circled in her mind. Her muscles failed to fight any longer and her lungs begged for air as Lucy's screams grew distant.

A crack of bone hitting bone knocked Hugh sideways against the wall.

Rebecca rolled the opposite direction, dragging in precious air and coughing, but caught the sight of her avenging protector standing over her like a guardian angel.

Daniel had come for her.

He grabbed Hugh by his shirtfront and landed another blow that rolled the footman's eyes back. Daniel released his hold, and Hugh slid down the wall into an unconscious heap.

Lucy knelt by her, sobbing.

"Blue." Daniel aided Rebecca to a seated position. "Are you all right?"

Rebecca nodded, and after her coughing subsided, she wrapped her arms around Daniel. "You came. You found us." Her voice was a raspy whisper, and tears flowed down her cheeks.

"Just in time." He pulled back and cradled her face in his hands. "Thank you, Lord."

Embracing her again, he held her until a hand lowered a lamp through the trapdoor.

"Need assistance?"

Rebecca didn't recognize the voice.

Daniel released her. "Let's get these ladies out of here." He aided Rebecca to stand and moved her under the trapdoor, keeping his hands around her waist.

"Wait." She pulled Lucy over. "Take Lucy. She's weak and dehydrated."

The lamp retreated and was set aside on the upper floor. A young lad knelt at the opening next to another man Rebecca hadn't seen before. "Lucy? Are you down there?"

"Giles?"

"It's me. I came to rescue you." Giles extended his hand. "You've been down there long enough."

Lucy stood on her tiptoes and reached toward him.

He grabbed her wrists. His forehead pressed against the floorboards. He grunted as he heaved but struggled to pull her out.

The other man reached through and also clasped Lucy's wrist, and together they pulled her up.

"Your turn, Blue." Daniel hefted her up. Strong fingers enveloped her wrist, and she ascended out of the darkness into the lamplight. She squinted against the brightness and scooted into a seated position out of the men's way next to Lucy, but the narrow storage room didn't offer much space.

"Now you, Wolston," the older man said.

"Lower the pulley's rope first, and I'll tie up our perpetrator."

Giles did as requested, and shuffling noises sounded below before Daniel called, "Ready."

"You first," the other man said and reached down.

Giles followed suit, and they both pulled. They shifted to get their feet underneath them and gave one last yank. Daniel pressed his forearms on the corner edge of the opening and heaved himself the rest of the way up.

He crawled to a stand and reached for Rebecca, enfolding her in his embrace. She inhaled that beautiful sandalwood scent and savored the moment, searing it into her memory.

"Praise God, you're alive and safe." His words were breathed against her hair. He spun her around, then stopped and gazed into her eyes. "You are to never leave my side again. Where you go, I will go."

His lips crushed hers as if he couldn't get enough—as if he'd never be able to get enough—and all her fears drained away in the strength of his love.

Suddenly, he tore away with a ragged breath. "Do you understand what I'm saying? I love you. I don't care what your real name is or if you're not the daughter of an earl. It doesn't matter if you're a penniless pauper. I love you. You're my beloved bluestocking."

Oh, to be beloved for who she was, who she truly was.

"I love you too." She stroked his cheek, soaking in the warmth of his gaze.

"It's good to see you, Lucy." Beside them, the Giles's gaze dropped to his worn shoes, and he clasped his hands behind his back.

"It's grand to see you, too, Giles." Lucy pressed a kiss to his cheek, and the lad's eyes lit brighter than the glow of the lantern.

Rebecca smiled at the young couple. It seemed Lucy held sentiments for him—and he for her. "Lucy, is this the young man you told Madeline about?"

Dirt smudged Lucy's cheeks, and her hair was tussled and falling around her shoulders, but Giles peered at Lucy as if she were the fairest maiden in the land as she introduced him.

Rebecca's own hair must, too, be in a similar state, but Daniel seemed not to care.

The man who helped her out of the hidden room cleared his throat.

"Forgive my manners." Daniel smiled at the man. "Lieutenant Scar, may I introduce you to Miss Rebecca Prestcote?"

The lieutenant bowed. "Lovely to meet you."

She bobbed a curtsy. "Thank you for rescuing us." She glanced at Daniel. "I owe you my life."

His arm snaked around her waist. "Come on. Your family is waiting to see you."

"Madeline?"

He gave her a light squeeze. "She's safe, Lady Corinne also, and thank God, you are too."

"Wait." Rebecca froze. "Professor Bell orchestrated Miss Blakeford's murder and planned Lucy's and mine."

"Bell is under arrest." Lieutenant Scar grabbed the rope, preparing to hoist. "You run along. I'll take care of Bell's henchman."

She sagged against Daniel, and he hugged her tighter.

"Let's get you back and warming by a fire."

Rebecca followed Daniel up a narrow flight of steps to the upper bin floor and back down through the stone level to the main exit. She'd expected when he'd referenced her family, he'd meant her sister and cousin, but cheers erupted.

The sight she beheld as she left the old mill stole her breath.

Madeline rushed over from the front of a crowd and hugged her.

Rebecca held her sister. She now understood how Madeline could willingly place her life in God's hands. Madeline trusted Him, knowing how deep His love was for her. Rebecca had just endured the most terrifying event of her life, but through it, God had opened her eyes.

He'd been with her in the secret room. He was with her always.

Over her sister's shoulder, Rebecca spied her cousin

standing front and center in the group, looking...contrite. It was an expression she'd never seen on her cousin's face.

Rebecca held out her hand, and Corinne hurried forward and hugged her, whispering apologies.

It seemed Rebecca wasn't the only person who'd learned lessons through this event. She whispered her forgiveness and love back to Corinne.

And there were Sarah and Professor Matthews, Lady Coburn with her motherly smile, Lady Farsley with her arm hooked through her husband's, and Mr. Kim standing on the periphery. When she caught his eyes, he bowed to her.

Behind them, the staff and even some of the townsfolk were gathered.

She felt motion at her side and turned as Lucy and Giles exited the mill.

The crowd cheered again with some extra whoops from the staff.

"Everyone came." Rebecca turned and peered up at Daniel. "We might be a bunch of misfits, but we are family."

Daniel took her hand in his. "I meant what I said earlier." He lowered to kneel on one knee and bowed like a knight might submit to his queen.

The crowd grew silent, and anticipation swirled in the night breeze.

Rebecca's breath stuck in her throat. Was he...? But she wasn't...Corinne...or of his class...or good enough.

When he raised his head to look at her, the love shining in his eyes had Rebecca's legs threatening to collapse.

"Rebecca Prestcote, would you do me the great honor of becoming my wife?"

"Why? I mean...I love you, Daniel, but why me? I can't fathom why you would want someone like me." She needed to understand, or she would always wonder, always question. "I lied to you and pretended to be someone I wasn't. I have nothing to offer a marquis—not a dowry or a title, not exquisite beauty. Even my knowledge isn't much of an offering, considering how wise you've proven to be. I have nothing to offer you."

"Always questioning." He chuckled. "It's one of the many things I love about you."

The heat of a blush pushed the chill from her cheeks.

His expression grew serious. "You're right. You were untruthful."

Her breathing stilled. She deserved his public chastisement for what she'd done.

"You made mistakes, and so did I, but God is a forgiving God. I forgive you because of what has been forgiven me, and I pray you will do the same for my failures and untruths."

She shook her head, not understanding. *Untruths?*

"I'll explain later." His gaze held his promise, and his voice dropped to a whisper. "Once we can be alone. Blue, please hear me." He held her hands near his heart. "You can't offer me anything but your love, but you also can't earn mine. I'm not a man who can be bought. My love is freely given. I love you because you love me, because we are good together."

He stood, peering into her eyes. "Let me tell you what I see. I see a woman who is humble and doesn't know how beautiful she is. A woman who is grace and wisdom rolled up into one. She may turn to books and knowledge too often"—his lips quirked—"but she has shown godly prudence. I see a woman who cares for others and readily gives second chances, who wants to please people not for personal gain but because she has a heart for them. I see a woman who'd sacrifice her life for her sister and to save a friend. I see a woman who sees others through God's eyes. I have no doubt that one day, this woman I adore will be a loving and forgiving wife and, God willing, mother. Most of all, I believe she'll want to use the gifts and talents God has given her to be a marchioness, because I can no longer picture my life without her."

Though nothing had changed...

Everything had changed.

It was as though God shone His face from heaven upon them, for her heart overflowed with love.

"Blue?" Uncertainty flashed in Daniel's eyes. "Will you marry me?"

"Yes! Most definitely, yes." She fell into his arms.

He rose, clasping her to his chest, and they stood together in front of friends and family, who also hugged one another with joy.

"God led me to you." Daniel pressed a gentle but sensual kiss to her lips, leaving her longing for more.

She peered into his warm gaze, her heart running over with love for a man she'd never have hoped would give her a second glance.

She couldn't help but tease him. "Actually, I believe God led me to you, since I was the one who tripped down the stairs into your arms."

"Quite right." He chuckled. "And don't forget running head-long into my wet cloak."

She giggled. "Ah yes. If I do forget, I suspect you'll remind me."

"Indeed." His expression turned serious. "Whether God led you to me, or me to you, what matters is that what He brings together, no man can separate."

He swooped in for a second kiss, and another cheer rose from the crowd.

EPILOGUE

$\mathcal{R}$ebecca shifted the restless baby, who'd grown tired of being cooped up in a carriage fifteen miles ago. She'd known traveling with an infant would be a challenge, but they couldn't miss Lady Coburn's party. She looked forward to seeing everyone each year. "We must be getting close."

Daniel pulled aside the carriage window drapes as their conveyance slowed and stopped in front of Griffin Hall. "We're here."

Junior slid off his seat and onto his Papa's lap to look. "It's Charlie, Papa!" He waved with both hands to his friend, the son of Professor and Sarah Matthews, who was only three months older than Junior's five years of age.

Their conveyance drew to a halt, and the footman opened the door.

The boy leapt from the carriage.

"Hold on, young man," Daniel said. "Wait for your sister."

Molly rubbed her sleepy eyes and blinked. With her father's aid, she pushed off the seat and tottered to the door.

Junior helped his sister, Molly, jump down the two stairs to the crushed-stone drive before the pair ran to greet their friends.

Daniel exited and extended a hand to his wife and infant.

Rebecca placed her gloved fingers in his, careful not to jostle six-month-old Evan.

"Welcome." A few more gray streaks lining her hair, Lady Coburn greeted Rebecca with a kiss before taking the baby from her arms. "And welcome to you, Master Evan." She grinned, and the baby smiled, pumping his little arms and legs. "So precious, and the spitting image of his father."

Rebecca peered at her husband, who beamed with pride.

The rest of the guests gathered close to greet them and have their first peek at baby Evan. Lord and Lady Farsley, who looked as if they hadn't aged a day, handed Junior and Charlie their shuttlecock rackets.

Lord McGower, still dressed in Indian garb, offered to teach them how to play. "Did you know the game is called Poona in India?"

"Can you also teach us how to wield your India-sword?" Junior jumped up and down.

Charlie joined in, adding a drawn out, "Please."

"You keep strengthening those muscles so you can lift it, and in a couple of years, I'll teach you the proper way to take down a foe." Lord McGower tussled their hair and sent them off to play.

Madeline approached with Professor Duval a step behind. Rebecca wrapped her sister in a big hug. "Oh, how I've missed you." Rebecca pulled back and studied her sister at arm's length. "How are you faring?"

"Quite well." She clapped her hands and opened them toward Evan. "Come see your Auntie Madeline."

Lady Coburn handed Evan over to his aunt, who smiled and rubbed noses with her nephew, speaking high-pitched nonsense until she coaxed a big smile.

"Great to see you, my friend." Daniel clapped Duval on the shoulder. The professor had to drag his gaze away from Madeline holding the baby.

Rebecca squeezed Professor Duval's hand. "How is she faring, really?"

"Marvelously well, actually." A lovesick grin curved his lips.

Madeline had written how she'd grown an attachment to the humbled professor and how changed he'd been by his experiences at Griffin Hall.

"She's taken to the treatment very well and hasn't shown any symptoms in over six months."

Tears welled in Rebecca's eyes. Placing a hand over her heart, she whispered, "Thank you, Lord."

Daniel's arm slid around her waist, and he pulled her to his side.

She blinked the tears away. "She said as much in her letters, but I wanted to hear it from you. I've been praying for this moment for so long."

Daniel kissed her temple before addressing Professor Duval. "I received your inquiry, and you have my blessing."

Rebecca's brow furrowed. "Blessing for what?"

"Lucy!" Madeline waved to her newlywed friend, who approached up the lane holding Giles Shepherd's hand. "I wasn't sure you were going to make it."

"Are you funning me?" Giles nudged his wife with his elbow. "She made sure our honeymoon coincided with the party so that we wouldn't miss it."

The butler opened the front door of Griffin Hall, and Corinne, her husband, Lord Marshall, and their daughter, Eveline, joined the gathering guests.

"I heard all the commotion and knew you must have arrived." Corinne extended her hands to Rebecca. "It's lovely to see you, cousin."

Rebecca pulled her in for a tight hug. "It's wonderful to see you too."

"Eveline..." Molly handed her friend a newly picked bouquet from Lady Coburn's flower garden. "I got these for you."

Rebecca glanced at Lady Coburn with a *sorry-about-the-flowers* grimace, but Lady Coburn merely smiled and took the girls' hands. "I have a flower blooming in one of Professor Matthews's pots that will look beautiful in your hair. I'll show you after teatime."

At the sound of rumbling wheels, Rebecca turned to see who was approaching.

"Here comes the lieutenant," Giles said.

The Scarcliffe carriage rumbled up the drive and stopped behind the Wolston coach, which was still being unloaded.

Lieutenant Scar hopped down and then aided his wife, Lady Abigail Scarcliffe. After her came their twin sons, who were on holiday from Eton, and their daughter, Emma, who was a year older than Molly. The lieutenant nodded at Giles. "Fresh out of training and already married. How's being wed?"

"Grand. I'm blessed to have a wonderful wife, a job with the Home Office"—Giles nodded his appreciation—"and a chance to be here. We think of everyone here as family."

Rebecca squeezed Lucy's hand. "As do I."

"The agents were strict during training on no outsider information, but I heard Professor Bell attempted to escape Newgate." Giles clasped the lieutenant's shoulder. "Did he dance from the hangman's noose?"

"No." Lieutenant Scar shook his head, and he glanced at Daniel. "But he'll never step foot out of prison."

"Attention, attention." Lady Coburn moved to the front stoop and clapped her hands. "Now that everyone has arrived, please make your way inside. Tea will be served shortly."

Rebecca allowed Daniel to guide her into the house while she called the children and waved them inside the foyer.

Molly stopped just inside. Staring at the ceiling, she moved in a slow circle. "It's beautiful."

Rebecca remembered her first time stepping into the Coburn's grand entrance and the awe she'd felt. So much had changed since then. Instead of fearing she didn't belong, she now experienced an overwhelming sense of family and being loved.

The guests circled the perimeter of the foyer, and Rebecca peered at each of their faces, thanking God for the impact this group of misfits had made in her life. They'd attended her and Daniel's wedding, joining Corinne and Lord and Lady Mercer on the Prestcote side of the aisle, while Daniel's proud grandfather, mother, sisters, and their husbands sat on the other. Her friends had traveled from all over England after Molly's challenging birth to ensure mother and daughter were well.

Rebecca still chuckled over Lord Farsley's comment. *Lady Farsley had to see you with her own eyes to make sure you were all right, and I had to smell you with my own nose.*

Now, Professor Duval cleared his throat and stepped into the center of the circle.

Draping an arm across her shoulders, Daniel gave his full attention to the professor. A pleased expression creased the thin lines of her husband's handsome face.

"You know something I don't, don't you?" She eyed him, but his smile only grew. He put a finger to his lips.

"The past five years have changed my life," Professor Duval said. "And each of you has had a tremendous role in my modification. One particular person has opened my eyes to a loving Creator, how He made us equal in His sight, and how science reflects His glory." He extended his hands to Madeline, who stepped forward and placed her hands in his.

He lowered to one knee.

Rebecca gasped, and her hands flew to cover her mouth.

"Miss Madeline Prestcote, would you do me the great honor of becoming my wife?"

Delight flooded Rebecca's heart. This was all she dreamed of for her sister. Professor Duval endeared himself to Rebecca by taking over Madeline's treatment with as much determination as Rebecca had shown.

Her sister glowed with love. "Absolutely, I will marry you. God has saved my heart for you."

Cheers echoed throughout Griffin Hall, and Rebecca was the first of their adopted family to shower the couple with love.

Did you enjoy this book? We hope so!
**Would you take a quick minute to leave a review where you
purchased the book?**
It doesn't have to be long. Just a sentence or two telling what
you liked about the story!

Receive a FREE ebook and get updates when new Wild Heart
books release: https://wildheartbooks.org/newsletter

FROM THE AUTHOR

Dear Readers,

Thank you for reading the Agents of Espionage Series. I had a delightful time conjuring stories of secrets, spies, and a bit of suspense.

I must say a special thanks to Misty and the Wild Heart Books team. It is lovely to work with such great and inspiring people. Thank you for all your hard work polishing my manuscripts, seeing my vision, and bringing my dreams to life. A special thanks to my editors, Robin Patchen, Robyn Hook, Denise Weimer, and Brenda at Threefold Edits, who help navigate the chaos of my imagination. Also, to my critique partners, launch team members, beta readers, and social influencer friends, you are a blessing to me. Thank you for making this series a success!

I praise God for my supportive family and His love, goodness, and faithfulness, as well as for blessing me with such a supportive family.

Although I hate for the series to end, I'm excited for what lies ahead with a Danforth Theatre Series.

So please, wonderful readers, stay tuned...
Blessings,
Lorri

ABOUT THE AUTHOR

Lorri Dudley has been a finalist in numerous writing contests and has a master's degree in Psychology. She lives in Ashland, Massachusetts with her husband and three teenage sons, where writing romance allows her an escape from her testosterone filled household.

Connect with Lorri at http://LorriDudley.com

GET ALL THE BOOKS IN THE AGENTS OF ESPIONAGE SERIES

Book 1: Revealing the Truth

Book 2: Reclaiming the Spy

Book 3: Redeeming the Rake

Book 4: Relinquishing the Agent

ALSO BY LORRI DUDLEY

The Leeward Island Series

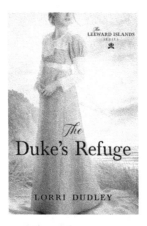

Book 1: The Duke's Refuge

Book 2: The Merchant's Yield

Book 3: The Sugar Baron's Ring

Book 4: The Captain's Quest

Book 5: The Marquis's Pursuit

Book 6: The Heir's Predicament

WANT MORE?

If you love historical romance, check out the other Wild Heart books!

A Summer on Bellevue Avenue by Lorri Dudley

In the world of the elite, reputation is everything...

Wealthy heiress Amanda Mae Klein is set to marry the man she loves, Wesley Jansen—the only person she trusts to help ease her anxiety among the social climbers of high society. Then the daughter of a union boss falls down a flight of stairs at Wesley's oil company's office in the middle of the night...and the woman claims Wesley pushed her.

Seeking solace from the growing scandal, Amanda flees to the mansion-dotted seaside of Newport. Wesley follows and sets about disproving the rumors while winning back the trust of Amanda. But soon, Amanda finds not only her social status but her life at risk. As grievous events pit the two against each other, will their love find a way to survive?

~

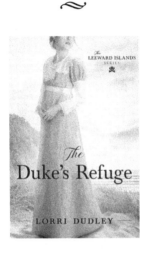

The Duke's Refuge by Lorri Dudley

When love comes in a tempest, who knew it would wear pink?

Georgia Lennox has traded in her boyish ways for pink gowns and a coy smile to capture the eye of the Earl of Claremont. However, on the day she's convinced the earl will propose, Georgia is shipped off to the Leeward Islands to care for her ailing father. But when she arrives on Nevis, the last thing she expects is to learn that her abrupt departure was not at her father's bidding but that of the infuriating, yet captivating, island schoolmaster. And now her plans may well be shipwrecked.

Harrison Wells is haunted by the memories of his deceased wife and hunted by the women who aspire to be the next Duchess of Linton. Desiring anonymity, he finds sanctuary in the Leeward island of Nevis. He's willing to sacrifice his ducal title for a schoolmaster's life and the solace the island provides. That is, until unrest finds its way to Nevis in a storm of pink chiffon—Miss Georgia Lennox.

As Georgia and Harrison's aspirations break apart like a ship cast upon the rocks, a new love surfaces, but secrets and circumstances drag them into rough waters. Can they surrender their hearts to a love that defies their expectations?

~

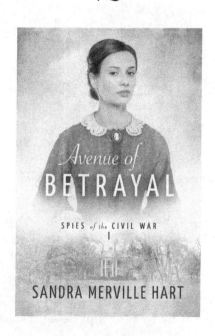

Avenue of Betrayal by Sandra Merville Hart

Betrayed by her brother and the man she loves...whom can she trust when tragedy strikes?

Soldiers are pouring into Washington City every day and have begun drilling in preparation for a battle with the Confederacy. Annie Swanson worries for her brother, whom she's just discovered is a Confederate officer in his new home state of North Carolina. Even as Annie battles feelings of betrayal toward the big brother she's always adored, her wealthy banker father swears her and her sister to secrecy about their brother's actions. How could he forsake their mother's abolitionist teachings?

Sergeant-Major John Finn camps within a mile of the Swansons' mansion where his West Point pal once lived. Sweet Annie captured his heart at Will's wedding last year and he looks forward to reestablishing their relationship—until he's asked to spy on her father.

To prove her father's loyalty to the Union, John agrees to spy on the Swanson family, though Annie must never know. Then the war strikes a blow that threatens to destroy them all—including the love that's grown between them against all odds.

www.ingramcontent.com/pod-product-compliance
Lightning Source LLC
Chambersburg PA
CBHW070919140325
23252CB00006B/10